SAVAGE RUIN

THE SAVAGES SERIES

STELLA BRIE

COPYRIGHT

Cover Design by Moonstruck Cover Design & Photography, moonstruckcoverdesign.com

Editing: Kaye Kemp Book Polishing

❀ Created with Vellum

INSPIRATION

This story is fiction and <u>takes liberties</u> with the current state or boundaries of technology. Some of the technology <u>exists today</u>, some *might* exist in the future, and the rest is *likely* pure fiction, meaning it's probably made up. ;-) If you're curious which ones are real, I've added a Technology page in the back.

Thank you to everyone who gave this unconventional why choose series a chance! It means a lot to me. Enjoy!

PLAYLIST

"Made For This" - City Wolf

"Fighter "- Royal Deluxe

"Last One Standing" - WAR*HALL

"Oh My God" - Adele

"Can't Stop Me" - Native 51

"Higher and Higher" - Outskirts

"Human" - Christina Perri

"Human" - Rag'n'Bone Man

"Amado (Ao Vivo)" - Vanessa Da Mata

"It's Only Love, Nobody Dies" - Sofia Carson

"Take It All" - Valley of Wolves

"Death of Me" - Daughtry

"Into Your Arms" - (feat. Ava Max) Witt Lowry

"Take My Hand" - 5 Seconds of Summer

AUTHOR'S NOTE

This book is a WhyChoose romance, which means the heroine does not have to choose between male interests. Please note—this book contains references to abuse and stalking that may be difficult for some readers. It also contains death, violence, and cursing. Please take care of yourself and read at your own discretion. Recommended for 18+ due to mature content.

CHAPTER 1

Awareness taps forcefully on the edges of my mind, but the excruciating pain it brings is too much for me to handle. I turn to the sea of nothing, and with a grateful sigh, slide into the inky darkness, letting the pain fade into the background. Yet a sliver of awareness remains and a voice slips into my world.

Drifting aimlessly, the low timbre of unintelligible sounds becomes a soothing lullaby accompanying me along my journey, stopping only to be replaced by another. Although different, the new voice seamlessly carries me through the darkness, and my cocoon remains intact—for a while. Somewhere along the way, the tone changes. Raw anguish pierces the veil of darkness, disrupting my peaceful interlude, until I'm unable to ignore it. Compelled to reassure them, I reach but never make contact. Restless, I strain against the darkness that once gave me such comfort.

Angry voices intrude. Expecting pain to follow, I flinch. Utter silence descends. When nothing follows, my body relaxes, but my mind is no longer content to just drift. It's alert and vigilant against the danger I sense.

The darkness softens to grey, and the pain returns. A whimper escapes. Warmth encompasses my hand, followed by a sharp prick. The pain eases. Sleep takes over.

When I wake, light and heat surround me, pulling from me from the lingering shadows. Gritting my teeth against the pain in my body, I lift my eyelids and squint against the brightness to check my surroundings. The lack of familiarity is both unnerving and reassuring. Instead of grey concrete and a dim room, sunlight bounces off cheerful yellow walls, flooding the space with brightness. A television, high on the wall in front of me, plays softly while beeping noises fill the air around my bed. A dark figure slumps in a nearby chair causing my muscles to tense, but the lean silhouette eases my fears. I'm no longer in the warehouse, and that's not Diego.

A cool hand clasps my wrist, startling me, and I jerk to find a woman in blue scrubs standing by the bed. "It's okay. You're safe and in the hospital. I'm Sam, your nurse, and I'm going to take your pulse. Okay?" She lightly circles my wrist but waits until she sees my slight nod before proceeding. "How are you feeling?" After a few seconds, she lays my hand on the bed and picks up the chart to write something down.

My voice cracks when I answer. "Fine. Sore."

She grabs a sliver of ice from a nearby cup and places it in my mouth. "That's to be expected. On a scale of one to ten, how is the pain?"

My body throbs in sync with the drummer in my head, but it's less intense. "Five?" It's hard to tell right now because everything seems muted.

She consults the chart and nods. "Good. You're not due to get a pain reliever for a couple more hours. I'll let the doctor know you're awake, and I'm sure he'll be in to see you shortly." After adjusting the covers, she continues. "Take it easy, and if you need anything, press this button." She hands me a remote and gestures to the red button with a plus sign on it.

I nod.

"Thank you, Sam," a voice states softly. The figure at the end of the bed strides toward me.

Mateo. My breath hitches when I see his familiar face and warm brown eyes. "Is this real?"

"Yes, you're safe. Diego is dead," he says reassuringly, his eyes never leaving mine.

I feel like I did when I had a car accident at sixteen... fine until I saw my mom's face. A dam bursts inside me, and my emotions come pouring out. Tears stream down my face while I silently tell him what happened to me, how scared I was, how bad it hurt, the moment I lost hope, and a million other things, including the overwhelming relief to find myself alive and here with him. I thought I'd never see anyone again. My hand squeezes his tightly, afraid to let him go, but it's not enough. I'm terrified this is a dream conjured up by my desperate mind.

"Minha linda, you're killing me," he says softly. "I can't even hold you right now. There are so many pieces of you stitched and held together by sutures and bandages." He reaches over to the nightstand and pulls a tissue out of the box. Wiping softly down my face, he carefully dries my cheeks. "I've got you. You're safe, and I'm not going anywhere. Okay?"

When he mentions holding me, I can think of nothing else but the feel of strong arms surrounding and protecting me, even if it's only for a brief second. I need it so badly I can barely breathe, almost as much as the moment I realized my mom was gone when I needed her the most. But I've been alone so long I don't know how to ask for comfort, especially from someone I've only known for a few weeks. All I can do is cry and stare at him, hoping he hears my silent plea.

With a curse, he lowers the bed rail and eases part of his body onto the bed beside me. His arm hovers over my chest, caging me in tightly, but without touching a single sore spot. "I'm right here with you, and I'm not leaving." His troubled dark eyes reflect his promise to keep me safe—even if I know it's just for tonight.

Diego's eyes promised death, and I believed him. Everyone says

3

your life flashes before your eyes, but I saw very little. Instead, despair and regret consumed me. How could I die when I haven't lived?

The image of the Santos men standing tall on the dance floor popped into my head during that final painful minute. A cruel vision, a subconscious dream? I don't know, but I'm done with hiding in the dark. Whether I live a month, a year, or fifty years, I'm going to throw away my fears and find my best life, whatever that means. My hand grips his shirt to hold him close. My tears slow. Exhausted but safe, I drift off to sleep.

———

WHEN I WAKE, Mateo is still lying beside me, his expressive eyes closed. Taking advantage of the moment, I blatantly study his beautiful features. Long dark lashes lie peacefully against strong cheekbones. Lean contours and sharp-looking cheekbones lend an aristocratic appearance to his face, but the dark stubble gracing his jaw makes him more approachable and appealing. Pouty lips relaxed in sleep offer their own temptation, making my lips tingle in memory of the last kiss we shared on the beach.

Beautiful, I muse. It's not only his looks that draw me to him, nor his mind, although he'd never believe his intelligence isn't his best asset. Don't get me wrong, his genius is incredibly sexy, but it can also be a bit too sharp and singularly focused to be the only draw. Nope. It's the vulnerability I sense beneath the surface that entices and calls to me, whispering of his secret need to let down his barriers and find a connection with someone.

A reflection of the ache in my own heart, I muse. I burrow a tiny bit closer.

"Ahem."

I turn my head toward the sound and find Cruz standing by the bed with a speculative look in his eyes.

"Looks like we've traded places," he states gruffly. "How are you feeling?"

I grimace. "Like a Mack truck ran over me a few times," I reply, rolling to my back. My voice is hoarse, and I can't help glancing over at the cup on the nightstand.

Cruz reaches over and picks it up. "The nurse said you could have small sips of water." As he slips the straw between my lips, the door opens and Thiago strides into the room.

Straight, almost black hair lies haphazardly across his broad forehead, deep scruff covers his jaw, and judging by the dark circles under his eyes, he desperately needs sleep. It's the worst I've seen him look. Although you wouldn't know it by his energy. His usual intense demeanor has been amped up by a thousand percent and easily fills every square inch of the small room. His presence should be suffocating, yet something in me shifts and settles knowing he's here and in charge. I let out a long, slow sigh, releasing the straw.

Obsidian eyes move from my lips to Cruz' fingers, to Mateo lying beside me. His mouth firms. "Cruz, I didn't expect to see you here."

Cruz raises an eyebrow and gives his usual nonchalant shrug. "I'm not sure why you're surprised. I check on Henley every day."

Thiago narrows his eyes. "I thought we agreed to shifts?"

"You dictated shifts. I never agreed to them," Cruz retorts. "Besides, Mateo's been here all day." He crosses his arms in challenge.

The tension is thick between the two of them, and I can't help but wonder what happened to cause the friction.

Mateo stretches beside me. "Everything was peaceful until you two showed up. Isn't that right, Henley?" He winks at me before carefully easing himself off the bed. Cutting a stern look at Cruz and Thiago, he heads to the door. "I'm going to find some coffee and food. Ease up. You're stressing Henley."

Thiago studies the ceiling for a second, then jerks his chin toward the door. "I'll be right outside." With a pointed look at Cruz, he walks out.

I dart a glance at Cruz and raise an eyebrow. "What's going on?"

His hand tightens on the bed rail. "Zane needs someone to set up surveillance on a potential rescue victim. In Mexico. He asked me to go. I'll be gone for a few weeks." He stares into my eyes when he delivers the news.

"You just got out of the hospital!" I protest. "You need at least a couple of weeks to recover. Zane's ridiculous. What did you tell him?"

"I told him I'd speak to you first," he replies softly, but his eyes are intent and watchful.

Bewildered, I frown. "Why would you need to speak to me? If this is about saving your life, I told you, we're even. If you want my opinion, I think you need more time to heal."

A resigned expression crosses his face, and he sighs heavily. "It's a pretty soft job with no action, practically a vacation, and I'll have plenty of time to recuperate." He reaches down and picks up my hand. "If you need anything, I've programmed my number into your phone. I'll—" He clears his throat. "Take care of yourself, Henley. At least try to stay out of trouble while I'm gone." With a final squeeze of my hand, he walks over and opens the door.

Thiago's standing in the doorway a second later.

Cruz steps up to face him head on with his shoulders thrown back. "You'd better take good fucking care of her."

Thiago nods and moves to the side to let him pass. Dark eyes find mine. "I will," he promises.

CHAPTER 2

HENLEY

After sleeping most of yesterday, I'm feeling a bit more normal this morning. The fogginess is starting to disappear, and if I don't move too much or quickly, the pain stays at a low-level throb. I can't imagine what it must have been like when they first brought me to the hospital. According to Mateo, it's been a long four days.

My mental state is an entirely different story. Thoughts bounce around like rubber balls in my head, but every time I focus on one, Diego's face and fists appear, so I let them continue their chaotic path.

I glance to my left, but the small couch Thiago slept on last night is empty. I'm not sure how he folded his massive body into it, much less slept, but he refused to leave. Even after the weird scene with Cruz, he continued to be intense and hypervigilant, his eyes constantly assessing me. For what, I'm not sure. Maybe he's waiting for me to ask about Diego, but I'm currently avoiding the topic.

For weeks, everything rushed by at warp speed until it suddenly stopped at the end of Diego's fist. For someone who's lived life vicariously via a virtual environment for the last few years, the world feels so real now. Sensations constantly bombard me until I want to find a computer and hide, but without a device readily available, escape is impossible.

A stranger enters the room followed closely by Mateo and Thiago. The obligatory white coat tells me he's a doctor. Mid-thirties maybe. Looks nice. Normal.

He flashes a bright white smile toward me. "Hello. I'm Dr. Rodriguez. Unfortunately, you were asleep when I dropped by yesterday. It's good to see you awake and alert this morning. How are you feeling, Henley?" Picking up the chart at the end of the bed, he glances between it and me, waiting for an answer.

Thankfully, the nursing assistant had been by to help me clean up this morning, and I'm feeling human again.

"Better," I reply.

"Do you mind if I check a few things?"

I glance at Mateo and Thiago.

"Do you want us to step out?" Mateo asks softly.

I thought they might be uncomfortable, but since they seem fine with staying, I'm happier with them in the room, especially with a strange male in here. "No, stay."

The doctor gives me a rundown while he checks everything. "You came in with a severe concussion, extensive bruising across your face and torso, and a few cuts." He presses softly on my chest and abdomen making me exhale sharply, then flashes a pen light in my eyes. "With rest, the most severe bruising should heal within a couple of weeks. Regarding the concussion, I'd like to get some new scans of your brain just to be safe. Mateo tells me it's formidable, so we need to make sure it's healing properly, okay?"

My hand reaches up to softly rub a sore spot on my ribs. "Yes."

He peers down at me. "Overall, you're very lucky. I know it doesn't feel like it right now, but your body is starting to recover, and we haven't seen any complications or internal bleeding arise. If the scans come back clean, you'll be able to go home tomorrow or the following day. Heavy exercise should be restricted for at least another week, but I encourage you to walk and move around to keep the blood flowing. You'll probably need help to do necessary tasks for about a week, but we can talk about it once we're ready to send you home. Right now, just keep resting. Do you have any questions?"

I glance down at my body, but the angry welts on my wrists brings flashbacks of Diego, so I hurriedly return my gaze to him. "No questions."

"Okay. I'll be back once I have the results." With a dip of his chin to Thiago and Mateo, he leaves.

"Well, that's good news, right?" I dart a glance at Mateo and raise my eyebrow. *Ouch*, even my eyebrow hurts. Getting out of the hospital sounds good, and although my loft is gone, I have several back-up places. But the need for help is worrisome. Maybe there's some type of rehab or recovery place where I can go for a week? My fingers twitch with the need to find answers. "Mateo, do you happen to have my phone?"

Thiago crosses his well-muscled arms. "You're supposed to be resting. Why don't you leave the phone with Mateo for another day or two?"

I narrow my eyes. What I wouldn't give to cross my arms without wincing right now. Unfortunately, I don't think it's possible, so I settle for a glare. "I appreciate your concern, but I'll rest better if I have something to occupy my brain. If you aren't inclined to give me mine, I'll simply get Sterling or someone else to bring me a new phone. This isn't a negotiation. I'm not asking your permission." The words nervously rush out, but I hold his unblinking stare with one of my own. It's like staring down a cobra. My heart races, wondering if he'll strike, but I can't back down. The sooner Thiago learns he isn't allowed to dictate to me, the better our... friendship will be.

He throws up his arms in exasperation. "Fine, but I want you to promise you'll rest frequently. And that is non-negotiable. Your health comes first."

"Well, of course," I return solemnly, hiding the tiny smile of victory that is dying to pop out. "Mateo?"

He laughs, pulls my phone out of his back pocket, and hands it over. "I figured you would want it today. It's been over a week since you held it."

I grip my lifeline tightly. With this, I can practically take over the world.

———

MY SCANS CAME BACK "CLEAN" yesterday. The doctor informed me I could leave today if I had help getting around for a week.

After researching the options on my phone, I made a reservation at a luxury relaxation center in Naples, Florida. Warm and by the water, they promise to pamper me with excellent food, nursing care and, more importantly, the no camera policy means it's also extremely secluded. It will be the first vacation I've had in a very long time. What more could I ask for?

This morning, I asked Mateo to pack some clothes and necessities for me, but he shook his head no and stormed out, cursing in Portuguese.

Sterling was significantly more helpful.

I pick up the ID he dropped off a few minutes ago and grin when I see the name and picture. "Henley Night." It's me in all my pink hair and blue-eyed glory. Henley from the past and future with a piece of Nyx thrown in for kicks. It's perfect. I might need to use other IDs for back-up accounts and safety reasons, but this will be my main identity. A new Henley. Alive and finding a life in the real world for the first time in a long time. It fits.

The door opens, and Grayson slowly limps into the room. I frown. He's impeccably dressed in a tailored suit, but his smooth stroll has been replaced by short, stiff steps, and dark circles sit prominently under his eyes. We didn't part on the best of terms in the hallway the night of the ball, and the virtual meeting later didn't give us time to chat. This is the first time I've seen him in a week. I bite the inside of my cheek to keep my worry contained, knowing he wouldn't want it, and wait for him to say something.

According to Thiago, Grayson has been on a rescue mission with Zane for the last two days. He didn't say what he'd been doing. Initially, I assumed he was helping them get set up financially, but those tasks wouldn't result in injury. *Hmm.* Another piece of the Grayson puzzle. Maybe one day, I'll have the full picture.

His eyes sweep over me, and his mouth tightens. He grabs the chair and brings it closer to the bed, then motions to the plastic in my hands. "A new identity, huh? Dare I hope you've chosen the name Rose?"

I hand him the ID.

"Henley Night," he reads aloud, then hands it back to me. Inscrutable blue eyes lock onto mine. "Does this mean you're going to be a real person again instead of a virtual ghost?"

Virtual ghost, I silently repeat. An apt description. "Not exactly. I don't know what it means right now. It's a step toward reclaiming myself. The last few weeks have reminded me what it's like to be seen and heard in real life. To be me, Henley." To be held, touched, and kissed, but I don't say those words out loud.

"Henley..." he begins, stops for a second, then continues. "Henley, I'm incredibly glad to see you're feeling better. We need to talk about the ball, and since it looks like you'll be around for a while, I want to clear the air, so to speak." He pauses and runs a hand through his immaculate hair. "I..."

With a forced sigh, I interrupt the speech he obviously took time to prepare because I honestly don't want to hear it. "It was a kiss, Grayson. A good kiss fueled by all the wrong things—champagne, anger, and a need to push each other's buttons. We can forget it ever happened, okay?" If I want to remember the intense moment in private, well, that's my business, right? It's not like I'm going to be here, anyway. "Besides, I'm getting discharged later today and leaving immediately for Naples."

He appears stunned for a second, but his expression quickly changes to anger. "That's not..."

11

STELLA BRIE

The door opens, and Zane pokes his head into the room. "Mind if I come in?"

Relieved, I motion for him to enter. "Please, I need to ask for a favor."

He chuckles. Coming into the room, he sets down a beautiful vase of flowers.

"If you'll excuse me, I need to make a phone call," Grayson spits out. He strides jerkily from the room, anger rolling off him in waves.

Zane's observant eyes pivot from him to me. "Everything okay? I can come back later."

"The usual," I reply, waving a hand vaguely in the air, not wanting to admit to the constant friction between Grayson and me. "They're beautiful! Did you know tulips were my favorite?" I beam at him. "Thank you."

"You're welcome, but I must confess to having an ulterior motive," he says mysteriously. "Last time I saw you, you mentioned a dance and two hundred and fifty thousand dollars? I've been dying of curiosity ever since."

I lean closer and grin. "I'm not sure if anyone told you yet, but I'm CJ Tech."

Pure shock crosses his face, followed by relief. "No, they didn't," he replies with a chuckle. "But they may not be aware of why it would be good for me to know. Marcos kept your donations to the charity a secret. Are you going to continue to support the charity or is that the last donation?"

"Not only am I going to keep giving my annual twenty-five percent, but I'll be donating Marcos' share, too. I inherited all his projects, and it's what he would want," I assure him. "Although, at some point, his projects will be zero unless I can find a secret stash of them somewhere."

"I might be able to help with that," Mateo interjects, walking into the room. "In the will, he left me his old notebook full of ideas. I wasn't sure what to do with it except treasure it because it was his, but now I know."

12

Excitement burns through me, and my mind races at the possible ideas he might have written down. It's like finding gold.

Mateo shakes his head at my reaction, but I see the matching gleam in his eyes.

"Regarding the two hundred and fifty thousand I paid for the auction tickets to get into the ball, I want to be sure it counts toward my share for this year," I state firmly, holding Zane's stare to let him know I'm serious.

He narrows his eyes, desperate to refuse. "Fine, fine, I know there will be more coming," he agrees grumpily.

"Also, I'll continue supplying the documentation and IDs needed for the rescues," I assure him. "It's important they have the necessary paperwork, along with quality fakes that hold up to scrutiny."

He chuckles. "Slick will be thrilled. He was dreading the responsibility," he says, only half-joking. "Anything else?"

"Nope, that's it," I retort with a cheeky grin. "Unless you want to dance?"

"No, he doesn't," Thiago states firmly from the doorway. "Where did the flowers come from?"

"Zane brought them. Aren't they gorgeous? Tulips are my favorite," I reply with a smile. "Unfortunately, he's only being nice to try and wrangle more money out of me." I chuckle at the expression of pained exasperation on Zane's face.

"Why don't I walk you out and you can explain," Thiago suggests to Zane, his mouth set in a firm line.

"Thanks a lot," Zane fires over his shoulder as he leaves with Thiago.

Grayson comes back.

Thiago steps into the room a few minutes later, his eyes filled with guilt, and I immediately freeze.

All three Santos men at once. This can't be good. "Why are all three of you here? Not that I'm not happy to see you, but it's kind of suspicious."

"Why didn't you tell us you gave twenty-five percent of CJ Tech's earnings to the Santos Foundation?" Thiago asks gruffly.

"Because it has nothing to do with you. What I do with my money is my business. I believe in the mission, and it's better than paying taxes to the government," I tell him, firmly closing the subject.

"You sound so much like Marcos sometimes, it's uncanny," Thiago admits with a heavy sigh. "We need to talk to you about the day we rescued you from Diego."

"Or we can wait until I'm feeling better. After I recuperate, I'll return, and I promise we'll sit down and discuss everything. The doctor said I need at least a week to heal, although I'm thinking two might be better, and I found a luxurious recovery center in Naples that fits all the requirements. They have an awesome menu, a view of the ocean, and medical staff. It's perfect." My voice trails off when I see Thiago shaking his head.

"Naples is out. It's not safe," he informs me. He shifts uncomfortably against the wall.

My fingers trace the welts on my wrist. They seem to be a little lighter today. More pinkish red, instead of the angry red they were two days ago. The soft pads of my fingers trail over the raised areas where the restraints bound my wrists together behind my back. At least I can feel things now. I can't help but rub the tips of my fingers, remembering how numb they were that day.

A warm, dark hand comes down on top of mine. Following it up to its owner, I see the concern in Thiago's eyes. And guilt. Loads of guilt. I tense.

"Mateo got the message you sent, but it didn't contain enough information for us to find you. We would never have made it in time." His voice is gruff and full of emotion as he admits this to me. The torment he felt at that moment is also reflected in his eyes. "We had help. Shortly after your message, Mateo received a video on the same channel you used to send the text. It was taken from a webcam, and it showed you sitting in front of it, beaten, with Diego behind you. Proof of its validity."

I can see he isn't going to be deterred, so I swallow and motion for him to go on.

"The video offered to exchange your location for unpublished software. We didn't have much because Marcos kept everything in his office, but we had the two projects he sent you in the will. Mateo found them in your backpack. We promised him the AR/VR glasses along with the code," he reveals slowly, as if he's not sure how I'll react.

I tilt my head while I think back to that moment. "I saw the webcam light on and knew someone was watching. I thought it might be the invisible man from the video since Diego seemed to delight in infuriating him. The request to trade for software sort of confirms it. He's desperate. I'm sure his boss is furious with him for failing to decipher the key to unlock the AR software. He needed something to stay in their good graces," I muse, satisfaction coloring my voice for a second.

When I see the guilt on all their faces, I realize I need to be just as transparent. Swallowing the lump in my throat, I continue. "Right before you got there, I figured you weren't going to make it. How could you? I didn't have a clue where I was, and the scant information I sent had been a Hail Mary in the last second of the final quarter. I thought—why continue to hope? Diego's patience was gone. My time was up. The enemy won the battle, and I would pay the price."

I clench my hands tightly together to help me get through the last bit. "I deliberately goaded Diego, hoping he'd make it quick and shoot me. Unfortunately, I pissed him off too much because he did the exact opposite of what I wanted him to do. At the time, I thought it was the stupidest decision I'd ever made, but it turned out to be the smartest. If he hadn't decided to drag it out, I likely wouldn't be here now." The beating gave them the necessary minutes to get to me, although to say it sucked is a gross understatement.

Thiago's face fills with a stormy expression.

Mateo shoves his hands through his thick hair and tugs hard. Grayson turns to look out the window.

"I'm thankful you didn't give up, and I couldn't care less about the glasses," I say fervently, although I'm not sure the last part is one hundred percent true. A couple of tears slip down my cheeks when I think about those last few minutes in the warehouse. The thought of dying without having truly lived had been brutal and devastating. Relieved to have a second chance, I look up to find all three men staring at me. "Another minute, and I wouldn't be here. Who took the shot?"

"Cruz," Grayson replies hoarsely, his voice filled with emotion.

Hmm, I wonder if that's the cause of the friction between Cruz and Thiago?

"Good. Cruz and I are absolutely even now. Once I get back, I'll have to…"

Thiago holds up his hand. "No. This isn't negotiable, Henley. The war isn't over by a long shot. We don't know who's behind everything, how deep the corruption is at SEI or how far they're willing to take things. More importantly, the enemy knows you're involved now, and they can identify you. None of us wants you out of our sight. Instead, we want you to move into our house. It will be safer if we stay together."

All three of them look like they're holding their breath, waiting for me to protest.

As if.

My sigh of relief is loud and long. I might have made it through the last few weeks by myself, but going forward, I'll take all the help and protection they're willing to give me. It's going to get ugly before the end, but I'm determined to make it out alive and find a real life not the half-life I've been living.

"Good." I pause. "Our enemies are going to be really pissed when I release the AR software."

CHAPTER 3

HENLEY

M ateo jerks at the bomb I just dropped. "Wait, you have the software? An un-encrypted copy?"

"Marcos left two copies of the software. The flash drive I retrieved from his office the night of the explosion contained an encrypted copy, but I needed the key to un-encrypt it. His instructions sent me to find two files, so I knew the key could only be found with both."

"But you didn't take the file from SEI's servers," Mateo interjects.

"Right, but I didn't need the actual copy. He named the file on the flash drive "Meus" and the file on SEI's server "Pequenos Selvagens", and the two together..."

"Meus pequenos selvagens," Mateo states hoarsely, looking over at Thiago and Grayson. All three of them exchange silent words. "He used our phrase to encrypt the software. Even Diego wouldn't have put much thought into an endearment he might have heard when we were kids. It only meant something to Marcos and us." He chuckles and looks to heaven like he knows Marcos is listening. "Always one step ahead, even when your back is to the wall and time is limited. Something so incredibly simple, yet known only to a select few. Brilliant." He returns his gaze to me. "How did you know?"

"Grayson and Marcos had the same picture on their desks, but Grayson's had the moniker engraved on it," I admit softly. "I snapped a pic when I saw the frame because I thought it might be a possibility. Unfortunately, the risk was too high to test the phrase because I didn't know if Marcos had included any type of lockout threshold to limit the number of attempts. But when I saw the second file name, I knew it was the key. It's why I didn't need to download the additional copy from the server."

"What are you going to do with the software?" Thiago asks gruffly, his voice strained with emotion.

"Get it into the hands of every doctor on the planet," I reply with determination. "I'm not sure how I'm going to distribute it yet, so I'm open to ideas. I don't want to put it up for auction again, but I'd like to generate some money for it. It took a lot of hours to create, and we put off finishing anything else. Without the revenue, we won't have a donation for the rescue foundation, nor will we have seed money for new projects." I bite my lip, thinking about the invisible man. "My biggest challenge is finding a way to prevent it from being pirated before it's widely available." I roll my neck to ease the tension creeping up the sides.

A firm hand cups the back of my neck and massages the tense muscles. "We'll figure it out together," Thiago states firmly. "For now, let's go home. We need to get you better first." His face is full of strength and confidence, and a tiny kernel of hope unfurls inside me.

———

THE IMPOSING black iron gate and matching fence stand tall, a menacing barrier blocking any view of the house and grounds from the street. I slide a questioning glance toward Thiago, but he's busy typing the entry code into his phone. The gate parts and the two sides swing open, allowing us access to the house. Impressive. I'm betting the gate isn't the only new security he's added since my last visit. I can't wait to take a peek.

Dark eyes meet mine, a fierce, protective glint in them, and for a second, I bask in the overwhelming feeling of safety he exudes. Wrapping it tightly around me, I hold on to it for a few precious seconds until all my fears are gone, then release it into the air. Too many times, the promise of safety has turned out to be nothing but an illusion. It's not that I don't want to believe, but I can't afford to discard the lessons of the past.

Parking in front of the door, he eases his long body out of the car. "Stay put."

Bemused, I unbuckle my seatbelt and watch his powerful legs eat up the short distance around the front of the hood. My door opens, and a large hand appears. Gripping it with my own, I use his strength to ease myself out of the low-slung vehicle.

"I should have brought the SUV," he mutters when he sees me wince.

My chest and stomach hurt the most. Well, my face too, but I don't need my face to move my body. "I'm not sure it would have been better."

We realized earlier that carrying me hurt a lot, so with small steps, I make my way into the house. Once inside, I grimace at the sight of the stairs, but Thiago stops me.

He motions to the hallway on the right. "I've put you in the guest room next to me. It's on the right past the office."

Startled to hear he's going to be in the next room, I pause to stare into his brown eyes, but the dark mirrors reveal little. "I don't want to bother you."

"It's a little too late for that," he responds wryly. When he sees the guilty expression on my face, he quickly explains. "I wouldn't be able to sleep if you were anywhere else. I need to know you're safe and have everything you need."

"Where's the nurse going to sleep?"

STELLA BRIE

He frowns. "What nurse? The doctor said you would need assistance getting up and down, dressing, and a few other things this week." Comprehension dawns and he clears his throat. "We didn't want strangers in the house, but if you're uncomfortable, I can ask Zane to recommend someone safe. A woman." Dark eyes assess me closely.

The thought of Thiago helping me dress and undress makes me flush with uncertainty and a hint of embarrassment. I hate being this vulnerable and reliant on someone else.

Not sure how I feel about being this intimate with them, especially him, I answer honestly. "It's one thing to stay in your house, and another to be dependent on you and have you helping me... change clothes." I turn down the hall, heading to my new room. "Is this going to cause problems with a woman in your life? What about Mateo and Grayson?"

He ignores the first question. "All three of us are planning to help, but if you have a preference, let us know." The hand on my back guides me into the room on the right. "This is your new room."

Draped in crisp white and creamy beiges, the bedroom and small sitting area are luxurious and peaceful. Perfect, actually. A yawn catches me unaware. I'm exhausted. I've barely done anything today, but the small amount of effort I've expended has sapped all my available strength. "It's beautiful."

Thiago eases me down on the bed. Squatting in front of me for a second, he pulls off my shoes, then walks over to the dresser to grab some pajamas. "You'll be more comfortable in your usual sleepwear." He returns and holds out his hands to help me stand.

No time like the present to test out whether this is going to work. With a deep breath, I stand and wait for his instructions.

"Would you like me to close my eyes?" he softly offers.

I shake my head no, my gaze fixed on the center of his chest.

His fingers find the hem of my t-shirt, blunt tips sliding against my skin as he pulls one side of it up. I suck in a deep breath.

He clears his throat. "Let's remove your shirt first. I'll leave your bra on, swap the shirts, then remove it, okay?"

At my nod, he eases one arm out of the left hole, then does the same on the right before tugging the shirt over my head. My body protests loudly, but I grit my teeth until the pain eases.

Without pause, he slips the sleep shirt over my head, but when he tries to ease my arm up through the sleeve, we realize the pajama top is smaller than the previous t-shirt. A sharp pain pierces my side, and a whimper escapes.

Thiago frowns. "Hold on. I'll be right back." He strides out the door, leaving me half dressed with the shirt hanging around my neck. Seconds later, he returns with a large white t-shirt. "This will be easier for you to wear. You won't have to lift your arms very high to get into it, and it won't constrict you when you sleep."

Without waiting for my reply, he slips off my shirt and puts his on me. The shirt sleeves are practically at my waist. Relieved, I slide my arms into the holes with very little effort. The light fabric floats across my body, its texture so incredibly soft it's like wearing a cloud. Rubbing a piece of the fabric between my finger and thumb, it's hard to tell if it's cotton or silk. Who knew t-shirts could be so luxurious?

"So much easier," I inform him. Looking up with a smile, I find his intense eyes narrowed on the shirt I'm wearing. Electricity arcs between us and my smile fades while my heart picks up its already rapid beat.

He leans over, pulling me in closer, his hard body dwarfing my smaller one, and wraps his arms around me. His masculine scent saturates the air, burrowing deep into my lungs and skin. Caged in his circle, I can't see, smell, or feel anything but him. I'm consumed by this moment. Fingers trail up my spine, causing me to involun-tarily arch into his chest. My hands grip his biceps for balance, unintentionally pulling him even closer to me. The man isn't even trying to turn me on, and yet I'm practically putty in his large, very capable hands. A soft groan escapes.

His fingers stop, pads pressing lightly into my back, holding me to him for a split second of time, then he shifts and unclasps my bra. I sigh when the soft band around my chest loosens, but I'm not thinking of the pain, only the need to remove the offending barrier between us.

He clears his throat and leans back to angrily question me. "Why did you put on a bra when it hurt so much?" Fingers deftly maneuver the bra out of the shirt.

The desire-drugged moment fades. Defensively, I shrug. "I was in public."

"Next time, let me know, and I'll shield you. But honestly, this is Miami. Nobody would blink an eye," he asserts. He moves my hands to his shoulders. "Hold on to me while I take off your pants."

A delicious shiver runs up my spine at his words. My hands trail nervously across his broad shoulders, sliding against hard, tense muscles, while I wait for him to remove my leggings. Thumbs hook into my waistband and slide them down until I can step out, leaving me almost bare before him.

Large hands slide back up my legs to my waist. He inhales sharply.

"Do you want me to grab you some underwear?" he whispers hoarsely.

My face floods with red. I don't wear underwear under my leggings or my pajamas. Living alone, I'd deemed them optional long ago, but I'll have to change that habit while I'm here. "No, the pajama shorts are fine."

With a loud exhale, he reaches for the shorts, puts my feet into the legs, and pulls them up. Once secure around my hips, his hands grip my waist for a second and it's all I can do to stop myself from leaning into his arms.

He stands and eases me into bed.

"I don't want a nurse," I blurt out, refusing to look too closely at the reasons why.

Satisfaction crosses his face. "Good. I promise we'll take good care of you." He strides out the door.

Easing down farther into the bed, I use sleep to escape the thoughts tumbling through my brain.

CHAPTER 4

THIAGO

O nce out of the room, I lean against the wall and rub my hands on the rough texture of my jeans needing to replace the feel of her silky skin, her silky *bare* skin, from my tactile memory. The bruises all over her face and body should have been a mood killer, but instead I wanted to strip her bare and caress every single mark until pleasure replaced the pain. That's the good side of my thoughts.

My fists clench. The flip side is the need to know every single inch of damage on her body, so I can sear it into my memory. Somewhere deep inside, in the darkest of places, pure rage lashes wildly against its cage, and it needs fuel. It's been like this since we found out about Marcos, but it worsened when I found her lying on the ground, her face barely recognizable, Diego standing over her with his fist raised to strike her. Again.

My finger twitches in memory of the shot I took, but Diego was already falling when it reached him. Cruz' training kicking in a second before my reaction. Damn spook. I hadn't even seen him move into the room. I'm glad he killed him, but the rage refuses to go away. Marcos. Jason. Henley. All of them mine to protect, and yet, I failed spectacularly every single time.

She doesn't belong to you, a voice inside reminds me. I snarl and push aside the image of her dressed in my t-shirt, nipples hard against the soft cotton, her body tuned into my desire. She may not *belong* to me, but she's mine to protect. Ours to protect. All three of us owe her our allegiance and protection.

But it isn't all innocent. I know Mateo is keenly interested in her. Grayson, too, if I'm not mistaken, although he's doing everything he can to run from her. She would be a good match for either of them... or both. They shared a girlfriend long ago, and it seemed to work out fine for them.

I smother the stab of jealousy that hits me and focus on the positive.

Once Mateo and Grayson are happy, I'll be able to find someone and settle down too. It's time. I've focused solely on my family and SEI for the last fifteen years, but I want a legacy. It shouldn't be hard to find someone to fill that role.

The beautiful, accomplished brunette I went out with a month ago is perfect for me. I frown when my mind draws a blank on her name. I shrug. I'm sure it will come to me after I get some sleep. Footsteps echo down the hall, and I straighten when Mateo comes into view.

He stops. "What are you doing in the hallway? Is Henley okay?"

"She's good. Asleep," I murmur, forcing myself to move away from her door. I motion for Mateo to turn and walk back toward the living room. "My guess is she'll sleep for a while. When she wakes, you can take her some dinner."

Ignoring the tug to go in the other direction, I follow Mateo to the back patio. Grayson's sitting on the couch, his head back and eyes closed, with a glass of clear liquid in his hand. I'm guessing it's tequila.

"Did she want us to call Zane and get a nurse for her?" Mateo asks, plopping down in the chair across from Grayson.

"No, she understands the safety concern and is fine with the current plan," I reply without looking over at him. Spotting the decanter of bourbon, I make my way over and pour myself a drink, then drop down beside them. "She'll need to wear our shirts for the next few days until her body is a bit more healed. They hang farther down and make it easy for her to slip her arms in and out." It will be better for my sanity if they supply her with their clothes.

Mateo pulls out his phone to make a note. He's so compulsively organized. I chuckle.

When I look over to share my amusement with Grayson, he's staring at me with a shuttered look on his face. I wait, but he says nothing.

Finishing my drink, I set the glass down on the table and lean back on the sofa. *I just need to close my eyes for a few seconds, then I'll get up*, I promise myself.

———

TINKLING LAUGHTER WAKES ME. Confused, I tense, waiting for the happy sound to return, but when I don't hear anything, my body relaxes, and my eyes drift closed again. The laugh returns, but this time, I force myself to wake up and listen. It's Mateo and Henley. I get up to go find them.

She's sitting at the dining room table with a pile of t-shirts in front of her when I walk through the patio door.

"This is plenty, I promise," she protests, her arm wrapped around her chest while she laughs. "I'm hoping I'll be able to wear my own clothes soon. Although I do like your taste in t-shirts. They're brainy and nerdy. Perfect."

"Thanks, but some of them..."

Grayson interjects. "Some of them are really old. Maybe you'll spill something on them, and we'll be able to get rid of a few." He pauses when he spots me. "Is everyone ready to eat?"

"Did you clear out your whole closet?" I tease Mateo, but the gleam in his eye tells me he's not the least embarrassed.

"Does everyone have something to drink?" Grayson calls out,

setting a vegetable dish on the table. "Mateo, can you put those in Henley's room? Thiago, would you mind setting the table?"

I follow him back to the kitchen to grab plates and utensils. "Interesting to see a few of your t-shirts in the pile, too. Why didn't you let Mateo tell her?"

"It's nothing. Just a couple of old shirts," he snaps. Picking up a plate of ribs and a bowl of salad, he heads back to the dining table.

"Methinks he doth protest too much," I mutter under my breath.

Although, I certainly understand the appeal. Seeing her at the dining table, in my t-shirt, her bright pink hair tousled from sleep, with those tight little nipples saluting me through the cotton, I could easily forget myself.

An impatient sigh comes from my right. Grayson reaches out and takes the plates and silverware from me to set the table himself. I hold back the snarl rising to the surface and rub a hand down my face to smooth my expression before following him.

After setting everything down, he fills the last plate in his hand with food and sets it in front of Henley.

"Everyone, sit. Eat," he demands, picking up his own plate.

"It's so good. Where did you learn to cook?" Henley asks Grayson after taking a bite.

We all three tense.

His voice is strained when he replies. "Something I picked up when I was a child."

"I'm impressed," Henley teases him, but her smile falters when she sees his vacant stare. Her eyes dart to mine with a question, but I subtly shake my head.

"How are you feeling?" I ask Henley while we wait for Grayson to return from the past.

"Tired. I slept all afternoon and I'm still tired," she admits, with an embarrassed laugh.

"It's to be expected," Mateo informs her and points to his head. "I still get tired, and it's been almost three weeks. It takes time to heal."

"Can I see it?"

He shoves his hair out of the way to show her the ugly scar on his forehead. The bright colorful bruising has faded, but the dark pink scar remains. He had the stitches removed while Henley was in the hospital.

"Sexy," she says jokingly, but the hitch in her voice tells me she finds his scar disturbing. "Although I could have done without the terrifying ride in the middle of the night and the brush of death it took to get it."

I shudder when I think of how close he came to dying. If Diego had succeeded in either of his plans, our table would be a devastatingly lonely place tonight. When I glance at Grayson, his pale face reflects my thoughts.

CHAPTER 5

<u>HENLEY</u>

Brutal fists slam down on my face and body over and over. I try to roll away, but there's no escape. Pain radiates with every blow. If I could only get my hands free... but they're trapped beneath me, useless and numb. A strangled scream erupts from my throat.

"Henley, querida, you're safe. He's not here," a strong voice states firmly, reaching into the dark to find me. "Diego's gone. Forever. I promise. He can't hurt you again." He repeats the same words over and over.

The nightmare recedes, but the fear remains. I open my eyes to scan the room for his ugly face, but he's not here. There is only Thiago holding me, his voice low and steady, repeating his message of assurance while his fingers softly stroke my face.

"I want to see it," I whisper.

He pauses to scrutinize my expression. With a fierce nod, he eases up from the bed and stalks out of the room, returning minutes later with his tablet.

Settling his large body beside me on the bed, he carefully repositions me until I'm sitting halfway up and using his firm chest to lean back on. Wrapping an arm around my shoulders, he props the tablet up on his knees in front of us and pushes play on the video.

The camera jumps wildly up and down while the person wearing the body cam runs toward the grey concrete building in front of them. Running feet, heavy breathing, and low murmurs are the only sounds. Upon reaching the corner, the camera swings a hundred and eighty degrees.

"In position."

"Two seconds."

"On the roof. No line of sight."

"Hold. Lone man running from the building. Not Diego. Detain him?"

"No, let him go, but follow." Thiago's voice is low and purposeful when he responds, but it's the only one I recognize.

"Thermal picks up two people. One on the ground. One standing. No traces of explosives found. Are we a go?"

"Go," Thiago commands.

The camera swivels to the left and stops. A few seconds go by while a man squats in front of something. He reaches out and opens the door, then silently motions forward with two fingers. When the camera gets close, I'm startled to find the man directing everyone is Zane, but instead of the calm, almost sweet man I've become accustomed to, this is a battle-hardened soldier. The camera briefly picks up a flash of cold eyes set in a fierce countenance before it moves forward into the building.

Everyone shuffles quietly through the door into an entryway. An open doorway is directly ahead, and the camera moves steadily toward it. Everything is quiet until the camera gets about two feet away. Then it picks up Diego's shouting and cursing, some in English, some in Spanish, and a low keening sound. The video speeds up, the person bursts through the door, and captures Diego standing above a bloody mess on the ground.

I reach out and pause the frame. It's me. You can tell by the flash of pink hair and the clothes I'm wearing, even if you can't see much else beyond the blood. Diego's gripping my shirt with one hand, his other is raised to punch me again.

His eyes swivel in the direction of the camera, and it's in that moment, I can see he knows he's about to die. Pure defiance and satisfaction blazes on his face, but no fear. No despair like I felt.

Angry, I push play. A gun appears in the camera's line of sight and fires. Diego falls immediately, but something doesn't add up in the timing. I frown and rewind to watch it again before pausing to peer sideways at Thiago.

"Cruz' shot hit him before mine," he bites out, eyes glued to the scene on the tablet, pure rage pouring from every inch of him.

I slide my hand over his clenched fist and look back down at the scene. "I know he got off easy, but I'm glad he's dead. I've been terrified of him ever since he killed Marcos. For weeks, his beady eyes and the gun in his hand haunted me. I could see him shooting Marcos over and over. Whenever he was near, fear would rise in my throat, choking me. Picturing him at the gun range helped ease the fear, but I couldn't shake it. Time was against me. Between murdering Marcos and the Dallas incident, he was my most dangerous threat. With him gone, it gives us time to clean house and figure out our next steps."

I push play again. Boots echo off the concrete floor and the camera races toward the two people on the ground. A man goes by and kneels to confirm Diego's dead, although the bullet hole in the center of his brain and vacant eyes is a good indication. The camera swoops downward, and hovers over my body.

The mic picks up a few words sworn softly in Portuguese, but I don't know their meaning. "Henley, can you hear me? It's Thiago. We're going to get you some help. Stay with me. Can you open your eyes?" The camera swivels around to find Grayson and Mateo standing nearby, staring past Thiago's shoulder, probably at me. "Mateo, get the computer. See if you can pull anything from it. Grayson, tell Zane to get a clean-up crew in here to dispose of the body. In pieces. No traces." With one last look back, the two take off, then Thiago turns the camera and his body back toward me.

30

"All clear."

The camera jostles when Thiago rips off his helmet and vest. The video goes dark.

"One enemy down. Two to go," I state softly. "Did you find the other guy?"

Thiago shuts off the tablet. "No, he slipped through our net. Another former member of our security team. We're looking for him." He tosses the tablet on the nightstand. "Raider, one of Zane's crew, is using his resources to hire an entirely new team for SEI. We can't take a chance the current team hasn't been corrupted by whatever bullshit Diego fed them."

"What about everyone else at SEI?"

Thiago heaves a huge sigh. "We know Carlton is in on it. He's the only other person outside of Mateo who has access to the server where we put our new phone numbers. Right now, we've got someone tailing him and we're monitoring all his work activity. We don't want to tip off our enemy, but we'll need to decide how to handle him soon." He gets up and paces around the room. I'm almost mesmerized by the sight of his powerful body striding back and forth in a pair of dark sweatpants and nothing else. Muscles bunch while he talks with his hands. "The worst part is we have no way of knowing who else might have been recruited by our enemy."

His last words bring me out of my musings. "Money. Give me access to their names and personal information, including their bank accounts, and I'll use a program I created to identify any anomalies or patterns associated with creative accounting methods. If they've received a payout, I'll know. Most people are not smart enough to use a third-party alias, nor do they understand how the banking system works. I do." I bite my lip, then warn him. "It's not legal, and while I can hide my tracks, you need to understand there is a risk."

Hard eyes turn in my direction, showing me the man who made SEI into the powerhouse it is today. "You'll have whatever you need. We're cleaning house. Work with Mateo." He strides over and sits on the side of the bed. "I know you're tired. We'll talk more about this tomorrow. Do you think you can sleep now?" Worry makes his brow furrow deeply.

I'm tired, but I doubt I'll be getting any sleep tonight. I smile and nod.

He chuckles and shakes his head back at me. "You're still a terrible liar." Moving around to the other side of the bed, he pulls back the covers, slides in beside me, and grabs the tablet. "How about a movie? The new James Bond?"

I gasp in disbelief. "Seriously? You want to watch a spy thriller? We're practically living in one right now." A picture from the condo flashes in my head. "Are you the one who has all those spy books in the condo?"

He shrugs defensively. "I like intrigue and action. Do you want to watch it or something else?"

I hold in the laugh threatening to burst out. One because laughing hurts right now and two because I don't want to hurt his manly feelings. "Absolutely. Let's see if we can pick up any good tips."

He narrows his eyes, but presses play on the movie. He positions me along his side, so I can comfortably see the screen, but having his half-naked body so close to mine obliterates any thought of comfort.

Tense, I lie there barely breathing in and out for at least a half hour, feeling every hard line of his warm chest against me, but his eyes never waver from the screen. My body slowly relaxes, curling into his until a dreamless sleep claims me.

CHAPTER 6

<u>HENLEY</u>

Mateo wakes me the next morning. I immediately glance to my right, but the only indication Thiago slept beside me is the masculine smell drifting up from the sheets. His pillowcase is even smooth.

Unable to lift my arms high, I settle for a basic shower, but the thought of going another day without washing my hair is driving me crazy. Walking slowly into the bedroom, I finger the ends of my dry and very dirty hair and eye the man in front of me. "Mateo, do you think you could help me wash my hair?" Silence greets me, and I frown. Looking up, I raise an eyebrow.

"Sorry, distracted. Seeing you half-dressed is becoming a favorite look for me," he reveals, his voice husky. "Yes, I've got a plan which should work. If you lie on a lounger outside, I can wash your hair as it hangs off the back. Hopefully, it will be easier on you because you won't have to hold yourself up or lean over a counter. But let's get you dressed first."

Such a small thing, but the fact he's already thought of a plan to wash my hair makes me smile.

He grabs one of the t-shirts off the bed and helps me slip it on.

I look down. It's a Green Day t-shirt. "Were you a big fan?"

When he looks puzzled, I point to the front of the shirt.

He smirks. "Actually, Grayson is the fan. I must have picked up one of his shirts."

The mischievous gleam in his eye makes me nervous, but I refuse to ask. If he stole one of Grayson's favorite shirts, he can pay the consequences. I'm not getting involved.

Instead of the intense desire I felt when Thiago undressed me last night, this morning's session with Mateo is full of fun and flirty moments. Soft caresses, a peck on my shoulder, and a wink when we're done.

Once we get outside, he helps me sit on the lounger, then slowly lowers it to an almost flat position. My head rests on the back edge and my hair hangs over. "Have you ever done this before?"

After gathering his supplies, he pours water over my hair to soak it. "Mmm, why don't you relax and let me concentrate?" Warm palms smooth shampoo on to my hair first, then strong fingers slowly work it into the strands. When they start massaging my scalp, my eyes close, and I sigh.

For the next however long, the world zooms out of focus, and I luxuriate in the feeling of complete bliss encompassing my entire body. Only the occasional murmur from Mateo to turn my head one way or the other penetrates the semi-aware state I've embraced.

A shadow eclipses the sun, but before I can open my eyes, his lips find mine for a long, unhurried kiss. It's sensual and yet, relaxed, stirring up the briefest of embers without fanning them into a flame. He pulls back and I open my eyes and lock onto his warm brown ones.

"Thank you. It was wonderful. It's been a long time since I've fully relaxed." My normally husky voice is deeper than usual.

"My pleasure. Let's get you up into a sitting position," he rasps. After raising the back of the chair, he gathers his supplies and takes them into the house.

A few minutes later, we're sitting in the sun, letting my freshly washed hair dry, when I bring up my late-night discussion. "Thiago and I had a chat last night about finding the rest of the SEI traitors, but I need your help to execute it." I explain the idea, then proceed to give him a list of items I'll need. "If you can get a few additional clean laptops, the search will go a lot faster. Do you have anything here? If not, I can order some to be delivered tomorrow."

It's as if I threw a switch. Mateo's mood shifts from lighthearted to focused in a nanosecond, and for most people, it would probably feel abrupt, but I find comfort in the familiarity of it.

"I've got a couple here I use for testing. I can wipe and reset them pretty quickly." He pauses. "And I also have your laptop. I grabbed it from the hotel room before the police could get there. I'll get it for you, but you must promise to also rest, or Thiago will have my head." He gives me a stern look.

"I promise. Nothing more strenuous than pecking at a few keys," I retort but with a smile. It's nice to have someone worried about me.

He raises an eyebrow in disbelief but finally leaves to get the laptops.

While he's gone, I pick up my phone and contemplate interrupting Cruz' mission to send him a text but decide a short one can't hurt. "Thiago showed me the video from the warehouse. Thank you. I'll sleep better knowing."

"I've always got your back, even when I'm not around. Text if you need anything," Cruz replies quickly, making me smile.

Sterling said Cruz' mission was going well, but that's it, and I didn't want to pry. It's enough to know he's safe. I set down the phone.

I'm lightly dozing when something cold touches my arm. Startled, I flinch away, only to be caught by a hand at my elbow. Following it up to a pair of dark blue eyes, I scowl at Grayson. "Don't sneak up on me. Or grab me when I'm sleeping." The memories of the past collide with the recent memories of Diego, causing my body to shake from a spike of adrenaline. Or fear. Maybe both. "Sorry. I don't mean to be rude, but it

35

triggers too... much." I don't want to admit to him how close the edge is right now, so I look away, hiding from those observant eyes of his.

I bite the inside of my cheek while I consider what my reaction means. I sigh, knowing what it means. I'm going to have to start up my therapy sessions again. On one hand, I'm relieved I already have someone familiar to talk to, but I'm also frustrated to find I've slipped back a few steps.

Grayson runs a finger down my arm. "I didn't want you to burn, so I brought some sunscreen out. Knowing your preference for applying it yourself, I'd normally hand it to you, but it might be tough to get to all the places right now." He waits, sunscreen in his hand, for me to decide.

My skin is already pink from the thirty or forty minutes I've been out here, and I doubt I'd do a good job of applying it right now, so I slowly nod my agreement.

He motions to the cold glob sitting on my bicep. "I'm going to start again. If it gets uncomfortable, all you have to do is say 'stop.' Okay?" Without waiting for a reply, his large warm hand reaches out and smooths the sunscreen down my arm to my hand. Soft, light strokes I can barely feel.

My eyes flick to his face, but he's concentrating on the job at hand, so I blatantly stare at him. The dark circles have faded a bit, and overall, his movements are more fluid.

His eyes dart to mine when he moves down the lounger to start on my leg.

I nod my agreement to his silently raised eyebrow.

My legs didn't fare too badly in the beating. My knees are black and blue, and my ankles have a few pink welts from the restraints, but honestly, pretty good.

His fingers stroke softly, up and down, rubbing the sunscreen into the skin. He's meticulous in his application, and it feels divine. My legs fall open to let him get to the inside, and I hear a breath whistle out of him, but he never looks up.

Needing a distraction, I throw out the question that's been on my mind for days. "What do you do for Zane on those missions? You were pretty banged up when you came to the hospital."

His hands pause, but he doesn't look up. "Why do you ask?"

"A question with a question?" I snort. Why am I not surprised? Fine. I'll answer. "I don't like seeing my... friends in that condition. You looked like you were in a lot of pain." I stare steadily at the top of his head, waiting for him to look up and meet my eyes.

Blue eyes filled with surprise find mine. "Zane's missions are dangerous. We rescue people from violent situations. Sometimes things don't go according to plan." He shrugs nonchalantly.

A vague answer, but an answer. "What's your role?"

Fingers stroke circles on the inside of my thigh, and tingles radiate up toward my core. I inhale, prepared to tell him to stop, but he's not looking at me or my legs. He's staring off into the distance. I quietly release my breath and focus on him.

"Zane calls me when he needs a negotiator or an interrogator. Both take advantage of my unique ability to tell lies from truth. Plus, people tend to gravitate toward me. Some even like me," he asserts with a smirk in my direction. He switches to the other side of the lounger and starts on my left leg.

"What about the danger? Aren't you scared?"

His hands stop rubbing the lotion for a brief second. "Yes."

"Why do you do it?" My question hangs in the air for a second while he considers answering it.

He finishes up my leg and moves up the lounger to my left arm. "Almost done," he assures me.

Disappointed by the lack of an answer, I frown and watch his fingers finish the job. My arms and legs tingle pleasantly everywhere he's touched, but my mind is a jumble of thoughts while I try to work out the why without his input.

He caps the bottle and turns back to me. "Now you can stay out here and work with Mateo for a while." He stands. "I go on the missions because I need reassurance that I can still separate the lies from the truth and haven't allowed myself to become lax. It helps Zane, too, but like all things"—he gives a self-deprecating laugh—"I do it for myself."

He walks off, and I hear him mumble something about Green Day to Mateo, who only laughs.

Mateo comes up beside me and hands me my laptop.

"Do you go on missions with Zane, too?" I blurt out.

He tilts his head and darts a speculative glance toward the patio, where Grayson just disappeared. "He told you?"

"I asked. He answered," I reply. Sort of.

He sits on the lounger across from me. "No, I don't go on missions with Zane. Neither does Thiago. Only Grayson. Sometimes the past drives us to do things we wouldn't normally consider." He opens two laptops and waits for me to open mine. "I've reset these. This is going to take a while, so let's get started."

CHAPTER 7

MATEO

After downloading the program and setting up the laptops, we write additional code to pull the employee information automatically from the list I created into the software, so we don't have to type new search queries each time. Since this isn't legal, I didn't want any APIs connected to SEI or our networks, but a simple table works fine in this instance.

My stomach rumbles with nerves while I wait for the first results to come back, but Henley is practically vibrating. "Do you find this exciting?"

She hesitates. "Yes, I do." Her chin rises high in the air. "When I first started hacking, I felt guilty. Why should I use my brain to help someone deceive the system or get something they didn't deserve? My first jobs were simple modifications to grades and degrees. They were quick, easy, and paid well. To stay hidden and flush with easy cash, I constantly pulled in the same jobs over and over. It was mind-numbing, honestly." Her mouth twists in memory.

I scowl, hating the thought of anyone changing their grades. "What made you... graduate into bigger things?"

"Two things. One: I needed a more secure identity for myself so I could establish bank accounts and find better living accommodations. Weekly motels are a bit hazardous. Two: if I learned how to make quality fake IDs for myself, I could use the skills to create identities for others. IDs are considerably more lucrative than changing grades," she replies matter-of-factly.

The image of a weekly motel near downtown Miami pops into my mind, and I can't help but look at her in shock. "You were living in weekly motels? How did you even stay safe?"

She gives me a wry expression, but I honestly can't fathom living in one. It really brings home the reality of her situation.

"I'm sorry. I'm just trying to understand," I promise her. One of our first real conversations pops into my brain. "And this is where Marcos stepped in to help you? He taught you to create the identities, create back-up accounts, and all the other stuff you needed to learn to stay hidden."

A radiant smile bursts across her face. "He did. I'll never forget it. When I tell you he saved me, I mean it. Not only from my stalker. Who knows what would have happened if I'd continued to live so precariously close to the bottom?" She purses her lips. "I never felt guilty again. People do a lot of terrible, terrible things out there. Marcos helped me establish my own moral code to guide me on my shadowy path. He pointed me to areas of the dark web where good people were desperate for help and made me research every job to ensure I wasn't helping the worst of humanity." She levels a serious look at me. "I survived and made a life. And slowly, Marcos and I found a new way to make money together. Although, as you know, I've never quit making IDs. They're too important."

"I wish I'd known all this before Marcos died," I rasp. "He must have needed those skills when we fled South America. I know Thiago often felt guilty for the things Marcos had to do, but I never understood it until now. Marcos came to get my mom and me when I was seven. Once we reached Miami, there was never a time I didn't have everything I needed, or even most of what I wanted, but I never realized what it took for him to give that to us." My brow furrows. Thiago's right. I really have lived in my own world, protected from everything. First by my mother and Marcos and now, Thiago. It feels so selfish.

She reaches over and grabs my hand. "Don't. Marcos wouldn't want you to feel guilty because you had a good life. He gave you a gift. Find a way to give it to someone else. Pass it on. Get involved with the rescue missions or with another cause where you can use your incredible brain to find solutions to help others. It's the best way to honor him." Her blue eyes are incredibly earnest in her quest to encourage me. The computer dings. She peers down at the results. "We found our first potential traitor. Paul Masterson. Name ring a bell?"

I think about it for a second. "Security team. High probability it's true. Now what do we do?"

"Basically, the program found several substantial deposits unrelated to normal income flow," she explains, reading the data from the screen in front of her. "We simply trace the money to see if it's legit income. Maybe he has a rich uncle sending him regular money or a side business. If it's honest income, it will be traceable." She wrinkles her nose, and I laugh at the irony of her statement.

"Excluding you and Marcos?" I tease.

Her mouth twitches, but she doesn't reply. It takes me a full minute to realize she's zoned out. I chuckle. This must be what it feels like when I go off into my own world. No wonder they get exasperated with me.

She suddenly leans forward, then gasps while holding her ribs. "Damn, remind me not to move quickly." Her face is ashen with pain despite the colorful bruises decorating it. She carefully straightens and breathes in and out for a few minutes.

"Okay. That hurt. A. Lot. Where was I?" She darts a glance at her computer to find the answer. "Oh yes, I might have found an interesting pattern that could help identify some of the early dissenters. All the early deposits in Paul's account can be traced to a closed account at a bank in Houston, Texas. The name on the account is fake, and the trail stops there, but it means our enemy wasn't quite as sophisticated in the beginning. That came with time, and possibly the hiring of our invisible man who is obviously a genius."

"If the trail stops, how does it help us?" I frown, not following her train of thought.

"If my stalker taught me anything, it's the fact that nobody is invisible, no matter how hard they try to hide themselves. Which is why Marcos let Thiago's father think he died and set up my death, too. People don't look for the dead," she informs me with a shrug. "Maybe Zane and his team can follow the trail physically or check old security footage. I'm not exactly well-versed in the more espionage aspects, but I'm sure they'll have some ideas."

I relay the information to Thiago via text, and he agrees with Henley. It's worth checking out. He's meeting with Raider and Zane in an hour to go over the new candidates for the security team, so he'll see what they say.

Her shiny pink hair catches my eye. It's completely dry. "With this new variable, we can separate the employee list into two tables with different search queries, which means we should be able to finish this afternoon. Before we start on this final batch, let's move to the couches on the patio. They're considerably more comfortable than these loungers." Helping her up, I get us moved and resettled on the softer furniture.

My list finishes quicker than I anticipated, and I glance over at Henley to see if I can pick up some of her names, but those beautiful blue eyes are closed. I reach over and set her laptop on the coffee table, letting the program continue to run, then make her more comfortable with a pillow and blanket. With her bruises, sleeping upright probably feels better, so I don't move her.

I grab a seat next to her on the couch to give her a bit of structure. A few minutes later, her head slides onto my shoulder and I decide to forego my usual rabbit hole tendencies to live in the moment with her. With a sigh, I lean my head back and close my eyes.

Our conversation from earlier has been silently weighing on my mind. The things she's done go against every principle of mine, but all I feel is admiration for her ability to survive and thrive with the cards life dealt her. In comparison, my life has been easy. Doors have never been closed to me. Either Marcos' influence or my intelligence opened them.

Even the bullying in my early years stopped once Grayson joined our family. He didn't even have to threaten most of them. He accepted me, and as a result, others did too. Some might have thought me odd, but they have never said it out loud because they didn't want to risk losing Grayson's friendship.

Growing up, college, the present. All seem to blur together with only a few high points standing out, like my degrees, SEI, and family events. The lows are barely a blip on the screen.

Women I've dated in the past follow the same pattern. High achievers, smart and extremely capable women, focused on their careers. The relationships were... satisfactory for all parties. A meeting of the mind and body. Except for one five-year relationship, none of them disrupted my life, and even when the more serious one ended, my heart might have been a bit bruised, but I can't recall thinking about it too much.

Why does it feel like I've been living on the surface of life? Before Henley, I never looked to deepen my experience in anything; my only focus was the accumulation of more knowledge.

But she makes me see the world differently, literally question the foundation of acceptance and latitude I've approached life with until it feels like it's turned on its axis. We haven't spent much time together, but there's something about her, something I haven't felt before, a connection. At first, I thought it might have been generated from the adrenaline rush of the car chase or the fact she reminds me of Marcos, but somehow, it's more.

What does she think of me? Affection, maybe. Chemistry, definitely. The image of her coming apart in my arms at the beach flashes through my mind, and my body throbs in response. It doesn't help that I've been semi-hard since I sat down and breathed in her delicious body wash. With a groan, I adjust myself and try to think of other things.

I don't know what she feels, but I refuse to stand on the sidelines of my life. Maybe I should do a little research. It couldn't hurt. We're a little restricted on the dating options right now, but I'm sure I can think of something.

When Thiago and Grayson walk out on the patio around six p.m., Henley is in my arms fast asleep and I'm mentally making a plan. The programs finished compiling the list an hour ago, but instead of falling into my usual obsessive behavior to chase down additional information, I stayed with her. My fingers glide through her soft hair, loving the feel of the strands against my skin.

"How long has she been asleep?" Thiago asks gruffly.

"Sleeping or sleeping peacefully?" I murmur in reply. "She fell into a restless sleep a couple of hours ago, so I pulled her into my arms. She's been sleeping peacefully now for a little over an hour."

"She had nightmares last night, too. Demanded to see the footage from the rescue," Thiago admits quietly. He meets my questioning glance steadily but gives little away. "She's going to need some help to get over things, especially with her past."

I nod my agreement, my fingers sliding through the strands again.

"Did you find any results?" Thiago questions tersely, determined to clean SEI's house quickly.

Motioning to the pad of paper on the coffee table, I wait for him to pick it up. "It's not quite as bad as we thought. We found twenty-two people at SEI who've taken bribes in the last four years. Most of them were in security and IT, but we did have one person in accounting." I dart a glance to Grayson, whose lips compress in anger. "Surprisingly, Philip Carlton didn't turn traitor until last year."

"They've been bribing people for four years, but we didn't even notice, which tells me they didn't have the right people in place until Philip Carlton. When did Diego become a traitor?" Thiago asks, his brain sifting through the strategic implications quickly.

"Diego was the first. Most of the security team came on board with him. He managed to recruit a few IT people, but nobody of note until Philip," I reveal. "Philip must have been the golden goose. If I recall correctly, the timing isn't coincidental either. Philip pitched new software to us about three months prior to him taking the first bribe. We declined to move forward with it because we were focusing all our resources on the new security upgrade we were planning to launch. I can't recall much about the pitch, but I'll look into it."

Grayson jerks his head toward me. "Actually, I remember this one. It's the first time I'd ever sat in on a software pitch for SEI, but because it focused on the financial sector and could benefit my clients the most, I attended. The software was intriguing, but not ground-breaking, and unfortunately, it wouldn't generate the same revenue we were forecasting for the update to our security prod-ucts, so we declined to move forward. We did tell Philip he could shop it around, or we would broker it for him, but he didn't want to go those routes."

I rub the bridge of my nose under my glasses while I think back on the pitch, but I'm still drawing a blank. "I'll have to pull a copy from the archives."

Grayson holds up a bag. "I picked up dinner on the way home. I'll get everything together." He strides back into the house.

Thiago stretches and follows him out. "I'm going to grab a shower."

Shifting my attention to the woman sleeping in my arms, I lightly place kisses on her cheeks and lips to wake her up. "Wake up, minha linda. It's time for dinner."

Her lashes lift and she turns a sleepy look my way. "Mateo?"

Her head lifts and I help ease her into a sitting position. She tries to subtly wipe her hand across her mouth, and I shake my head.

"You didn't snore or drool. Quite disappointing, really," I tease her.

She scoffs, but I see the relief in her eyes. "Did you finish running the lists?"

45

I nod and give her the same update I gave to Thiago and Grayson.

"I'm sorry," she offers softly.

With Philip being my personal recruit and a lead in my department, the betrayal hits me hard. "I was hoping we were wrong, but..." My voice trails off. "Come on, slacker. Let's go eat." I laugh at her mock fury, needing the moment of light-heartedness.

Philip is a punch in the gut. If there was one person, besides my family, who I'd have staked as loyal, it would have been him. Now, I must figure out a way to set a trap and catch him red-handed in the act. I want him to realize I've played him for a fool like he did me. A bittersweet victory, but I'll take it.

CHAPTER 8

HENLEY

Grayson brought Cubano sandwiches home for dinner. Massive concoctions encased in a grilled sweet bread and filled with pork, ham, pickles, Swiss cheese, and mustard. It's a masterpiece of flavors. I glance over and find him watching me with a satisfied smile. My mouth is full, so I give him a thumbs up.

He reaches across me and grabs the honey off the table. Pouring a spoonful onto my plate, he motions for me to dip my sandwich into it.

When I add the honey to my second bite, I can't help but moan at the flavors. Tart mustard and sweet honey fuse together in the most utterly delicious combination. I wonder if there's a Cuban restaurant nearby. If a sandwich is this good, the rest must be out of this world. A big glob of mustard and ham falls on my plate, making me laugh. It's certainly one of the messiest things I've ever eaten.

"I've never had Cuban food, but I definitely want to try more now," I say enthusiastically, barely able to get the words out between bites. *So freaking good.*

While I finish the rest of my sandwich, Thiago explains the new security team to Grayson and Mateo. "Our new head of security is an old Army Ranger buddy of Zane's, who he backs a hundred percent. His name is Jameson Bennett. Raider recruited the rest of the team through other contacts to ensure the team's loyalty is to SEI instead of one individual man. Most of the members are ex-military, comprised of men and women, and they're lethal."

He pauses to take a bite. "Since we were overhauling the entire team, we took advantage of the fresh start to create some necessary structural changes. Security branches out into three areas. Cybersecurity, personal security, and SEI's defense. We appointed leads for each branch according to their expertise. One man, Jaxon Pointer, spent quite a lot of time in cybersecurity for the Pentagon, and he'll head up cybersecurity for SEI."

He looks pointedly at Mateo, whose face fills with satisfaction. I know Mateo and Diego hadn't gotten along because of Diego's lack of cyber knowledge and his inability to prepare SEI against any attacks, but this new plan obviously has Mateo's full approval.

"Thomas Sanders will lead our personal security. He will be reaching out to speak with you about your schedule. Security is going to be more restrictive," he says, glancing at Grayson, who grimaces. "But right now, it's necessary. The third team will be focused on SEI's security. Employee backgrounds, buildings, the jets, and so forth. That team will be led by Allison Engles. Any questions?"

For the next few minutes, they talk logistics, but my mind drifts away to start a to-do list. I wonder if any of the rootkits burrowed into our enemies' computers. If they did, I need to set an activity alert.

"Earth to Henley," Mateo whispers in my ear.

Jolting, I turn and see his wide smile. "What? Sorry. I drifted off for a second."

"That's okay. We're used to it," Grayson says, his eyes darting to Mateo. "Would you like some dessert?" He motions to the stack of pastries in front of me. "They're pastelitos—pastries filled with various fruit custards and other ingredients. These have guava and cream cheese inside of them."

I grab one and take a large bite. Flaky bits fall off and float down onto my plate. "Mmm, they're kind of like a crossover between a turnover and a Danish. Pretty good." Guava cream squirts onto my fingers, and without thinking, I lick it off. Then immediately stop. I barely hold in the groan of disgust. I'm so used to eating by myself I didn't even think before licking my hand. My face heats with embarrassment, but I refuse to look up before I finish. Once the last bite is gone, my eyes dart to each of them, but they're busy finishing their own pastry. I sigh with relief. It's weird living with other people, and I haven't quite gotten used to it.

"Have we lost you again?" Mateo asks, laughter in his voice.

"No, I'm still here," I counter with a mock glare in his direction. Talk about pot and kettle. "Actually, I'm really glad to have my computer so I can check on the rootkits I installed on the videos and the drive."

Mateo stops eating. "What rootkits?"

Oops, I guess I forgot to tell him about the traps I set. "When the videos kept disappearing, I decided to install rootkits on the remaining copies in the hopes of catching some intel off an enemy's computer. In addition, I loaded mock AR software on a flash drive. I saw Diego pick it up when he came to get me in my apartment that day, and I'm hopeful he gave it to someone important. I checked once, but there wasn't any activity. I'm going to check again tonight and set up an alert."

"You're saying we could possibly have a spy in the enemy's computer?" Mateo asks in disbelief. When Thiago and Grayson give him puzzled looks, he goes on to give them a high-level explanation of a rootkit. "Basically, it's malicious software designed to enable remote access to someone else's computer. It's extremely intrusive and very hard to detect because it can literally hide itself or subvert a program looking for malware. While your computer security software might be able to detect and remove it, most don't have the capability. It usually requires you to replace your hardware to get rid of it. It's a digital Trojan horse." He grins widely.

"We don't know for sure if or who downloaded it. It could be an entry level goon for all we know," I interject, not wanting anyone to get their hopes up. "But fingers crossed, we find something."

"Keep me informed," Thiago orders in an arrogant tone.

I narrow my eyes at him, but he only raises an eyebrow in response.

Mateo chuckles but says nothing.

Expensive cologne fills the air when Grayson leans over me to get my plate.

"I can take my dishes to the kitchen, Grayson," I protest, feeling weird about him waiting on me all the time.

"It's always a pleasure to assist a beautiful woman," he replies smoothly.

I deliberately look at him and roll my eyes.

An ember appears in those blue depths of his. "Wouldn't you do the same for me?"

"Help you or give you fake compliments?"

"Ouch, you wound me," he says with a laugh. "Make no mistake, Henley, you're a beautiful woman. I don't lie. Ever."

Unsure of what to say in return, I sit there and stare at him.

"Thank you for dinner," I finally stammer out. Keeping my back straight and using mostly my legs, I manage to stand by myself. "If you'll excuse me, I'm going to the patio to check on the rootkits."

With small steps, I make my way outside and over to the couch. I'm considering the best way to sit when someone helps me. Breathing in deeply, I smell Mateo's fresh, clean scent and look up at him and smile.

He hands me my computer and takes a seat next to me while I check on the rootkits. The ones I installed on the videos haven't had any activity. I'm guessing they destroyed the files without downloading them. I set an alert, but with little hope they'll return anything.

The rootkit on the software is active. Right now. Fascinated, I follow the path I established into the heart of the enemy's computer. Unfortunately, the web cam is blocked, but I can see the code they're reviewing. It's the dummy code I'd installed on the flash drive. I can't help but smirk.

They're scrolling slowly through the lines, probably looking for some indication of its authenticity. It's a pretty good fake. The only way they'll know whether it works or not is if they test it.

"Wow, you really went all out to convince them it's the real deal," Mateo states with surprise.

"Honestly, we had extra code from tests that failed, which enabled me to create something quickly. I wasn't sure if it would work, but it needed to be convincing enough for them to install and test it out. At the very least, I hoped it would buy us time or insight."

Digging around in the directory, I find a lot of boring stuff. Going into the control panel, I dive into the advanced settings until I find "Show hidden files, folders, and drives." Presto! A slew of files appears. They all have names on them, like Emma, Amala, Hieu, Garrett, and so forth.

Opening the first one, I find software code and scan through it. A signature pops up in the meta description tag. <meta name="description" content="Emma Parker, Facial Recognition Algorithm developed for Computer Sciences 4001, Dr. Langford MIT."/> I scan through the code, and it looks completely legitimate.

I quickly move to another folder labeled "Amala." It's also code. I open it and scan the information in the head tag until I find the meta description tag. <meta name="description" content="Amala Vinya, Identifying Email Spam Algorithm developed for Computer Sciences, 4001, Dr. Langford MIT."/>

"Do you think he stole all these ideas?" Mateo's outraged voice brings me out of my rabbit hole.

"I'm not sure. Dr. Langford is one of the best algorithm professors at MIT. Since my scholarship was based on the algorithm I developed, they assigned him to me as my advisor, although I only ever met with his grad assistant. I couldn't wait to attend his class, but I never got the chance because I left after my sophomore year."

His finger sweeps down the folder. "Look."

The folder is labeled "Henley", and with trepidation, I open it. The banking algorithm I developed is in the folder, but I'm not outraged. "MIT published my code when I won the scholarship. It wasn't stolen."

I peruse the code but find nothing different from the one I created. There are additional files in the folder, so I glance through them until I find a pretty extensive chunk of code. Pieces of my work embedded within a slew of new lines. Intrigued, I scan the code to figure out how they built upon my original idea. When I see the commands in the code, I begin to get an inkling of what I'm looking at.

"Son of a..."

"What is it?" Mateo asks.

"I think it's the code they used to play the shell game with your money. The code builds off my original idea, but they expanded it to create this massive new algorithm. The work is impeccable, but there is no way they could do this quickly. This is the type of project one works on for a year or two." I turn the screen toward him and point out the new areas of code, which are quite extensive.

He whistles. "Going back to the others, let's write down the student's name and find out when they attended MIT. See if there's a common denominator."

Surprised, I look at him. "You're not just a handsome face, are you?" He looks surprised when I lean over and give him a quick kiss on the lips. "Got a pen and paper?"

It's tedious work, but we knock it out quickly. Then, we pull up the MIT archives and search for the names on our list.

"They all attended the same years I did, although they were a year or two ahead of me," I state, stunned by the information. "I wonder if we should find them and ask whether their work was stolen or simply picked up after publishing. Maybe we'll find something in common besides MIT, algorithms, and Dr. Langford."

Pulling up Google, I start to search for the first name, but Mateo closes the lid. "Tomorrow. You need to rest or Thiago's going to come down on both of us." He points to where Thiago stands in the doorway.

I purse my lips, contemplating defiance, but cave when I realize how tired I am from the long day. "Fine." I hold my hands up for Mateo to help me. "Take me to bed or lose me forever, Goose."

Mateo looks confused, but I hear a snort come from Thiago. Interesting. The man loves his movies and not just the spy thrillers, either.

CHAPTER 9

My heart's pounding and my entire body is clammy when I wake around midnight. The nightmares prey on me like my stalker once I fall into a deep sleep. Carefully sliding my feet to the floor, I continue to lie flat until my legs can support my weight, then sort of slide off while lifting my body. I inhale sharply when the expectant pain pierces my side, but surprisingly, it eases quickly, and I shuffle my way to the restroom.

When I come out, the light by my bed is on and Thiago's standing beside it with his hands on his hips and a scowl on his face. "Why didn't you call me to come help?"

Easing down onto the bed, I wave off his concern. "It's fine, really. I need to start trying to do things on my own. Go back to bed, Thiago."

He pulls the covers up for me and reaches over to turn off the light.

"Leave it on," I bite out, my tone sharp. Softening it, I tack on some manners. "Please."

His dark eyes are sharp while they assess me. "Nightmares?"

I shrug, not wanting to say it out loud.

With a decisive jerk of his chin, he strides around the bed to the other side, fingers already undoing the top button of his jeans. Sliding them off, he reaches back and grabs the neck of his t-shirt and pulls it off, too. He stands by the bed in his black boxer briefs for an itty bitty blip of time before easing in next to me.

But it's too late. The image of his body in those short snug briefs is burned into my retinas forever, and it's hard to hold back my groan. I thought his naked chest was incredible, but his legs are sculpted and stacked with muscle, too. Thiago's big, but I didn't quite expect all of that. The man must work out a lot. Like a lot, a lot. Maybe every day. Dark coarse hair graces a few areas of his body, but the rest is smooth dark skin and hard lines. My heart races for an entirely different reason when I envision tracing each line and groove with my tongue.

I clear my throat to tell him he doesn't have to stay with me. "Thank you." It seems the words about him leaving are gone. Poof.

His warm body slides up against mine, causing me to shiver. He must think I'm cold or scared, because he pulls me deeper into his arms and practically wraps his body around mine.

Every inch of muscle imprints onto my tactile memory. And if that's not enough, the combination of his subtle aftershave and the unique scent of him buries itself in my nose and lungs. Now, every time I see this man, I'll be thinking of his delicious-smelling, hard body wrapped around me.

My hands stretch across the inch of space between us to rest on his hips. Hard, angled muscles fill my palms, but I don't allow myself to grip him like I want. Instead, I force my hands to lie inno-cently on the surface.

His voice is gruff when he speaks. "I completely understand. For years, I had recurring nightmares about my father finding us, killing Mateo and Grayson, Marcos, and Tia Mariana. It took me a long time to feel safe. Talking to someone helped, though." He leans back to look me in the eyes. "You can always tell me whatever you want. I'm a good listener." Sincerity and a shared empathy shine brightly from his obsidian gaze.

"I..." I don't finish the sentence because I don't know where to start. The past and present have been thrown in a blender together and I can't tell one from the other. Maybe with the similarities? "He." I pause, my voice cracking with bad memories. "My stalker caught me once and held me for two weeks in a dark basement with only a single window up high." Thiago stiffens against me. "When I woke in the warehouse, it felt the same—dark with a window up high. Diego unknowingly created the perfect environment for the old memories to surface. The nightmares with him beating me eased after I saw him die, but the fear of being trapped and held in a dark place is harder for me to get over."

His hand strokes my back softly. "How did you move past it before?"

"Marcos demanded I see a therapist. She helped me expose my fears, and eventually, the nightmares stopped. I'll call her tomorrow," I promise him. Without thinking, I lift my chin and lean forward to kiss those stern, but tantalizing, lips in front of me. "Thank you for staying with me."

He freezes. "Let's get some sleep," he states firmly, his big hand pulling my head down to his chest.

Embarrassed, I lie there quietly. Obviously, him being here with me is just a sign of his protectiveness and not anything more. Should I apologize for the kiss? I don't even know what it meant or if it meant anything at all. I bite my bottom lip, trying to erase the feel of his firm lips against mine. He shifts and my face moves another inch, causing the side of my head to rest more fully against him. My ear catches the distinct sound of his rapidly beating heart.

———

OF COURSE, he's gone by sunrise. Unlike the last time, I wake the minute he slides out but keep my eyes closed until after he leaves.

When I open them, the smooth pillow beside me catches my eye. Is the secrecy for my benefit or his?

Taking a deep breath, I brace myself and move up inch by inch until I'm reclining against the pillows, then grab my laptop off the nightstand. Might as well get some work done.

I search for the individuals on our list and find a few of them are now professors or executives at large corporations, so I send them a couple of emails to ask about Dr. Langford and their code.

While I wait for the answers, I grab a file from the InterPlanetary File System, where I hid an extra copy of the AR/VR code, and un-encrypt it. Once I've checked to make sure it's the final version, I sit there for a minute, fingers tapping rapidly on the edge of the laptop while I consider the potential ramifications of what I'm about to do. I nod. It's worth the risk.

I sift through the directory of a gaming company known to be on the verge of getting their VR glasses to work and find the individual in charge of research and development. Crafting a carefully worded email, I dangle the idea of modifying their glasses to be both AR and VR and suggest a possible partnership. I hit send and smirk.

Yes, the swap for the technology saved my life, but they killed Marcos, kidnapped me, beat me, and threatened my life. I'm not stealing the code back. The enemy can still bring the software to market, but I'm determined they won't be the only player. We're in a race now and the first one to market is going to win the lion's share. Bring it on.

With a snap, I close the lid and lay the laptop beside me on the bed. A yawn catches me off-guard, and I snuggle down into the pillow and drift off. This time, my dreams are pleasant.

CHAPTER 10

<u>GRAYSON</u>

Blood fills my nightmares, choking me with anguish and guilt. The sight of Henley in a bloody heap on the floor of the warehouse triggered images of Kira on the floor of my bedroom. Pictures of them both swirl round and round in my brain until my head feels like it's going to explode. The two won't leave me alone, and the urge to escape beats at me. This would usually have me jetting off to find the nearest adrenaline-filled rush, but not this time. The thought of leaving my family, and Henley, unprotected stops me in my tracks.

She's been here two days. The last time she stayed with us, I felt the tiniest crack appear in my walls, but I deliberately ignored it. I admit to being intrigued by her but kept my distance. Until the night of the ball.

Watching her twirl around in that outrageous peacock dress, laughing and dancing with that idiot actor, made me feel a pang of emotion I thought I'd conquered long ago. To feel it again was a punch in the gut. Jealousy is destructive. It ruins lives. And it pissed me off to feel even a kernel of it.

When I joined Mateo and Thiago on the edge of the dance floor to discuss our next steps, I heard every word the punk said, but it didn't bother me. After all, I'd spent a lot of time making sure everyone sees the surface me. I shrugged it off until she jumped in and defended me. Her words shook me. I'd done absolutely nothing to deserve them from her.

Still angry at myself for feeling jealous, I followed her out of the ballroom, determined to shut down the connection between us. At least that's what I told myself. It didn't quite go the way I planned. I mentally snort.

The picture of her standing against the wall—spitting mad and firing back at me, her chest heaving and her obscenely short skirt fluttering back and forth across those incredible legs of hers—makes my breath catch even now. A switch flipped and all I could think about was getting a peek. Just one, to satisfy my curiosity. I convinced myself it would be enough. Except it wasn't.

The semi-sheer flesh-colored underwear almost brought me to my knees. In public. Consequences be damned. Thankfully, she had more control than I and pulled me back from the edge. Only to push me right back to it a second later with that scorching kiss. I laugh. I don't know whether to be grateful Ava called out or not.

Something shifted inside me in that moment, and no matter how hard I try, I can't get back to the old me. The cavalier attitude I'd adopted is disappearing, but what that means, I have no fucking clue.

Pulling myself out of the introspective sinkhole I've dropped into, I roll out of bed with a groan. I don't want to think of the past or the kiss or work or anything. An idea pops into my head. Maybe we all should escape.

She's been here two days now and all she's done is work. Mateo and Thiago might be okay with that scenario, hell, Henley is probably fine with it, but she's not going to heal if she doesn't take some time to relax. Without a computer or a phone.

Thiago stops beside the kitchen island where I'm sitting and shoots me a contemplative stare. I know he's looking at the dark circles under my eyes, but I refuse to acknowledge his worry. He's always been overprotective, but this situation has given him an excuse to level up a notch or three.

"I'm not going into work today," I coolly inform him. When I hear him drop his bag on the counter, I hold up my hand. "Stop worrying. Everything is fine. I'm fine. We're all safe in this new fortress of security you've forced upon us. I've got everything under control." I don't tell him my plans to take Henley to the beach, because he'll worry himself to death, force a bunch of rules down my throat, then decide it's too risky. Sometimes what Thiago doesn't know...

His head tilts to the side while he considers his options. "If this is triggering you, I need to know about it." When I simply raise an eyebrow, he jerks his messenger bag off the island. "I mean it, Grayson. I need to get to the office, so I'll drop the subject for now. If you want me to pick up something for dinner, text me. Try to be nice to Henley today, too." He grunts at my lack of response and walks out.

When Mateo walks in an hour later, rubbing his eyes and yawning, I inform him of our plans. "Help Henley get ready. All three of us are taking the day off and going down to the beach to relax. No excuses. No computers or phones."

Expecting him to argue, I'm startled to see a slow smile break out on his face. "Fantastic idea. I completely agree." The phone in his hand rings and he answers. "Thiago, what's up?"

Waving my hands in front of Mateo, I shake my head back and forth, silently telling him not to say anything to Thiago about our plans.

He rolls his eyes but agrees. "I'm here. I just got up and haven't really thought about it. Let me get Henley up and dressed and get some stuff done. I'll call you back later." He mumbles an agreement to something Thiago says, then hangs up.

"Why are we hiding our plans from Thiago?" He quirks his eyebrow while he waits for an answer to his question.

"You know why," I reply with an exasperated expression.

"Thiago will veto a perfectly fantastic idea. Now, go. I'll get the food and drinks together. You get dressed and help Henley."

Twenty-five minutes later, Henley walks into the kitchen, her hair in a ponytail, wearing one of Thiago's white tanks over a swimsuit, with her long legs bare and on display. I chuckle and snap a pic. I won't send it to him now, but it's a sight worth capturing, and I'm sure it will mess with his mental control.

I motion to the island where I've laid out scrambled eggs, toast, and coffee, knowing morning is not her favorite time of the day. With a sigh of relief, she eases onto the barstool and takes a big gulp.

We usually have a maid service, but none of us wanted to take the risk right now. I snatch up the pan and quickly wash and dry it. Once Henley is finished, I take her stuff and add it to the dishwasher. When I look up, she's watching me with a fascinated look on her face. I raise my eyebrow.

"You love being in the kitchen," she says with a smile, but her tone is questioning. "Have you always been this way?"

Feeling the back of my neck tighten, I focus on scrubbing the counter while I answer. "If I hadn't learned to cook, I likely would've starved. Foster kids are sometimes forgotten." I rinse out the dishcloth and leave it on the side of the sink, then walk over to her side of the island. "More than that, it gave me a sense of control and independence, not to mention something to leverage." She tilts her head in confusion, so I explain. "When they assigned me to new foster parents, I always volunteered to cook. Once I made them something incredible, things usually eased a bit. They'd bring in more groceries, give me a little freedom, and generally, treat me better. It was a win-win situation."

She tilts her head to the side, blue eyes entirely focused on me. "I'm surprised you still want to do it. You've got so much going on already with work, your boats, the NFTs, and everything... else. I'd have thought you guys would have a chef."

"I don't want another chef in my kitchen," I inform her with a mock glare. "Honestly, if I didn't cook, we'd never see each other. Thiago would exist on protein bars and salads. Mateo would eat takeout every day." She flushes. I'm guessing she's guilty of the same bad habit, and I just shake my head at her. "If I cook, we have dinner together. Even when Marcos was here. Except on Sundays, when we used to go over to Mariana's." It pangs me to realize we haven't gone to Mariana's for Sunday brunch in a long time. With this threat hanging over our head, I'm not sure if it's a good idea, but maybe we need it. Something to discuss with Thiago later.

"Well, I severely lack any ability to cook, so I'm truly grateful for all your meals," she states firmly. "And I love eating dinner with all of you. It's nice. Like a family. My dad died when I was little, and as a single parent, my mom worked a lot. It sounds like you didn't have much family until you came here. Given our backgrounds, maybe it's something we both need." She slides gingerly off the barstool.

Exactly, family dinners, I muse surprised to find something in common.

Mateo strolls into the room. Trunks on, flip flops, and no shirt. I watch Henley swivel toward him with a smile on her face and a hint of desire in her eyes. The same heat graces his face. Something is sizzling between them.

Riveted, I watch him lean down and capture her lips in slow motion. A hand snakes round her back and slowly glides down her tight left cheek to give it a squeeze before settling.

She gasps, and it goes straight south. With an almost silent groan, I reach down and shift myself so it's not obvious how turned on I am by watching them. Damn Mateo. He knows exactly what this is doing to me. Watching a woman being pleasured by another man, hearing her involuntary cries, makes me harder than steel. Most women don't mind having another man watch them, and Mateo and I have indulged this habit in the past, but we've always been sure to ask permission. I wonder whether Henley would be open to it.

I tear my eyes away, pick up our picnic basket, and head out.

"I'll see you two on the beach." She moans when I pass the patio doors, and it takes everything I have to keep walking. I don't dare look back.

When I get to the beach, I set up the umbrellas and chairs, put the picnic basket in the shade, and practically race to the water to cool off. I dive into the first wave and swim out a bit before riding another back to shore. Striding out of the water, my eyes lock on Henley's, and her pink tongue swipes across her bottom lip. Without breaking my pace, I turn around and head straight back into the water.

After I get my body under control, I manage to drag myself out of the water and over to the lounge chair beside Henley. With a flop, I lie in the sun drying off while I catch my breath.

"The water looks incredible," Henley states softly. "Mateo, would you mind helping me up?"

I open my eyes and look over at her. "Do you think you should get in the water? The waves can be pretty strong."

Mateo helps her up. "I'll go with you," he offers.

"No, I need a few minutes by myself, and I'll only go in up to my knees. Stay here with Grayson," she replies. She tugs at the tank but seems unsure on whether she should take it off.

"Henley, nobody cares if you have bruises. Take your tank off. Enjoy the feel of the sun on your skin. Soak it in. Enjoy the day," I encourage her.

She bites her lip for a second, then slips her arms through the holes. Mateo slips it off her head. Without turning around, she makes her way down to the water.

I whistle. The bruises are stunning. Every color of the rainbow graces her creamy skin, and in the bikini, every one of them is on display. No wonder she felt self-conscious about taking her cover up off.

Mateo groans. "Tell me about it. I've dressed and undressed her three times over the last couple of days and spent all day with her yesterday. I can't even remember what it's like not to be turned on."

I tilt my head and give him a WTF stare. "I was actually

surprised by the bruises, but now that you've brought the topic up... You were both sizzling earlier, but damn, Mateo. You know what that does to me."

"Sorry, sorry," he replies with a grimace. "Either you or Thiago need to help her tonight." He darts his eyes to me, and when I nod in agreement, he turns back to watching her. "Thanks. I appreciate it. The body wash is getting to me." He chuckles at my confused expression. "Never mind."

We both lie there watching Henley splash around in the ocean. She's only in the water up to her knees, but I can't look away.

"Do you think I'm self-centered?"

I peer over at him, but he's not looking my way. I guess it's one of those talks. "No. Self-absorbed, maybe, but you're not self-centered. Why? What brought this up?" Did Henley say that to him? I tilt my head and wait for his answer.

"I don't think I ever realized how hard everyone around me had it," he states, looking directly at me now. "I'm sorry. I should have tried harder to be more... present, I guess. To look up from a book or a computer once in a while. I honestly didn't realize how easy my life has been until recently. Until her." He smiles when he glances over at the woman by the water.

"You made my life better," I insist. When he turns to me with a skeptical expression on his face, I give him a wry smile. "You're the first person who ever needed me. That meant more to me than anything you could have said or done. Don't worry about it."

He lifts a shoulder in response. "You're my brother. Of course, I need you. Thiago needs you, too, although he rarely shows it. But I think some change is in order." He gets up and heads toward the water... and her.

With a roar, he runs into the ocean near Henley, deliberately splashing her. She squeals, and he laughs loudly before pulling her in front of him. He points out something in the water, and they both grin. He's so carefree with her and present.

It suddenly hits me how much he likes Henley. In the past, his relationships were a bit one-sided. He lived his life, and they integrated into his schedule and plans. This is different. He wants to change for her. And I must admit, he would be good for her, too. Much better than me.

CHAPTER 11

HENLEY

H is lips grace my shoulder with a kiss before he dives into the next wave, leaving me on the shore. I stare longingly into the water, but I've got at least a week or two before doing something strenuous like swimming will even be possible.

Turning away from the sparkling blue ocean, I dig my feet in the sand and make my way back to the lounge chair calling my name. The pink tint on my arms catches my eye. Definitely time for some sunscreen.

Walking toward Grayson, I see him tense, but the mirrored sunglasses hide his thoughts from me. When I get closer, he stands and reaches for my shirt, but I hold up a hand to stop him.

"I'd like to lie in the sun for a while," I explain. "Would you mind repositioning the umbrella?"

He leans up and releases the umbrella, so it collapses in on itself. "When you're ready for some shade, it will be easier to just reopen it." He motions to the chair. "Do you want to sit up or lie down?"

"Sit up but also relaxed back a little," I reply.

When he gets the chair in position, I sit down with a heartfelt sigh. One of these days, I'm going to stop feeling so tired, but it doesn't look like it's going to be today. The sunscreen lies at the foot of the lounger, but I can't make myself get up to get it. In a minute, maybe.

A loud exhale sounds beside me, and I peer up, only to find Grayson scowling down at me.

He grabs the sunscreen and holds it out. "I'd be happy to apply this for you," he informs me quietly. "It's okay to ask for help, Henley. It doesn't mean you're weak."

My eyes move from his face to the bottle, and I drop the hand reaching for it. He's right. This is stupid. He put sunscreen on me yesterday and nothing happened, and I certainly didn't feel indebted to him.

"Would you mind putting sunscreen on me again, Grayson?"

"It would be my pleasure, Henley," he responds promptly. He sits beside me, then leans forward to start applying it to my arm.

The muscles in his abs bunch tightly together, and I bite my lip to hold in the groan threatening to escape. I've been aware of his nearly naked state all morning, but any time I'm tempted to look, I switched my focus to Mateo. With Mateo still swimming, there isn't anything to distract me. Maybe if I keep my eyes fixed firmly on his abs, he'll think I've zoned out.

He's more ripped than Mateo, which suggests some type of regular workout routine, but he's not stacked like Thiago. With his wide shoulders and lean hips, his body resembles the swimmers I drooled over during the Olympics a couple of years ago.

He shifts farther down the chair to put sunscreen on my legs and my view changes to brown sand. Blinking, I shift my gaze to my leg and watch him rub the lotion into my skin. Strong brown fingers glide in circles on my legs, making the white liquid disappear. Mesmerized, I watch him finish one leg, then switch to the other side of my chair to get the other one.

His hands rub closer to the top of my thigh, and I pull in deep, quiet breaths and force myself to lie perfectly still. While my body is locked down, my mind is free to wander, and I slip into a half-dream state where his hands don't stop at the top of my thighs. Instead, they flirt with edges of my suit, before slipping underneath to touch me where I so badly wanted him to the night of the ball.

I'm so deep into the little fantasy playing in my head, I don't even realize he's done with my arms and legs. When his hands slip to my waist, I lick my lips and let out a breathless, "Yes."

He freezes. "Hell, Henley," he says gruffly, his voice rough with... something. His hand grabs mine and wraps it around the bottle of sunscreen. "I think you can do your stomach."

His eyes are still hidden behind those damn sunglasses, so I can't tell if he's irritated or turned on. Until he stands and I get an eyeful.

He's definitely turned on, I muse.

He frowns when I stare at the impressive sight in front of me. I guess he's kind of irritated now too.

I wait for him to say something, but he only looks toward Mateo, who's striding out of the water, then walks away.

"Thank you," I tell him, my naturally husky voice deeper than usual. With little attention to the task, I slather sunscreen on my stomach while I watch Grayson from the corner of my eye. He stands with his back to me for a few seconds, then slowly squats to open the picnic basket.

Mateo strides up to us, looking invigorated from his swim in the ocean. Darting a look from me to Grayson, I'm surprised to see a slow smile cross his face.

"Looks like Grayson applied sunscreen to protect you from the wicked sun, minha linda," he observes with laughter in his voice. A brown finger reaches out and draws a line down my leg, making me gasp.

Grayson whirls around and glares at Mateo.

I tense, but Mateo strokes soothing circles on my leg until my muscles relax.

68

Locked together in a sort of limbo, they stare at each other for a few minutes, while I wait for them to figure out whatever it is they need to figure out. When Grayson breaks the standoff by turning his back to us, Mateo silently shakes his head like he's disappointed in him.

I pull my bottom lip between my teeth while I try to grasp what just happened. All morning, I've been wrapped up in Mateo. His playfulness a beacon, drawing me to him, making me crave his sweet, sensual kisses. When I'm with him, I like how I feel about him and myself. Relaxed and invigorated. And I don't have to be anybody else. Just me.

Yet a minute ago, I'd been consumed with Grayson, picturing us together under the sun, his hands caressing every inch of me. The kiss at the ball woke a fire in us that keeps flaring up even though I feel like we're both trying to douse it. I'm not sure I like Grayson, or if he likes me.

Thiago pops into my mind, but I brush his image away. The man exudes raw power and sexuality. Any red-blooded woman would want to be near him, with him, but I'm nothing like the gorgeous and voluptuous Amazon women he typically dates. He's not even remotely interested, just protective of me, like he is with everyone else. The first night was a single moment of pure chemistry. Since then, he hasn't shown one iota of desire toward me.

My fingers tap against the chair in a familiar pattern. It's like I've fallen into an alternate universe. Two months ago, the only man in my life was Marcos, and he didn't generate any feelings except admiration. The rare times I forced myself out of the house to go on an app date, it usually ended up in either disappointment or meaningless sex, a brief moment spent trying to feel something.

Now, I'm all feelings. Is it because I finally decided to come out of hiding? Has this attraction been here all along and I didn't know? And what do I do about the three, err, two men? Do I choose one? Ignore it? I don't have anybody to ask for advice.

Lean fingers grip my chin and pull me around to face him. "It's

69

fine, Henley. Stop thinking. Relax and enjoy the day. Everything will sort itself out. I promise."

My eyes find his warm brown ones and I blink at the conviction in them. "I don't like promises," I remind him. "They never come true." Although I wish with everything in me they would.

CHAPTER 12

<u>MATEO</u>

The tension between the three of us hovers like a cloud the rest of the day, but I might be the only one happy about it. Henley is worried and confused, and Grayson has retreated into his shell, but both are good signs. If Henley is worried, it means she cares about my feelings but also feels something for Grayson. And he only hides when he's avoiding reality. In this case, Henley.

When I walked up earlier, you could cut the sexual tension with a knife. I waited to feel upset or jealous, but it didn't happen. Instead, an image of all three of us popped into my head, and it felt right.

What I said to Grayson earlier is still true. I want to change, but I'm also realistic enough to know I need to fall into those computational rabbit holes to keep my sanity. If not, the numbers drive me crazy with their incessant tapping on the edges of my mind. And I don't want to ask Henley to fit into the edges of my life like the other women in my past. I want her to have what she needs... whatever that is. If she's not happy, she'll leave, and it would be impossible to find her.

A massive, scowling brute moves in front of me, and I smirk. I knew Thiago sensed something earlier. I'm surprised it took him this long to hunt us down. Squinting up at him, I see him decked out in swim trunks and carrying a towel.

"Thiago, glad you could join us," Grayson remarks in a pseudo excited voice. "How was work? Did you work out a deal?"

Thiago scowls at him and flashes an image of Henley on his phone, then shows me. It's the picture Grayson took earlier of her in Thiago's tank top.

I chuckle.

Thiago glares at me, then turns his attention to Henley, who's asleep in the lounger next to me. His eyes skate over her from head to toe, assessing her well-being. Once he's reassured she's okay, he answers Grayson's question. "The company came back with a better offer, but they want shares of SEI to be a part of the deal. I turned them down. With Marcos gone, I'm not sure there's any reason to pursue a partnership."

Henley stretches on the chair beside me, waking from her nap.

I must look puzzled because Thiago explains further. "Marcos asked me to look into partnering with a medical device company. Maybe this was for the AR technology he and Henley developed?"

"Or the breast cancer detection vest?" I remind him of Marcos' other project.

Henley sits up a little straighter and reaches for her shirt. "Right now, doctors, especially surgeons, view CT, MRI, and ultrasound scans in 2D. The software would convert the scans first to 3D models, then to AR images. Marcos and I always planned to offer an AR headset or glasses with the software, although it's not required to view the disease or condition in 3D. But with the addition of the optical device, surgeons can view the AR images overlaid directly on top of their patient. It would be an incredible advantage during surgery to not only know, but see precisely where to cut, how deep their target is, and other various physical data needed for the surgery to be successful."

I smile, remembering how excited Marcos was when he

explained the idea to me. The same look is on Henley's face right now.

She shrugs. "The original intent was to make a deal with an existing manufacturer, but once Marcos got his AR/VR glasses working, maybe he thought it would be better to partner with someone. Or he might have been thinking of the vest or a combination of projects. Who knows? Marcos was always thinking ahead."

Thiago pinches the bridge of his nose. "Should I start looking for another device manufacturer?"

Henley hesitates, then blurts out. "I sort of already did. I reached out to a gaming company who I know is on the verge of launching their own VR glasses to see if they'd be interested in a potential partnership. Instead of limiting their scope to VR only, they could offer AR/VR glasses and immediately expand their target market. I told them I was actively shopping a finished solution around and would need their answer within forty-eight hours."

She raises her arm to tap her wrist as if she's wearing a watch. "They have forty hours left to respond. I didn't give them any demands. I want to see if they're interested first." She darts a glance at each of us, waiting for us to react.

Shocked, I swing my legs to the side of the lounger to sit up straight. "We exchanged the AR/VR glasses and code for your life. Why would you risk making our enemies even more angry?" Shoving my hand through my hair, I contemplate the ramifications of what she's done. Damn it.

She shrugs nonchalantly. "I'm thankful to be alive, and they have a copy of the code. They can manufacture it, enter a partnership, or sell it—whatever they want. But I have a copy of it, too."

Her face is fierce when she looks at me. "They killed Marcos. Kidnapped me. Beat me. Threatened my life. They don't get a reward, especially for something Marcos spent hours and hours creating. Fuck them."

She compresses her lips, so I turn to Thiago for help.

A slow smile spreads across Thiago's face. "I didn't know you had a copy, but I agree. Fuck them. This is war. Maybe we can also

73

use it to draw them out from wherever they're hiding. Do you want to broker the deal yourself, or do you want some help?" He's practically vibrating with energy at the thought of striking a blow against our enemy.

She contemplates Thiago's offer. "I'd prefer to have SEI go into partnership with them vs. CJ Tech. For one, you're a legal entity." A wry smile crosses her face. "Honestly, deals aren't really my wheelhouse. All I want is the physical product. Although I've come up with an option for launching an MVP, or minimally viable product, for the first version of our AR product."

Grayson gets up and moves closer to the three of us.

"We'll need you to go with us to make the deal. At the very least, they'll want a demonstration of the technology, but we'll also need you to lead any technical discussions," Grayson informs her.

"I definitely want to go, although I'd prefer to be introduced as an SEI tech lead or something," she agrees, adding the stipulation.

"What's the name of the company?" Thiago asks, ready to type it into his phone. "I'll get a meeting set up for the earliest available time."

"VRDeck," she answers, naming one of the biggest VR gaming companies in the market.

I whistle. "They're one of the biggest, but you'll need a company big enough to get to market fast and they can certainly pull it off. Good thing Thiago's one hell of a negotiator, because having leverage will help."

Grayson and Thiago look at each other with a competitive gleam in their eye. I have no doubt those two will put together an incredible deal and get Henley what she needs. "Wait, what is your MVP solution?"

"Most mobile devices support AR technology now, so we launch the product as an AR app. The original solution would only need a few modifications to use a mobile operating system instead of a desktop, but mainly due to their inherent limitations. Once complete, the 3D model could be viewed through any phone or tablet. If they already have their own AR headsets that work with mobile, they can use them."

She reaches a hand toward Grayson to help her stand. "Thank you," she murmurs. "It's actually a better solution than our original idea. Doctors will be able to view a patient's organs, nerves, blood vessels, or other body parts, segment the disease or problem areas, zoom in or out, and even consult with other doctors using a device they carry with them every day. It's truly amazing. Not only will this revolutionize surgery and patient treatment today, but in the future, it can be extended to emergency services to use in the field to quickly identify hidden injuries like internal bleeding or ruptured organs."

She holds up a finger when Thiago opens his mouth. "Distribution of an app is easy. With an annual licensing model, we can create a low-cost entry point for doctors and an annual revenue stream for our companies. There are over nine million doctors in the world. If we estimate fifteen percent of the total, or one-point-three million doctors, will download the software and license it at a cost of one hundred dollars a year, we could generate over one hundred and thirty million dollars a year. Some of the revenue would need to be reinvested for maintenance and upgrades to the technology, but the remaining would be a significant source of revenue for all three companies. The model might have to change as competitors hit the market, but I'd look to SEI to manage the ongoing business." Her eyes dart to the three of us to gauge our thoughts on this solution.

Grayson's eyes light up when she speaks about the revenue. He's a walking financial machine.

"Are you suggesting a three-way partnership between SEI, JF Technologies, and CJ Tech?" Thiago questions her, his voice sharp. "It would be tough to create a legal contract between us given that two of the companies don't legally exist."

She shrugs. "I never thought about it. Marcos and I trusted each other and never relied on legal documents. Plus, we didn't want the companies to be legal. If they were legit and paid taxes, we'd have considerably less money to give to the foundation."

"What if SEI made JF Technologies a wholly owned subsidiary? It would make it a legitimate business, but we could account for the taxes and other necessary expenditures across SEI's in-house entities. With the kind of money we're talking about, it would be tough to conceal the source. This mitigates the issue and still allows JF to operate without directly paying taxes. For CJ Tech, we could continue the partnership using a private purchase deal." Grayson throws out his suggestion to Thiago and me.

Thiago thinks about it for a second, then nods. "It could work. We need to iron out the details before I completely agree, but my main concern is keeping SEI legitimate."

Henley looks relieved to find a possible solution.

"Can you create the app?" I interject.

She wrinkles her nose. "I can complete all the development necessary to use the iOS or Android operating systems, but someone else should probably build the apps. I'm not the best creative or user experience design person. It needs to be simple so we can get it to market quickly. Maybe three primary sections—a demo of the technology, a registration and payment section for the annual license, and finally, the main AR display and segmentation functions. Plus, the usual minor stuff like legal, account and password creation, forgot password, blah, blah, blah."

"I agree. We have a few developers on staff I can pull in to create the interface and a library of components to pull it together quickly," I tell her before looking at Thiago. "Do you want them to come here or for us to go there?"

"Neither. Virtual meetings only," he informs me. "We're not taking any chances right now."

I look around for my phone to send them a meeting invite.

"No phones," chimes Henley beside me.

"Right," I retort with a chuckle. "Are you ready to go inside?"

Her attention returns to Thiago standing there in his swim trunks. "Let's stay for a while. It's been nice to play hooky today. Exactly what I needed."

Thiago lifts an eyebrow toward Grayson. "Good call," he drawls.

Henley's face looks surprised for a second, then swivels to face Grayson. "Thank you. It's been... wonderful."

His mouth lifts in a half smirk. "Thiago, I'll race you to the water." Before the words are out of his mouth, he takes off. Even with his head start, the two end in a tie.

"Thiago's fast!" Henley exclaims in disbelief.

"For a big guy, he can move," I confirm with a chuckle. "While they're gone, I want to talk to you about earlier." I pause until she turns toward me, but she's still too far away, so I shift over to sit on her lounger and look her in the eyes. "It's okay to be attracted to Grayson. To both of us. I..." I pick up her hand. "I want to tell you something, but I don't want you to think badly of us. Or jump to conclusions, okay? Promise me you'll listen and keep an open mind?"

Her breath whistles out. "Okay." While she might look calm, her fingers are squeezing mine a little bit tighter.

"Grayson and I had the same girlfriend in high school. She liked us both, and neither of us wanted to give her up, so we all three made the decision to be in a relationship together. We didn't tell anyone but family because we didn't want her to suffer at school," I confide to her.

She frowns. "That isn't what I thought you were going to tell me, but okay?" Confusion and uncertainty cross her face. "Why are you telling me?"

I hesitate for a second. "She's the only girlfriend we shared, but we have had threesomes with other women. With their full consent, of course." The words stop flowing while I try to figure out where to go from here.

With other women, it was easier. They were more experienced and often suggested it to us. Henley says nothing, and I'm not sure if that means she's offended or shocked or.... I shove my fingers through my wild hair in frustration. What do I do now? Maybe I should have waited for Grayson to have this discussion with Henley. He's better at the whole communication thing.

Her fingers start tapping against my hand. "Is this something you want with me? I don't... I haven't ever..." She stops and lifts her shoulders. "I like you, and I'm attracted to you. Both of you. Maybe Thiago, too. I don't know. It's kind of confusing. You're all beautiful or handsome... whatever. Sophisticated. And smart. But I don't know if the isolation of the last few years is causing me to react to all of you or what. I know you, Mateo, more than the others, and I like you, but I'm not sure about Grayson. Although I'm sure the sex would be great. With all of you." She pulls her hand from mine and slaps it over her mouth.

"Merda," I spit out. "I'm not... We're not expecting you to do anything with any of us. Although, I definitely hope it's going that way. With me." I wiggle my eyebrows, hoping she might laugh. She doesn't. I sigh. "I want you to be comfortable reacting to us the way you want without worrying about jealousy or whether it's the right or wrong thing. That's the only thing I meant. We'll take our cues from you. I swear. Not a promise, but I swear you're the one who decides what steps we take. Although we might try to persuade you, we will never take it further than you want to go. Okay?"

She looks relieved, which makes me feel like I finally accomplished what I wanted to say instead of royally fucking this up.

"And you're sure nobody will get upset?"

I pull her hand to my chest. "I swear."

CHAPTER 13

<u>THIAGO</u>

Mateo has lost his fucking mind. "Que porra é essa? You told Henley she could do whatever she wanted with each of us? What is wrong with you?" I roar, unable to keep my temper under control. Share my woman with my family? He's crazy. Louco. I pace around the gym, trying to calm down before I say something I'll regret. "Look, I know you two have shared in the past, but why the hell did you drag me into it?"

Mateo looks at Grayson for help, but he simply crosses his arms and leans against the wall. "I didn't bring you up. She did. Henley is attracted to all three of us. Although she's not sure if she likes Grayson." He smirks at the irritated expression on Grayson's face. "Thiago, I don't think you two have seen each other much since she arrived, right? Maybe she's just attracted to the idea of you."

I run a hand down my face to clear my expression before I turn to Mateo. "Not exactly. She's having nightmares. Since I'm the closest, I've been helping her get through them."

Mateo raises an eyebrow and gives me a smug look that makes me want to wipe it off with my fist, but he's not wrong, damn it.

Grayson straightens from his lounging position against the wall. "Care to tell us how you're helping her get through the night-mares?" Dark blue eyes flare with anger.

"Sometimes we talk, watch a movie, or I stay until she goes to sleep," I say with a shrug, as if it's not a big deal. Walking over to the punching bag, I push it a few times to expel some of the energy burning inside me. "I understand what it's like to need someone to help you get through the dark nights." I turn back to Grayson. "Don't you?"

He narrows his eyes. "You're sleeping in her bed, aren't you?" He scoffs. "No wonder she's confused."

I clench my fists tightly and remind myself of the reasons why I don't want to punch Grayson. He's family. You protect your family. Marcos drilled that into me at an early age because he knew if my father ever caught up to us, either he or I would have to get the family to a safe place. But he's also right. I growl in frustration.

"You're right. I fucked up, too. Maybe we've all fucked up. Henley isn't innocent, but she's not a sophisticated woman of the world, either. I agree with Mateo. From now on, let her make the moves. If she wants you two, it's up to her to decide," I say resignedly. "As for me, I won't stop helping her at night, but I'll stop sleeping in her bed. I'll make it clear any attraction isn't recipro-cated. Deal?"

Grayson snorts. "Good luck with that." He turns to Mateo. "I'm not sure I want this with her. It's too much. She triggers something inside me, but I can't be anything... good for her. I just don't know, Mateo."

Mateo whirls on Grayson. "This is the first time you've felt anything in years. Are you going to hide forever because of Kira? She wasn't well, Grayson. You didn't drive her to do it. You know the investigator said she'd been mentally unwell her entire life." He points a finger at him. "And honestly, Henley is a hell of a lot stronger than Kira. Look at all she's gone through and come out the other side. You're running scared. You know it. I know it. If you don't want anything to do with her, be honest."

Turning to me, he gives me a hard stare. "The same goes for you. Be honest with her, if you can. Honestly, I think you're both fooling yourselves, but it isn't the first time I've been smarter than you two." With a last disgusted look at both of us, he stomps out the door.

A smile curves across my lips. I'm impressed. "Did someone switch bodies with Mateo the last few days? Or is this all Henley's doing?"

Grayson's staring at the floor. "I think some of it is her. Some of it is him realizing life is a bit more complicated than he thought and he can't hide behind the numbers forever." He walks slowly around the room, sliding his finger along the equipment. "Do you think Mateo's right? Is Henley stronger than Kira?"

He keeps his eyes averted, not wanting me to see the darkness crawling through him, but I hear it in his voice. The thoughts that torture him the most. "She's stronger. Against all the odds, she kept going. She's a fighter." It's what I admire about her the most, but I don't admit it to him.

Straightening his shoulders, he stands and meets my eyes. "It takes one to know one, I guess. Thanks, Thiago."

"Look at the path in front of you, Grayson, not the one in the rearview mirror," I remind him.

He nods and leaves the gym.

Stripping down to my workout gear, I pick up the wrap on the bench and methodically weave it around my wrists, through my fingers, across my knuckles, and back to my wrists. I do the same to the second hand, then pull on my gloves. Punching hard on the bag, I block out the words reverberating through my head and concentrate on laying it all out on the bag.

I SET the iPad on her bed with a note on how to access my movie library. Mateo's right. I can't keep sleeping in her bed. Hopefully, this will help her when she wakes from her nightmares.

"What are you doing in here?" Henley asks from the open doorway. "I mean. This is your house…" She gives an exasperated sigh. "Do you need something?"

You. Under me. I hold up the tablet for her to see. "I thought you'd want to help yourself to my movie library." My stomach clenches when I see the understanding dawn on her face, chased by an expression of hurt.

"I see," she says stiffly. "Thank you. I appreciate your thoughtfulness. I'll try to keep the volume down so you can get some sleep." Her eyes dart around the room but never return to me.

"Good night, Henley," I reply softly.

She says nothing, only dips her chin in reply.

When her cries come later that night, it's everything I can do not to go to her. Feeling sick, I shove the covers off and lean over the side of the bed with my head in my hands, trying to ignore the sounds. Just when I can't stand it anymore, they stop. A few minutes later, I hear a movie start. It should make me feel better that she found her way through it without me, but instead, I feel like shit.

CHAPTER 14

<u>HENLEY</u>

he sun is barely rising when I wake. Damn Thiago. Crack of dawn. I'm a night owl not an early bird. I turn over, close my eyes, and start counting back from 4000. 3999. 3998. Did I do something to make him leave? 3997. Was it the kiss? 3996. 3995. 3994. Arrrgghh.

Gritting my teeth, I ignore the pain and use the anger to dress myself this morning. It's time I started doing things again. Rely on myself. I kind of let them call the shots and take care of me the last few days, but I need to get back to my usual self-sufficiency. If they weren't here, I'd be doing this alone, anyway.

I groan when I pull up my leggings, carefully gripping the fabric to tug them into place, then straightening the seams because leaving them crooked would drive me crazy. When they're finally in place, I'm a hot, sweaty mess and in pain. Dropping down to the bed, I give myself a few minutes to rest from the ordeal. Who thought my favorite item of clothing would be so damn hard to get on?

After sliding on a large t-shirt that uses a formula to say "I ate some PI... and it was delicious", which obviously belongs to Mateo, I slip my feet into my worn out running shoes.

When I get to the hallway, I ignore the door to my right and head to the foyer. Once there, I contemplate a walk on the beach, but I need to get away from everything Santos for at least a few minutes and breathe. Reset. Punching in the code on my phone, I turn off the security alarm and head out.

The sky is sort of grey with a hint of the sun popping up to the east. I swear I would flip off the sun if I didn't think it would make me look crazy.

With a quick pivot to the right, I hit the street. The urge to run is a drum beating inside of me, but I ignore it and stick with a steady, slow walking pace. I can't afford a setback now. I need to get better, figure out my next steps, and find a life. Less virtual, more real world. With people who want me.

Mateo's grin appears, and I slow my walk. I like Mateo and I know he likes me, too. He definitely wants to be with me. But can I be with him and ignore the others? Why couldn't I just be attracted to him? Someone cool, fun to hang out with, smart, caring, good-looking—essentially Mateo.

Maybe I should stop thinking for a while. Enjoy my time with Mateo. Keep things polite, but distant, with Grayson and Thiago.

There are immediate things to do, like getting the software into the hands of doctors and defeating our enemies. Longer term, I need to figure out whether I want to run my company from Miami or work with SEI remotely. We're tied together whether we like it or not —the shares Marcos left me cemented it, but it doesn't mean we need to physically be near each other. The work can continue anywhere. It would be for the best. After the threat is eliminated, of course.

Resolved, I turn around and make my way back to the house. Beads of sweat roll down my face. With all the thoughts swirling in my brain, my walk was longer than I originally planned, but it felt so good to be moving again.

As I near the gate to the house, Thiago's standing there in a black tank and shorts, hair matted with sweat, and a ferocious scowl on his face. I falter for a second, then force my shoulders back and meet his eyes.

"Where the hell have you been? It's not safe for you to leave the house by yourself. You didn't tell anyone or leave a note. What if something happened? How would we find you?" His hands are moving rapidly while he fires question after question at me.

"Thiago, the whole neighborhood is going to hear you. I went for a walk. You can easily track me with my phone. If you'll excuse me, I'm going inside to get a shower." I walk slowly through the gate and up to the house, ignoring the man beside me every step of the way.

He takes a deep breath. "Henley," he says gruffly. "If you want to take a walk, let me know. I'll go with you, okay?"

"No," I refuse to comply with his request. "If I want to take a walk, I will. We're in a gated community, and honestly, I'm a bit tired of hiding. Please excuse me." I enter my room and close the door behind me.

A thud hits the door. "We're not done with this conversation," he informs me. "We'll pick it up later."

Ignoring him, I head toward the shower. A grin breaks out. My grumpy mood is gone. Maybe this early bird thing isn't so bad after all. I scoff at the thought. Let's not get carried away...

———

MATEO'S WAITING for me when I get out. "I hear you dressed yourself and went out for a walk this morning?" He smiles broadly. "Good for you. Do you want help or have you got it?"

The leggings were hard to pull on, but dressing didn't kill me, and it felt good to do it myself. "I've got it. Are we having a meeting today with the app development team?"

He lifts his arm and checks his watch. "In two hours. Nine a.m. Are you going to come down for breakfast?" He tilts his head, assessing me closely.

"I'll be down in an hour. I want to check my email and take care of a few things," I assure him.

"I miss helping you dress already," he states with mock sadness. "But on the bright side, if you're getting better... maybe I'll be lucky enough to undress you someday soon." With a whistle, he strolls out of the room.

He makes it so easy to like him.

Instead of leggings, I find a loose pair of joggers in the stash I ordered before I left for Dallas. I run my fingers across the clothing Grayson bought me. I should really get Peyton over here to help me put some outfits together. I haven't a clue what's appropriate or not, and while the invites are scarce right now, I'm hoping I'll have more events to attend in my new "life." Maybe a date or... another ball. I smile when I see the fabulous peacock dress hanging in the back of the closet. It would have been a shame to lock this up as evidence in the police department's basement.

The club chair in the room is perfect for getting some work done this morning. With a pillow added to the back, I prop myself up and get comfortable.

Opening my email, I see a request from Sterling for a new ID and passport. The picture inside is a beautiful young woman with dark brown hair and eyes. Twenty-two years old. With her dark complexion, I can easily choose from a variety of backgrounds.

Accessing my files, I flip through the options and decide to use Isabella Rossi. Once I've chosen her identity, I quickly set up her background and pay a hacker friend to print the necessary materials and overnight them to Sterling.

Getagoodlife: *You've been gone longer than usual this time. Glad to have you back and spending all that beautiful BTC with me.*

Nyx: *Ha! You only care about my bitcoin. ;-) Let me know if you run into any issues or delays. Thanks for rushing this one.*

Although I paid for the rush, it's considerably less than what he charges others. Getagoodlife appreciates frequent customers, and since he's one of the best forgers in the business, he's my number one resource for passports and IDs. It's still expensive. Thankfully, I can set up the backgrounds myself.

I shoot off a text to Sterling to let him know the background's done and details have been uploaded to the designated spot. The physical IDs will be in his hands tomorrow morning. He returns with *ta, simply smashing, darling.*

The next email is from Amala Vinya, replying to my inquiry. She reassures me the code we found on our enemy's computer was not stolen. Amala published it at the same time she turned in her paper. Her professor at MIT, Dr. Langford, required his students to publish their solutions to get exposure and generate job interest. She lists the journal she published it in.

Although, interestingly enough, she admits the code has been updated and finds the changes a bit concerning. The original algo-rithm identified email spam and classified it according to its threat risk. It was intended to assist corporate email systems with auto-matically identifying and ranking the threat caused by malicious email. The revised code allows an email to be classified as internal, even if it originates from an outside source. With a low threat risk, it can easily penetrate firewalls.

A good solution flipped on its head. Sounds familiar. They took my original banking algorithm and code, expanded upon it, and turned it into a tool for their impressive shell game.

Pulling up the list of files we found on the enemy's computer, I head to the journal's website and conduct a search for each of the papers. They're all here, published to this journal. I check the board of directors and find Dr. Langford, MIT, but instead of the standard portrait picture, the professor is sitting at a desk, his head down grading papers. The rest of the directors are various professors at MIT, but I don't recognize their names. I'll ask Mateo about them later.

My alarm goes off on my phone, telling me my allotted time is up. Setting aside my laptop, I stand and carefully stretch to ease some of the soreness. Time for breakfast.

CHAPTER 15

HENLEY

The meeting with the app developers goes well. Thankfully, we can pull a majority of the functionality, like account creation, from existing code and with only a few changes adapt it for this app. There's also a database we can replicate and use for this project. It's basic, but we're only looking to get up and running. Enhancements can easily be made once it's live.

The biggest piece is integrating the code Marcos and I developed, but I need to update it for the new platform. I flirt with changing the modeling software to take advantage of a potentially more mobile-friendly solution but decide to keep the existing for now. It's imperative we get this live quickly.

"I've kicked Thiago out of his office and made it ours," Mateo states a little too gleefully. I think he's enjoying the shift from security systems to working on a more exciting project.

With little time to waste, we get started. Mateo is managing the rest of the app build while I focus on the main functionality.

The rest of the day flies by. Food appears by my elbow on a periodic basis, but I'm lost to code. Defining new components, building each one out, testing, modifying, and finally, passing it. Each one slips from me to QA to be tested with various devices and mobile operating systems, but thankfully, they find very few bugs enabling me to fly through the tasks I set for today's build.

The screen blurs, making me blink. The next thing I know, I'm being carried in someone's arms. The sexy smell is achingly familiar.

"Thiago?" I frown. "What are you doing? I need to get this done."

"Shh, querida," Thiago murmurs. "You'll wake Mateo. You need to sleep for a few hours. Okay?" He carries me to my room and sets me down.

I look at the bed and grimace, knowing I won't be able to sleep once I'm in it, but instead of trying to convince him, I nod agreeably.

He grunts. "I'll stay and keep the nightmares away."

Irritated, I stiffen and turn away from those laser sharp eyes. I don't need his charity. "I'll be fine," I reassure him. "I'm exhausted and will be asleep the moment my head hits the pillow."

The door quietly shuts behind me. After waiting ten minutes, I open the door a crack and peer out. The hallway's empty, allowing me to slip out and return to the office. When I get there, Mateo's still asleep on the couch. Quietly cracking open some caffeine, I sit down and immerse myself in my creation.

Two or three hours go by before I stop again. More errors are appearing in the code than is acceptable, a sure sign I need at least a couple hours of sleep. The thought of returning to my bed alone makes me tremble, though. My eyes dart over to Mateo sleeping peacefully on the couch. Biting my lip for a second, I contemplate whether there's enough room for both of us and decide it's worth a try.

Grabbing a blanket, I slide my body onto the edge of the couch in front of Mateo and cover us up. He shifts, but by the sound of his breathing, he never wakes. Relieved, my muscles relax into a puddle and within seconds, I'm gone.

STELLA BRIE

The warm hand pressed against my stomach wakes me a few hours later. I shift and stretch but leaving the cocoon I'm wrapped in feels entirely impossible. Relaxing back into Mateo, I sigh and close my eyes.

He leans down and kisses the side of my neck, making me shiver. "This is a delightful surprise," he murmurs. Lips trail up to my ear, peppering small kisses along the way, and I turn my head to give him better access.

When he hits a particularly sensitive spot by my ear, I arch back into him. He hisses and holds me against him while he rubs the bulge in his jeans enticingly back and forth against me. "I'm usually hard in the morning, but waking with you in my arms..." He groans, then stops.

Dropping his head to my shoulder, he breathes in and out a few times. "Give me a second to calm down. We need to stop. You're injured, we've got work to do, and you deserve better than an old couch."

All the touches and kisses the last few days have been simmering beneath the surface of my skin, temporarily eclipsed by the pain of my injuries, but not this morning. Need bubbles up inside me until all I can think about is being with him.

With my hand on top of his, I guide his hand down to show him how much I need him. "I don't want to stop. Touch me," I implore him. Arching against his hand, I drag his fingers through my wetness.

He stills for a brief second, then slides one of his lean fingers down the center and plunges inside me. "Meus Deus," he breathes out. While his finger slides in and out, his thumb stretches up to rub enticingly across my nub.

I raise my leg to make it easier for him, and he slides his leg in from behind to prop me up. While his hand plunges in and out, his body thrusts in time behind me until it feels like the motions are one.

My body flutters, and I catch my breath. Seconds later, an orgasm rolls through me, and I moan, clamping down on his

90

fingers. Heat spirals outward, and I press against his palm, needing to keep him close, wanting him to experience it with me.

His hips slow but don't stop completely. Harsh breathing against my neck tells me how turned on he is right now, but he says nothing, only pressing the occasional kiss against my skin.

When the tremors ease, I breathe in and out a few times before sliding off the couch to stand on shaky legs.

He sits up and looks at me with a satisfied smile on his face. "You're so beautiful when you come," he says huskily.

I hook my fingers in my waistband and peel the top half of my joggers down. "Mateo, help me undress," I demand breathlessly.

"Henley, I..."

I place two fingers against his lips. "I'm sore, not dead," I remind him. "You've been driving me crazy the last few days. Feeling your hands against me while you help me dress or undress has been pure torture. I want you. Now. Unless you don't want me?"

Warm brown eyes study me for a second. "I'm not sure it's possible to not want you. I've been hard for days, dressing you, caressing your creamy skin, and watching you wear my shirts around the house. Are you sure?"

Leaning down, I capture those pouty lips of his with mine, nibbling and sucking on them until the kiss changes from playful to urgent. "Take my pants off, Mateo."

His fingers hook into my pants and slide them down to the floor. As I pull each leg out, I place it beside his on the couch until I'm sitting on his lap. With his head between my hands, I take my time kissing him, wanting to savor this moment and reassure him I'm not making a flippant decision. I want him to feel my desire with every cell in his body.

He pushes up against me, the rough denim a delicious friction against my sensitive body, and I moan. "I want you too, minha linda," he rasps, need straining his voice. "I can't wait any longer either."

I reach down and unbutton his jeans before standing and

helping him pull them off, along with his dark briefs. When his cock springs free, I reach down and grasp it tightly. With a twist, I stroke up and down a few times, watching the pleasure roll across his face until his hand stops mine.

"It's going to be tough enough lasting long. Save the playing for another time," he tells me. He rolls on the condom he grabbed from his jeans and pulls me over his lap. "I think this will be better for your injuries. You can control the pace."

With a knee on either side of him, I line up and sink inch by inch onto him, feeling him expand and fill me completely. We both groan. It's been a long time, and it takes a minute for my body to adjust. I think about taking my shirt off, but I'm afraid he'll see the bruises and stop, so I don't.

His hands settle on my hips, and he holds me down tightly on top of him for a second. "I want to feel you wrapped around me, wet and tight... memory..." He hisses when I clamp down, and his golden-brown eyes narrow. "Damn it, Henley. I'm on the edge."

I lift up and slide down. Again and again. "Me too." I'm so turned on. I spear my hand through his hair and yank his head back so I can kiss him while I ride up and down.

Kissing Mateo is the sweetest of drugs when everything is calm, but it's as if grabbing his hair flipped a switch. Pouty lips turn hard while his tongue plunges into my mouth, devouring me in a kiss so filled with fuck me vibes, it makes me even wilder.

His hand comes up and cups the back of my head, pressing me into him, barely letting me breathe. His other hand moves from my hip to my clit, to pinch and stroke it, making me ride him harder and faster.

He swells, and I know he's right on the edge.

With a jerk, I pull back from his lips, but I don't release his hair. "Come with me," I pant, barely able to get the words out before my orgasm slams into me. Moaning at the feel of him inside of me this time, I stare into his eyes while I let it take over.

Brown eyes flare with gold, both hands move to grip my hips, he pushes up into me hard, then holds me down on top of him. His body pulses as his release chases mine.

My orgasm eases, and I loosen my grip. Massaging the place where I pulled his hair, I smile ruefully. I don't even know what came over me. I've never been aggressive with anyone during sex, but with Mateo, I wanted him fully present and so turned on all he could think about was me.

Pouty lips caress mine, nibbling and licking softly. "Are you okay? Your lips are swollen. I didn't hurt you, did I?" He pulls back to look over me. A hand lifts to rub a thumb lightly across my lips and down my side.

"Stop worrying. I feel better than I've felt in a long time. I might be sore in a couple more places, but it was totally worth it," I state firmly. When I lift my body, he grabs the condom to hold it in place until I've totally slid off. With him gone, my body feels empty. "I'm going to grab a shower. Then, I'll be back to work. Okay?" I can't help the kiss I place on his lips, needing one more taste of him.

He quickly stands up and pulls me into his arms. "Henley, wait. Tell me that meant something to you, that it wasn't just a moment of incredibly fantastic sex." He pauses, his eyes scrutinizing every expression crossing my face, but when I don't say anything, he nods.

"I'll go first. I like you. You're loyal as hell, even putting yourself in danger to find out who murdered Marcos. Despite the past and your odds, you keep pushing forward until you're not just surviving, but thriving. You give yourself and your skills to others without asking anything in return. You're fun, sweet, and beautiful. I don't know what the future holds, but I'm asking you to make room for me in it. You don't have to say anything right now. I know things aren't ideal and you have a lot to think about, but I can't let you walk away thinking this was only a physical thing for me."

His eyes search mine while he waits for an answer.

"I like you, too." I blurt, unable to deny what I feel. "But I don't know about everything else. Living in the real world, instead of hiding, will be a lot for me. What if I can't do it?" I don't mention

Thiago or Grayson because I realize they don't matter to how I feel about Mateo. Initially, I kind of thought of them as this package deal, but when Mateo and I were joined, it was only the two of us. "Can we take it a day at a time?"

He smiles, then leans down and kisses me. "Absolutely."

He wraps the blanket around me but stands deliciously defiant, and very naked, in the center of the room with a cocky grin on his face while he watches me walk out.

The moment is going to be seared into my brain. I grin. Smart man.

CHAPTER 16

<u>HENLEY</u>

Over the next three days, Mateo and I work non-stop on getting the project finished. They're the most grueling days I've ever worked in my life, but the mornings are spent exploring each other. It's a good thing I'm sitting a lot the rest of the day because I don't want Thiago or Grayson to see me walking funny. I laugh silently.

It's been an idyllic moment in time, and even though our bubble of solitude can't last, we've made the most of it. I might even have to ask Thiago if I can keep his couch. I smirk imagining the look on his face. Maybe I'll get Mateo to ask him.

And miracle of all miracles, we're close to finishing the app. The last of the development is going through the QA cycle, and if there are only a few bugs, we could finish today. It's such a huge difference to have a team working behind the scenes to build out the rest of the project. Is this what it would be like working with SEI? It's exciting. My ideas could get to market so much faster than my current average of one to two a year.

Loud voices penetrate my thoughts, and I tilt my head to listen.

Someone is shouting. Outside, I think. Puzzled, I get up and go to the window, but I'm on the side of the house and can't see anything. I listen again. It's Thiago. Who's he shouting at?

I head out of the office and pass through the front door. When I hit the driveway, I see Thiago pacing on the street and shouting into his phone. Grayson and Mateo stand beside him. All three look upset, and Mateo's face is bone white.

Worried, I run over to find out what's going on. Right before I get there, strong arms wrap around and pull me to a stop. I glance up at Grayson and frown.

"What's going on? Is somebody hurt?"

Thiago spins around. "Get her out of here. She doesn't need to see this," he orders Grayson.

Mateo pulls me out of Grayson's arms. "I've got her. Stay with Thiago," he assures Grayson.

A familiar feeling passes over me, and my stomach tightens knowing beyond a shadow of a doubt a sucker punch is coming. "Mateo, what's going on? Don't keep me in the dark." He pauses. "Please."

His arms drop, and I take off. Swerving around Grayson, who's now yelling at Mateo, I slip through the gate and collide with a wall. In this case, a large well-built wall named Thiago. He whirls around to grab me, and that's when I see him. Or at least I think it's a him.

The body is wearing a man's suit. Generic, black. White shirt. Or at least it used to be white. The collar is entirely a dark reddish-brown now. Similarly colored streaks run down the rest of the shirt like small rivers. His arms lie folded in his lap. A band adorns his finger, and he's wearing a plain black watch around his wrist. He's propped against the corner of the gate with a box beside him.

I brace myself to look at the area I've been avoiding since my first glance. There is nothing where the head should be. Somebody cut off this man's head.

"Do you know who it is? Is there a note, or is this the message?" I whisper to Thiago.

"Henley, go inside, now. I'm taking care of everything. Grayson,

96

come get her!" he yells. The voice on the phone says something to him, and he goes back to yelling at the lucky recipient.

Before Grayson can round the corner, I hurry over to the box to look inside. Soulless blue eyes peer back at me, and I shove my fist in my mouth to hold back the scream rising to the surface. If I let loose, Thiago will freak out. Don't scream. Don't scream. It's just a head. Plus, he was an asshole, right? He actually urged Diego to hurry up and kill me so he could escape before the Santos men arrived.

Diego's right-hand man. Blondie sure ended up in a bad way. But why deliver him here? Is the enemy cleaning up loose ends? If so, we may need to move up our timetable before we have dead bodies littering the driveway.

A note is... stapled to the back of the man's head. Gross. I shudder, but step around the box to read it. I hear Grayson swear behind me.

Little Brain, Little Brain, my heart stopped when I saw your beautiful beaten face in the webcam. A gift. He shouldn't have left you to die. You can thank me later. Word of warning. The Savages are my targets. Don't get in my way. I'll come for you soon.

The world darkens, and I sway. Strong arms wrap around my body and pick me up. The subtle smell of cologne tells me it's Grayson. Soothing sounds spill from his lips, but I don't understand a word. I stare helplessly into those blue eyes silently pleading for him to tell me everything's going to be okay. But he doesn't. A confused expression crosses his face, and he frowns.

I tap his arm. "D... own," I stammer, barely able to get the word out. When he shakes his head no, I explain. "Sick."

He sets me down, and I stumble over to the grass and fall to my knees, barely making it before I lose whatever I last ate. Tears roll down my cheeks while I heave and heave until there's nothing left in me. Except bitterness.

The deep, dark bitterness that comes with losing the one thing I want most in this world: freedom. A life away from the shadows I've lived in for so long. I open my fist and stare at my palm. It was right there. Gone now. I rock back and forth, trying to figure out what to do next.

He reaches for me, but I jerk away to stand on my own. What if he's watching? Anyone around me is a target. He's proven it over and over. "I'm okay. Fine. I... need to brush my teeth."

Hands brush the hair back from my face, but I guess my expression isn't very reassuring because Grayson shakes his head. "Don't lie to me, Henley. We'll get through this together, okay? Let's go inside, brush your teeth, and wait for Thiago to figure out what to do next."

I pull my head back and away from his hands. "Don't touch me. Please. You don't understand. He hurts everyone around me, and I can't stand the thought of him..." I stop. Grayson's not going to listen. "I told you. I'm fine." I turn my back on him and start walking toward the house.

He grabs my elbow to stop me. Dark blue eyes filled with worry stare down at me. "It's okay to need help, Henley."

There's only one thing I can use. "I'm going to be sick."

When he lets go, I sprint toward the house and straight to my room. Slamming the door shut, I head to the bathroom and turn on the water to brush my teeth. My head spins while I brush and try to think of what to do next. Run?

Several of my safe houses are within driving distance, but where's my car? I haven't even thought about it since I parked it in the hotel garage. Is it still there? Could he trace it to me? I didn't register the vehicle under Henley Night, but I can't remember if I gave the license plate to the front desk clerk.

Blondie was there the night Diego took me from the hotel. In fact, he knows—umm... knew—quite a bit about me, including the name I used at the hotel, which is the same freaking name I'm using now. Why did I use Henley Night? Damn it.

Plus, there's all the media pictures with my new name. It seems so incredibly stupid right now. It doesn't matter if I have a thousand wigs. He knows exactly what I look like.

I told myself I didn't believe in the promise of safety here, but I did. A sob escapes. I let the illusion lull me into a false sense of safety. If I hadn't, I would have an exit plan, but I have no plan. Zero. Nada. I yank my fingers through my hair nervously. So stupid.

I finish and rinse my mouth. The wild woman in the mirror catches my eye. Breathe, Henley. Stop spiraling and focus. You've escaped many, many times. You can do this. You've got the resources.

I go to the closet and pull down the duffle bag I saw in there the other day. My side twinges a little, but I ignore it. The bruises have faded to a yellowish-brown color and I'm healing fine, but I can't afford to escape one man and fall into the trap of an even worse one. The thought is sobering and exactly what I need.

Within minutes, most of my clothes are packed. You don't need much when you're on the run. Leggings, t-shirts, and running shoes. The foundation of every professional runner's wardrobe. After packing, I put it back into the closet.

Just in time, too. A knock sounds on the door. I open it to find Grayson standing there wearing the same worried expression.

Relief flashes across his face. He pulls me into his arms, squeezing me tightly. "Sweet Rose, it's going to be okay. Lean on me, okay?"

His arms feel so good, too good. I pull back and nod. "I'm sorry for being rude earlier. I just…" I purposely let my voice trail off. The man is a walking lie detector and I can't afford for him to suspect something's up. "I brushed my teeth, and I'm not sick anymore. That's better, right?"

His eyes narrow, but I must pass his test because he agrees.

As if worried I'll run again, he tugs me into his side and locks an arm around me. We walk into the living room and find Thiago and Mateo having a conference call with Zane, Sterling, and some guy I've never met.

Mateo leaps up and rushes over to wrap his arms around me. Breathing me in, he holds me tightly, as if he needs a hug as much as I do. I grip him hard in return. Tears clog my throat, but I can't let them fall. Not now. I don't want him to know I'm on the edge looking down.

"I'm okay," I tell Mateo.

He eases back and studies the look on my face. "You're not okay, but you're strong. And you have us. All of us." His lips capture mine in a short, but sweet kiss.

My lips cling to his when he pulls away. I frown as his words register, but my attention is caught by Thiago, who's standing in front of me, brows drawn, mouth tight.

His obsidian eyes sweep me from head to toe. His anger from earlier is gone, but so is the relaxed Thiago I've gotten to know better since I moved in here. He's been replaced by the ruthless predator I met at SEI by the elevator. "Why can't you listen when I tell you to go inside?" He sighs heavily, like the weight of the world is on his shoulders.

He pulls me from Grayson and guides me over to the couch to sit in front of the open laptop. "Who's the message from, Henley? Is it him?"

I bite my lip but say nothing.

"The nickname, the personal tone, and the reference to William not saving you. We know the message is for you, but we need you to confirm it's from your stalker." Thiago squats down to face me. "Tell me, please. I don't know how to protect you if I don't have all the details."

William must have been blondie's real name. I remember the ring on his finger and wonder if he's still married. Poor woman.

I glance at Mateo, who's sitting at the table with his laptop in front of him, looking worried to death. I sigh and return my gaze to the powerful man in front of me.

Thiago's dark eyes are fierce, like he's willing to slaughter the world for me, and surprisingly, it's this silent reassurance that helps me get the words out.

"It's him. My stalker. He's always called me Little Brain. I don't know why, but since it all started at MIT, I'm guessing he knew me somehow. He's incredibly smart. Smarter than me. Mateo's level.

Obsessed. I don't know what he looks like because the few times I've seen him, he wore a mask. He's tall. Maybe 6'2" or 6'3"." I stop and take a deep breath. My hands are shaking with pumped up adrenaline or fear. I don't know. Every time I tell someone about him, he destroys them. Well, except for Marcos, but as Marcos reminded me, you can't hurt a ghost.

Thiago darts a look at the three men on the screen in front of me who are taking notes.

"Can you introduce me?" I ask Thiago, nodding my head to the stranger on the screen.

"Henley, Raider," Zane interjects. "Raider, say hi to Henley and be nice."

The man beside Zane has absolutely zero expression on his face, but his eyes are cold as ice. Light blue in color, they contrast sharply with his dark skin, but it's not the color that makes them appear cold. Those are the eyes of a killer. I shiver.

He grunts out my name. "Henley."

Sterling shakes his head and whispers something in Raider's ear, but all he gets in return is a negative headshake. Sterling looks disappointed.

Thiago glares at Raider for being rude, but it has zero impact.

"Nice to meet you, Raider," I murmur, although I'm sure he knows I'm just being polite.

"What about his voice?" Zane asks.

Back to my stalker. I try to remember the few times he's spoken to me. "It's moderate and cultured, kind of like Sterling's but without the British accent."

Sterling tilts his head in interest. "He sounds like he came from a wealthy background. No slang?"

"Exactly. He doesn't seem to have an accent, and his speech is very precise," I state with surprise, having never really thought about it. "MIT is full of rich kids, though."

"Any scars?" Raider questions with an impatient sigh.

I've only seen his neck and hands, but nothing comes to mind, so I shake my head.

"Hair?"

"The mask covers his entire head except for his eyes and mouth," I tell them. "And it's a different mask each time, with nothing in common. I've tried to think of things over the years to find out who he is, but I've come up blank." I sigh. "There's very little to go on. He spent most of his time terrorizing me and ruining the lives of my friends and family from a distance." He doesn't sound very scary when I put it that way, but the things he's done to those who have protected me... "I've only seen him in person a few times."

Thiago motions behind me, and Grayson comes around to sit on one side of me while he takes the other. "Mateo is searching the cameras of every house around us right now."

I shake my head. "You won't see him. The cameras will be blank. Every single one. He's good," I warn them.

"We'll check, anyway. Don't forget, Mateo is smart, too," Grayson reminds me.

Mateo looks up and gives him a half smile.

Thiago takes my hand in his and my attention returns to him. "Henley, let's talk about the few times you spent with Stanley." When I look puzzled, he smiles gently. "Sometimes naming the thing that scares you the most helps give you a bit of perspective and takes away some of its emotional power. I named your stalker Stanley because it's absurd, and it will help ease the terror in your mind when you think of him."

Why didn't I ever think about naming him? "Stanley... I've only seen him a few times. The first two times, he showed up in my dorm room. I woke to find him sitting beside my bed. When I screamed, he slipped out. Nobody ever saw or caught him on camera. They thought I made him up."

Anger flashes across Thiago's face, but he nods encouragingly.

"The first time he spoke to me was in my room at my mother's house. I didn't scream because I didn't want my mother coming to save me," I reveal, my voice tight with terror from that night. "He spent an hour talking to me, telling me he thought I was a worthy partner for someone of his intelligence. Of course, he needed to be sure, so he informed me he'd give me a series of tests, and if I passed, he'd marry me. If I didn't pass, he'd kill me. Then he left."

My whole body starts shaking when I think of how I had lain in my bed, listening to him calmly tell me about our future. He never held me at gunpoint or threatened me with a weapon of any kind. Listening to him speak was more terrifying than if he'd waved a loaded gun because it revealed his madness.

"I was so angry with myself when he left. Why didn't I run or fight or even cuss him out? I promised myself I would the next time. A month later, he returned. I had rented an apartment from this nice old couple. It was more like a room in their basement with a kitchenette, but it was perfect, and more importantly, my mother was safe in her own apartment across town." I stop there.

How do I explain what happened next?

"This time, I tried running. He caught me by the throat and... smiled at me, like he was proud to see me run. His fingers tightened until I thought I was going to pass out, so I kicked him in the balls. When he dropped me, I grabbed the lamp and hit him on the head. He tackled me to the ground." I pause for a second. "The old man from upstairs came down with his gun and ordered him to get out of the house. Stanley... and he fought. The gun went off. He killed the old man. In shock, I stood there for a minute, but then I heard the man's wife on the stairs. I ran toward her, shouting for her to run and call the police, but she continued down the stairs, calling her husband's name. He shot her, too. While he was busy with their bodies, I ran. He set fire to the place. I became a wanted felon."

Tears roll down my face. I'd brought that psycho to their door, and I didn't even have the guts to warn them. If I had, maybe they would have called the police instead of trying to save me.

"So, he killed two people in a matter of minutes," Raider recounts with a thoughtful expression on his face. "Did he look remorseful or worried to you?"

I think back to that night. "He calmly informed me that it was my fault he'd had to take the action he did, and he expected me to act better in the future," I whisper, knowing he was right.

"It wasn't his first time killing someone," Raider states firmly. "Even sociopaths have some type of reaction the first time they kill someone. Glee, shock, anxiety, anger."

"I think he killed my mother," I reveal with a sob, having kept this secret from everyone. "The next night, I went to her apartment to say goodbye, but it was empty. There was a note saying she couldn't handle the mess I'd made of my life, and she was leaving. She left an envelope with a few hundred dollars in it. I took it and ran." My chest heaves, and Grayson wraps his arm tightly around me while I stare at Thiago. "The note wasn't in her handwriting."

His large hands reach out and gently wipe the tears from my face. "Henley, he took away all your support to make you vulnerable. It backfired. You never gave up. No matter how many times he caught up with you or you had to start over, you kept going. You're a fighter, Henley. He didn't break you. He made you."

With one last hiccup, I stop crying. Could I have been viewing this all wrong? I barely remember the girl I was when it all started, but I remember being constantly scared, jumping at shadows, and worried about supporting myself. I'm still scared, but things have changed considerably. I'm stronger, much stronger.

"Is that the last time you saw him?" Thiago asks gently, although he already knows the answer because I told him about the basement my first night here.

Grayson's arm is wrapped tightly around me, and desperately needing something to hold on to, I reach up and grip it with both hands. I clear my throat a few times until I can get the words out. "The last time I saw him, he kidnapped me in the middle of the night. I woke up in the basement of a house. For two weeks, he kept me there." Grayson's arm twitches, then tightens.

Zane grunts. "Did he say anything personal during that time?"

I glance at the laptop, but they're wearing their best poker faces. My eyes dart to Mateo, who's no longer looking at his computer. He's staring at me with horror on his face. I swallow.

"I can't think of anything. He mostly made me jump through a series of tests. As a reward for passing all my tests one day, I asked to pet the horse I could hear outside." I pause and feel the heat flare on my face. "He agreed, but he made me go without my clothes. I think he thought I wouldn't try to escape naked. When he turned his back to me, I jumped on the horse and rode it out of there."

The utter silence following my escape is unnerving, and my stomach twists into more knots.

"Tell us about the house," Raider commands, interrupting the tense moment.

I flash him a grateful smile. "White, farmhouse. Stables nearby. It was in Kentucky. Near Lexington. About twenty miles out in the country. It's abandoned now. I could never find the owner."

He raises an eyebrow, and I give him the address.

"I never told anybody. When I escaped, there wasn't any point in going to the police, especially with the warrant out for my arrest. Once I found clothes and money, I made my way to one of my back-up safe houses. I was prepared to keep running, but as you know, Marcos decided to 'kill' me, so my stalker would believe I died," I finish with a sigh and lean against Grayson, needing to borrow some of his strength. Between the last four days of coding and today, mine is almost gone.

He shifts, bringing me in closer to him.

Thiago gets up to pace and Mateo sits down beside me.

He grabs my hand tightly, his thumb rubbing softly against the back of it in a soothing manner.

"So, what's next?" I ask lightly.

"Well, it seems your stalker, err, Stanley, is somehow tied up with the Santos' enemy. Whether he's the tech guy or someone else, he's got enough power to find the Santos house and enough latitude to kill one of his own and not care about paying the price. Of course, that could be because he's a psycho, but I doubt it. Even they have self-preservation instincts," Zane recaps the conclusion we've all come to based on this morning's delivery.

"So, even if I left, he'd still be here, an enemy to them?" I question Zane, knowing he'll tell me the truth.

Mateo protests loudly beside me.

"Yes, and he's got even more reason to go after them now," Zane replies, eyes narrowed on me.

I nod. Instead of the fear I expected, relief floods my body.

"It's not much, but we'll dig for any new information we can find," Zane informs Thiago. He slaps Sterling on the back. "Slick has a knack for finding the most obscure details. He'll keep you all in the loop. Get some rest while the waters are still calm. We're going to need it."

When my intruder alarm went off that morning in Dallas, I thought my stalker had found me, and even alone, I contemplated staying and fighting it out until the bitter end. At the time, I wasn't willing to risk my small life and the safety I'd found. But now? The chance for true freedom and a real life is up for grabs. Maybe it's time I showed my stalker what he created. There will be no exit plan.

CHAPTER 17

When I wake early the next morning, it's still dark outside, and I'm tucked between Grayson and Mateo in Mateo's bed. I'd only been in his room once, but it's all about work. A large desk takes up one corner of the room. Several monitors, a couple of laptops and a desktop sits on or around it. Small Post-it Notes are tacked everywhere. A couple of abstract prints in black and white grace the white walls. The remaining room is filled with a king bed, a dresser, and a TV.

There are a few personal items and pictures, including the meus pequenos selvagens photo Grayson had on his desk. My attention is captured by a picture of Mateo holding a surfboard and smiling broadly at the camera. Or someone behind the camera. He's tan and athletic, and several years younger. He looks good. Happy.

"It's too early to be awake," Mateo whispers in my ear.

He snuggles in tighter against my back, and I can't help but feel his morning wood against me. This is the exact reason our mornings have been so delightful lately. I push back against him, immediately wanting my wake-up call.

His mouth sucks lightly on my earlobe. I gasp, then quickly look over at Grayson, but he never even twitches.

A muscular leg inserts itself between both of mine, making me realize I'm at least partially naked under the covers. His hand slides up my thigh until it's nestled between my legs. I open wider, silently telling him what I want, and a low chuckle sounds in my ear.

A finger moves my underwear to the side and strokes a line through my wetness to flick my nub. I bite my lip hard, keeping my moan locked in my throat, and push against his hand for more.

A finger pushes inside and strokes me. "Is this what you want?" I move my hips like I'm riding his hand. "Or what about this?"

Two fingers plunge into me, and I inhale sharply. *Yesss.*

With incremental movements, my hips continue to meet every downstroke. I don't want to wake Grayson, but it isn't nearly enough. Reaching back, I slip my hands into Mateo's briefs. I pull his cock out and stroke up and down, but it's an awkward position. Giving up, I slide it between my legs and arch back, so the tip slips inside.

"Are you sure? What if Grayson wakes?"

I stop and look at the man in front of me whose eyes are still closed. I picture those blue eyes open and watching, and my breath catches.

"I need you," I whisper, although I'm not sure if I'm whispering it to Mateo or Grayson in that moment. I tilt my hips back farther to get closer to the man behind me.

He pulls my panties completely to the side and slides inside, filling me up. This is a new position for us, with my legs almost completely closed, and him sliding in and out from this angle. It's shallower but hits the best spot from this angle, making my body quiver. Plus, it feels almost secretive, like you wouldn't know what was happening if you walked into the room and saw us.

Under the covers, he steadily strokes in and out, never increasing in pace, winding me tighter and tighter. A small moan slips out, and worried, I snap open my eyes only to meet Grayson's dark blue gaze. I tense in surprise, causing Mateo to moan softly in my ear.

I wait for Grayson to say something, but he doesn't. Does he know Mateo is inside me, or does he think he's fingering me?

Mateo's hand moves to play with my nub, and I arch into it but stifle any noise.

My breaths come faster, and my body coils tighter.

Grayson's eyes flick to the covers and back to my face. A devilish smile graces his face before his hand reaches over to play with my tight nipple.

I gasp. Mateo takes it as a sign to rub faster, and even though I desperately try to wait, I can't. Arching against both their hands, I come. My body clenches down on Mateo's hard cock, and the waves crash over, carrying me under, then spreading out to reach my entire body.

Throughout it all, I stare into Grayson's eyes. His cheeks are flushed, and his dark blue eyes glitter with his own desire. I watch his hand steal into the covers in front of his body, and I can't help but wonder what his cock feels like. I lick my lips.

Mateo groans, and his body continues to slide in and out for another minute, until I hear his breath catch and feel him pulsing inside me. He grips my hips while his breath flares hotly on the back of my neck. A sweet kiss lands on the side of my neck.

"Beautiful, I'll be right back," he murmurs. He slides out of bed and heads into the bathroom.

Grayson picks up my hand and I hold my breath, wondering where he's going to place it. He brings it to his mouth and places a kiss in the center of my palm. I stare at him, wishing I could hear his thoughts, but the silence of the moment is more important. Too many times, the words get in our way.

He places my hand on the center of his chest, quirks an eyebrow in a silent challenge, then lets it go.

I lick my dry lips and run my hand lightly back and forth across the smooth skin and muscle of his chest. Carefully watching his face, I flick his nipple, but all I see is a tightening around his eyes. Maybe he's not very sensitive there.

An image of his abs from the day at the beach flash into my mind, and my hand drifts down, until my fingers can caress each individual line. His breathing picks up a tiny bit and his abs harden under my touch, but his reaction isn't close to what I want.

I inch the tiniest bit closer and glide my hand lower until it's sliding around his cock, taking its measure. He groans, and I smile. My fingers caress his length and width, and I realize he's wider than Mateo. My body shifts restlessly.

His hand clamps down on top of mine, holding it still. We stare at each other, but neither of us speak.

The toilet flushes, and I pull my hand back. With one last look, I turn and face the other way, not wanting to see him reject me again.

Mateo comes out and helps me out of bed so I can use the restroom and clean up. When I return, I slide in on Mateo's other side, pushing him toward the center.

"Is everything okay?" he whispers in my ear.

"Yes," I reply with a soft kiss on his lips.

———

WHEN I WAKE a couple hours later, the sun is up and brightening the day—and Mateo is watching me sleep. I blush. This is the first time we've slept in a bed together. Thankfully, the other side of the bed is empty, so it's just the two of us.

"I like waking to you in my bed," he informs me, his voice husky with emotion. "How are you feeling?"

"How could I feel anything but good after my early morning wakeup call?" I teasingly reply. When he doesn't smile, I sigh. He's like a dog with a bone. "Resolved, maybe? I want a life, and the only way I'll get one is if he's gone. Maybe this was inevitable from the beginning. Him or me. Locked in this long, drawn-out life or death battle. I just didn't realize it until now. Interesting enough, I don't think he did either. He's been playing games for so long he's lost touch with reality."

Mateo leans over me. "I don't think our enemy understands the beast he's unleashed. All three of us will go to war right by your side. Your death isn't an option, minha linda. I refuse to even put it into the universe. The past doesn't matter anymore. You're strong and so are we. Zane and his team aren't too shabby, either."

"Ha, I dare you to say that to Cruz," I challenge him.

He gives a mock shudder. "No way. Spooks are crazy. Have you taken a hard look at Cruz? And Raider?"

"They worked for the CIA?" I whisper loudly and snicker.

"Cruz did. Raider never said, but I don't want to know his dark past. Even for me, some things need to stay buried," he says with emphasis. "Enough about those two. What do you think about sharing my bed?"

I lay my head on his chest. "It's nice," I say hesitantly. "What was Grayson doing in here?"

His hand sifts through my hair. "Nice isn't quite the answer I was looking for," he states ruefully. "Fabulous, incredible, awesome, or something similar would be infinitely better."

My hand glides across his chest. "It's incredible, but it can't last. You live here, and so do I—right now. When this over, I'm going to need to get my own place. Maybe you could come over and spend the night with me?"

His hand pauses. "Incredible. Exactly what I wanted to hear. Thank you." His hand strokes down my arm softly. "We don't know what things are going to be like when it's over, but we'll find a way together. Let's table that discussion for now, okay?"

He pulls my chin up. "Did you mind Grayson being here? He was worried about you, so I invited him to sleep in here with us."

"Yes and no," I return honestly. "He confuses me. One minute he's rejecting me, and the next... He constantly blows hot and cold."

"He's working through a few things. Give him time," Mateo urges me. "Did you like him watching us?"

I narrow my eyes. "You knew?"

"Grayson's never slept that soundly in his life," he says with a chuckle. "I wasn't sure if he simply pretended to be asleep the whole time or if he watched. Based on your answer, I'm guessing you knew he was watching."

"Yes, he watched us," I admit. "And I—I liked it. His face... He seemed so focused and turned on just watching. It was... kind of flattering, I guess."

Mateo leans down and gives me a slow kiss. "Thank you for being honest and telling me. I don't want you uncomfortable. Ever. Remember, you call the shots." He swipes a finger down my neck. "One more thing I want to talk to you about from this morning. We didn't use a condom. Are you on the pill, or do we need to watch for a potential surprise?"

Surprised myself, I shake my head at my utter disregard of something I'd never forgotten. "I've never forgotten to use one, but I'm covered. I have the shot, and I received a new injection while I was in the hospital." After I was kidnapped, I wanted something to protect myself, just in case, so I'm diligent about staying on it. But I love the way he asked me. I raise a hand and place it along his cheek. "You're incredibly sweet and understanding, Mateo. Most men would have freaked out, but it wasn't even the first thing on your mind."

He flops back on his pillow and throws an arm over his face. "No, I'm not sweet. Strike that word from your vocabulary. I'm fine with geek or nerd, but not sweet. In high school, when a girl called me sweet, it always meant she wanted to be friends. Just friends."

"I like sweet, but I definitely want to be more than 'just friends'," I murmur, gliding my hand down his body playfully. "Have you ever been in a serious relationship?"

He shifts uncomfortably, making me raise my eyebrows. "I was once in a relationship for five years," he reveals, moving his arm from his face to my back. "I met a girl in California when I went out there to get my master's degree from Stanford. Her name was Ashley, and we clicked easily. We both had plans to get our doctorate degree, so I stayed, and we moved in together. For the first few years, it was wonderful. We worked on our individual thesis and lived our daily life. But SEI started to need me more and more, and as I got involved with the research and development of new products, I found I enjoyed the real-world application more than the theoretical. I'd lose myself for days in the work and our relationship suffered. We drifted apart. When I was ready to go back to Miami, we broke it off. I hear she's a professor at a university, married with two kids now."

I think about the normalcy of her life and envy her for it. Would that have been my track if my stalker hadn't decided to derail my life?

He flips us over until he's on top. "I can't promise I won't immerse myself in my work, but I already see a difference in myself when I'm around you. You make me more aware of the world and the people I care about in a way I'd never considered. I want to change. Not just for you, but for me and for Thiago and Grayson who've always had to pick up the slack. I want you in my life, Henley, front and center, not on the sidelines."

I push a swath of hair out of his face and look into his serious eyes. "If... when we come out on the other side of this war, I promise..." I grin when I see the look of shock cross his face. "Yes, promise, to give us a chance. You push me out of my comfort zone, too. And I like it. I like you—very much."

His warm brown eyes shine with happiness. Pouty lips descend on mine, demanding and needy, making me want him. His hands grasp my shirt and strip it off me. Subconscious, I cover the worst of the bruises and part of my small breasts. I've always been so self-conscious of my flat chest.

"Move your hands, Henley. I want to lick and kiss every inch of your body, and they're in the way," he orders me.

I slide them to his shoulders, and he bends down and places a light kiss on the worst bruise. He moves to another and does the same. Over and over again.

The feather soft touches make me shiver and not from the cold.

My body opens beneath his lips, luxuriating in the sheer admiration each kiss conveys. My nipples harden, and he switches his attention from my bruises to my breasts. His mouth hovers over my breast, nibbling and licking my nipple until I'm writhing beneath him. In a sudden move, he covers it completely and sucks hard. Need arrows through my body, making me cry out.

When he switches his attention to the other one, I'm murmuring nonsense, only to hear him chuckle. "I'm taking my time. Being in the present. Remember? You're so beautiful when you're aroused, Henley. Are you sweet, though?" He scoots down on the bed between my legs.

I nearly come off the bed when his mouth latches onto me. My fingers clench the sheets, needing something to hold on to while he takes his time tasting me. I'd only had someone do this once before, and I wasn't that impressed. I honestly thought it was a waste of time. Until now.

My body spirals tighter and tighter. "I need you inside me," I plead with Mateo.

"After," he mumbles. "I want to see you fall apart from my mouth first."

He's focused entirely on my body. His mouth descends, and I cry out when he sucks my nub like he did my nipple. Everything darkens until my only focus is his mouth. Sensations roll through my body until it suddenly all rushes to the center, then explodes outward.

When the world comes back into focus, Mateo is sitting up, watching me, his hand stroking his cock in anticipation. "Minha linda. I can't say that enough. You're mine and so beautiful."

"That was amazing," I state softly, feeling a little shy.

His mouth curves in a sexy smile. "We're just getting started."

His body covers mine, the delicious weight a reminder of the differences between us. He slides inside, and I groan. This morning's been full of so many good surprises, I can almost forget yesterday. Almost.

Once I'd calmed down and understood this was happening,

whether I was prepared or not, I knew I had to be all in. This time is different. I'm stronger and mentally more prepared to fight for what I want. Having the Santos men and Zane's crew backing me makes a world of difference, too. He's one man, a psycho, who deserves whatever is coming his way.

Mateo playfully nips my shoulder. "Your attention, please. Stop thinking," he commands me. "Today is for us. Tomorrow, we'll regroup and plan our attack."

CHAPTER 18

THIAGO

My fists drive hard and fast into the bag, snapping forward with controlled force, but my thoughts are anything but composed. The rage burning inside is straining to unleash itself on our enemies but targeting a ghost has been damn near impossible. Thanks to Henley, we have a chance to splinter their alliance and potentially draw them out.

My mind immediately goes to Henley. The pure terror on her face when she saw the note will haunt me forever—another fucking example of my inability to protect her. If I hadn't been yelling, she wouldn't have even known something was going on. At the very least, I should have closed the lid to the box. She's like Mateo, with this obsessive need to know every detail, unable to leave something alone. I should have anticipated she'd look.

When she'd realized running wouldn't save us, she made the choice to stay and fight. The biggest monster in her life, and she chose to stand with us. Part of me wants her to run and find a safe place. But the other half wants her here beside us, taking down our mutual enemies and getting her revenge.

My phone dings with an alert and a modular voice informs me the patio door is open. Immediately tense, I pull off a glove and open the security app to see what's going on. Part of me hopes it's him. He hasn't the fortitude to withstand the damage I plan to inflict on him. Can he play with the big boys? We're not two old people or a young girl on the run. We're ruthless men who know how to fight and are willing to do whatever it takes in this war. Is he?

Disappointment and pleasure war with each other when I see Henley on the back patio. She's looking east toward the sunrise, and... scowling? Her lips move, a slim hand rises, her middle finger extends, and she flips off the sun. What in the hell? I snort. She told us when we first met mornings were not her favorite time of the day. What is she doing up this early?

Except for yesterday, she's practically ignored me since I gave her my tablet. The few times I have seen her, she's been excruciatingly polite, and it's been driving me crazy. I hate this distance between us. Every time I think about breaking the rules and climbing in her bed, I watch her with Mateo, and I know it's for the best. But damn, I miss the smell of her on my skin and the sweet defiance she exhibits when I give her orders.

She strolls back into the house, and I put the phone down. A second later, it pings and informs me the security system has been disabled and the front door is open.

Furious, I yank off the other glove and storm out of the gym. I can't believe she's going for a walk with that psycho out there. Does she have no common sense? Breaking into a jog, I round the corner and run out the front door after her. I swear, there's going to be some damn rules put into place. How the hell am I supposed to protect her when she walks right into danger?

When I get to the gate, I'm puzzled to see it's closed. I double check the app and there are no alerts. Scanning the front yard, I don't see her anywhere.

"Garage door is open."

What is she doing in the garage? Striding around the side of the house, I find her leaning against the wall with a frown on her face.

"Henley, what are you doing? Do you want to go for a ride?"

Her face is troubled when she looks over. "I'm looking for my car, but it's not here." Fingers tap restlessly against her arm. "Do you have the list of evidence seized by the police?"

"Your car is at SEI. Mateo grabbed your keys from the hotel room and paid a valet to take it over to the office," I inform her. "I'm sorry. We should have mentioned it sooner. With everything going on, it slipped my mind. Do you want me to bring it home this afternoon?"

Relief chases the worry away. "Yes, please. I like having it close by."

A vehicle is a lifeline. Like her phone and computer. Marcos always made sure a vehicle with a full tank of gas was in the garage, too.

"I understand. I'll have Thomas take me to the office this morning, and I'll drive your car back. Okay?"

"Thanks, I appreciate it," she replies. Her eyes drift to my hands, over my legs, and back up. "Have you been fighting?"

The flare of heat in her eyes is so fucking tempting. "I was working out when the alarm informed me the front door was open," I explain, leaving out the part with the patio.

Comprehension dawns, and she snorts. "You thought I planned to take another walk, didn't you? I bet you stormed out of the house ready to lay down some rules." Her laughter echoes in the garage.

I grit my teeth but say nothing.

She closes the garage door.

"Garage door closed."

"Interesting, I didn't know it did that," she says, laughter still coloring her voice. "Can you show me the gym? Since I'm not allowed to take a walk outside, a treadmill will have to do. You have one, right? I remember seeing several purchases for exercise equipment in your bank account."

I give her an incredulous look. "When were you snooping in my bank account?"

She waves a hand like it's nothing. "Before we met. I needed to know if SEI was a legitimate business or if you were doing illegal things, like laundering money. Your account is pretty boring. Tons of exercise equipment, jewelry for your... dates, tailored suits, and flowers every Sunday." She points over her shoulder. "Oh, and super excessive luxury vehicles."

Most of the women I've dated would love to have access to my bank account, but I can't say any of them would care what I'd bought with it, only the number on the bottom line. My mouth twitches. "Sorry to be so boring. Did you look at all our accounts?"

She rolls her eyes. "Of course. Mateo likes to spend a ton of money on education." Her lips quirk like she approves. "Grayson is the interesting one. The amount of money he spends on yachts is obscene. What do you even do with that many?"

I close the front door and lead her past the living room and down a set of stairs. "The ocean is his escape. The gym is mine. It's in the basement," I reveal. "And yes, I have a treadmill. Several, in fact."

We land on the bottom step, and she gasps at the sight in front of her. The entire basement is one large workout center. "We have the main area with treadmills and other cardio equipment." I point to the right. "Free weights." I point to the left.

I wave a hand toward the various doors. "They lead to a sauna, a pool, and hot tub. And a restroom."

She stares around in disbelief.

I grab her hand and pull her to the back of the gym. "This is what I call 'the arena' and it's where we train using various fighting techniques. Plus, I use the bag to work out when I need to get rid of some stress. What do you think?"

"I think you're probably better equipped than most professional gyms," she states with a chuckle. Her hand reaches out to push the heavy bag. "Can you teach me?"

I frown, not sure I heard her correctly. "Teach you... what? To box?"

"Can you teach me to fight? To defend myself? Enough to bring someone down or get out of their hold? I watched a few videos, but I must have done them wrong because they didn't work," she states matter-of-factly, but her voice trembles slightly with fear.

A fierce wave of protectiveness rises in me. This is something I can do for her. "Yes, I'll teach you some moves, and we'll practice every day until they become second nature, okay?"

Her eyes shine with relief. "Thank you," she says fervently. "I want a few surprises up my sleeve when he comes for me."

I inhale sharply, then reach out and pull her to me. "He's not going to come anywhere near you," I respond with a growl. "We're going to flush this bastard out and remove him. Permanently."

She pats me on the chest but shakes her head. Her blue eyes are dark with determination. "Maybe, maybe not. Teach me the best and worst moves you know. Teach me as if you know he's going to take me. The probability is a lot higher than you think, and you might be giving me an advantage."

I recognize the fierce determination in her gaze. She's a fighter, and if I can put another weapon in her arsenal, she'll use it. "You're right. Go change. We'll start today," I reply, to her surprise. "I understand more than you think. It's the reason I started working out. If my father found us, I wanted to have more options than running."

She lifts her chin at my confession and smiles. "Thank you. I'll be back in ten."

While she's gone, I unwrap my hands and organize my thoughts on the best moves to teach her. We don't have years to perfect her skills, so she needs the most impactful moves she can master in only a few sessions. I hear her on the steps and turn to find her entering the room wearing leggings, one of Grayson's t-shirts, and running shoes.

I grab the loose fabric of her shirt and yank her toward me. "Tie it close to your body. Loose clothing can be used against you."

She nods earnestly and ties a knot in the bottom of the shirt.

I dip my chin. "Good. Now, I want you to yell."

She frowns, clearly uncomfortable with this simple order.

Crossing my arms, I wait.

"Aaarrggh!" she semi-yells.

"That was terrible. Do it again. Louder."

"Aaarrggghhh!"

I grab her from behind in a choke hold. "The only way you can get out of this is to yell like your life is on the line."

She yells, a little louder this time. "AAAarrgghh!"

I drag her backward. "Yell, damn it. If you don't yell, he's going to kidnap you to an abandoned place where nobody will be able to find or hear you. YELL!!"

She takes a deep breath and yells with everything she has in her. "AAARRRGGHH!"

I let her go. "Your first line of defense is to run, but if you can't, use your voice. Make a scene, and don't stop yelling. Wave your arms. Make it apparent to anyone nearby that you need help. It's uncomfortable. Women are programmed not to make a scene and we need to eliminate those barriers. We're going to integrate yelling into every aspect of our training. You will yell at the beginning and end of each session, and you will yell when we're attacking each other. Got it?"

Her face loses some of the embarrassment and gains a bit of determination back. "I've got it. No loose clothing. Yell like hell."

"I'm going to teach you how to properly kick a man in the balls. Like the yelling, you need to throw yourself into this move at full force. No half-ass kicks. Got it?" I demonstrate how I want her to kick, making sure to put force into it.

I motion to her legs. "Which leg is dominant?"

"Right."

I place my legs in a staggered stance with my right leg behind me. "The first thing is getting your body into a position of power. Mimic my stance, with your dominant leg in the back position and your hands and arms raised. This will help give you more momentum when you kick. Good. Balance more on the balls of your feet, not the heels. It will help you move quicker, adjust faster, and stay more balanced when you kick or hit your attacker."

She shifts to the balls of her feet.

"Good. Rock back and forth. Get a feel for it. Bring your hands up for balance. When you're ready, bring your dominant leg through and straight up as hard as you can, then step back into the stance. The entire time you're kicking, I want you to yell. Got it?"

She brings her leg through and kicks me hard between the balls. I block with the pad in my hands.

"You didn't yell. Do it again."

Her yell is softer than I'd like, but she does it.

"Again. Louder and harder."

"AAARGGHH!" she screams.

I pump a fist. "Yes! Let's repeat that a few more times."

She flushes with pride and proceeds to yell and kick like a demon.

"Every day when you come in, I want you to practice that maneuver. Do you think you could take me down?"

She scoffs. "Not a chance. You're stacked muscle and I'm obviously not."

My mouth twitches at her description, but I refrain from laughing. "Everyone has soft spots. When attacking or defending yourself, these vulnerable areas can incapacitate them, even the big ones. I want you to repeat them several times a day until you can't think of one without the others. Okay? If you know them, you're more likely to look for opportunities to strike them in those locations and do the most damage. I'll demonstrate what I want you to do. Stay very still, okay?"

She stands in front of me with her feet shoulder width apart.

Bringing up my fists, I use my hands in short strike motions to get her used to someone attacking her. "Eyes." I punch forward, and she staggers back a step. "Nose." Punch. She wraps her arms around her head and squats down.

Shit, shit, shit. I didn't think about my fists triggering her.

I squat down beside her and gently pull her into my arms. "Shh, querida, I've got you. I'm sorry. It's okay." With careful movements, I sit on the mat with her in my lap while I continue to reassure her. My hand runs through her hair a few times. It's so soft. No wonder Mateo's always playing with it.

A few minutes later, her hand flexes against my shirt. "I'm sorry. Maybe I can't do this," she says dejectedly, looking down at her lap.

I sweep the pink hair back and pull her head up. "No, I'm sorry. This is entirely my fault. I didn't think. We need to get you used to someone striking against you but without triggering you. I think if I use exaggerated slow hits, it might be okay. Do you want to try or call it a day?"

She scrutinizes me. "If you have time, I want to try again."

Ouch. "I have time," I reply firmly. I lift her onto her feet, then vault up. We get back into position. "Ready?"

"Eyes." I slowly push toward her eyes. So slow, she laughs.

It might be silly but getting her used to hands punching toward her is necessary. If she's triggered during an attack, she'll lose any advantage. I go through the rest of the spots using the same technique. Nose, ears, jaw, throat, groin, knees, Achilles tendon.

"Now, you do the same to me. Ten times. Go."

She runs through each of the spots, thrusting her small fists forward, until I'm satisfied.

"We'll go through this exercise every morning, too. Except give me your hand," I order her. "Thumb stays on the outside. Try to use your knuckles when you hit. Punch straight forward, snap back quick." I wrap her fingers into a correct fist and demonstrate how to punch, then make her repeat the maneuver over and over until I'm satisfied.

She places a hand on my arm. "Thank you, Thiago. I know how busy you are, and this only adds to your plate. Plus, it cuts into your workout time. I'll try to be a quick learner."

I clasp her hand in mine. "This is important. I can always get up earlier to get my workout done. Be here tomorrow at five-thirty a.m."

She grimaces but agrees.

"Feel free to use the treadmill or anything else," I tell her. "I'm going to shower and get ready for work. And I'll bring your car home this evening. Good job today, Henley."

She beams at me.

As I hit the stairs, I look back and find her practicing her kicks. I smile. She sees herself as weak, but she's one of the strongest people I've met. We have to make her believe it, too.

CHAPTER 19

HENLEY

M y muscles protest loudly when I bend over the desk to look at the app. But I'm excited to learn something physical I can use. Given the lack of ability I've displayed in the past, he'll never expect it, which already gives me a slight advantage. I can't always count on my brain to get me out of a situation, and who knows if I'll have a gun with me.

Another thing I'm going to need—a new gun. I wonder if Zane could get me one. I add it to the long mental to do list in my head.

My thoughts drift back to this morning's session with Thiago. Yelling seems silly at first, and excessive. But if someone is trying to kidnap or assault me, don't I want excessive? I never thought about it until today, but if I'm not going to go all in to fight for my life, why fight at all?

I take a deep breath to clear my mind and focus on the phone in front of me. The app is installed, and it's time to put it into action.

I tap display and watch the 3D image appear through the phone and on the flat table behind it. Time for the second view. Setting the phone down, I slip on the headset and look at the same 3D image, but this time, I see it overlaid on top of the dummy we've placed on the desk.

It shows the exact size and location of the tumor in the patient's brain along with the myriad of blood vessels and nerves wrapped around the tumor, which is something incredibly difficult to see on the 2D scan.

Both devices will provide doctors with something they can't see today.

I pull off the headset and beam at Mateo.

He throws a fist in the air, then picks me up and whirls me around until we're both dizzy. "You and Marcos built something truly incredible and life changing. The phone makes it accessible and portable for all doctors, and when paired with the headset or glasses, it can revolutionize surgery. Amazing."

Grayson claps from the doorway. "Congratulations. I didn't get to see it when Marcos did the original demonstration because I was out of town, but it's truly remarkable." He claps Mateo on the back, then leans down to pull me into a hug.

Startled, I return his hug. "I'm glad you're here," I state, much to his surprise, then look at Mateo. "I know we talked about pushing it live tonight, but this could be a huge opportunity for us to divide our enemies. When you broker technology, don't you set up a live demonstration for the bidders?"

Mateo nods. "Yes, we usually show the demo, then open the bidding. Why?"

Thiago walks into the office and hands me my keys. He circles around the desk to look through the phone and view the brain. "Remarkable." Dark eyes full of pride and heat catch mine. "You should be very proud of yourself."

"Thank you," I reply huskily, then turn back to Mateo. "What if we set up a live demonstration for our doctors? We could have them send CT or MRI scans to us in real-time and show how the software converts and displays the image in a matter of minutes. We let the solution sell itself," I say excitedly. "At the end of the demonstration, we tell them the app's available for immediate download in their preferred app store, give them the name and price. But until that moment, we keep it secret from everyone."

Mateo thinks about it for a second. "We've never done anything in real-time with unknown data. It has a few risks, but if we pull it off, it could be the jumpstart we need. But what does that have to do with our enemies?"

"What if you told Carlton it's a demonstration to kick off the bidding? Wouldn't he run straight to our enemy and inform them?" I throw out the suggestion.

Mateo follows the breadcrumbs. "When the app is announced, they will all know we set a trap for Carlton." He frowns.

"I like it," Thiago states firmly from his chair by the desk. "She's right. We need to start moving offensively. If we can take one player off the board, we need to do it."

Mateo hesitates. "They'll kill Carlton when they find out. I'm not sure I can do it."

Thiago dips his chin, acknowledging Mateo's statement, but says nothing.

Grayson offers a suggestion. "We could make his presence a requirement for the demonstration. It would save his life, but also give us an opportunity to question him and gain some intel. Maybe even find out who the fucker stalking Henley is or the name of our enemy."

Mateo places his hands behind his head and stretches while he thinks through the scenario Grayson just laid out. Then he looks at me, and I can see he's made up his mind. "Let's do it."

Thiago's eyes gleam with satisfaction. "Mateo, start getting the demonstration set up, but don't announce what it's for yet. If anyone asks, tell them we're still in negotiations. Timing is going to be critical on this trap. I want to give them only enough time to make a move, not plan against us. And send the app team on an all-expense paid vacation for the next two weeks. Tell them it's a reward for their hard work. Remind them that they're under a non-disclosure agreement, and they're not allowed to speak to anyone about the project, not even an SEI colleague, or they'll be fired."

Mateo pulls out his phone and starts making notes.

"I'll go ahead and package up the app and all the information. It usually takes about twenty-four hours for the app to go through the app store approval process. In addition, I'll run real-time scenarios to help mitigate the live aspect," I inform Mateo, already making my own list in my head.

Thiago narrows in on Grayson. "How quick can you pull a party together on that fancy yacht of yours?"

Grayson's slow smile tells me he's caught on to Thiago's plan. "If I meet with a party planner tomorrow, I can get all the booze and everything brought on board within two days. Food is tougher. Maybe a Miami theme? We could pull in food from area restaurants instead of having a catered event. We're looking at three to four days, especially if I throw some incentives into the pot."

"Get everything but the food. When we have the bid set up, we can add the last part. Maybe we can use the event to flush out more than one bird," Thiago commands him, then turns his attention to me. "We've got a meeting with VRDeck at the end of the week. It looks like the app is ready, correct?"

"It's ready," I confirm, then dart a glance at Grayson. "All three of us?"

"Just the two of us," Thiago replies. "Do you have business attire, or do we need to order some clothes?"

I'd been wanting to ask Peyton out to the house to help me go through my closet, but I knew Thiago wasn't keen on having anyone in the house but us. Now I have the perfect excuse. Clothes, and maybe some time on the beach. "Do you remember Peyton from the ball? My escort?"

Thiago nods cautiously.

"He's a stylist. Grayson bought me plenty of clothes, but I'd like to get Peyton's help to pull some outfits together. For the business meeting, the demonstration, yacht party, and other events. I'd like to invite him to the house," I finish in a rush. Why does this man make me so nervous sometimes?

He thinks about it for a minute. "Okay. Don't give him the code. I want someone here at the house the whole time. Promise me."

"I promise," I swear. There's safety in numbers these days.

Thiago stands and looks at the dummy lying on his desk. "Is there any chance of me getting my office back soon?"

I look around the large room at the mobile devices, scans, computers, and dishes scattered about and wince. "Not this week? I need to set up tests for the demonstration." The couch is a huge neon sign blinking at me. "Also, could I buy the couch? It's incredibly comfortable, and I've kind of grown attached to it. It would be perfect in my office."

Mateo mutters something under his breath, but I can't hear what he's saying.

"You want my couch? Wait. Your office? Did I miss something?" Thiago interjects, looking at Grayson and Mateo.

I shrug. "I meant my future office. You know, for when I move out?" His brow lowers. "After all this over." I quantify my last statement, so he doesn't think I'm planning something stupid with Stanley the stalker out there. I snicker. That kind of has a sing song quality about it. Stanley the Stalker. Maybe I should start singing it? It could help turn down the fear a decimal or two.

Thiago narrows his eyes and studies the couch. With a sharp inhale, he swivels to stare at Mateo.

Mateo glances at Thiago, then Grayson, and lifts a shoulder.

I raise an eyebrow. The room is utterly silent, all three of them having some kind of silent man discussion. "The couch?" Nobody says anything. "Ok, well, I have an appointment with my therapist." I hold up my hand when Thiago rumbles something. "It's virtual. If you don't mind." I point to the door of Thiago's office.

All three shuffle out with different expressions on their faces, but I ignore them and shut the door. Hurrying to the computer, I bring up the conference number and dial in to meet with my therapist. This is going to be an interesting call.

CHAPTER 20

GRAYSON

She's killing me. Slowly, but surely. Sleep is more elusive than ever to the point I'm barely functioning these days. When I'm lying alone in my bed at night, the image of her coming apart in front of me plays the second I close my eyes. Each time, the scenario changes, just a bit, enough to keep me coming back for more. One thing stays the same. In every instance, she's holding my cock when she comes.

I can't stop seeing it, and if I'm honest, I don't want to.

My mind and body are at war with each other, and my mind is losing. Logical reasons to stay away from her are disappearing like smoke.

You're a damn fool, I tell myself.

I take a drink of coffee, hoping it will wake me up. Mateo strides into the kitchen, followed by Thiago. Both are dressed for work. Thiago grabs a protein drink from the fridge. Mateo beelines for the coffee pot beside me.

"Mateo and I are going into the office today. He needs to work on a few preliminary bid items, and I need to prepare for the meeting with VRDeck," he informs me.

"You've gone into the office every day. It's almost as if you're avoiding some... thing," I taunt him, but he only raises an eyebrow in return. "Someone needs to stay with Henley." I slide my gaze to Mateo.

Please don't let it be me. I just took a cold shower.

"Actually, nobody is staying here today. I've arranged for Thomas and a team to go with you and Henley to your yacht. The arrangements for the launch party can't wait," Thiago explains, his voice gruff with emotion.

He hates the thought of her leaving the safety of the house. "Why don't you have the team guard her here?" I suggest, desperate to get some space to think without her nearby.

"She doesn't have a gun, and I promised her I would never ask her to stay with strangers again unless she had her phone and gun with her," Thiago replies. He hesitates for a second, then continues. "And honestly, I don't know our new security team that well. Can I trust them with Henley's life? Yes, I believe so, but I'm not a hundred percent sure yet."

Thiago rarely explains himself. He must feel strongly about it. And, if I'm honest, could I leave her here with a house full of strangers? No. Look what happened last time I left her. "I'll take her with me to the yacht. She doesn't need a gun today, but she does need one. Do you plan on getting one from Zane?"

"He's working on it. Hopefully, I can bring one home today," Thiago confirms before looking at his watch. "Are you ready, Mateo?"

Mateo leans in close to me and whispers, "Give Henley a good morning kiss for me." He chuckles at the expression on my face. "And remember, I'm an excellent kisser, so do it right."

I roll my eyes at the last statement and shove him toward Thiago. "Get out of here."

"The team will be here in twenty minutes," Thiago calls out on his way out the door.

Surprisingly, Henley walks into the kitchen a minute later.

"What are you doing up so early?"

She wrinkles her nose and makes a scrunchy face. "I've been up since five. Thiago's teaching me self-defense, and it's the only time he has available in his busy schedule." Bringing the coffee to her nose, she inhales deeply, then takes a few sips.

I laugh. "How's that going? Thiago's extremely intense about self-defense. When Mateo and I were growing up, he forced us to join every martial arts class with him, even if we didn't want to do it. I'm glad I did it now, but we had to sacrifice a lot of flirting time with the girls in high school," I jokingly confide.

Her eyes spark with interest, then she laughs and explains what he's taught her so far. "It's mainly the basics, but I didn't even know that much. And it isn't really something I could learn from watching videos, although I tried."

Tried and failed, I'm guessing from the tone of her voice. My fist clenches, but I shove it in my pocket. It's hard to hear anything about the time she spent with that fucker, but at least she's starting to open up to us. I clear my throat.

"Are you going into the office? I thought Mateo was going today?" she asks, a confused expression on her face. "You're not leaving me here alone, are you? Or worse, with a bunch of strangers from your security team? If so, I'm going to need a gun. There's no way I'm staying here without one."

Fear rises in her eyes, and I raise a hand to stop the slew of questions. "We're going to my yacht to meet with a friend of mine who's a party planner and get the event kicked off. How does a day out of the house sound?"

"Like heaven," she responds with a sigh of relief. A broad grin appears. "What time are we leaving?"

"The security team is going with us, and they won't be here for at least another fifteen minutes. Sit down, and I'll make you a quick breakfast," I reply, motioning to the barstool on the other side of the island. "Eggs and toast?"

"Sounds delicious, thank you," Henley returns, sliding around to grab a seat. "You look tired. Is everything okay?"

I contemplate answering with the entire truth, but I don't want things to stall before we get to the yacht. "My dreams have been keeping me awake at night," I confide to her. "Maybe this afternoon, I can grab a nap and catch up on some sleep."

She sighs. "I know the feeling. The past and present have been mashed together. The only time I can get some sleep is if I work myself to death or Mateo sleeps with me."

I turn around and set her plate down in front of her. "Maybe we can both catch a nap this afternoon. Over the years, I've learned the nightmares tend to stay away from the light of day." Or maybe we can nap together this afternoon. A groan rises at the thought of us in a bed, but I strangle it before the sound escapes. "I'm going to change into something more casual. I'll meet you at the front door in a half hour."

Her brow furrows while she scrutinizes my face, but doesn't say anything, just nods her agreement.

I give Claire a call as I head back to the bedroom to change. "Hey, Claire, it's Grayson Santos. I want to confirm a time to meet today." Quickly calculating the time to get there, I add another thirty minutes in case we run into traffic. "How about sometime between ten and noon? Give me a call back if the time doesn't work for you."

Claire has thrown various events for us over the years, so I know she'll do a great job. I dress quickly and head downstairs to meet Thomas and his men.

Several SUVs line the driveway, and I scowl at the sight of them. I hate traveling in a convoy. Smoothing my expression, I glance around to find the man in charge. "Thomas?"

Surprisingly, a short, stocky man steps forward. Instead of the suit Diego always wore, he's dressed in black combat fatigues and boots. In addition, he's armed to the teeth with a side pistol, a large knife, and a shoulder holster with two pistols in it. And probably several hidden weapons, too. A professional. I already like him.

"I'm Thomas Sanders. Nice to meet you," he says, shaking my hand with a firm grip. "Grayson, right? I'll introduce you to my team and walk through the security procedures for today. If everything sounds good to you, we can leave whenever you're ready."

Direct, too. "Yes, Grayson. Thanks, I appreciate it."

With a short signal, each bodyguard steps up and introduces him or herself, and provides a brief summary of their expertise. I'm grateful to see a few women in the group. They can accompany Henley to areas men can't go.

"We'll travel in two SUVs and one sedan. The car allows us to hang back and see things from a different angle. Two will accompany you in your SUV. Four will ride in the second SUV and the sedan. We've got our route mapped. I've texted it to you," he states the details with military precision. "Once we arrive, the team will spread out over the yacht and on the ground, but one man and woman will stay close to you and Henley. Everything sound good to you?" He waits for my nod.

"Sounds excellent, thank you," I state firmly.

Henley walks out the door in a pair of silky shorts and the blue blouse that matches her eyes. The one I told her was designated for going on a date. I swallow.

"Henley, let me introduce you to Thomas, who's heading our personal security."

I watch him closely, and the man's eyes never drop to the gorgeous legs she's got on display, winning my wholehearted approval.

"Good morning, Henley. If you need anything, let me or one of the members of my team know," Thomas says quickly before introducing everyone to her. "So, are we ready to go?"

"Shall we?" I open the door with a flourish and help her into the vehicle.

Once she's in her seat, I lean over and whisper, "I knew that blouse would look good on you. If only this were a date."

Pink creeps up her neck and graces her beautiful cheeks. She turns and stares into my eyes. "I don't recall you asking me on a date."

I raise an eyebrow. "Touché, sweet Rose. Does that mean you'd be interested in going on a date with me?"

"You'll never know unless you ask," she returns nonchalantly, but her fingers are nervously pleating the edges of her shorts.

"Maybe I needed some encouragement," I quip and shut the door. Walking around to get in my seat, I can't help but anticipate the day I'd originally dreaded.

It takes little time to get to the yacht. Once the security team clears it, we board.

"This is insane," Henley murmurs. "It's bigger than I imagined. Ninety million dollars. That's a hell of a lot of money, Grayson. And this isn't even the only one. You have the fast boat we took out a few weeks ago, a sailboat, and this one."

I tilt my head. "How do you know how much I paid? Ah, wait, never mind. Thiago informed us you were snooping in our accounts." I snicker at the look on her face. "It's fine. I don't care. Most of my precious boats were bought with the money I made from NFTs. I consider it... play money, I guess. Why? Does it bother you?"

To my astonishment, she has to think about it. "Yes. No. I guess not. I mean, I wouldn't want you telling me what to do with my money, so why should I care what you do with yours?"

I grunt. "Would you like a tour of my gorgeous girl, or do you want to relax while we wait for Claire?"

She swivels her head around to look at the deck we're standing on. "Tour, definitely. What did you name this one?"

I hand her a bottle of water. "It's called Redemption." Ignoring the look on her face, I keep going. "This 278-foot yacht has four decks. The entry deck on the bottom is where we house the toys and the dinghy." I let her look around, then motion to the stairs. My phone pings, and I pull it out to see a text from Claire confirming a time for the meeting.

Her shorts flutter in the breeze, and I get a long look at her beautiful legs. I sigh. "When you get to the top of these stairs, swivel and keep going. We'll start at the top and work our way down."

She continues up to the top deck, but she doesn't wait for me. Her feet are already carrying her to the edge to look out, then down. "Wow, we're so high." She rests her arms on the railing. "It's an incredible view. It's going to be spectacular at night with the Miami lights and buildings surrounding us." Her hand waves toward the buildings nearby.

"It's amazing," I confide. "Okay. This deck is mainly a lounge, although we do have a small fridge up here. It's all about the view on this deck. We're meeting Claire on the entertainment deck, but I'll show you the main deck first. It's two levels down."

When we get to the lower deck, I explain this level is reserved for close friends and family. "There's a pool, jacuzzi, loungers, a small kitchen, dining table, and a living area with a huge TV for watching games."

Her eyes practically bug out when she sees the glass swimming pool ensconced on the deck. "If there was an apocalypse, you could live here quite easily."

I laugh. "Ok, Claire should be arriving in a few minutes. We'll go up one deck to the entertainment area."

She nods and heads up. When she gets there, she steps onto the deck and twirls around in a circle. "The view is still good from this level."

"This is the main bar and entertainment area. We host most of our parties on this level. There's a large living room with doors that open completely to the outside. The main area is clear for mingling or dancing, and the back area is set up as a dining area," I explain, showing her the various sections.

"When you say we, do you mean you and your beauties?" she asks breathlessly.

"We have in the past, but no, I was referring more to Thiago, Mateo, and myself. Marcos, too," I admit freely. Glancing at my watch, I realize we have about ten minutes before Claire gets here.

I pull her into my arms and twirl around the deck. "If I'm lucky, this is where you and I will have our first dance." Humming along with the song in my head, I spin, leading her in a wide circle. Her lithe body fits mine perfectly, and I bend my head toward her. "Pretty good, don't you think?"

"Mmm," she replies, a tiny line appearing on her forehead.

I tense.

"Mateo's pretty smooth on his feet, too," she teases. "But honestly, I bet Thiago's the best dancer in the family. Maybe I'll dance with all three of you and compare."

"What on earth makes you think Thiago would be a good dancer?"

"The man is light on his feet and moves incredibly fast," she whispers conspiratorially.

My lips twitch, but I can't hold the laughter in. "You'd win that bet. He loves dancing, and he's incredibly good at it, but don't you dare tell him I told you. It must be his Brazilian heritage." I give a mock sigh.

"There you are," Claire exclaims from the rear deck. "I must have gone to the wrong level. Handsome as usual. How are you doing?" The sound of heels striking the deck tells me she's almost to us.

Henley gives a wry smile and steps out of my arms.

Claire immediately steps into them and kisses me on both cheeks. "Hello, Grayson." She spins around and thrusts a hand toward Henley. "Hello, I'm Claire Delgado."

"Henley Night. Nice to meet you."

Claire briefly slips her hand into Henley's then turns to me. "Tell me you're not serious about having a party here in less than a week. I mean, seriously, Grayson. What's the rush?" She wraps an arm around me and pouts. "Are you trying to give me a heart attack?"

"We may have an occasion to celebrate soon, but it's top secret. We won't know the exact date until two days prior to the party. I assume we can get everything but the food on board." I pause when I see Claire start to panic. "Don't worry. It's casual." I tell her my idea about bringing food from different restaurants on board, and she blanches.

"It's a Miami theme," Henley interjects. "Miami has fabulous restaurants with food from everywhere. It's perfect."

Claire runs her hand down my arm. "Let's go sit down some-where, with a drink, and iron out the details. You know I'll drop everything for you. We can figure out what to do together."

I motion to the lounge behind me. "Why don't you ladies take a seat, and I'll bring you something to drink. What would you like?"

"White wine," Claire calls out. She saunters into the lounge and starts laying items on the coffee table in front of the couch.

Henley shakes her head and holds up her water. "I'm good." Her phone pings, and she laughs. Turning it around, she shows me an image of Mateo's lips. The phone pings again. She shakes her head.

"What?" I ask, grabbing a water for myself and wine for Claire.

"Nothing," she replies with a blush, making me wonder what he said. She strolls into the lounge, typing furiously, and sits on a chair by the sofa.

"Here you go," I tell Claire, handing her the wine. I look down at the coffee table and see swatches, paper, and inspiration boards. "What's this?"

"Invitations, decoration, linens, and all the things that go with planning a party," Claire says, exasperated.

"Make everything white. Clean, crisp. Hand delivered personal invitations only for three hundred people. Champagne to celebrate. Local food. Done," I state firmly, flashing my most charming smile to get Claire on board.

Claire lays a hand on my thigh. "There's no way I can get every-thing ready and loaded onto this gorgeous yacht in two days. It's impossible. Give me at least two weeks."

I lay my hand on hers. "You have two days, and I'm prepared to pay incentives to get it done. You're the best, aren't you?" I raise her hand and squeeze, then lay it on her own leg.

She giggles. "Ohh, Prince Charming, you know I'm putty in your hands and can't resist your flirty ways." Her finger taps the wineglass in her hand. "I may have to call in a lot of favors to pull this off, but you're worth it. Who are we inviting to this impromptu secret party?" Claire asks, a slight strain in her voice.

"Henley, who should we invite to this party?" I ask, drawing her into the conversation.

She looks up from her phone in surprise, then holds up a finger. "I have a list. Marcos and I came up with one when we were finishing the project. Let me dig it up."

Claire looks surprised. "This is a work function? Why didn't you say so? I thought Miami's elite were attending."

"Oh, they'll be here, too. After all, we're celebrating a win for SEI," I assure her, knowing the power we wield.

"Sent to your email. If you'll excuse me, I'm going to call Peyton," Henley drawls, flashing a smile toward Claire and me.

Stunned, I watch her walk off, phone to her ear, with an expression of relief on her face.

CHAPTER 21

HENLEY

W hen I walk away, Claire scoots closer to Grayson, and I can't help but shudder. She was driving me crazy with her high-pitched voice and giggling. I'm just happy I don't have to deal with her.

Peyton answers the phone, but instead of his usual joie de vivre, his voice has a sharp edge to it, "Henley, you beautiful girl. Where have you been?"

"Sorry, sorry. I know I promised to call, but I had a bit of an accident, and I was in the hospital for about a week. I've been recuperating until today. Forgive me?" I cringe at the word accident, but he doesn't need to know we have lunatic enemies kidnapping and targeting us.

"Are you doing better? Do you need me to bring you some food or anything?" he replies, his voice filled with contrition.

"Ahh, thank you, that's incredibly sweet of you to offer! But I've got plenty of everything," I assure him.

"Well, now I feel bad for calling you all those terrible names," he jokes, in a half serious tone. "My only excuse is I'm used to people blowing me off, and I assumed the worst. I'll forgive you if you forgive me."

"Done. How has everything been since the ball? Did you get any new clients?"

"I picked up several regular clients, but without any splashy events lately, it's been tough to get new ones. I'm thankful I get to spend part of my time doing what I love," he says cheerfully.

"I may be able to provide the splashy event, but I also need some of your practical expertise and styling help," I inform him.

"I'm in," he returns quickly.

"You don't even know what it is yet," I retort.

"Who cares? The last time you called me, I got to attend Miami's ball of the year. So, even if it's a boring charity event, I'll do it," he says dramatically. "It's not, though, is it? A boring event? I mean, I'll still do it, but I'm not sparing my best outfits on it."

"How about a party on Grayson's yacht? Is that exciting enough?"

"I knew you wouldn't let me down," he crows excitedly. "Formal?"

"Semi-formal, I think," I reply. "The affair will be casual, but it's a launch party on a huge freaking yacht. I'm guessing Miami's idea of informal doesn't quite match mine. It's kind of short notice, though. I need it by end of week. I have clothes in my closet, but if you have something, I know it will be beautiful."

"Why is everything always so last minute with you?" he exclaims. "Just kidding. It's fine. I have more dresses than clients right now."

"Bring whatever you think would look good on me. I trust your judgement," I tell him. "Also, bring some swim trunks and we'll hit the beach afterward. I'm dying to know what happened with that good-looking man you met at the ball." We finalize the timing and I hang up.

Grayson and Claire are ending their meeting, so I take the time to use the restroom. When I come out, I'm startled to find a female bodyguard in the hallway. I smile at her and slip past.

Unfortunately, Claire is still here, clinging to Grayson, but he's slowly moving her toward the stairs. Another hug and a few more kisses, her fingers wiggle a goodbye in my direction, and she leaves.

I walk over to stand by his side. "Did you get everything worked out for the party?"

"I should punish you for leaving me with her," he grumbles. "She's the best at what she does, or I'd have thrown her off the top level."

I giggle and lay a hand on his chest. "Oh Grayson, only for you, darling. For anyone else, it would be simply impossible."

His eyes narrow, and he sweeps me into his arms.

I laugh.

Striding across the deck, he comes to a halt in front of a wooden door. Opening it, he steps in, carrying me with him.

"Are we in an elevator? This is over the top. Can you put me down?" I plead.

He releases my legs and eases me down until my entire length is pressed against his. For a few seconds, he holds me to him, dark blue eyes staring into mine. Finally, he lets my feet touch the ground.

The doors open into a long, carpeted hallway. "This level is where all the sleeping quarters are located. We have seven guest bedrooms with ensuites and additional rooms for the staff. Plus, the galley is on this level." He grabs my hand and pulls me along.

"Seven bedrooms?!" I state with a laugh, then give him a side glance. "What are we doing down here?"

"I want to show you my favorite place on the ship," he explains, tapping on the double doors in front of him.

He swings them open and gestures for me to enter. It's his bedroom. My eyes widen. This one room is bigger than my old loft. There's not much in here beside the bed and a bookcase, but it screams luxury. From the lush fabrics on the bed and windows to the plush carpet under my feet. Even the air smells expensive with its subtle undertone of the cologne Grayson wears.

Walking further into the room, I see the large bookcase is filled with unique knickknacks and art. A black sculpture catches my eye and I wander over to look at it.

"I got that in Greece. Isn't she gorgeous?" he drawls with excitement. "There's a school where they teach restoration and sculpting. One of their incredibly talented students created it. It's one of my top five favorite pieces."

I run a hand over the smooth ebony surface of the female bust. "It's gorgeous." Another piece catches my eye. It's a rough-looking wooden fish. I point to it.

"I picked that up in Portugal. A little girl was selling them on the street, and I couldn't resist."

My eyes drift from piece to piece. "This is amazing. I never really thought about traveling but seeing all your treasures makes me want to explore."

He points out several more items and explains their origin. His enthusiasm is contagious.

"I thought it was all about the prestige of the yacht, but it's more than that, isn't it?" I stare at him, waiting for an answer.

He smiles ruefully. "My parents died in an apartment fire when I was a baby, and for almost nine years, I was in the foster system. Every year, I'd dream of running away to somewhere exciting. I'd look up places, and if they looked interesting, I wrote them on my list." He points to a list framed on the wall. There must be over fifty places listed on the ruled paper. Every one of them written in a child's hand and in pencil. They're all crossed out.

"I think I've only been on two vacations my entire life," I say, marveling at the list of places he's visited. "Once to the beach when I was a kid. I think it was in North Carolina." I shrug, not remembering much beyond the waves and sand. "Then, when I was thirteen, my mom and I took a road trip to visit all the schools I was considering for college. That's when I fell in love with MIT." The trip was fun, but I never forgot the reason we were doing it.

Shaking off the melancholy, I slip over to the bathroom to take a peek. "Seriously? The shower is gigantic. You could hold a party in there." I dart a look at Grayson. "Maybe you have."

He rolls his eyes but doesn't confirm or deny it. "That's not even the best part," he says with a tantalizing smirk. He gets on the bed and props himself up against the headboard. He winks and pats the space beside him.

My heart beats faster, wondering what he's up to. The last time we were in bed together, I held him in my hand. My hand flexes with the thought. I cautiously stroll over and get on the bed next to him.

He looks at me and grins. Pushing a button on the small remote in his hand, the curtains around the room slide open, revealing floor to ceiling windows until water is the only thing I see.

"When I'm out in the ocean, I fall asleep with the waves slapping against the hull and a water view that goes on forever. It's amazing," he murmurs in my ear.

I shiver when his breath caresses my ear. "This might make the yacht worth ninety million," I concede to him. My eyes are glued to the water. It's almost hypnotizing.

When he's quiet for too long, I turn my head and see his eyes close for a brief second, then open again. "Grayson, you're falling asleep. Why don't you lie down and take a nap?"

He slides an arm around me and pulls me down with him. "Only if you'll stay with me."

My eyes trail over the dark circles under his eyes, and I can't help but agree. "I'll stay with you." Feeling a little chilly, I pull the blanket up around us, then snuggle down into his arms. It feels decadent to take a nap in the middle of the day, but the early mornings have been tough. My eyelids close.

———

A FINGER RUNS down the side of my cheek and I smile. But it's not Mateo's face I see when I open my eyes. Instead, Grayson's blue eyes and chiseled features greet me. Although his eyes are fixed on me, his mind seems a million miles away.

The sun is still shining through the windows, but with a little less intensity than when we went to sleep.

"How long did we sleep?" My hand sweeps the bed for my phone, but I can't find it.

"Three hours," he replies huskily. "The best sleep I've had in weeks. Thank you for staying with me." His finger swipes lightly over my cheekbones. "The bruises are almost gone, although the memory of what you looked like when we found you that day pisses me off whenever I think about it." He places feather light kisses on each cheekbone.

Somewhere along the way, we took a step closer today, but what does it mean? Is he aware of the shift?

"Grayson, what are you doing?" I ask quietly. "Every time I think I've figured you out, you throw me a curve ball. Like today. I expected the extravagant yacht, but then you bring me in here and it's almost like a secret glimpse into your soul."

I cup his jaw. "But if you run true to form, you'll revert to the distant, polite roommate when we get home. You only have two temps—blazing hot and ice cold. What do you want from me?"

His breath rushes out. "A kiss," he rasps. "With no anger, no regrets. A kiss you would only share with me, no other. That's what I want." His eyes are almost navy with desire while he waits for my answer, but it's the look of contemplation that entices me.

The heat and passion of our first kiss flickers in my mind. Without the anger and adrenaline, would it be the same? Maybe it's time we found out. I lift my chin toward him. "Yes."

His arms pull me in tighter, until I'm almost underneath him, and his warm body settles firmly into mine like he's intent on staying a while. His lips descend, lightly tasting and sucking my bottom lip, before delving a little bit deeper into the kiss. Tongues slip and stroke languidly, almost lazy in their approach. The kind of kiss that could last all day.

Reaching up to cup his neck, I turn my head and pull him deeper into the kiss, replacing the languidness with heat. Thoughts vanish, the world follows, until it's him and me and this moment. The passion building rapidly between us.

He groans and settles his hips fully against me. Rock hard, he deliberately pushes against my body, making me feel every inch.

Gasping, I turn my head for air, but his lips chase mine, capturing and holding them hostage. This time, the heat changes to an inferno, driven by the need passing back and forth between us in equal measure. Now I'm burning from the inside out, and I can only quench my thirst with his lips.

Suddenly, we're at the peak and teetering on the edge. We force our lips apart and stare at each other. Breathing heavily, the aftermath of this intense kiss thrums in our veins calling to us like a siren to finish what we've started, but unlike the desire-filled moment at the ball, this is more than a turning point. Its repercussions are deep and full of the unknown.

At almost the exact same time, we step back from the precipice yawning before us. I stroke my fingers down his jaw, then let gravity take it down to my side. He slides off me and rolls over to his back, neither of us ready to leap.

CHAPTER 22

Thiago's thick arm wraps around my body in a move he calls a rear choke hold. Whatever it is, I can't get out of it, and I've been trying for a half hour. He patiently waits while I move through the motions he's taught me, but nothing happens. I must be missing something.

His gruff voice is low in my ear, causing shivers to run down my spine. "Walk through the steps, okay?"

I blow my hair out of my eyes and shake my head. "Grab onto the attacker's arm to create some space between his arm and my neck and put my chin down to prevent him from moving it closer." My movements follow the words closely.

"Good. Next."

"Take a step forward with the foot on the opposite side of his elbow. Bring my other foot into his body, bend down, swing around, and push off his chest to flee." I stop talking and follow through with my body. But it doesn't matter what I do, I can't manage the turn and bend part of it. I blow my hair out of my eyes.

"We'll keep working on it. Make sure to keep your chin tucked,

STELLA BRIE

with a tight neck. Protecting your neck is your first priority," he instructs me. "You can't get away if you're unconscious." His body moves in behind me.

We practice for another twenty minutes, but I'm not getting it. Frustration beats at me.

Hard fingers gently grip my chin and pull my head up to meet his eyes. "You're doing great. Even when you think you're failing, you're not. Your body will remember more than you think it does. Just keep putting in the practice."

I bite the inside of my cheek for a second, hesitating to tell him my worst fear. "Don't give up on me, okay? If I can't get this one, can we work on another move and come back to it later?"

He blinks and his face fills with fury. "Why the hell do you think I'd give up on you?"

I shrug and try to look away from his furious stare, but he refuses to let go of my chin, so I blurt it all out. "When I first got here, I felt like I was getting to know you. The person you are here, not Thiago Santos, CEO of SEI. But when you withdrew, I thought maybe I was becoming a nuisance or a burden or something. And it's okay. Seriously. I understand you're busy, and waking up every night to deal with my nightmares is exhausting."

He blows out a breath and throws up his hands.

I grip my shirt. "I'll practice until I can get it right. I'm sure Mateo can help me figure out where I'm getting hung up. Just don't give up. This is too important."

He lets go of my chin and turns his back to me.

My heart sinks. Maybe I can ask one of the others. Or even Zane.

"The reason I stopped coming to your room is because I was becoming too attached to our late-night movie sessions. To holding you while you slept. It's not because you were a nuisance," he says gruffly. "Mateo thought I was confusing you, and you were becoming attracted to me."

Shock, embarrassment, and anger collide with each other. "He assured me it was okay to be attracted to you—that it wasn't

148

wrong. I don't understand." I shake my head back and forth to clear the fog. Only one thing is important right now. "You don't have to worry. I know you're not attracted to me. The lack of response to the kiss I gave you put that to rest."

I contemplate the man in front of me, then step around to see his face. Maybe logic will put us back on track. "We've been working out for days now, and neither of us has become over-whelmed with lust." There have been a few close calls, but he doesn't need to know about them. "So, if you're good to continue teaching me self-defense, I promise to keep giving it my all. Okay?"

He sighs heavily. "I'm angry because you think I'd give up on you. This is important to me. You're important to... us."

"Grayson told me you three learned martial arts together," I murmur.

He lifts a shoulder. "Everyone needs to know how to defend themselves. Life can be damn ugly. You know this better than most. I made sure they would always have a fighting chance, and I'll make sure you have one, too. I promise. I won't give up on you, Henley. Ever."

"I wish I'd had a big brother like you growing up," I say wistfully. "Or I guess you're Mateo's cousin, even though you three act like brothers. Do you consider each other brothers?"

He looks pained. "I can't be your big brother, Henley," he croaks. "I... it's just that I... never mind. I'm going to be late for work. Tomorrow, we'll walk through this maneuver again, and if we need to, we'll move on to a different hold. Have a good day with Peyton. I'll see you tonight."

———

MATEO, Peyton, and I collapse on the floor of my bedroom. The once tidy interior is overflowing with fabric, shoes, dresses, and accessories galore. Something pokes me in the back, and I arch up to pull it out from under me. A strappy black heel with rhinestones winks back at me.

Scooting backward until I'm halfway propped up by the bedframe, I fold my arms and raise an eyebrow at Peyton. "This is a lot more than a few dresses, Peyton. Did you bring all your creations?"

He eyes me between the feathers of the boa wrapped around his neck. "I might have gone a little overboard. You did say you needed outfits. Plural. And if you're going to represent my brand, every aspect of your wardrobe must be perfect."

Mateo chuckles. He rolls to his feet, then holds out a hand to help Peyton and me up.

I glare at his hand, still mad at him for the whole Thiago thing this morning. Ignoring his offer, I push myself to my feet.

He sighs and leans over to give me a hard kiss on the lips. "I'll see you later." His hand shoves his hair back. "Nice seeing you again, Peyton. We'll catch up later." He strolls out.

Peyton flashes a look that promises pain if I don't spill the dirt.

"Yes, we're dating, and it's serious, but like all things, it's complicated. We've got a lot going on right now, and we're figuring it out day by day," I end my announcement and point to the closet. "Why don't you look in the closet? We can add any clothes you feel are necessary."

His eyes widen. "Anything? Nobody ever gives me carte blanche. Maybe you're crazier than I thought." He laughs but heads straight to the closet before I change my mind.

I lean against the doorway and watch him sort through the beautiful clothes. He separates most of the clothes into four separate areas of the closet and organizes them within their sections. A small pile of clothes lies at his feet. Once the last item is placed, he turns to me and explains what he's done.

"I've separated your closet into four sections. Casual, business, informal, and formal." He points to each section as he lists them out. "Your gorgeous peacock dress is formal, but you can't wear it again. It's too remarkable. We'll keep it there for now, but it should be cleaned and stored in a bag." He waits while I pull out my phone

150

and take notes. "You need several formal gowns of varying lengths. I have three or four with me, but we can work on getting you more."

"What if I donated the peacock dress to a charity for prom?"

His eyes light up at the thought of the dress being worn again. "If you do, I want to participate. Not only would it be good for my brand, but it will be fun. Plus, I'd love to help them style their look."

"Deal," I reply. "Once this launch business is done, I'll work on contacting an organization. I should be able to reach out in a couple of weeks; plenty of time for prom."

He nods his head absently. "You only have one informal event outfit," he tells me, pointing to the silky black jumpsuit in the corner. "Don't worry, I have a lot of those with me. Most should fit you, but I can take measurements and finish them up while you're on your trip."

I'd told him I was leaving on a business trip for a couple of days. "Fantastic. The only event I know of right now is the yacht party. If you have something that works, we should focus on finding an outfit for it first."

He pulls three or four outfits from the rack in the middle of my bedroom. "I think one of these will work, but we'll try them on and see."

Going back into the closet, he points to the business and casual sections. "Most of these can be mixed and matched. For example, this black blazer could easily pair with a pair of jeans for a casual look, with a dress or pants for dinner, or with a button-up for a business meeting. It's an extremely versatile piece, and I'm impressed with the quality. Did you buy these clothes?"

I make a note in my phone about the items I can wear with the black blazer, and he raises an eyebrow in disbelief.

Pink rises on my face. "Hey, this is not my area of expertise. I need notes and pictures. And Grayson purchased the clothes."

His mouth quirks. "I knew it. He's got truly incredible taste and knows how to dress a woman's body."

My mouth turns down at the thought of how many clothes he's

probably bought for women over the years. "The man definitely has great taste."

He quickly helps me pull together a few business outfits for the trip. "What about dinner? Don't most of those things include dinner at a swanky restaurant?"

I lift my shoulders. "This is my first business trip. Pack it if you think I'll need it."

"Nope, you're going to pay attention and learn how to do this yourself," he says sternly. "First outfit—business. This cream blazer, matching blouse, and these navy pants. This works for a business dinner, too. Or you can pair it with jeans for a more casual look. We'll do shoes in a minute. Take a picture." He continues to pair options and hold them up for me to snap a picture of each one.

"I think that's enough. I'm only going for a couple of days, but I love this approach. I can scan through the pictures and pick. It's a great way to help me find outfits quickly," I enthuse. Smart man. "Okay, what about shoes for the trip?"

He pulls a pair of navy wedges from the pile on the floor. "Try these on." When he sees them on my feet, he gives a satisfied smile. "Those shoes will work with any outfit. Always take a pair of flip flops." He hands me a plain black pair. "Those are from the store. Tag is on them."

I peel off the tag and lay it on the bed.

He hands me a pair of white chunky-looking tennis shoes. "These are street tennis shoes, and they're perfect with anything casual, even a dress. I'm not sure if you're going to do a lot of walking, but it's good to have a pair with you, just in case."

"Anything else?"

He picks out a few accessories and adds them to the pile. "You can mix and match the jewelry. This camel-colored belt goes with all the outfits. Done."

"Wow, we're done already?" I exclaim.

He laughs. "We're done with packing for your trip and organizing your closet. Now, we're getting to the good part—dress up!" He shoves the dresses he picked out for the yacht party in my hand

and gestures to the closet. "Go, change, and parade them for me to see."

For the next three hours, all I do is try on clothes. Mr. Perfectionist looks at every single line, hem, strap, and whatever else is on the item of clothing to make sure it's up to his very, very high standards.

"Okay, I'll alter these and get them back to you. Don't worry, I'll tag them with the correct area of your closet," he assures me. "The rest of the rack won't work for your coloring or body type. You might want to return or donate the additional pile in the closet. And now, we're done."

I walk into the closet and look at all the clothes hanging from the rack and the shoes lining the shelves. "I don't think I've ever owned this many clothes in my life." Our house was simple and cozy. We didn't have a lot, but I never lacked for anything. Clothes were never a priority for me. Studying was always first.

Peyton comes to stand beside me. "It's an excellent start. You need a few more dresses for events, but we can add those later."

I wrap an arm around his waist. "It's fabulous. You're fabulous. Thank you. Now, how much do I owe you? Am I going to have to hock my car?"

He's silent for a moment. "I'll send you a bill." He laughs. "The business has been a side dream of mine for a while, but I didn't take it seriously enough. Things changed when you forced me to attend that ball. For the first time, I could see what it would mean to be a full-time designer. Now, my brain is on fire with all the creative ideas that are popping into my head night and day."

He bends my head down to look at my roots. "Speaking of... I brought the hair supplies, too. They're in the bathroom. Why don't you color your hair, and I'll get the rest of this cleaned up and back to my car. Then we can go to the beach and relax."

My mouth quirks. "Oh, thank goodness. My roots have been showing pretty badly."

"You know, I'd have guessed your hair would be light brown, not blonde," he replies with a curious look on his face.

"I've always liked playing with color. Why be blonde when you have a whole rainbow at your disposal? Pink's my current favorite." I shrug, telling him the truth. "Although my absolute favorite was a pretty lilac color, it was too hard to maintain." I head into the bathroom, letting him clean up the disaster in my room.

———

"OKAY, spill. What happened with that gorgeous man you met at the ball?" I take a sip of the frosé he brought while I wait for him to answer my question.

He gives a dreamy sigh. "We're dating. It's serious, not complicated, and hot, so very, very hot." His hand waves back and forth. "His name is Cole. He's a lawyer, but I try not to hold that against him. Some baggage, but nothing I can't handle. Confident. Knows what he wants. I kind of keep expecting the other shoe to drop. It's that good."

"That's wonderful! I'm so happy for you. If you two get married, I'd better be invited to the wedding," I warn him with a smile.

He shudders. "Marriage is too conventional for my tastes. A piece of paper isn't really what I'm looking for. I want an interesting and confident man, who supports my dreams as well as his own. Someone who isn't afraid of life and all its messiness. And above all, a man who doesn't cheat on me. It doesn't sound like a lot, but do you know how hard it's been to find a man like that in Miami? Who wasn't already taken? Impossible, damn near impossible."

Maybe unconventional is better. "True. Too many people get hung up on the established criteria for a proper, successful life and forget to live." I shake my head in approval. "I'm glad I had a small part in helping you find happiness. What kind of law does he practice?"

"Corporate law. His eyes light up when he sees a thick, complicated contract," He replies with a roll of his eyes. "Outside of work, he's full of surprises, and we love to go dancing. You should come with us sometime. It's a blast!"

I sip the drink and relax on the chair. "It sounds like fun. I'll do that next time. I swear, I could live out here on the beach. It's so peaceful."

"If I'm honest, I prefer to splurge for a pool pass at one of the luxury hotels. They set everything up and bring you food and pretty little drinks the whole day. Next time, we'll meet up at one and you can compare the two," he says magnanimously.

I frown and point to my drink. "Someone did bring me drinks."

He narrows his eyes at my subtle cheekiness. "Just remember that for next time. It will be your turn to get us drinks." He gets up and stretches. "I've got to go. Someone created a lot of work for me." His eyes dart to me. "Thank you, Henley. I'll send the bill via email. Also, I'll let you know which dress to wear for the yacht party. They all look good, but none are really hitting the right note for me right now."

My mouth quirks at his perfectionist tendencies. "You know you're invited to the yacht party. Be sure to bring your boyfriend. An invitation will be hand delivered." I wave him off and relax. It's only four o'clock.

CHAPTER 23

HENLEY

Mateo is waiting for me when I get out of the shower. It's obvious by the look on his face he wants to talk about the Thiago situation. I sigh and get dressed. He groans softly behind me, and I barely suppress the evil smile rising to the surface. He deserves to suffer a little.

When I turn around, he moves closer. "I'm sorry the discussion with Thiago was awkward this morning. Was I wrong when I told him you were attracted to him?"

"First of all, a woman would have to be dead not to be attracted to Thiago. I'm not that much of a unicorn. But I didn't think you would discuss me and the way I felt. It blindsided me, and it was embarrassing," I admit to him. "And honestly, I'm kind of confused. I thought it was fine for me to be attracted to all three of you?"

Mateo runs a hand through his hair. "It is, but there is more to this when it comes to Thiago. He might not be aware he's flirting or how it might impact you. And he needed to know you were attracted to Grayson and me. I told him if he wasn't interested in you, he needed to be honest. He decided to back off."

"I don't even know what to say. He wasn't interested which is fine. I think knowing he knew is what kills me. It's one thing to get rebuffed in the dark after a kiss, but it's an entirely different thing to have your feelings discussed behind your back," I tell him.

"I get it, but Grayson, Thiago, and I always make it a point to give it to each other straight." A long, heavy sigh fills the air. "Too many people get hung up on what's right or wrong in this world. Why is it wrong to want to be with more than one person? Because current society dictates it? If the world's population was decimated tomorrow, would it suddenly be okay or even expected to build the population up? Feel what you want, Henley. If we're all honest with each other, things will work out," he states firmly.

Inching closer, he pulls me into his arms. "I'm sorry you were embarrassed. It wasn't my intent. Forgive me?"

My arms wrap around him. "Yes, I forgive you. I'm sorry, too. I know you're looking out for me, but I've been on my own for a long time and can take care of things myself."

His lips slide down my neck. "Is the argument done? Want to make up?"

Instead of replying, I capture his lips with mine while my fingers work on the buttons of his shirt.

He backs up and turns, pushing me onto the bed.

While he strips off his shirt, I sit up, unfasten his jeans, and pull out his cock. I stroke him from bottom to top a few times, but he looks so good, I can't help leaning forward and circling the head with my tongue. He tastes and smells so good, like soap and man. So sexy.

He moans.

The sound arrows through me, turning on all the delicious parts of me. Fascinated, I close my mouth over him, and flick the under- side of his head a few times, making his hips buck a little. With a moan, I circle the tip again, then draw him deeper inside my mouth. At about a third way down, I suck lightly while my hand rolls him from root to lips.

Pulling him out, I breathe on the tip and look up at him.

"Minha linda, I'm getting so turned on watching your beautiful mouth enjoy my cock," he rasps. His hand cups the back of my head, fingers spearing through the wet strands. "Do it again, please."

With a wicked smile, I concentrate on tasting and sucking on him in several spots. One hand strokes his cock, but I use the other to explore his body and find what turns him on most. My finger grazes the small smooth spot under his balls, and his cock leaks cum. Licking it up, I take him farther into my mouth and suck while I play with the sensitive spot.

He moans loudly.

The need to see him lose control is riding me hard. My mouth and hands work harder and faster. His cock swells.

"I'm going to come. If you don't want it in your mouth, tell me now," he groans, barely able to get the words out.

There's no way I'm giving this up now. I shake my head and keep up the pace. His hand tightens on my head, and a few minutes later, his release hits him and he jerks a few times in my hand and mouth, coming hard.

Swallowing a few times, I ease him out of my mouth.

"You're incredible," he murmurs. "Thank you."

Phew. I'd only done that a couple of times, and I wasn't sure how it was going to turn out. I guess enjoying yourself is the key. I stand and kiss him on the lips.

"Thank you. Why don't you give me a moment and I'll meet you at dinner?"

He drags me into his arms and gives me a tight hug. "See you in a moment."

When he's gone, I hurry over and pull out another pair of under-wear. Peeling off the soaked ones, I toss them into the laundry. I grin. I didn't realize how turned I'd get.

I take a moment to get everything packed like I'd intended to do after my shower. It would have taken me forever to pick outfits if Peyton hadn't helped me. I pull them from the closet and fold each item carefully, then pack them into the suitcase. Done. I'll add toiletries in the morning.

The dining room table is surprisingly empty. I head toward the kitchen, where I find Mateo and Grayson drinking a beer at the island. "Are we having dinner together, or should I grab a sandwich or something?"

Grayson throws a dirty glare my way. "We're having dinner together, but it's just the three of us. Thiago's getting a shower and packing. We're going to eat here at the island. Have a seat. Stir-fry will be ready in a few minutes." His eyes linger on my lips for a second.

I bring my hand up and subtly wipe across my mouth. Nothing. Surely Mateo didn't tell him. I whisper the question in his ear.

He chokes on his beer. "Absolutely not," he croaks when he stops coughing. "I would never discuss those details."

Relieved, I blow out the breath I'd been holding. When I look up, Grayson's eyes are darting from me to Mateo. I immediately look at my phone.

Dinner is quiet. I'm too nervous to say anything, and Grayson seems lost in his own thoughts. Mateo's typing a to do list.

After eating, Mateo heads to the living room and I help Grayson clean up. "Thank you for dinner. It was delicious, as always."

He catches me by my elbow and swings me around. "Is every-thing okay between us? After the other day?"

Mateo's voice rings in my ear. *Be honest.* "You mean after the incredible kiss we shared?" Somebody's got to bring it up.

He backs me into the counter and cages me in his arms. "Yes." His voice is ragged. "All I want is to kiss you again, but I know I won't be able to stop a second time. I know this is confusing for you. Hell, I'm confused. But I promise, I'm trying to work through things."

"Tell me the kiss meant something to you," I urge, needing reas-surance I'm more than a passing flirtation.

"I care about you. More than I thought," he admits grudgingly.

"But you're different, Henley. You pull at something I'd turned against a long time ago."

"What scares you so much about me?" I ask, concerned about the darkness I see in his eyes.

A pained expression crosses his face. "I'm not sure I can be serious with one person again. It almost destroyed me last time."

My eyebrows flick up. At least there's a reason behind his need for an entourage. And if there is anyone who understands, it's me. Change is hard. Letting go of fear is even harder, but at some point, he'll have to decide.

"I understand, and I don't want to rush you, but I can't be one of your 'beauties' and share you. I know it's incredibly unfair, given my relationship with Mateo, but it isn't what I want for my future. If you need those women in your life, and they make you happy, then be honest and tell me. I'm not going to be angry or throw a fit or anything. We all make our own decisions."

His forehead leans against mine. "I promise I don't need them to make me happy. The only thing they've ever been is a distraction. That's it. I'm… it's me. I don't know if I can give you what you need to be happy, and I know it sounds like it's an excuse, but the last thing I want to do is hurt you. I just need time."

"We all do," I murmur, feeling the minutes rushing by at warp speed again. My hand slips between us to lightly rub his lips. "I'll be back in a few days. Maybe the space will help."

———

IT'S dark when I meet Thiago in the basement for our lessons. Yesterday, I thought I'd be too embarrassed to see him again, but I'm too tired for it to be an issue. With everything on my mind last night, I couldn't sleep and decided to get some work done. Based on what I found, it's a good thing I did.

Thiago's standing in the arena, his big, muscular body dressed all in black, exuding a menacing air. Something or someone has royally pissed him off.

"You look exhausted," he barks at me. "Did you get any sleep last night?"

Not in the mood to explain myself to another Santos man, especially one who seems more than a tad grumpy this morning, I raise an eyebrow. "Are we working on the rear choke hold this morning or something else?"

Please, please, say something else, I plead silently.

He motions me over to stand in front of him. "Face me. I'm going to reach out and grab your wrist, and I want you to try to get away." His fingers lock around my wrist.

I pull and twist, but they only tighten. "I can't."

He places my hand on his wrist. "Grab my wrist. I'm going to walk through the move slowly, okay?" He swings around a hundred and eighty-degrees to grab my wrist from the top, thrusts forward, and I suddenly find myself on the ground.

I press my lips together. He grabs my wrist, and I swing around, grab his, and push. The next thing I know, he's on the ground with his arm at an awkward angle above him. I blink. I did it.

"You have all the control in this move for a few seconds. Push your attacker's arm hard, then run away," he tells me. "Again."

Every time we practice the front hold, I get it right. Then he slips in a rear choke hold, and I can't do it.

"Is there another way to break the rear choke hold?"

He thinks about it for a second. "There is. I threw them out because this is more effective, but if you can't do it, it's a moot point. Let me think about it on the plane. I'll find something for us to work on at the hotel. Grab some breakfast. We leave in an hour."

CHAPTER 24

THIAGO

H enley's gripping the armrest next to me so tightly her knuckles are completely white. We haven't even taken off yet. Why didn't she tell me she was afraid of flying?

"Nervous flyer?" I comment casually.

The plane starts taxiing to the runway, and I hear her inhale sharply.

She lifts her shoulders. "Never flown before," she reveals, her voice cracking with nerves.

Shocked, I stare at her. Twenty-eight and she's never flown?

When she sees the expression on my face, she blushes. "We didn't vacation much when I was younger, and I couldn't exactly fly the last few years. Too many cameras at airports." She turns her face to the window.

Even before her stalker, her life was limited. No wonder she adapted to a life in hiding so easily. I pry her hand from the armrest and grip it with mine. "Squeeze as hard as you want. You won't hurt me."

She looks down at our joined hands. "Thank you, Thiago. That's really sweet of you."

My teeth grind together when I hear the word sweet. First the big brother comment, now this. It makes me want to show her I'm far from either. The tight grip of her fingers gives me some satisfaction, at least.

The plane revs and takes off down the runway. In seconds, we're in the air and turning in the direction of our destination.

She's looking out the window, and when we bank, she squeaks at the sight of the ground.

I chuckle. "We'll level off in a minute, and the flight should be smooth from here on out." My thumb skims lightly back and forth across the top of her hand to help ease her anxiety.

Opening my laptop with my other hand, I skim through the information accounting sent over. It's a copy of VRDeck's last four quarterly reports. Her hand flexes in mine, and I lose my train of thought.

"Coffee?" the attendant asks. I nod, then turn to Henley to see if she wants anything, but she's fast asleep. Her head is tilted to the side at an awkward angle. Motioning to the flight attendant to get me a pillow, I lean over and push the button to recline her seat, then place her head in a better position. A smile appears, but she doesn't wake.

When she came down for training this morning, the dark circles under her eyes told me she hadn't slept much. I didn't hear her call out with nightmares, but she might have slept in Mateo's room. The thought of something else keeping her awake makes me scowl.

When I'd come home yesterday, the moans coming from her room had made me hard as a rock until only a shower could help me find relief. Not willing to face her or Mateo across the dinner table, I'd thrown myself into SEI reports. It worked until I went to bed. Images of them together played repeatedly in my mind, and I'd tossed and turned for hours.

"We're thirty minutes out," the flight attendant murmurs beside me.

With a snap, I close my computer. Standing and stretching, I refresh myself and let the security team know we're landing soon.

She's still sleeping when I return. "Henley, querida, wake up," I murmur near her ear, not wanting to startle her. "We're landing soon."

"Hmm, you smell minty," she replies softly. Bright blue eyes open and stare sleepily into mine. "Hello."

My mouth curves. "Your first flight, and you slept the whole time," I remark, with a shake of my head "Did you get any sleep last night?"

"Too much on my mind," she reveals. "It's a good thing, too. The dark web is buzzing with rumors around VRDeck shelving their VR glasses to bring a new AR/VR product to the market."

I freeze while my mind races through the possibilities. "So, either they're a hundred percent on board with our potential partnership or our enemy has gotten to them first. I wonder which one it is?"

"We won't know until we meet with them," she returns with a shrug. Stretching out, she groans and rolls her neck. With a flick of a finger, she opens the seatbelt and stands.

I get up and she slides past, barely brushing her body against mine, but my mind reacts the way I've trained it—automatically reciting numbers from the last report I read. The morning sessions have been tough, especially the rear choke hold. Feeling her curves rub against me has driven me almost mad. The only way I've gotten through each session is by distracting my brain with numbers. Oh, and cold showers afterward.

She thinks the attraction is gone, but it's only gotten worse. Still, nothing's changed on my end. The thought of sharing... When I heard her with Mateo last night, I wanted to storm in and rip them apart.

Fifteen minutes later, she's back, but instead of leggings and a long t-shirt, she's wearing business attire. Her bright pink hair is pulled into a low bun behind her head, and she's wearing make-up.

She's transformed her usual natural bohemian look into something utterly sophisticated.

"Perfect," I state firmly when she slips by me and into her seat.

She snickers. "Of course, it's perfect. Peyton picked it out."

————

THE IRRITATINGLY SMUG kid in front of me smiles broadly at Henley. He might look twelve, but in actuality, Blake Mason is Henley's age, and the founder and CEO of VRDeck. Ignoring him, I take a second to get a feel for the office beyond the glass walls and the brightly colored room we're sitting in.

It's the epitome of a start-up environment. People are working in industrial looking cubicles, sitting at café style tables, or raiding the pantry for snacks. It looks like there's even a lounge for people to play video or VR games, but given their products, it's understandable. It's a surprisingly well thought out office. Maybe I should introduce a few of these features into SEI to attract younger talent.

I write a mental note and tune back into the discussion.

"We've been approached by another party offering the same product," he divulges, confirming the rumor. "Good news, though! I'm looking to make the best deal for my company. What are you offering?"

Henley turns to me.

Too many details can fuck up a deal, and I only want two things from this deal. "SEI is offering the code in exchange for the following—one million units delivered to us within the first six months and thirty percent of the profits for the first three years." It's an excellent deal. Even if production costs are in the higher range, it will still leave VRDeck with a healthy profit margin. And their reports say they're cash-poor.

He looks disappointed. "I'm looking to diversify our offerings and really hoped you'd offer shares of SEI."

I raise an eyebrow, knowing he's just flexing his non-existent muscles. Everyone is aware SEI is a privately held family company and we never offer shares. My eyes dart to Henley. Almost never.

"What is the other company offering?" Henley asks.

"A true partnership," he quips. "Splitting costs and profits fifty-fifty. Can you beat it?"

"Sounds like a great deal. What's the name of this other company?"

Blake hesitates for a second. "LCW Holdings."

She smiles at him. "Sorry, I've never heard of them, but I'm sure you've done your due diligence and checked them out. If they're the powerhouse SEI is, you'll be set."

His brow furrows. "I'd like forty-eight hours to consider the deal."

Good move, Henley.

"The deal is on the table for twenty-four hours," I state firmly.

"But it's not exclusive or guaranteed," Henley pipes up. "Right, Mr. Santos? We're offering the same deal to the entertainment company next, right?"

My cock twitches when she calls me Mr. Santos, but I order it to stand down. I frown and shake my head.

"Oops, sorry, I probably shouldn't have said anything," she winces.

I stand and look at Blake, whose head has been swiveling back and forth. "The first company to accept the deal will be the one in business with SEI. I know I'll get the best deal for my company, because it's the only one I'm willing to make. Run the numbers, talk to your lawyers."

Henley shakes Blake's hand. "I've sent the demo to your email. Sorry, we don't have time to stay and chat. Maybe if we do business together."

I grip her elbow and escort her out the door.

The security team falls in behind us when we get to the lobby. We load into the two waiting SUVs.

"Four Seasons hotel," I tell the driver. "Brilliant. He…"

"Stop," she commands the driver before turning back to me. "Is there a place around here where we can grab a late lunch? I really did make us an appointment with Epic Entertainment for four p.m." she says, chewing her bottom lip.

I tap her lip with my thumb until she releases it. "Thomas, please find a suitable restaurant nearby. Tell me about this meeting you've set up," I order her.

"Well, when I saw the rumor last night, I dropped an email to Epic. They replied right before we went into the meeting with Blake. They want to meet today," she explains. "Would you be interested in meeting with them? If not, I'll cancel."

"SEI and Epic are both powerhouses. We'll be two wolves in a cage, but if we don't kill each other, it could be a cornerstone deal. I'll pull their quarterly reports while we eat and email Grayson to see what he thinks. But the idea fires me up," I remark with satisfaction. "And honestly, I'm not sure I like Blake or VRDeck. They've got a big cash flow issue which concerns me." She laughs. "What?"

"I'm one hundred percent sure you didn't like him. To be honest, I didn't either. It doesn't seem like he did his due diligence on the other company," she says with a shrug. "I wonder what LCW stands for. Our enemy's initials maybe? When I created CJ Tech, I named it after my mother and father—Catherine and James. Marcos named his company after his wife, Juliana—and his sister— your mother, Francisca. If they did the same..."

"We may be dealing with three enemies. I wonder if the C stands for Carlton?" I ponder the idea of investigating it, but a letter isn't much to go on. It won't hurt to have Sterling run a check, but I doubt they're legit.

We arrive at the restaurant. Thomas splits the team. Two secure the vehicle while Thomas and another enter with us. We request two tables.

Henley peruses the menu quickly. "I'll have a cobb salad."

"Hamburger, medium rare, and a salad with olive oil and balsamic," I add, then point to the table where the security team sits. "Also, combine their order with ours." I pull out my phone and send a text to Thomas telling him to order the team whatever they need. We'll be here for a couple of hours.

Getting out my laptop, I pull up the Epic's reports and quickly scan them. The phone rings. "Go."

Grayson gives me his analysis of Epic's financials. "To summarize, they're solid. The only advantage we have is the tech. Go for it."

"Thanks, we'll let you know how it goes," I reply and hang up.

Henley arches a brow.

"We're going for it. I'm going to offer the same deal we gave to VRDeck. If we complicate it, Epic will walk away. The hardest part will be settling on a profit percentage," I speculate.

The food arrives, and I pick up the burger and take a huge bite. "Is the rumor the only reason you set up the additional meeting?"

"Probably should have done it in the first place. More leverage if there's more competition, and you should always have back-ups, right?"

I grunt. "One of Marcos' rules. I don't always follow them. Maybe because I like more risk in my life, but I understand why he tried to avoid it. He had to protect five people. Having a back-up plan probably saved us more times than I want to know," I reflect.

"It's been a lifesaver for me. I still believe in having options, but maybe I don't need a back-up plan for everything," she says, to my surprise. "In fact, for the first time in years, I don't have an escape plan. Some days it makes me panic, but I'm not going anywhere until this is finished. The next time I leave, I want it to be out in the open."

I put my fork down, disturbed to hear she might leave us. "What do you mean? Are you planning on leaving Miami?"

"I can work from anywhere," she reminds me.

"What about Mateo?"

"He doesn't want to talk about it until all this is over," she says with a sigh.

Smart man—buying more time—but I hate the thought of her not being nearby. For the first time in ages, I've been coming home at the end of the workday instead of staying until seven or eight at night. "I see. Probably good to wait."

She takes a bite. "Maybe. I have one piece of good news—the app received approval from the app store. I pushed it live in an obscure country to limit its exposure for right now, but we're in business," she reveals with a grin. "The product is ready for distribution. How about the bid?"

"It's been started but hidden until we get through these meetings. I've been thinking about the glasses, and if everything goes to plan, I think we should donate a pair of glasses to any surgeon who requests a pair instead of pairing it with a future software update. The goodwill will stir up publicity, SEI will offset the revenue with a write-off, and it may help generate faster adoption in the hospitals," I tell her. It's a win-win for the project and for us.

Her eyes light up. "That's an excellent idea."

My phone chimes. "It's time. Ready to go?"

"Lead on, Mr. Santos," she says excitedly.

CHAPTER 25

<u>HENLEY</u>

T he minute we arrive at Epic, we're greeted by the director of research and development who immediately escorts us to a boardroom on the top floor. Unlike VRDeck, this is not a fun, casual atmosphere. It's big business. People move with purpose here.

When we step into the room, all discussion ceases. A tall, good-looking man with a charming smile strides over and introduces himself. "You must be Henley Night. I'm Beauregard Whitman, but you may call me Beau." He shakes my hand and turns to Thiago. "Thiago Santos, I presume?"

Two wolves in a cage—an apt description. Beau might look charming on the surface, but the intelligent glint in his eye says differently. Ignoring the other most powerful man in the room, even for a second, is a bold move. I glance at Thiago and watch his lips curl in anticipation.

Spreading his feet apart, he immediately expands his presence in the room and shakes Beau's hand. "Yes, Thiago Santos," he says, nothing else. He simply waits for Beau to invite him into his domain.

Beau tilts his head. "Unfortunately, we've only got a half hour to discuss this opportunity, but we're intrigued by the potential. Let me introduce you to everyone, and we'll get started."

Thiago's face tightens, but he nods. "This is Henley Night. If you have any questions on the tech, she'll be able to answer them. I'm Thiago Santos, CEO of SEI."

Beau introduces his executives. Every single one is at the director or vice-president level, which tells me he's at least got the right people in the room.

"Would you like refreshments?" Beau's PA points to the drinks and food on the buffet beside the table.

Thiago clears his throat and all chatter and movement ceases immediately. "I'd like to be respectful of your time," he states smoothly, but the sardonic gleam in his eyes tells me he's irritated with the thirty-minute limitation. "Our deal is very simple. If you're interested in hearing it?"

Beau leans back in his chair, his demeanor casual, but his eyes hold a hint of their own irritation. "We're not entirely sure. Who developed this code? Who owns the rights to it?"

"My uncle Marcos developed the code, and he left it to Henley in his will. It's all completely legal and binding," Thiago informs him.

"How do you know if the code even works? Our team has been working on a solution for years, and we haven't managed to get a dual unit operating yet," Beau returns.

"We've used it to enter the metaverse, and we've tested it against new AR software we're launching soon. I've sent proof to your email," I assure him.

He picks up his phone and finds the email. "Forwarding."

Beau's team immediately responds. Opening their computers, they start to hit play.

If I don't do something, we'll be walking out the door in eight minutes without putting the deal on the table. I take a deep breath. "Stop. The video is roughly an hour and twenty minutes long, and we only have six minutes left."

Beau raises his hand.

I pause to gather my thoughts. "We're talking about a lot more than a pair of AR/VR glasses here. While that is the only deal on the table, the true impact won't be measured by a single product. It's an accessory, but an invaluable one. We've developed a product that's going to revolutionize the medical field, and it's going to happen fast. The exposure Epic Entertainment will receive from being tied to this project is immeasurable. It will open a whole new industry for your company."

Every eye turns to stare at me. Thiago grunts, but he doesn't say anything. Guess he approves of me taking point. "We believe in this project so much we've drilled the deal down to two terms, which is probably unheard of, especially by two industry giants like Epic Entertainment and SEI. Are you interested or should we leave?"

Beau abandons his pseudo relaxed position and leans forward. "Let's hear it."

"In exchange for the code to the AR/VR glasses, we'd like one million units delivered to us within the first six months and thirty percent of the profits for the first three years," Thiago says, presenting the offer.

Silence continues to reign, but the expressions on his executive's faces range from disbelief to outrage. Beau's face never changes.

"What are you planning to do with the glasses?" Beau asks casually, but the one question tells me he's intrigued by the offer.

"Donate them to any surgeon who asks for one," Thiago replies. "We have no interest in producing or selling this product. As Henley said, it's only an accessory to the software we're releasing soon."

"What is this revolutionary product?"

Thiago raises an eyebrow. "The information is confidential at this time."

"Everyone thinks their product is going to revolutionize the world. What if you're wrong?" Beau taunts him.

"Write a clause to void the contract contingent upon the release of the product," Thiago inserts smoothly. "If you decide not to pursue it, we can easily find another company to be our partner."

Thiago leans forward. "Although, it would be a missed opportunity not to announce the accessory when we reveal the product. Along with Epic Entertainment, of course."

"Epic Entertainment is the largest entertainment company. If we turn you down, who are you going to go to?" Beau's broad smile is smug when he asks.

The furrow in Thiago's brow tells me he's getting irritated and we only have a couple of minutes left.

"Biomedical Health Corporation," I interject before Thiago can answer.

For the first time, Beau looks confused.

"With the way AR is moving into the real world, everyone is looking for a solution. Gaming, entertainment, fashion, healthcare, military, you name it, all of them need this device. Add VR into the mix, and you have a whole other group of companies. We need a production partner who can be up and running within a month, which is why we're only targeting conglomerates like yourself, regardless of industry. We have the code and production specs for a fully functioning product. It's not going to be hard to find a partner," I state confidently and look at my phone. "We have one minute left."

Thiago's mouth twitches, but he stands. "Regretfully, our time is up. If you're interested, throw us a counteroffer tomorrow morning. If we don't hear from you, we're moving to the next company on our list. We'll be at the Four Seasons. Thank you for your time."

He pulls my chair out and puts a hand on my lower back to guide me out the door.

Standing in the elevator, he leans down to murmur in my ear. "You were magnificent. Maybe I need to take you to all my negotiations."

Surprised, I look up. His eyes are glittering with fierce emotion, making me inhale sharply. The elevator dings and I tear my eyes

STELLA BRIE

away. Releasing the breath I've been holding the whole way down, I follow him out to the SUV.

Thiago calls Grayson immediately to give him an update. While they're talking scenarios, I watch the scenery go by. Soon, we're pulling into a portico, and a doorman is moving to open my door. Thomas is there before he can touch the handle. He opens it and helps me out.

The doorman steps back and smiles. "Welcome to the Four Seasons. Can we help you with your bags?"

"We're traveling light, thank you," I reply with a shake of my head.

Thiago comes around to my side and looks around. "Where's the bellhop?"

"We only have one bag each," I remind him. "And they roll." I demonstrate the three-hundred and sixty degree turning radius on my suitcase. He continues to stare at me. "What?"

"Nothing," he replies with a chuckle. He pulls his suitcase along behind him. After checking in, we head up to our rooms, which are on the same floor. When I mention this to Thiago, he jerks his chin at Thomas. "It's a safety precaution."

I dart a glance at Thomas, who acknowledges the statement with a nod.

"We're eating here tonight," Thiago says when we get to my door. He makes me wait while security checks out the room. "The reservation is at seven-thirty. I'll come get you."

"Seven-thirty," I repeat, then roll my suitcase into the room and close the door. The room is luxurious with a capital L, but I couldn't care less. Stripping the beautiful clothes off, I change into leggings, a t-shirt, and fuzzy socks and climb into the fluffy bed sitting in the middle of the room. I need a nap.

———

AT SEVEN-FIFTEEN SHARP, there's a knock on the door. I look through the peephole and see Thiago's large body standing in front of me.

"Let me grab a sweater," I tell him. Sliding open the closet door, I pull one from the hanger and sling it over my arm. "Ready."

Thiago's standing in the doorway checking his phone. "You look beautiful," he murmurs without looking up.

"Hmm, thank you," I reply. "Do you think these pants look black or navy?"

He lowers his phone and arches his eyebrow. "Your dress is navy."

I laugh. "Just checking to see if you're paying attention."

He grumbles but puts his phone away. "Better?"

I beam at him.

The restaurant is elegant, but the warm night calls to me. "Can we eat outside on the patio?"

He raises an eyebrow toward the maître d, who bows his head respectfully.

Pocketing the tip Thiago slips him, he motions to the young lady next to him. "Certainly, sir. Sienna will take you to your table. Have a good evening."

The warm sultry air feels much better than the air-conditioned interior. Thiago orders us a bottle of wine and an appetizer of sweet corn empanadas. Quickly deciding on my dinner, I put down the menu and look for the lake I saw from my hotel window, but the trees are blocking my view.

The man beside me is quiet. When I turn toward him, he's studying me with a bemused expression on his face.

I quickly look at the front of my dress to make sure I haven't buttoned it wrong. Everything is in its place. "What?"

"The meeting would have ended in a stand-off if you hadn't stepped in today. If the deal gets finalized tomorrow, like I think it will, you and I will go out and celebrate. Maybe go dancing. How does that sound?" he asks with a sexy smile.

Wait. He doesn't have a sexy smile. Nope. Put those thoughts away. But it would be nice to leave the hotel, and if Mateo and I are serious, it will be better if Thiago and I get along outside of the gym. "That sounds wonderful," I tell him.

The server sets down the empanadas and presents the bottle of wine to Thiago, who approves. "What can I get for you this evening?"

After ordering the filet, I take a sip of wine and listen while Thiago orders the duck. The server leaves, and we dig into the appetizer.

"Wow, this is delicious," I say after finishing the first bite. "Good call."

He takes a big bite and nods.

"Thank you for taking this on. I know your plate is full with SEI business, but I honestly didn't want to do this on my own," I tell him.

He hums. "I should be thanking you. You're going to make SEI a hell of a lot of money, and all I had to put in is a few hours of work."

"We're even?"

"Not a chance," he replies. "I'm trying to catch up from every-thing you've already done for my family and SEI. I..."

"Henley? Henley Davis? Is that you?" A blond man walks over to our table.

The security team intercepts him before he can get near me.

He chuckles. "Henley, it's me, David. From MIT. I know it's been a long time, but I don't think I look that different," a voice says from behind the wall of security.

Shocked, I kind of freeze. Do I acknowledge he's got the right person or deny him? David's sweet face drifts into my mind. I sigh and nod to Thiago.

"Thomas, let him through," Thiago orders his security lead. Standing, he reaches out a hand toward David, who stops and stares at him. "I'm Thiago Santos."

His face hardens briefly, but he quickly smooths his expression. "David Perry," David says, introducing himself. "Henley. It is you. I thought it was when you went by, but the pink hair threw me. How are you? What have you been up to?" He reaches out to give me a hug, but I step back.

Instead, I hold out my hand for him to shake. Does he not remember dumping me? I was devastated. "David, it's nice to see you again. How are you?" I can't tell if his broad smile is forced or authentic.

"Henley Davis. Wow, I never thought I'd see you again. Or have the chance to apologize for my behavior. My only excuse was I was young and dumb," he says, raising his hands. "You look amazing. It wasn't the same when you left MIT." He drones on and on until I want to scream.

"Do you live here?" I ask, trying to move him off the subject of me.

He looks around nervously. "Here? Oh, you mean Austin. No, I live on the east coast. Just here on business. How about you? Is this your husband?"

"No, Thiago is my boss. I'm here on business, too," I reply.

A weird sound comes from Thiago, and I turn toward him with an arched eyebrow. He returns it with one of his own.

Our dinner arrives, and I can barely stop myself from kissing the server in gratitude.

I move to sit in my seat. "Well, it was nice seeing you, David. Good luck with everything."

He jerks forward with his arm outstretched. "Here's my card. Call me sometime. I'd love to catch up," he states with a grin. He gives Thiago a side glance. "Nice meeting you."

Thiago stares at me while he eats.

"What?" I ask, bewildered by the expression on his face.

"How long has it been since you've seen David?"

I think back. "Sophomore year at MIT. He and I dated, but he broke it off when he heard some rumors about me. They weren't true, but he believed them. Why?"

He leans back in his chair. "In all the years you've been running, have you ever seen someone from your past?"

"No, not really. Or if I had, I didn't recognize them or they me.

What's going on in your head, Thiago?" I question him, putting down my fork. He's starting to make me nervous.

"I don't believe in coincidences, and there's something off about David. I'm going to have Sterling investigate him," he informs me picking up his phone.

I frown and think about it, but I can't see this being anything but a coincidence. An unpleasant one, but still, just a random thing.

Thiago snatches up David's card and takes a picture before handing it back to me. "My gut is rarely wrong, Henley."

I give him an incredulous look. "Really? It was wrong about me, wasn't it?"

His mouth compresses. "You're an extremely rare exception. A onetime thing, I assure you. My gut is right ninety-nine percent of the time. Just ask Mateo or Grayson."

"If you say so," I retort.

My stalker slips into my mind, and I compare David's height to Stanley's. It's not even close. David might be six feet, if he stretches. Damn it. Now this is bugging me, too. I slip his card into my purse. Maybe I'll do some of my own digging.

CHAPTER 26

<u>HENLEY</u>

Epic sent a courier early this morning with an invitation to have brunch with Beau Whitman at his house. Thiago accepted, and we're headed over there now. We pull up to the gate, and it immediately swings open. Thiago squints at the metal box by the gate and shakes his head. I'm guessing he finds Beau's security system lacking.

When we reach the end of the driveway, a large rambling ranch house with a façade of stone and wood waits for us. Thomas assists me out, then gets back in. They decided it would be best if they returned for us later.

An older gentleman in a suit stands by the front door. "Good morning, Mr. Santos, Ms. Night. I'm Carmichael. If you'll follow me, Mr. Whitman is on the back patio."

Carmichael leads us through the house. I'm surprised to see it's a home, not a cold mansion like I expected. Wooden beams cross the ceilings, the floors alternate between a rough wide-plank wood and terracotta tile. The big furnishings are high end, but extremely comfortable-looking. We walk through large wood-framed French doors onto an extensive stone patio.

Beau Whitman is reading some documents when we find him. He hands them off to the man beside him and stands. "Welcome to my home."

After shaking hands, he shows us to the buffet that's set out along one wall. It includes a variety of food from breakfast to lunch, and I can't resist filling my plate with all the deliciousness.

Thiago sticks to his usual healthy selections of wheat toast, egg whites, fruit, and coffee. Surprisingly, Beau loads up his plate like me.

"I thought it would be better if we had a more relaxed atmosphere to talk about our potential deal," Beau explains after taking a few bites. "The boardroom has its uses, but given yesterday's meeting, this might be more conducive."

I snort. "It's certainly friendlier," I remark lightly. "And I'm usually happier when someone's feeding me."

Beau's mouth quirks. "Good. I've run the numbers, and given the volume of production we need to start with in order to fulfill your requirement of one million units in six months, while still hitting our revenue targets during the same time frame, I propose twenty-two percent profit for the first three years."

Thiago puts his fork down and reaches for his coffee. "Why don't we mix it up? Twenty percent profit for the first year, thirty the remaining two years. Unlike most products, you don't have research and development costs to recoup. Once the initial production investment is zeroed out, the rest is profit. Plus, you'll have the foundation for future enhancements."

Beau punches in some numbers on his phone. "The numbers work for me. Done. I'll have my lawyers draw up the papers this afternoon and send it over. We will not be including a contingency clause to void the contract based on your product release. If it is what we think it is, we'll reap a huge benefit from the exposure."

I narrow my eyes. "What have you heard?"

"Let's just say I reached out to a few healthcare individuals who were invited to a bid demonstration earlier this year," he quips. "With a gentleman named Marcos, I believe."

Not wanting to confirm or deny the rumor, I go back to eating my meal.

Beau chuckles. "When you're done eating, I'd love to show you the lake. The view from here is incredible." He slides a glance at Thiago, whose eyes are narrowed on him. "You too, of course, Thiago."

I mentally roll my eyes at the posturing, but Beau was right. The relaxed atmosphere was infinitely more conducive than the board-room, and more importantly, we have a partner. Within the year, the glasses will be in the hands of surgeons everywhere.

———

I SLIP the earrings into my ears and step back to make sure everything looks good. My pink hair falls in waves and is a pretty close match to the YouTube video Peyton sent for me to follow. My make-up is simple and neutral. My black silk dress is deceptively simple, but elegant, with its halter style neckline and flirty A-line skirt. The bare back is my favorite part, adding a hint of sexiness.

And unlike the peacock dress, I don't have to worry about acci-dentally showing anyone my underwear. This skirt falls only a couple of inches above my knees. I twirl around but smile when nothing scandalous shows.

The firm knock on the door tells me Thiago's here, and I grab my clutch and open the door.

Dressed entirely in black with a slightly menacing air surrounding him, he's pure devastation and the epitome of every woman's fantasy of what a mafia don might look like from the tips of his straight dark hair to the tips of his elegant shoes. Power in a package. I try to remember to keep breathing.

His dark obsidian eyes drop to my shoes and travel slowly back up again. The heat in his gaze makes me shiver, but he doesn't say anything.

"Peyton said this dress would work. If it doesn't, I can change?"

"We're going to be late if we don't leave now," he says gruffly. "You look beautiful."

"Thank you. You look handsome yourself," I reply, trying to keep things on an even keel. "I'm excited to go dancing. What's a supper club?"

He ushers me through the hotel and into the waiting SUV. "It's a restaurant that focuses more on the social experience of dining and upscale entertainment. The one we're going to tonight has dancing. It should be fun."

Minutes later, his hand rests lightly against my back as he escorts me from the SUV into the club. The hostess parts black velvet curtains and I almost whistle at the view in front of me. It's so… swanky. Almost like the room is from another era when restaurants were reasons to dress for a night out.

Plush velvet is everywhere, from the barstools at the bar to the booths in the dining area to the individual chairs surrounding the stage. Dark, moody colors of blood red and black with heavy gold accents set the tone for the evening.

We're immediately seated in one of the booths near the stage. Fascinated by this place, I can't decide whether to focus on the beautiful décor or the gorgeous people dressed in their finest. It's another world.

A dark chuckle tickles my left ear, and I turn my head to find Thiago practically curled around me in the booth. "You should see the look on your face. I'm guessing you like the place?"

Every word out of his mouth is almost torture. Small puffs of air travel down my neck, making me shiver. "It's amazing. I've never been somewhere like this before. Everything is beautiful and sophisticated. It's almost like we stepped back to a time when restaurants were more glamorous, and an evening out meant something."

His mouth curves. "Exactly. Do you trust me?"

"Yes," I say without hesitation.

He calls the server over and orders a couple of cocktails. When my drink arrives, it's a dark purple concoction in a champagne glass. Surprised, I sniff it, but I can't smell anything.

Thiago raises his glass toward me, and I bring mine up to touch his. "To Henley. Thank you for loving Marcos as much as we did. Everything you've done, including today's deal, is in honor of him. He would be so proud of you, not for what you've done, but for who you're becoming. Saúde!"

"Saúde!" I repeat. The first sip of the concoction is divine. I can't even tell what's in it, but I'm not sure I care. "Mmm... delicious."

Thiago bends down and murmurs in my ear. "Drink, eat, dance, and let loose tonight. I'll take care of you."

The thought is so tantalizing, I can't even breathe for a second. My eyes drift up to the man beside me. "Are you serious? I don't have to worry about anything?"

His strong hand grips mine. "I've got you, Henley. Enjoy yourself."

Soft jazz starts playing in the background, adding to the haze of ambiance, and I slowly allow myself to let go. The drinks are flowing and the intensely attractive man next to me is in full charm mode. Instead of his usual surly self, Thiago's regaling me with stories of all of them when they were children.

"Marcos would get this stern look on his face when he was disciplining us, but I'd always see him and Tia Mariana laughing about our antics later. He was a different father to each of us. For Mateo, his father left after my aunt became pregnant. My aunt is wonderful, but he needed someone who could speak to him at his level. Besides being a father figure, he was Mateo's mentor."

He takes a bite of his steak, then continues. "For Grayson, he was the only father he'd ever known. They probably had more of a true father and son relationship out of all of us." He lifts a shoulder. "For me, he was everything. An uncle who became a father the instant he saved me from death and the man who taught me how to survive and thrive in this world. Probably similar to your relationship with him."

"I'm not so sure. He was so stubborn and wanted everything

done a certain way, which meant we argued quite a bit," I state with a laugh. "We'd try to outdo each other with logic to explain why one of us was more right than the other. Suddenly, his big belly would start shaking and he'd be laughing instead of arguing."

Thiago brow furrows. "Big belly? Marcos didn't have a big belly."

"In the metaverse he did," I quip, and describe the avatar Marcos used in our lab. "I think he thought I would be more at ease. It was a shock to see him in the video that morning and realize he was handsome. I wouldn't have guessed it was him, but he exudes intensity whether he's an avatar or an image on a video."

The emcee announces the singer, and Thiago's eyes light up. "Dance with me."

On the dance floor, he swings me into his arms. The woman on stage is singing the cover song for Adele's "Oh My God." It starts out slow, but switches quickly to something fast and upbeat. She's singing about a woman having fun and letting go. I throw my head back and laugh.

He lets my hands slide out of his, and I dance in a circle by myself for a minute. I dance back into his arms, and he expertly twirls me. I raise my hands in the air and dance around him, my body barely brushing his with each circle. The song starts to come to end, and I slip back into his arms.

"Thank you," I say breathlessly. "I needed this."

His strong arms wrap around me, and we sway to the slower song they're playing now. "I've been waiting to dance with you since the ball," he admits, his voice husky. "This was worth the wait. Do you want to keep dancing or go back to the table for a drink?"

Enraptured with this version of Thiago, I can't bear to return to the table. "Dancing, definitely." Feeling free and unencumbered, and a little tipsy, for the first time in ages, all I want is to dance the night away with him.

The songs vary wildly, but most of them stay in the realm of romantic. The singer switches to a new song from Sofia Carson, called "It's Only Love, Nobody Dies," and I turn my back to his front to dance. I love this song, but I can't stare into his dark eyes when she's singing about kissing.

It makes me want to sing the same words to him, to kiss me now, but it wouldn't be fair. I shove it all away and lose myself in the dancing. He wraps his body around mine, front to back, together and apart, face to face, and everything in between.

After another hour, I'm exhausted. "I'm going to the restroom. Meet back at the table?"

He signals to someone off to the side, and I swivel around to see the female bodyguard I saw on Grayson's yacht the other day. "She'll be nearby if you need her."

The haze of the night lifts, and reality starts to creep back in. "Thank you," I tell her on my way to the bathroom.

"Absolutely," she replies with a smile. After sweeping the restroom, she positions herself outside the door. "It's all clear."

With all the dancing, I expect to see a mess in the mirror. My face is flushed, but surprisingly, most of my makeup is still intact. I use the restroom and reapply my lip gloss. When I come out, she's waiting to escort me to Thiago.

"Here," he says, handing me a glass of water. "Do you want to stay longer or leave?"

I sway slightly and laugh. "I'm ready to go," I confirm after taking a sip.

His arm swings around my waist and he pulls me in close. When we get outside, I hear the music start up again, and I can't help swaying to the beat. He smiles down at me and shakes his head.

A few minutes later, he glances at his watch. "It's been too long."

The female bodyguard from earlier is standing with us. "I agree. Let's get you both back inside. I'll call Thomas and let him know we have a situation."

She steps in front of me and twirls her finger, but before we can turn to go back inside, she's collapsing. Her body falls forward, and I automatically reach out and grab her. Vacant eyes stare back at me, and I start screaming. I lay her on the ground. Blood pools around her head.

Thiago pulls the gun from her holster, grabs my hand, and jerks me up.

"Wait," I scream, and bend down to get the radio in her hand.

When I stand up, something whizzes by my face and strikes the brick next to me. Thiago's arm comes around my head the same time the brick splinters, sending shards in every direction. I hear him grunt. Did he get hit? Or shot? Panicking, I run my hands over his body.

"Get inside now," he orders, pushing me in front of him.

The doorman is bravely holding the door open for us. When we get close, Thiago takes the radio and shoves me through but doesn't follow.

"I need to check on the other guard. I'll be right back."

"NO! Thiago!" I scream, but he's gone.

Please, please don't let anything happen to him, I keep praying silently over and over.

The entire club is silent now except for the occasional sniffle from someone crying. People stare at the blood on my arms, but nobody says a word. The hostess quietly hands me a towel.

We all wait, unwilling to step outside until it's safe. Finally, the sirens get closer, and we hear several cars screech to a halt outside the club. Officers stream inside and the eerie stillness breaks with a collective sigh of relief.

The police quickly separate the witnesses from the rest of the club. An hour later, I'm still here by myself. I've given my statement to the police. Thiago hasn't returned or called, and I don't have Thomas' number. I can order a rideshare, but the thought of getting into a stranger's car right now is tough to swallow.

Shivering, I wrap my arms around my body, trying to hold myself together, but the same thoughts keep going round and round. Thiago should have been back by now. What if he's lying some-where in a ditch? God, what if he's dead? The worry builds and builds.

A large man in a black coat walks in, and I sigh in relief only to discover it's not Thiago. The man informs me he's part of my security team, and Thomas sent him to get me.

"Do you know where Thiago is? Is he okay?" I question him, but he doesn't answer.

He holds out a hand to help me up. I stare at it, then down at my blood encrusted hands and shake my head. "I'm only leaving with Thomas."

He clicks the radio on his belt and speaks into for it for a second. When he gets confirmation, he informs me of the change. "He's on his way, and he's proud of you for thinking on your feet and refusing to go with me. Most women would be hysterical right now."

I half laugh, half cry. "Plenty of practice." Where the hell is Thiago?

CHAPTER 27

THIAGO

S econds. One, maybe two seconds. Henley living. Henley dying. The prompt action of Henley's bodyguard is the only reasons she's alive. The blood and horror on her face won't be so easily forgotten, but it's better than her death.

Another mark on the tally sheet against our enemy, and... another debt owed. Every time I fail to save the people around me, the deck gets higher.

God, I miss Marcos. He always knew the way forward. Focus on the solution, not the problem, he would tell me. The only solution I see: eliminate our enemies before they eliminate us.

This was a bold move tonight. Striking against us in a public place. Involving the police. What did it accomplish? What was the purpose? To take out Henley? Why? It doesn't add up. Until now, they've been primarily focused on us and SEI.

In frustration, I pound the seat with my fist. At least the bastard who killed our two guards tonight is dead. When I saw the blood on Henley, I lost it. The rage I'd been holding back for weeks exploded, and the need to hunt him took over. When I found him, I gave him one chance to surrender, but the minute he fired on me, he was dead. No ID. The only item he had on him was the burner phone in my hand. I slip it in my pocket.

My phone buzzes with a text from Sterling. My gut was spot on. David Perry is the son of a wealthy single mother, father unknown. She inherited family money from a legacy thoroughbred horse racing stable and breeding farm located about twenty miles outside… Lexington, Kentucky at the same place Henley's stalker kept her. Is David her stalker? My hands clench.

Sterling admits it took him a while to dig up the information. The property and house were repossessed by the bank ten years ago, then divided up and sold to several different owners.

Upon David's graduation from MIT, he went to work for a tech company in Silicon Valley but was fired a year later when he got caught committing corporate espionage. Disappeared off the radar for a few years. Pops up infrequently on the dark web as a contract for hire—black hat jobs. Company on the card doesn't exist. Phone untraceable.

At the very least, he's either Henley's stalker or they know each other. But why show his face to Henley? He essentially outed himself as a player in this deadly game. I send the picture Sterling took from the hotel's security cameras to my head of security, Jameson Bennett, to cascade down to his team.

My phone buzzes. It's Thomas. "Where is she?"

"She's with me at the hotel. I'm the only one she would leave with," he states with satisfaction. "Still thinking on her feet, even with everything that happened tonight. Are you on your way back? The police need to get a statement from you, and they're not leaving until they do."

"I'll be there in twenty minutes. Have them meet me in the lobby," I order him. I hang up with Thomas and call Grayson to fill him in on what's happened. "She's okay. Shook up. It was close. Too fucking close." My voice is hoarse with emotion I can't control.

Grayson's cussing up a storm. "Tell Mateo to give her a call. I've got to handle the police and won't get to her for at least another hour."

We pull up and I stride into the brightly lit lobby. Two policemen in uniform and two in suits greet me. "Detectives? Why don't we go into the business center where it's quiet?" And private.

Thankfully, they'd done their due diligence and pulled the footage from the supper club. Unfortunately, their main interest is where I've been for the last couple of hours. "I left Ms. Night safely in the restaurant and went to check on our other guard. He was dead by our SUV. Shot. A car peeled out of the parking lot. I shot at it but missed. I ran after it, calling the police and my security team, but it turned out to be a witness to the murder of my man in the parking lot, not the murderer. Which I believe you know, since it's your men who stopped them."

They nod.

"I was headed back over the bridge toward the club when a car jumped the curb and headed straight toward me. I fired but missed. I dove out of the way, and it crashed against the end of the bridge. Someone got out and took off. I followed them for a while, but it's dark and eventually I gave up."

The senior detective frowns. "Why didn't you call us?"

"No phone. When I dove out of the way, it must have slipped out of my pocket. I retraced my steps, found it on the bridge, and called my team to pick me up." I don't tell them I purposely left it there where it couldn't be used to trace my whereabouts.

They nod. "We'll take the gun from you now," the detective offers.

Spreading my hands wide, I shrug. "I don't know where it is. When I dove, everything left my hands, including the gun. If you have a map, I can show which bridge I was on."

The two detectives silently communicate with each other. One pulls up a map on his phone, and I point to the bridge. "Are you sure you don't have anything else to share?"

"No—wait, I lost my wallet, too. If you find it on the bridge, can you send it to the hotel? I would greatly appreciate it. Now, if that's all, it's been a long evening, and I'd like to check on my people." I tap to share contact info with them. "Here's my lawyer's number. If there is anything else I can do to help find the bastard, let me know," I state firmly, standing to shake their hands. "Thank you."

She's on the phone with Mateo, crying, when I enter the suite. Her hair is wet, and the blood is gone. She looks so fucking beautiful I can't stand it.

Her eyes widen when she sees me. "He's here. I'll talk to you later." She's breathing heavily and crying, but instead of dying down, it gets worse when she sees me.

The emotion is building in her, and I know she won't want Thomas to see her lose it. "Thomas, we'll talk in the morning. Go get some rest and take care of your team."

The minute the door closes, she falls against the couch. "You're alive. This whole time, nobody would tell me where you were or if you were alive or dead. For three hours, I thought the worst. Until Mateo called me." Sobs rack her body, and she sags against the back of the sofa.

Her words blow a hole in my heart. Fuck me. I didn't know. Why would she think the worst? I yank her into my arms, but she pushes back in fury.

Her fists pound against my chest over and over and I stand there and take it, knowing I deserve it and much, much more. "Damn you, Thiago, for putting me through hell. Did you not think of how it would make me feel? How would you feel if I were dead?"

The image of the guard falling is easily replaced with one of Henley, and I grab her arms tightly. "Don't say that. Don't ever fucking say that to me."

She lifts a shoulder. "Why not? You don't care about me."

The dam I've been shoring up for weeks shatters into a thousand pieces. Crushing her to me, I kiss her like the world is ending, because that's how I felt tonight when I heard the shots. Like the sun would cease to shine and the world would be a thing of darkness without her in it. I can't continue to let her think I don't care when, in fact, it's the opposite. I care too fucking much.

She yanks her shirt off. "I need you, Thiago."

I pull her up in my arms and she wraps her legs tightly around me. Groaning, I find the nearest wall and prop her against it. My mouth latches onto her breast, sucking hard until she cries out.

She grips my head, pulling my lips back up to her mouth. It's a carnal kiss, full of need and urgency. My tongue plunges into her mouth, dueling with hers, and she moans and thrusts against me.

Her hands are everywhere. "Need. Inside," she gasps. "Thiago, please."

Reaching down, I yank her leggings halfway off, and she pulls one leg out, then wraps it back around my waist. I thrust my fingers in her. Thank the fuck, she's wet. Freeing myself, I line up and surge into her hard. She moans. This. Me inside her. Over and over, sinking to the hilt. Yet it's not deep enough. I want to sink into her bones.

"More," she cries, grinding down on me.

I yank her off the wall and stride over to the bed. Laying her down, I pick her leg up and thrust hard, going all the way in. Groaning, I set a rapid pace, driving into her without stopping. My cock is so damn hard I feel like I can go forever.

Her body quivers, and I reach down to stroke her nub. It doesn't take much until she's coming, her sweet body clenching my cock. "Thiago!"

With her body still trembling, I switch to a slower pace. Her blue eyes lock with mine, and I can see the emotional turmoil from this evening lingering in their depths. I slide all the way into her and watch her eyes drift shut from the pleasure.

"Open your eyes, querida," I rasp. "I need to see you're here with me. Alive. It was so close tonight. Being inside you is the only thing saving me right now." I keep up the steady pace, feeling the stretch of her body over my cock, and the pleasure begins to build.

Her beautiful face is flush with desire. "I can't get enough of you, Henley. Come for me one more time."

My fingers find her nub, and I play with it until she's writhing beneath me. Part of me wants to keep her on the edge until she's begging, but not tonight. Her body quivers and I pick up speed until she falls over the edge again.

The sight of her surrender triggers my own release, and I moan, coming hard enough the edges of my vision turn black.

Breathing heavily, I pull out and drop beside her. The control I've been holding on to for weeks is gone—splintered beyond reason. I turn my head and find her looking at me with a solemn expression on her face.

Worried, I sit up and lean over. "Did I hurt you? What's wrong?"

"I'm wondering if you're going to tell me that was a mistake or caused by the adrenaline of the night," she states softly.

Mateo told me to be honest... "I didn't plan it," I admit softly. "And I don't believe it would have happened without the events of tonight. But I won't hide from whatever this is between us anymore. I can't. Something inside me shifted and I don't want to live without calling you mine."

I lean over and kiss her hard, then grip her head between my hands. "I can't imagine a world without you in it. I'm sorry, so fucking sorry. I didn't know you would worry or think the worst. Forgive me?"

Tears slip silently down her cheeks. "But why did you leave?"

"I needed to get the bastard," I tell her, my voice tight.

"Couldn't you let someone else do it? Why did it have to be you?"

"Because I'm the one who keeps failing you," I roar, unable to hold back the guilt weighing me down. Standing, I pull my pants up and face her. "With Diego, your stalker, our enemies. Not to mention the rest of my people." I throw my hands in the air. "Marcos, Mateo, Jason, Roberto, and I just added two more to the list tonight. Melissa and Paul. Oh, and let's not forget Agent Antonio. When does it stop?"

"Oh, Thiago," she says softly, her anger dissolving. She yanks off the rest of her leggings and wraps the sheet around her body.

"Nobody blames you. We're at war. The only time we fail is if we don't try. And I'm not sure if you noticed, but we have a hell of a lot of people on our side. It's not just you on this battlefield. It's Mateo, Grayson, me. It's Zane and his team. And SEI's new security team."

She stands and lays her hand on my chest. "Everyone has a reason to fight. Blood's been spilled everywhere. It's personal for all of us. Don't rob us of the chance for vengeance by trying to take it all on yourself. The only way we're going to win is together."

The need to believe her is there, but it's slightly out of reach. Too many years spent trying to protect everyone. My thumb comes up and traces the lines on her face. "You looked so beautiful tonight. So carefree. I told you to let loose, let me take care of everything and look what happened."

She scans my face. "Don't leave me tonight."

"I'll be with you all night," I promise her, laying my forehead against hers. "Let me grab a shower, okay?" I grip her chin and kiss her until she's breathless. "I'll be back soon."

In the shower, the water turns pink with blood from where the shards of brick hit my arm, and I lean against the wall and watch it flow down the drain. How do I protect them against an enemy I can't see? Tonight was bad, and it's only going to get worse. I close my eyes and let the water wash over me, sending my sins and doubts down the drain.

When I return, she's fast asleep, with a little furrow in her brow. Still worried about something, maybe everything. The chemistry is explosive between us, and I still can't imagine how I'm going to share her with Mateo or react to seeing them together when we get back, but I'm willing to try. To be honest, my only priority right now is keeping all of us alive.

A low buzzing noise near the window draws my attention. I tilt my head, trying to pinpoint where it's coming from, and walk closer to the noise, finally tracing it to the jacket I was wearing earlier. I'd thrown it in the chair by the window at some point. I lift it up and when I hear the buzz again, it dawns on me. Scrambling, I grab the phone from the inner pocket where I'd left it.

"Lo'," I grunt, trying to sound like the guy I shot tonight.

"Is she dead?" the voice on the line asks impatiently.

Shock holds me hostage for a second. "No, but you will be soon," I vow.

Click. I shut the phone and stare at it. It was a woman.

CHAPTER 28

HENLEY

The warm hard chest beneath my fingers and the thump of his heart reassures me this is real. He's alive and here, naked in bed, with me. It's early, but it's not pre-dawn dark, so I know he's awake.

I tilt my head back until I can see him. Serious eyes drill into mine. Too serious. "What—no workout? I'm disappointed in you, Mr. Santos."

His mouth quirks and in a flash, he's on top, looking down at me. "You were asleep when I came to bed last night. I've been counting the minutes until you woke." He scoots down in the bed, trailing kisses until he captures my breast in his mouth.

Heat rises and my body arches into his. "Mmm, Mr. Santos, are you throwing our entire schedule out the window?"

His lips trails across my stomach. "Hmm, I'm seizing the moment."

The phone rings. I rise.

He moves between my legs and nibbles his way down my hip

until he reaches the most sensitive part of me. "Ignore it." His mouth settles between my legs, and I open without thought.

The tongue he wields with such wicked dexterity has me begging in minutes, but he refuses to give me the release I desperately need. "Thiago, please, stop teasing."

"I'm exploring your delightful body, learning its curves and valleys," he drawls huskily. "The depths." His tongue spears into me, and my body clenches tightly. "The sensitive spots." Lips close on my nub, and he sucks, making me buck up into his mouth. "The pieces made to fit my body." Fingers slide into me and hook to caress the spot on the inside.

"What do you want, querida? Tell me and it's yours," he murmurs.

"You. I want you," I cry out.

With his incredible strength, he easily moves us both until I'm sitting on his lap. "Lift up."

We both moan when he slides inside me. He leans back until we can both watch him thrust in and out. Between the sight of him sliding in and out, and the cut abs he's displaying with the angle he's maintaining, I'm practically drooling. It's the sexiest thing I've ever seen.

"Look at me, Henley," he orders.

My eyes jerk up and lock with his. The dark obsidian stones glitter with need. Mesmerizing.

"Tell me what you feel," he says, his voice savage. Not once does he stop moving, and I can do nothing but give him the truth.

"Your body, moving in and out of mine, stretching me, until I feel so full I can't imagine taking one more inch. But I want more. I want all of you," I cry. "Don't hold back. Not anymore."

"Are you sure?" he asks gruffly.

I pull his head to me. "Every single inch of you," I whisper. With my lips, I demand his surrender with every stroke of my tongue.

"Deal," he snaps back.

"Deal," I echo. My body locks onto his and squeezes hard. I'm so close. I slip my hand between our bodies and circle his cock tightly. Wanting to feel him and me together.

"Fuck, Henley," he swears.

"Mmm," I respond, sliding my hand from him to myself, circling and stroking, until I fall over the edge. My breath catches, and my body pulses on his, over and over.

He lays me at an angle with only my upper back on the bed, but my hips are still in his lap meeting his. Rising, he thrusts in and out quickly, driving himself higher and higher, while I watch. His mouth drops open for a second, and he stops, but inside, the warmth fills me up.

Not a minute later, the phone rings, making him chuckle. Then mine rings. Both stop but start again almost immediately.

He frowns and slides out of my body, making us both groan. Grabbing his phone from the nightstand, he leans down and presses a hard kiss on my lips. "Much better than my usual work-out. Thank you."

"Anytime, Mr. Santos." I say cheekily, watching his eyes flare at the name. Interesting. I blush, thinking about role playing with him.

"Mateo, what's up?" He moves toward the end of the bed and stands. "Are you fucking kidding me? I didn't give them permission to release his picture. What does the article say about the fire?"

I get up and head for the shower. Whatever this is, it's not good, which means we'll be heading out soon.

———

THE CASKETS ROLL up the belt and into the plane. My eyes drift to Thomas and watch his hands clench at his side. "I'm so sorry."

"It was my fault," he remarks. "I underestimated the enemy and deployed my team ineffectually. I won't make that mistake again. They're escalating. We will too. Military tactics from here on out." He dips his chin and heads out the door of the plane.

The big guy from the other night ducks his head and enters. With his finger on the trigger of his gun, he takes a stance near the door and waits. The rest of his team is outside watching the loading and preparation of the plane for take-off. This isn't the same process we followed on the way out here. Vigilance is high.

Thiago steps onto the plane and the guy turns to let him pass, then moves back into position.

He eyes him with satisfaction, then strides down the aisle toward me. "Another team will meet us when we land. I'll go to the ATF offices with my lawyer, and you'll meet Mateo at SEI. Okay?"

The ATF released Marcos' picture this morning along with the findings of their investigation—the deliberate bombing of SEI's satellite office. They've named Diego their prime suspect based on the video of him killing Marcos, and his subsequent coverup of the crime. They listed the other eight victims, including Jason, along with their pictures.

The publicity is bad. Thiago's been on the phone with his lawyer and PR team since he picked up Mateo's call this morning.

"I'm going to try to get the ATF to make a statement at the press conference tomorrow regarding the full cooperation we've extended to them. We set up a fund for the victim's families the day after the fire, which will hopefully lend some credence to our intent to support the investigation and help them through this terrible situation. At the end of the day, Diego was our head of security, and it was our building. We're responsible, and we'll own it," he states firmly. "Are you doing okay?"

"Good. Ready to get home," I reply, looking out the window to the team below. Thomas makes a circle with his hand, and they load onto the plane. Thick fingers lace between mine and I squeeze them tightly. It's going to be a firestorm.

CHAPTER 29

<u>HENLEY</u>

T he airport is a mad crush of press. Thankfully, they're contained on the other side of the fence and not allowed in SEI's private hangar. Two SUVs and a security team will go with Thiago. Two will go with me. The hearse will leave once the press is gone. One SUV will remain here for Thomas, who is staying with them to make sure they're delivered safely to the funeral home.

When the convoy hits the gate, the press tries to follow, but the split confuses them. Most follow me to SEI, allowing Thiago to keep his meeting with the ATF relatively quiet. Word will slip out, but it buys him a little time.

We roar into SEI's parking garage. Thankfully, security stops any of the press from entering behind us. Mateo is waiting for me when we pull up. He yanks me from the car straight into his arms, inhaling deeply, and holding me tightly in his arms. The tension from the morning eases along with the tight band around my chest. Security taps him on the shoulder, and he raises a hand to acknowledge the need to move.

Releasing me, he links our hands together while we follow the team into SEI. "Minha linda, I let you go away for two days, and you almost get yourself killed. Again. I refuse to let you leave ever again. Do you hear me?"

Puzzled, I raise an eyebrow. "Again?"

"Dallas. Huge fire. Destroyed your loft," he bites out, punctuating each word with his hands. "You never did tell us how you escaped and what caused the fire."

We enter the security room filled with televisions. "I had the loft modified to accommodate an escape plan with a hidden, secondary sprinkler system containing a Class B accelerant, a timer-based ignition switch, and a tunnel into the drainage system below."

Heads whip around to stare at me. The big guy from the security team points to me. "She's good under pressure."

"Maybe we should hire you," an older gentleman comments from behind me.

I swivel around to face him. A military man. Hard, almost stern features, eyes constantly moving and assessing. Buzzed cut dark hair and brown eyes.

"Jameson Bennett," he announces, holding out his hand.

The head of SEI's security and Zane's recommendation. "Henley Night. I'm sorry for your loss." The loss of two team members will be keenly felt in this small, close group.

He dips his chin. "Thank you, they will be missed." His stance relaxes, and he waves an arm. "Let me introduce you to the rest of the team. Allison Engles, she's heading up SEI's security." A pretty brunette on the phone in the corner raises her hand. "Jaxon Pointer, head of cybersecurity. He's been working closely with Mateo." The lean, serious man sitting on my right stands and shakes my hand.

The big guy from the plane steps forward and grins, knowing I don't remember his name. "Mitch."

Jameson continues, introducing those who are in the security room with us, although I see many more on the monitors in front of me.

The monitors are extensive but on par for a company whose

main product is security. They have several different types of cameras, including infrared and three hundred sixty degree views, with some cool features like the ability to tap and zoom, plus facial recognition.

The man on the monitor to the right catches my eye. Philip Carlton. He's currently walking out the lobby doors. I point to the monitor. "Can you follow him?"

Philip stops halfway across the courtyard in front of a blond man. He gives him a brief hug and pat on the back, then they chat for a few minutes. "Are we capturing everyone he has contact with?"

The security team manning the cameras nod.

"Have you seen him with this guy before?" His face is turned away from the cameras, but there's something about his mannerisms that's captured my attention.

The security guard on my left answers. "He usually meets him for lunch."

I lean forward. "Can you get closer?"

The guy looks to Jameson and Mateo, who both nod, and he taps the keys to zoom in on Carlton and his friend. The guy's head turns toward us for a brief second when he faces the wind and sweeps a hand through his hair.

"Son of a..." I whisper.

Mateo steps beside me. "What is it? That's Philip's son... I can't remember his name."

"David Perry. His name is David Perry. Damn. Thiago's gut was right. Austin wasn't a coincidence." I grit my teeth when I reveal his identity. "Who's the lackey? Philip or David? My money is on Philip. Solid, upstanding employee until his son enters the picture. If he's his son."

I turn to Mateo. "When did you meet David?"

He drags a hand through his unruly hair. "Officially, I met him at the pitch he and Philip gave us last year. It was for financial software of some sort. We could pull up the information if you want?"

I bite the inside of my cheek. "Maybe later. How many times do you think he's been here?"

"Here at SEI?" Mateo asks. He lifts a shoulder. "He's been here several times for lunch, but I haven't really spoken to him since the pitch."

"If they're close, we might be able to take both down at once," I remark, trying to think of how this could work. I've still got David's card with his number, although I wonder now if it's false. "I'm not sure yet, but let's keep it as an option on the table."

Jameson leans over. "When you figure it out, let me know. We'll make sure you have whatever you need. Let's get you both upstairs." He raises a hand and Mitch comes over, along with another guy... Russell, maybe?

They hold the service elevator for us, and we take it directly to the executive floor without stopping. Mateo pulls me into Grayson's office.

"What are we doing in here?"

"I've been avoiding the fourth floor and working from this office," Mateo informs me.

I glance at the digital frame on the wall and notice the NFT is different. He must have changed it. "What about Grayson? Is he working in here too?"

"I don't mind sharing," a smooth voice murmurs in my ear.

I whirl around and face the man who had me in such turmoil when I left. "Grayson." Without thinking too much about it, I launch myself into his arms and hug him tightly—the same way I did Mateo.

"Rose, you fucking scared the hell out of us," he mumbles into my hair.

"I can tell," I remark pointedly, the litany of curse words a sure sign of his worry. "It scared me, too. One second, she was standing in front of me smiling, and the next, she was gone. Then Thiago disappeared."

"Only because I had to," Thiago states softly from the doorway. He comes in and closes the door. "Only two good things came out of this trip—our deal with Epic Entertainment." Prowling toward me, he leans down and gives me a hard kiss on the lips. "And Henley and me."

He shakes his head in response to Mateo's silent question. "We'll all talk later. God, it's good to see you two, but we don't have time to visit. There's a lot to go over."

We move to the couch and chairs. "The meeting with the ATF went well. We crafted a solid cooperation message, and they're willing to be here to deliver it at our press conference tomorrow. In addition, they'll give an update on their investigation into Diego and his whereabouts." The three men exchange silent glances.

Thiago's face hardens. "They asked why I thought Diego might have wanted to murder Marcos. I told them we didn't know. Gave a bit of history of how he'd been a good friend growing up and a good employee until this point, how shocked we were when we saw the video, and we could only guess his motive was money. Make sure you stick to the same."

Mateo and Grayson both nod in agreement.

"Any updates while we were gone?" Thiago asks them.

"Party supplies are on board. Once we have a date, we'll need two days to get the food prepped and invitations delivered," Grayson replies.

"The fake bid is set up in the system. When we're ready, we need to schedule the live demonstration. Philip is aware something new is coming," Mateo adds.

"Oh, your gut was right... David Perry is in on this somehow," I exclaim. "We saw Philip Carlton and him chatting in the courtyard this morning. Mateo says Philip introduced David as his son during a pitch last year. Although who knows if that's true or a just a cover. If it is true... we might be able to use that information to catch them both."

Thiago winces and runs a hand over his head. "I completely forgot about Sterling's text when I got back last night. Totally slipped my mind." Reaching into his pocket, he pulls out his phone and relays the information on David. "Could he be your stalker, Henley? It was his mother's farmhouse."

The gut punch is brutal. It's one thing to think of David as a bad guy, but another to think he might know my stalker, or worse, helped him kidnap me.

"He's not my stalker. Too short. Wrong voice. I honestly thought he was the first victim of my stalker," I stammer. "David and I dated at MIT. I was crazy about him. Someone sent him videos of me and another guy. I tried to tell him it wasn't me, but he wouldn't listen and dumped me. Everything with my stalker snowballed after that point. He started sending me messages and videos of me on campus."

"He knew him," Grayson speculates. "But how well? Maybe Sterling can dig a little more into David's life at MIT and see if there is any indication of whether Philip is his father." He darts a look at Thiago, who replies to Sterling's text with Grayson's suggestions.

Thiago leans forward. "The press conference will be held at eleven a.m. tomorrow morning. Outside in the courtyard. We expect quite a big crowd. Jameson is calling in a few favors to make sure there aren't any incidents. All of us need to be there, including Henley."

Mateo folds his arms across his chest. "Henley doesn't need to go."

"I agree. Why in the world would you want her there... unless." Grayson's voice cracks and a look of disbelief takes over.

Mateo catches on quickly and jumps up. "Tell me you aren't intending to use her as bait!"

Thiago stares steadily at Mateo.

"No fucking way," Grayson interjects.

Mateo shakes his head. "What the hell are you thinking, Thiago? I can't believe you, of all people, would want to put her in danger."

Thiago jumps to his feet. "She's already in danger. You didn't see how quick it happened. Seconds. There was no time to react or protect her. If Melissa hadn't followed protocol and shielded

Henley's back…" His hand covers his eyes. "It was so fucking close."

He rolls his head around a few times to relieve some tension. "If she's standing with us at the press conference, it makes a powerful statement. It tells the world she's part of us and under our protection. But you're right, it also puts her in the target with us, but it could be the catalyst we need to bait one of our enemies… one of her enemies. He'll be watching." Thiago is confident Stanley the stalker will be watching the press conference.

"I'm not putting her in danger," Mateo roars, every bit as loud as Thiago.

"I've already agreed," I remark softly. Bait sounds like a worm on a hook without any choice in the matter, but I want to pull our enemies out of the shadows. It's preferable to a bullet from long distance. "Hiring snipers? Our enemy is escalating. We need to do everything we can to force them out into the open."

"And one of them is a woman," Thiago reveals to Grayson and Mateo, explaining about the burner phone he'd lifted from the guy he'd shot.

Thiago told me before we left Austin because he didn't want me to be blindsided. "It's the reason Mitch is my assigned bodyguard now instead of a woman."

Grayson runs a hand through his perfectly styled hair. "Fuck me. Do we have any clue who it might be? If Kira was alive, she'd have been number one on the list, but honestly, I can't think of a female who hates us enough to want to take us down."

Who's Kira? My eyes dart to Mateo, but he subtly shakes his head. Okay, then. "What happened to the guy after you shot him?"

Thiago clears his throat. "He's not surfacing any time soon, and the weapon's been returned to the security team for recycling."

"Well, that's handy," I reply. "Speaking of guns, I need one." I refuse to go anywhere without one now.

Grayson strolls to his desk and pulls out a pink box with roses on it. "We had Zane pick one up for you. It's a gift from us. We figured it would be better than flowers, especially right now."

I open the box to find a gun case with a Glock 19 in it. "Phew, based on the box, I was kind of afraid it would be pink. I'm all for pink, but I've already got that covered." I laugh and twirl a lock of my hair. "Thank you. I've missed having one with me." Taking it out of the case, I quickly load it and put it in my purse.

Thiago stands. "I've got to stay here and iron out the speech for tomorrow. Why don't you all head home?" He drops a kiss on my lips and strides out the door.

"I'm worried about him," I confide to Grayson and Mateo. "He thinks it's all on him to figure out how to atone for the deaths, protect us, and eliminate our enemies."

Mateo heaves a sigh. "He was the eldest, so Marcos made him second in command. When Marcos wasn't around, it was Thiago's job to be diligent and make sure we stayed safe. They would run escape plans once a month when we first moved to Miami. It eased when we got older, but with Marcos gone, he's automatically picked up the reins again," Mateo offers quietly.

"It's up to us to show him we're in this together," Grayson says determinedly. "Starting with the tomorrow's press conference."

CHAPTER 30

<u>GRAYSON</u>

Hearing the raw anguish in Thiago's voice when he explained how close Henley came to dying killed me. The sheer emotion he displayed told me more than words how he felt about it, too. I'd only heard that tone in his voice twice. When Mateo was shot, and when he told us Marcos had died.

I pace back and forth in my bedroom. Right after she left, I knew I'd been fooling myself, hiding from the truth. The house felt sad and empty without her here, and the resounding silence echoed inside me. I'd been alone in a crowd for a long time, but I've been hiding it from everyone. Until Henley. She makes me want more.

The need to spill everything and claim a spot by her side is making me crazy today. I take the stairs down to her office, but when I get there, I stop in the doorway. She's sitting on the couch with her head in her hands.

She lifts her head when I sit beside her. "Are you okay?"

"Just thinking about earlier," she states softly.

I clear my throat. "Me too. I need to talk to you. Tell you about Kira. She's a big reason I've had such a hard time with us. But not because of what you might think or know or don't know... I'm rambling. I need the ocean right now. Everything is in turmoil, and it's the only thing that helps me calm down. Come with me, and I'll tell you everything."

She fingers the jeans she's wearing. "Do I have a second to change?"

"Yes, of course," I reply. "Go, I'll wait for you."

She returns in a pair of running shorts and a t-shirt. Her feet are bare, and her hair is in a ponytail.

"Let's go," I say gruffly. The ocean better bring the magic today.

We see Mateo on our way out. "We're going for a walk on the beach. Dinner is in the oven. Listen for the timer, will you? All you need to do is pull it out of the oven and set it on the stove. That's it." I make a mental note to text him in thirty minutes to make sure dinner doesn't burn.

"I've got it," he assures me. "Go."

Henley and I walk down to the beach. When we get there, I stand in the water for a few minutes and stare at the roaring waves, each thunderous sound a testament to nature's power. Breathe in... and breathe out. A small hand on my back has me turning toward the woman at my side.

Her pink hair is whipping across her determined face, and she's staring at me, not the ocean. "Feeling better?"

"Yes," I state firmly. "The ocean is in my blood. It was the same for Marcos. Anytime either of us needed to escape life or the family, you would find us here or on one of my boats. When I was a kid, he'd jokingly search for gills and pretend he found them." I chuckle at the memory.

She laughs. "I can see it on your face. What the water does to you. It's like the cares of the world fall and the lines on your face smooth out. Want to sit or walk?"

I contemplate the question and decide to sit. "Let's move back from the water and sit here." About ten feet back from the waves, I plop down in the sand and bring her down beside me. "Are you comfortable?"

What if she hates me after she hears the story? Or worse, blames me? I clear my throat a couple of times. "I went away to a university in Texas. Kira and I met at a fraternity-sorority mixer, and it was pretty much love at first sight. For both of us. One date and we were joined at the hip from that moment. The whole first year of college was amazing."

I pause, thinking back to my freshmen year. Every single aspect of my life was perfect. "All of these new experiences, along with an incredibly fun and gorgeous girlfriend? It was heaven. Until it slowly started to tarnish. Being in a fraternity meant I met a lot of people, including a lot of girls. When we'd walk across campus, both guys and girls would come up to say hi, but Kira only noticed the girls."

I dig my fingers into the sand and scoop it up. "She started making snide comments about my behavior or the girls. If we were around my friends, she'd flirt with one of them to try and make me jealous. To be honest, I thought it was my fault. Maybe I was being too flirty. So, I went out of my way to compliment her, support her, and reassure her of my feelings. But no matter how many times I told her I wasn't interested in other girls, she didn't believe me."

I open my fingers and let the sand fall through the cracks between them. "Fraternities hold a lot of parties. A girl I knew from high school came to one of our parties. She seemed lost. I took her around and introduced her to everyone to help her. We talked a lot about home and high school. The usual stuff. It was completely friendly and platonic. Kira heard about it and went ballistic. We had a huge fight. It was the end of our sophomore year and the whole year had been filled with these jealous scenes. I couldn't take it anymore. For the first time, I refused to apologize for anything."

The sun begins to set. It's such a beautiful backdrop to this ugly story. "After the usual tears, silence, and threats didn't work, we broke up. A few days later, her mom calls me from the hospital to tell me she had taken a bottle of pills, but she would be okay. She asked if I was coming to get her, and I immediately went to the hospital. When I got there, she insisted it was all a big mistake. That she'd accidentally swallowed too many while she was drinking. It shook me. We started talking again, and by the end of the summer break, we were back together.

"The first semester of our junior year went by, and things were great. I even brought her home to meet my family for the holidays. Relieved, I thought we were past it all, and I loved her so much. She would tell me I didn't know how flirty I was being, and maybe she was right, and I was too flirty. She needed me to be better, so I started trying to do better. When we went back the next semester, we got an apartment. Most of the time, we stayed home together. I cut back on a lot of the fraternity stuff. There were a few incidences, but she made me feel they were my fault," I admit hoarsely. Even thinking about everything I did to change myself to accommodate her jealous tendencies makes me cringe.

I sign. "I didn't realize the overdose was the first in a vicious cycle of abuse and psychotic episodes. Even with the changes I'd made to my life, she couldn't stand it when I spoke to another girl. My friends tried to tell me it wasn't healthy, but I repeatedly brushed it off. She loved me and I loved her. I just needed to try harder."

I lay my head on my arms and stare at Henley. "Things came to a head the following summer. We fought, broke up. I moved out. The usual. But this time, I could see how much I'd changed to accommodate her. I'd isolated myself for her. I refused to return and wouldn't even speak to her. That's when things really escalated. She had some guy beat her up, threatened to kill herself, threatened to kill me, she chased down girls I spoke to on campus, and a ton of other shit. My entire senior year was fucking crazy."

Her knuckles are white where she's clinging to her knees, so I lace my fingers with hers and pull her hand into my lap. "Without telling anyone, I applied to Wharton's School of Business. Their master's degree program was exceptional, and more importantly, it was far away from Texas and her. Eager to get on with my life, I completed the accelerated program in a year, then moved back to Miami and joined SEI. For the next two years, I was either working or hunting for the next extreme sport to try. It worried Marcos to death, but he knew sometimes you had to fight your demons yourself.

"It's also when I started going on rescue missions with Zane. The first mission was bad. I was so green, I thought he would kill me himself," I admit with a chuckle. "It helped, though. Gave me back my sense of truth. After years of swallowing her lies and believing her account of things, I'd struggled with telling the truth from the lies."

She squeezes my hand. "You definitely got back all your super lie detector powers because you can always tell when I'm lying."

I tap her on the nose. "That's because you're a really, really bad liar."

She shrugs. I can tell she doesn't really care, and it makes me very, very happy.

"I rejoined the dating world, but it didn't go well. I found myself constantly scrutinizing my behavior to see if I was flirting too much, or worse, examining every word that came out of my date's mouth to see if she was lying. It was horrible."

My leg starts to cramp, and I stand to shake it off. "Want to walk?"

She eagerly nods and jumps up.

We head back to the water line to walk, splashing through the waves when they crest on the beach in front of us. "I ditched dating one on one and started going out in groups. Suddenly, all the pressure was off. It was fun. I was me again. My life felt like it was finally getting back on track. Then Kira showed up. Everywhere. No matter where I went, she found me."

I stare out into the water, searching for the words to tell her the last part. "One night, I lost it. Told her she was crazy, and the world would end before I'd ever go back to her. The next day, I went to the police for a restraining order. Two days later, I came home to my condo and found her dead on the bedroom floor. Blood everywhere. She'd slit her wrists." I don't tell Henley about the vitriolic note Kira left me. Nobody will ever see the ugliness she spewed in her final moments because I'd burned it immediately after reading it.

Her hand covers her mouth. "Oh no. I'm so sorry, Grayson."

She moves to hug me, and I stop her. "The worst part? I was relieved. Relieved," I yell. "What kind of person does that make me? This person I'd once loved so much was dead, on the floor in a pool of blood, and yet, I wanted to get down on my knees. I was so thankful she was gone."

She wraps her arms around me tightly. "Oh, Grayson. She abused you. Mentally and emotionally. Of course, you were relieved. When you're constantly battered by the same person, escape is the only thing that matters. When we hear stories of abuse, we always think it's the woman, but men are abused every day, too. She used your love to control and manipulate you. You didn't deserve it. Do you hear me? There is never a time when abuse is okay. Did you think I'd blame you?"

I tighten my arms. "Maybe. I don't know. As a man, it feels like I should have known better or been able to fight it, but I believed she was right, and I was wrong. At the end, it took everything in me to find myself again." I lean back and look her straight in the eye. "When I met you, I was immediately attracted to you, but I pushed it aside. Slowly, I started admiring the sheer guts you displayed in coming to Miami to hunt for Marcos' killer and the clever tactics you used to get the software."

I slip the errant strand of hair blowing in the wind behind her ear. "But it also made me angry. I didn't want to feel anything for anyone, and here you come along, and I'm intrigued, and I feel myself changing and wanting more. I tried to convince myself it was an infatuation. Until the night of the ball when you defended me. Me. I'd done nothing to deserve your defense, and yet you stood in front of everyone and passionately put that punk actor in his place." My breath hitches. "Then, the kiss. It broke me."

I lower my head until my lips are an inch above hers. "I've been fighting and fighting against us. Until yesterday. This entire time I've been worrying about the wrong thing—whether I could let another person in, give them—you—the power to hurt me, and trust it wouldn't end the same way as Kira. But the question I should have been asking is whether I could live without you. Last night, when Thiago told us what happened, things became crystal clear for me. I want this chance with you. More than anything, including my fears."

She moves her lips closer. "I know how hard it is to trust, and I'll do everything in my power to make sure you never regret it. I want us. And when you need space to breathe, tell me, it's yours," she says breathlessly. "Kiss me, Grayson."

With the sound of the ocean roaring in the background, I close the distance, unable to do anything else. Alive. In my life. It's enough. The rest will come with time and trust.

Her lips taste of sorrow and joy. I kiss her deeper, using the heat between us to burn away the ashes of the past. Since our kiss at the ball, I knew this thing between us had power, and I'd been fooling myself by calling it an infatuation. Drawing her in tighter, I kiss her until I can't feel anything but hope and her.

CHAPTER 31

<u>MATEO</u>

The lobby is filled with whispers and the sound of feet shuffling impatiently. Employees are crammed into every available space, waiting to hear the press conference. The emotions on their faces range from curiosity to fear, which is why we invited them to attend—to hear the words of assurance delivered with confidence from the man they look up to—Thiago.

The outside courtyard is packed as well. Members of the press rush to air opening remarks to audiences watching from home. Our PR team gives the five-minute warning, and reporters make their way to the seats we've assigned them. We learned long ago that it's better for us to control the press environment versus letting them push and shove their way into our faces.

Thiago strides out a side door with Jameson beside him. Security is thicker than usual with the extra men we brought in to control the crowds and keep us safe. I glance over at Henley. The big guy, Mitch, stands slightly in front of her, alert and ready. He'd better do his job well.

When Grayson and Henley returned from the beach last night, I knew he'd finally given up the battle he'd been waging with himself. A miracle. I'd been hoping he would cave, but the odds were stacked against me. Until I saw it, I wouldn't let myself believe it.

It took him years to recover from the number Kira did on him. He did it, but it changed him. To shake off the shackles of control, his motto became indulgence. Work hard, play even harder.

Until Henley. I chuckle softly.

Thiago pulls us together with a wave of his hand. Determination and confidence are the name of the game today. Adopting the casual confidence I project to the world, I stroll out SEI's front doors by his side, with Henley and Grayson following behind us. Along with a ton of security.

The press quiets the second Thiago stands at the podium. "Thank you all for coming today. We want to be as transparent as possible with the families, our employees, and the public. The bombing of our satellite office is a tragedy. Eight people lost their life that night. We lost two employees, Jason Peters, and Luis Hernandez, who worked security for SEI." The press starts murmuring to each other. "The remaining six people worked for other offices in the building. I'd like to take a moment of silence to recognize their loss and to pray for their families."

The sound dies for a few seconds while we take a moment to remember them. Memories of Marcos fill my mind. Some days, his absence hits harder than others.

"Thank you," he states solemnly. "We, the Santos family—not SEI—donated a million dollars to each family the day after the incident to help with their immediate needs. In addition, we started a fund for the victims and their families. Money received from friends, colleagues, and other businesses have been collected in the fund and it's at their disposal. If you would like to contribute, the information can be found on our website. This tragedy occurred at our building, and while we're not responsible, we're absolutely accountable. We embrace the role given to us because we have the power to help find the answers."

Hands shoot up in the air, but Thiago ignores them. "I know

some of you are wondering why we're only counting eight instead of the nine victims first reported. Marcos Santos was our uncle and friend. We initially thought his death was caused by the explosion. Unfortunately, that is not the case. The ATF has a video of his murder a few days before the incident."

The air explodes with shouts from the reporters.

Thiago holds up a hand. "Please direct all questions regarding the investigation to the ATF and the FBI. The ATF will join us shortly. They will only answer questions pertaining to the explosion. The FBI will be taking over the murder investigation of Marcos Santos."

"I'll take questions now," he informs them.

"If Marcos was murdered before the bombing, it seems to indicate this was a personal hit. Is that accurate? Can we use it as an official statement?" the reporter from the Miami Herald asks from the front row.

Thiago nods. "Based on the information given to us by the ATF, we believe this tragedy was a targeted hit against the Santos family, not SEI."

"Several employees have contacted our offices with concerns of safety. What are you doing to prevent further incidents?" she asks as a follow up.

"The safety of our employees is our number one priority, and if we believed for one minute they were in jeopardy, we'd shut down this office. As a precaution, we've brought in additional security and increased video surveillance of the entire office," Thiago informs them.

"What did Marcos Santos do for SEI?" a voice calls out in the back row.

Thiago turns his neck, but he can't see the person speaking. "Marcos led a lot of our technological advancements, from invention to execution."

A young man in the second row stands up. "The ATF is reporting Diego Gutierrez, the former head of SEI's security, as the primary suspect. Are any of you under investigation for the death of Marcos Santos?"

Thiago dips his chin to stare at him. "No, we're not."

The guy follows with another. "My source claims the video shows Diego Gutierrez murdering Marcos Santos. Have you seen the video? Is that correct?"

Thiago jerks his chin. "We have viewed the video, but until the ATF or FBI closes the investigation, we're not allowed to share any of the details."

A young woman stands up. "The Gutierrez family is denying any wrongdoing. They claim you are setting up Diego to take the fall. Is there any truth to that allegation?"

Thiago stills. "None. Diego Gutierrez was my friend and a trusted member of our executive team. We were devastated to learn of his involvement in the death of Marcos Santos."

A reporter from a local gossip rag stands. "Who is the young woman with you?" He winks at Henley, and I stiffen.

"Henley Night worked closely with Marcos. He was her colleague, friend, and mentor. During this time, in our shared grief, we've become close and consider her part of the Santos family now," Thiago states firmly.

He starts to ask another question, but Thiago gives him his "don't fuck with me" stare, and the man immediately sits down.

When there are no other questions for us, Thiago turns the podium over to the lead investigator for the ATF. A lady named Cassandra Stone.

She waves a hand toward us. "First, I want to thank the Santos family and SEI for their full cooperation in this investigation. This is a very difficult time for them personally, and yet, they've stepped up to give us full access to their staff, video surveillance, and any additional information we deemed necessary to conduct our investigation and pinpoint the suspect."

With a series of answers and non-answers, she quickly informs them Diego Gutierrez is the prime suspect in the bombing because of his involvement with the murder of Marcos Santos. The ATF believes the bomb was set to cover up the deed. They are unable to locate Diego Gutierrez at this time, but he's wanted for questioning in the bombing of the office building. If anyone has any knowledge of his whereabouts, they can call their Miami office. She cannot answer any questions on the murder investigation because it's been turned over to the FBI. At this time, there is not a warrant out for Diego Gutierrez.

The press conference comes to an end. Reporters race to get their closing thoughts on camera. Cassandra and her team leave immediately.

Thiago motions for us to return to the building. When he walks by Henley, he pulls her in front so he can shield her from behind. Grayson, in turn, shields Thiago, although he's unaware of it.

As I turn, an old man standing at the back of the crowd catches my eye. He's glaring at Thiago with eyes full of hate. Uneasy, I stop and grab Jameson's arm. "See that man in the back of the crowd?"

Someone steps between us, and when they move, he's gone.

"Let's inform the guys in the video control room. They'll bring up the footage and we'll see who it was," Jameson says immediately.

Our new security team is exactly why I'd fought so hard against Diego. Instead of bullies and thugs, we have professionals and state-of-the-art security.

"Let's check it out," I urge him.

When we get inside, I motion to Henley and explain where we're going.

She turns back to Thiago and informs him she's going to the security room with me. He frowns and raises a single eyebrow.

"Thought I saw something in the crowd. We're going to pull up the footage," I inform him. The crowd of employees are waiting for the Q&A session he promised in order to answer their questions. "Go. We'll let you know if we find anything."

When we get to the control room, it's a hive of activity. They're checking the faces in the crowd for David and anyone looking suspicious or out of place.

I stand behind one of the tech guys and point out the area where I saw the man. Sure enough. He was standing there the whole time. To my surprise, he's the one who asked the question about Marcos' role at SEI.

They pull his face from the camera to run a facial recognition search on him.

"Pull his fingerprint, too," Henley suggests. "Sometimes people use software or a disruptor to obscure their features from the cameras. They forget about their fingerprints, though. With the level of detail your video picks up here, we might be lucky enough to zoom in and capture it."

"Good idea," he remarks. He taps the keys to get closer and when the man raises his hand to ask the question, we're able to capture the print from his right forefinger. It's not the only thing we see, though.

Henley leans in closer. "Are there a bunch of numbers on his hand?"

The guy sharpens the image and cuts in closer.

"It's a phone number with the country code +55," the guy says, quickly grabbing a piece of paper and writing it down. "We'll run the number, too." He jumps up and runs over to a guy at a nearby computer and hands him the number.

He comes back a few minutes later. "Burner phone. What do you want to do?"

Jameson comes over. "Call it."

The guy dials the number. A gravelly older voice picks up. "Have Thiago call me. 011 55 11 3310 9976." He hangs up.

"Merda!" I say, grabbing the number and Henley's hand. I motion for Jameson to stay. "I'll take care of this."

"Do you know who it is?" Henley asks breathlessly when we enter the elevator.

"I think it's Thiago's father," I return with a groan.

CHAPTER 32

<u>THIAGO</u>

Twenty-five years is not enough time. Whatever the bastard wants, I can guarantee it's not going to be sunshine and roses. Money probably. Regardless, it's the last thing we need right now. Grabbing the burner phone, I dial.

He picks up on the first ring.

"Meu filho, back from the grave," he drawls in his signature gravelly voice.

It's cold and brutal, like the harshest of winter days, and brings back so many memories. Not the good kind either.

"A morte não me quis," I remark sarcastically, telling him death didn't want me.

"Death is truly capricious," he returns. "But fortuitous, too. Meet me at your private hangar. Thirty minutes. Come alone." He hangs up.

I relay the information to the three sitting in front of me, who immediately protest the meeting.

"He's a wily old bastard, but I'll be fine. He wants something, and he can't get it if I'm dead."

"No," Henley states firmly. "This could be a trap. What if he's the enemy?" She throws her hands up in the air. "If you go without your security team, then you open the door for us to leave without ours. Which is it? Leave them here or take them with you?" She crosses her arms across her chest, waiting for me to decide.

The sight of her passionate blue eyes staring me down stirs certain parts of me, but I tamp it down. Leaving without our security is non-negotiable for all of us. She's right. Damn it. "I'll take Thomas and one other."

"Mitch," she says immediately.

The big guy will be seen as an immediate threat. "No."

Mateo holds up a finger. "Allison Engles. She's the lead for SEI's security, including the hangar. Her military background is impressive. And, most importantly, your father will not see her as a threat."

Good call. I pick up the phone. "Jameson, are Thomas and Allison on duty? Have them meet me in the lobby in five. Thanks."

The phone rings.

Mateo notices the caller's identity and arches a brow.

I shake my head, not wanting to discuss it right now and silence the ringer.

They all three share a glance. Wonder what that's all about? Is there something else going on? I sigh.

"Head home, and I'll meet you there when I'm done," I advise them.

The phone rings in my hand. "Sterling, I'm on my way out the door. Can this wait?"

He spews a ton of information at me, but my brain can't get past the fact that I'm meeting with my father in twenty minutes. Merda! I've got to go. Running a hand over my face, I try to find my focus.

"Sterling... I know this is important, but I can't talk right now. I—"

The phone is taken out of my hand. "Sterling, Grayson. Call me. I'll be taking point on Henley's stalker." He pauses. "Yep, that too. Great. Give me five minutes." Hanging up, he tosses me the phone.

"Go! What are you waiting on? I'll take care of things with Zane and his team."

I hesitate. It's my job to manage these things, not Grayson's. I don't have time to debate, though. Scooping up both phones, I give Henley a hard kiss and head out.

Allison and Thomas are waiting in the lobby. We load up the SUV and head out. How do I explain my father? Nobody knows we fled to America and took a different last name, and I don't want the information to get out.

The only reason I'm meeting with my father is because he could make our lives extremely complicated. "Marcos' picture drew my father here. We haven't spoken in twenty-five years, but the reason I need you on alert is he works for the cartel. He's pretty high up—their accountant, in fact. The exterior might look like a weak old man, but inside he's pure evil. Don't underestimate him."

Ten minutes later, we screech to a halt outside SEI's private hangar. A small jet is waiting nearby. "Ready?"

We get out and head toward the jet. An old man appears at the top of the stairs. "I told you to come alone."

The voice stops me cold. "The years haven't been kind to you, have they?" I smile maliciously. "And I don't answer to you. If you don't like them here, we can leave."

He's silent for a second. "Fine. They stay on the ground."

"Door stays open. One stands at the top of the stairs." I spit out my own conditions. Henley's right. This isn't the time to be lax.

Instead of answering, he jerks his head.

I head up. Thomas follows but stops at the entrance. He pulls his weapon out and holds it ready.

The plane is empty except for my father. "Where are your guards?"

"I sent them to get dinner. Their loyalty is to Paulo," he states, with an offhanded shrug.

Paulo Costa Fontes, the leader of the cartel and my father's boss. I smirk. "I know you're not here for a reunion. What do you want?"

He chuckles. "To the point. I like it. I need an exit plan, and you're going to help me."

My brow furrows. He wants an exit plan from the cartel? Fuck, that's the last thing I expected to hear. "What can I do?"

He gives me a wry look. "It's simple. You have the means to fake my death and put me on a plane. Not too much to ask after all this time, right?"

"Why should I?"

His eyes gleam from the volley between us. "If you don't, I'll bring everything down on top of you. Imagine everyone's shock when they find out the CEO of SEI is an illegal immigrant. Oh, and let's not forget about Mateo. Marcos, too, although he's dead. A pity."

I lunge for his shirt and jerk him up. "Don't you ever say their names. None of them. Got it?"

The need to remove this threat is tearing a hole in my gut, but if I kill him, the cartel will come down on us like a ton of bricks. If I help him escape and they find out, they'll kill me. Somewhere in the middle is the answer I need, but what?

He smirks, knowing he's got me over a barrel. "Is that a yes? In two days, I want to be on a plane to a destination of my choice."

"Two days is impossible. We need four days," I insist.

"Three. Final terms," he retorts. His dark eyes gleam with satisfaction and victory.

"Fine. Three," I tell him. "Remember, you have as much to lose as I do. I'll be in touch. Same number?"

"I wouldn't be so sure about that," he replies with a laugh. "Same number. And Thiago—someone will be watching you and your pink-haired girlfriend."

"Fuck you," I snap, and head off the plane. "Let's go. We'll drop Allison off and pick up the rest of my security for tonight. Then home."

———

224

THE HOUSE IS in an uproar when I walk in the door. Zane, Sterling, and Raider are here. Henley's staring down at the kitchen island. Her face is furious and swollen from crying. What the hell is going on now?

When I get closer, several photographs are spread out over the surface. A pretty blonde woman laughs at the camera in a couple of them, but the rest are sick. Documented torture. The pressure builds behind my neck.

Henley looks up and meets my eyes. She hurls herself into my arms. "It's all my fault. I brought him home, and he killed her." She sobs, pointing to the images.

Jerking out of my arms, she paces rapidly around the island, unable to take her eyes off the pictures. "It wasn't enough for him to take her out. He was angry at me for escaping the night before, and he took it out on her. He tortured her. I can't... I can't breathe. Oh God. Why? Why did he do this to her? She never hurt a fly." Her breaths are coming quicker and quicker.

I grab her by the arms. "Deep breath in. Come on, you can do it. Breathe in, Henley." She draws a shaky breath. "And out. That's it. Again."

Raider comes over. "He would have done this for the sheer pleasure of it. Nothing you did would have caused or prevented it. It was a move in the game he was playing. The goal was to isolate you. He succeeded. Memorize these images. Use them to burn away the fear."

She eases out of my arms and tilts her head to study him. While the tears still flow, something he said resonated in her. Her chin lifts, and she returns to the photos, but with an air of purpose this time.

Grayson comes up to stand by me, his eyes glued to Henley and filled with... emotion.

When did that happen? Are they both involved with her? My gut tightens. Jealousy rushes over me like a wave, and I stagger.

"The sick bastard tortured her mother," Grayson murmurs. "The photographs were in an envelope on our front gate, along with a blonde barbie doll hanging from a rope."

225

"The press conference must have pissed him off," Mateo rasps.

Henley raises her head. "Maybe we should keep pushing him. This is the first sign of impulsiveness I've seen him exhibit. Everything he's done to this point has been meticulously planned."

We need him to show himself and act recklessly. "I agree. We'll go out and take pictures and I'll have my contact at the Miami Herald put them in the paper. Might as well make a big splash, right?"

She looks startled for a second, but then a fierce smile takes over. "Absolutely."

This day has been hellishly long and brutal, and the hits keep on coming. I stride over to the bar and pour myself a bourbon. My eyes close while I take a minute to regroup.

"Got one of those for me?" Zane asks beside me.

Pouring one for him, I stand there looking down in my glass. The deck is getting higher. How can I keep it all from falling on top of us? There's got to be a way. I'm just not seeing it yet.

"You look like hell," Zane grumbles. "We need to pull everyone together and get a game plan here. Do you want to or should I?"

I down the rest of the drink. With a flick of my hand, I catch Mateo's eye and motion for him to bring Henley into the living room. "Grayson."

Zane pulls in his team, but none of them sit.

Grayson walks up. "Why don't we each give an update?"

I move back to the bourbon and pour a second glass.

"Sterling was able to confirm David is Philip's son, which means there might be a way to leverage the information and trap them both. We'll work on a plan and let you know," Grayson states firmly. "He couldn't find much about David's life at MIT, or his friends, but he did discover—through Henley—that David often helped Dr. Langford's grad assistant, Aaron. It was he who introduced David to Henley. We're trying to track him down, as well as Dr. Langford. It could be a dead end, but it's worth tracking every lead to get this fucker."

"When Mateo and I used the rootkit to access our enemy's

computer, we found a lot of code solutions and papers written by Dr. Langford's students. I checked with the authors, and none of them were stolen. A few people were disturbed by the enhancements made to alter the code for less noble purposes, but it's all perfectly legal," Henley says, bringing us up to date. "Aaron is tall enough to be my stalker, but for some reason, I can't picture it. That's all I have for an update tonight."

Mateo leans forward to speak directly to me. "Maria Gutierrez will not be calling you anymore."

I cross my arms over my chest. "What did you say to her?"

"I told her we have proof Diego's been taking bribes from our enemies for the last five years, and if we turn the information over to the government, they will come in and seize her house and all her assets," Mateo replies in a hard voice. "As his wife, she had to have known something was going on given the significant amount of money in their joint account. I told her we wouldn't turn over our evidence unless it was necessary. She got the point."

A weight lifts from my shoulders. When I'd spoken to Maria, she'd been screaming about a lawsuit against SEI. While I don't think it would have gone anywhere legally, the additional publicity would have been a nightmare.

"What did your father say?" Henley asks quietly.

"We have three days to stage his death and pull together an exit plan," I say, tiredly. When is this all going to end? "If not, he'll tear us down and take SEI with it."

"How can he do that?" Henley asks with a puzzled expression on her face.

"We're illegal immigrants. If anyone found out, it would open a huge can of worms and could give the government a foothold into SEI. Plus, it would kill our credibility," I explain. "Any ideas?"

"Turn him in," Raider inserts smoothly. "Let Paulo Costa Fontes take out the trash."

"How do we get to Paulo?"

"I know him," Raider reveals. "I can set something up. Immediately. It would be a huge show of good faith if we went to him first."

"My father's got eyes on me. If I disappear for a day, who knows what he'll do? It's too risky," I say with a frustrated sigh. "Any other ideas?"

"I'll go," Mateo interjects.

"No, I'm not sending you into the lion's den," I retort.

"It's our best shot. I'll go to Brazil with Raider. You set up the accident and get his death listed in the paper," Mateo insists.

I slide my gaze to Raider, and he nods.

I hate not being able to handle this myself, especially since Mateo's not experienced in dealing with dangerous situations. Grayson could handle himself, but he speaks very little Portuguese. If Raider wasn't going, it would be a no go, but I know he'll get him out alive. "Okay, but any sign of danger and you're out. Got it?" I tell Mateo.

He smiles at Henley. "Oh, believe me, I won't take any chances." His lips buzz her mouth.

"How much money does he need?" Henley asks suddenly.

"It's the one thing he didn't ask for," I reply with a grimace. Wait a minute. It hits like a ton of bricks. He needs an exit plan but not money? "When I was a kid, they caught him stealing. Once a thief, always a thief?"

"I'll work with Jameson's team to see if they came up with any aliases using the facial recognition or the fingerprint scan. If he's hiding something, he's likely not doing it under his own name," Henley points out.

With her past, she would know.

Zane clears his throat. "Sterling's going to Mexico to help Cruz set up some surveillance. The mission is turning into something bigger than we thought. He'll be back in time for the yacht party, but our time in Miami is limited. We can give you another week or so, but we can't leave Cruz hanging. You understand, right?" Zane looks at me steadily.

I walk over and clap him on the back. "You've got to take care of your family," I assure him. "We appreciate any time you can give us. Let me know if we can help."

228

He shakes my hand. "You're a good man, Thiago. Take after Marcos." With a few goodbyes, they head out.

I look at Grayson and Mateo with new eyes. I've been protecting them all my life, making sure they had everything they needed while simultaneously taking care of anything life threw at us. Tonight, they picked up the reins beside me. The burden of guilt I've been carrying all my life eases. Maybe I don't have to take on everything.

Mateo stands up and comes over to me. "Are you okay? I know you've been preparing your whole life for the day when he would come. I understand it now. He looked like an evil old man, but I'd say his days are numbered. One way or another."

Surprised, I contemplate his words. He's right. These are his last days. "Are you sure you want to go down there? It's incredibly dangerous."

Mateo smiles grimly. "I'm proud to be able to finally do something for you and our family. It's about time, don't you think? We've got your back, Thiago." He points to Grayson, Henley, and himself. "And remember, I have years of martial arts under my belt, but more than that, I have the greatest weapon of all."

"Raider," Mateo and I say at the same time.

The fact he knows Paulo Costa Fontes is telling.

"Take care of her while I'm gone," Mateo orders me. He gives me a tight hug, then grabs Henley's hand and pulls her along to help him pack.

Once all this is done, we need to figure out how this relationship with Henley is going to go. Can we all live here together, or is it asking too much?

CHAPTER 33

T hiago's not in his office at SEI when I drop by. I text him and he replies with an order to stay put. I snort. The man needs to learn how to ask instead of dictating all the time. Thiago's office is sparse and boring. Unlike Grayson's, there isn't one personal item in this room. With a sigh, I lay the photographs I'm carrying on the pristine glass coffee table and drop onto the leather couch.

Mmm, this couch is so comfortable.

Lips caress mine, slowly waking me from my nap. I blink. Thiago chuckles. "You seem to have a thing for my couches."

I blush. "Good nap couches," I reply.

"Hmm, good for a lot more than a nap," he teases. "Although I haven't tested it out myself. Maybe we should take advantage of this rare moment of quiet." He continues to place kisses on my neck and by my ear.

The offer is so tempting, but when I find myself sliding farther down into the couch, I stop and groan. "We need to talk about your father."

He jerks up. "That's a mood killer." He sweeps his hair back with his hand and straightens his jacket. "What have you got?"

"Jameson's team is good, really good, and they have legal access to a few areas I don't. We might have found your leverage," I tell him, spreading out the three photographs on the table. "This is Ronaldo Hernandez Silva. Your father." I point to the second image of a man in a beard wearing a Panama hat. "This is Roberto Costa Fontes. I'm assuming the cartel makes him travel with that alias when he's doing business for them." I point to the third photo, where it shows a man with a cane wearing a New York Yankees hat and polo shirt. "Meet Ron Silva from New York City, who goes to Switzerland every three years for vacation."

"Based on the patterns, our guess is he travels to Africa to exchange money for diamonds on behalf of the cartel. On his way back, he detours to Switzerland to put the diamonds in his boss' account. While he's there, he makes a separate deposit of his own. Based on the bank footage, he enters and leaves the bank by himself. The bodyguards wait outside," she explains.

"He keeps his account in the same bank?" Thiago questions, disbelief ringing in his voice.

"An account and a safety deposit box. The bank offers a key safekeeping service. When the customer needs to get into the box, they give them the key and at the end of the visit, the customer gives it back. This is a huge benefit for your father because it means he doesn't have to carry the keys to his box which would be highly suspicious if Paulo or his men found them.

"They keep a pretty close eye on him during these trips. Every time we caught footage of him in the airport, two men were with him," I respond, and hand him the piece of paper I brought with me. "Here's his account number for the first Switzerland bank and the deposit box number. The balance is around a million dollars. I don't know what is in the box."

"First bank?"

I shake my head. "I was curious when we found the third identity. When he returns as Ron Silva, he removes the contents from the safety deposit box, liquidates the diamonds, and deposits the money in a second bank account. It's smart. If Paulo ever suspected him, he could legitimately claim the first account as personal savings or something." I hand him the paper with the second account. "The balance is close to twenty million in this account."

Thiago stares at it for a couple of minutes. I assume he's thinking through the options. He dials Mateo and gives him the information to share with Paulo, but not the account numbers. They're leverage.

Mateo informs him the meeting is set for this afternoon. If all goes well, he and Raider will travel back tonight.

Thiago calls his father next. "I need your DNA—blood and hair, at least. Courier it to my office by end of day." He hangs up. "Hopefully, this buys us some time. If not, it will be available if I need to go through with staging his death."

The air is thick with tension.

"Let's get out of here," he suggests.

"Where to?"

"Have you been to Little Havana yet?" he asks with a smile on his face.

Alarmed, I don't know what to say. "Havana, Cuba?"

"No. Little Havana in Miami. You're in for a treat," he assures me with a carefree grin. "Let me change and we'll go." He goes to the wall of cabinets by his desk and opens it to reveal a rack full of clothes.

"Wow, you have a closet in your office?" I get up and stroll over. Suits, button-down shirts, polo shirts, a tuxedo, and other assorted clothes hang neatly together.

He reaches past me to grab a pair of jeans and a black t-shirt.

When he whips off his suit jacket, I realize he's going to change right here. I lean against the cabinet to watch every second of his unintentional strip tease—but really, I'm waiting for him to get down to those sexy boxer briefs that show off his incredible assets.

When they're finally revealed, I bite my bottom lip to hold back any potential sounds of admiration that might come bursting out of my mouth right now. This man's legs are unbelievable.

His eyes dart to mine and widen. "If you keep looking at me like that, we won't get farther than the couch."

My gaze slides to the couch. It's comfortable. And I already know it works really, really well for all kinds of positions.

He grabs my hand. "Stop. We're running away for a couple of hours. Get with the program, Night."

I laugh. "Fine, fine. You'd better make it up to me, though."

His hand caresses my butt. "It will be my pleasure."

———

LITTLE HAVANA IS AMAZING. Riotous color is everywhere... from the walls to the windows to the roosters. Yep. The vibrantly painted statues are everywhere. Apparently, roosters are a symbol of strength and power.

We stroll down the sidewalk, peering into shops. The only time we stop is to watch the Masters Cigar Rollers roll cigars by hand in the store windows. It's incredibly meticulous work and mesmerizing to watch.

Both of us had eaten lunch earlier, so we grab coffees, a piece of caramel flan, and a guava and cream cheese pie and take it to the park. Every square inch is packed with people, but we manage to squeeze ourselves into two seats by a group of older men playing dominos.

Thiago's face is completely relaxed. "I can't remember the last time I took a couple of hours off in the middle of the afternoon."

I reach over and slide my hand into his larger one. It engulfs mine. Entwining our fingers, I play with them while we eat. "In the last five years, the only time I spent outdoors is on my runs. On my way down to Miami, I smelled the ocean and saw the waves, and couldn't stop myself from finding a place to eat by the water. It was the first time I'd eaten out in public in years." I wave my other hand. "Now look at me. Out here, walking around the streets of Little Havana, with a handsome man at my side. What a leap."

He slips a bite of the flan between my lips. "Actually, five men at your side, but who's counting?" His mouth twitches with the laughter he's holding inside.

I slide my eyes to Mitch, but he's not even looking at me. "I don't see anyone but you," I drawl in my best Southern voice and flutter my eyelashes.

The phone rings. It's Mateo. My stomach cramps with nerves.

———

PAULO COSTA FONTES insists on flying home with Raider and Mateo on SEI's private jet. With a contingency of guards, of course. He feels it's important to attend Ronaldo's sendoff personally. Plus, he needs to pick up the jet Ronaldo used to get to Miami.

Everything is going down tomorrow night.

Our Little Havana outing is cut short, and we head back to the office.

On the way, he calls his contact at the Miami Herald. "I need a favor. Would you mind coming to my office?"

When he hangs up, I turn and face him. "I assume we'll want to give Paulo the money your father stole from the cartel?"

Thiago's brow furrows. "I didn't think about it, but yes."

"Your father has two-factor authentication set up on his account. I can view the information in the account without triggering it, but to access it and change the password, it will require the security code," I explain to him. "He'll receive the code as a text on his phone."

"Which means changing the passwords to give Paulo access will have to be done at the last minute and you'll have to be there," he summarizes the dilemma. "Damn it. I didn't want you anywhere near the airport." A slew of curse words in English and Portuguese leave his mouth.

We're making the exchange at the hangar. Logically, it makes sense for Ronaldo to be hopping on a plane after his "death", but it also allows Paulo and his men to leave on their jet without the US government ever knowing they were here.

"Are you sure Mateo can't do it?" His voice is raw when he asks.

"My program," I quip, refusing to add any emotion to the already charged atmosphere. "It will be fine."

He reaches over and grips my chin. "I hate putting you in this position. And I don't care if you've done it in the past. It wasn't for me."

"Hmm, I could say the same about Austin. Remember the shooter?" I don't say anything else knowing he'll get the point. "We'll do whatever it takes to come out of this alive and on the other side."

A glint of admiration and heat shimmers in his eyes. "You're right." Hard lips plant a kiss on my mouth. "Let's go."

The rest of the afternoon is spent crafting an article for the fake paper we're printing. It takes thirty minutes to craft a story and add realistic images to it. The reporter also brought a ton of stories and ads from the past in an electronic format we can use to create realistic pages. Thankfully, It's only the front-page section—a few pages—but it's still a lot of work to add the advertisements and stories. In exchange for helping us create it, the reporter gets exclusive access to the yacht party.

He hands us a piece of paper with the address of the printer they use for the Miami Herald. Details matter when you're trying to con someone.

Dan, Thiago's contact, gets up to leave a few hours later. He pauses and wags a finger between us. "Any chance I can get a pic of the two of you? A bit for the gossip column? It could net me a favor for the future."

Thinking of our Idea last night, we both nod.

I hold up a finger. "Why don't we take it outside in the courtyard? It would look less staged. Like we were saying goodbye or greeting each other."

Dan's face lights up. "Great idea!"

We inform the security team, and they secure the outside for a few minutes. Thiago pulls me into his body and bends his head toward me. I grip his biceps and raise my chin. For a minute, we stand there staring at each other.

"Fantastic!" Dan shouts. "You two are fire. Thanks a lot." He packs up. "I'll be on the lookout for my invite to the party."

I turn back to Thiago. "We need to get to the printer. Let's go."

"Just a second," he rasps. His lips descend on mine, and he gives me a deep, very thorough kiss. "Now we can go."

Dazed, I look up at him and wonder where all this is coming from. It's not like him to be spontaneous. "Lead on."

Thiago gives the printer a substantial incentive to print several copies of the newspaper for us. We want it to look like a stack instead of a single copy.

It comes out perfect. I sigh with relief. "This was the last item, right? Zane and his team are ready. The other SEI jet has been moved to the hangar. I've got everything set up on this extra laptop to make the changes to the accounts. The only thing left to do is call your father. Why don't we head home to eat with Grayson? You can call after dinner."

He rolls his shoulders to ease the tension. "Maybe after dinner and a session on the bag. Let's go home."

CHAPTER 34

"It's done. The accident is set for tomorrow. Heart attack while driving. Natural causes. Documentation with your real name is in the vehicle, along with your DNA. Once it happens, I'll go down and identify your body and sign off on the cremation. I'll let my press contact know a friend of the family was killed, and he'll get it in the paper," I calmly lay out the plan for the death he wants so badly.

"Very good. I always knew you were a smart boy," he jokes. "And the exit?"

"Tomorrow night. Eight p.m. at SEI's hangar. The jet will be ready. You can give them the flight plan once you're on board."

"I'll be there," he says, hanging up.

A second later, a text comes in from an unknown number. It's a picture of me kissing Henley in the courtyard. "Don't fuck me over or you'll regret it."

I toss the phone down on the mat, pick up my gloves, and go to town on the heavy bag. Every time my fists hit the bag, I picture his bony face smashing into his skull. Repeatedly. By the time I'm done, he's a bloody, unrecognizable pulp, and I'm drenched in sweat.

With a loud groan, I bend over and pick up my phone. There's a text from Henley telling me goodnight. Startled, I glance at the time in the upper left corner of my phone. Eleven p.m. No wonder my body hurts. I'd been whaling on the bag for two hours.

The hot shower eases the soreness and tension in my muscles.

Is she sleeping with Grayson tonight, or is she alone in her room? For once, the thought of her with someone else doesn't punch me in the gut, but the need to hold her in my arms is making me ache, and not just physically. I want her in my bed tonight. A twist of the knob and I step out of the shower.

Drying off, I wrap the towel around my hips and stalk from my bathroom to her bed. She's sitting up in bed with the iPad in front of her, watching a movie. Without saying a word, I throw the covers back and pick her up.

"I need you in my bed tonight."

She wraps one arm around me, but the serious expression on her face makes me pause. "I don't know. Are you prepared to pay up?"

"In spades," I murmur, walking across to my room to put her in my bed. I toss the iPad onto the nightstand and pull off my towel.

She glances between my legs and licks her lips. "It looks like you started without me." Her hand reaches out to take my semi-hard cock in her hand.

My hips automatically push into her grip, needing to feel her holding me tightly. I wrap my hand around hers. "Tighter."

She grips it more firmly, and I watch her face while she watches our hands move up and down on my cock. She inches closer, and desire rips across her face. My cock goes from hard to steel in seconds.

Her teeth nibble on her bottom lip. "Should I go faster?"

"No," I reply huskily. Sliding her hand off my cock, I lay it on the bed beside her. "Let's get rid of this, shall we?" My fingers grasp the hem of her shirt and pull it off, only to find she's naked underneath. I look at her in surprise.

She blushes. "I was hoping."

I lie down beside her and look her in the eyes. Smoothing my hand down her body, I take a few minutes to enjoy the feel of her soft skin. "You never have to hope. If you want me, tell me—words or actions. Unless I'm sick or dying, I promise, I want you. Got it?"

"Yes," she breathes out. Her hand slides between us to grip me again. "I want to touch you tonight."

I close my eyes, sending a silent thank you to the universe. Sliding my hands under her, I roll over until she's on top of me. "I'm all yours."

Her leg slides across my body and she pulls herself up to sit on my lap. Sweeping her pink hair to the side, she bends down and places her lips on mine. Instead of the deep kiss like I expect, her lips and tongue explore mine with light, nibbling kisses and shallow thrusts. If I try to take it deeper, she backs off. Her tongue slides against mine, sucking lightly, before releasing it with a sigh.

It's driving me crazy. The need to take over and dive into the kiss makes my hands clench, but I continue to hold myself back.

Finally, her lips quit torturing mine and move on.

The tip of her nose glides up my neck while she inhales. "I love the way you smell," she whispers in my ear.

Goosebumps break out on my arms. "You're going to push me to my limits, aren't you?"

She sits up, and the movement makes us slide against each other.

Moans escape both of us.

Her hands glide over my upper body, lightly exploring every inch.

"Maybe." She gasps, then slides down before bending over to lick the groove along my abs. "I've been wanting to do this since the first time I saw you without a shirt. Let's count them. One." She licks the next groove. "Two."

Beads of sweat break out.

"Three." Her voice is muffled the lower she gets. "Four." She starts back at the top and counts down on the other side. "Mmm, I love all your muscles."

I look down and see the mischievous expression on her face. "Is it my turn yet?"

She rocks back and forth above me, causing her hard nipples to slide against my cock.

I lift my hips and angle it down the center of her cleavage. "I love seeing my cock cradled between your tits."

Her chin jerks down to look at us, then shifts back to me.

"Push them together," I plead, wanting her softness wrapped around me.

She pushes in from the sides. "Like this?"

"Fuck," I return. "Yes, just like that, sweetheart."

She rocks slowly back and forth, but her grin tells me she knows the light touch is only making me crazy. "How about this?"

I swivel my hips until I'm pulling in the opposite direction. A drop of cum leaks out.

She stops, and I grit my teeth. Why did I give her full reign?

Swooping, she licks the drop from the tip, and my cock jumps in response.

"Beautiful," she murmurs.

Opening her mouth, she takes me fully inside, and I arch my hips to encourage her to take me all the way in. Her tongue curls around the head, teasing its sensitive spot, and I can't help the small thrust to go deeper.

Breathing out, she slides me into her throat until she's more than halfway down, then sucks. Her mouth sets up a steady rhythm and swear words spill from my lips. The delicate touch holds me completely in her control.

My fingers grip the sheets. "Enough." I watch her pink lips compress when she pulls my cock out of her mouth. "It's my turn."

"You don't get a turn tonight," she huskily informs me, moving up my body to settle on my lap. "I can't wait," she admits, and slides over me, letting me feel her wetness. Rising up, she positions me beneath her, then lowers her body down onto mine.

I surge up, burying myself to the hilt.

She moans and grinds down on top of me.

Her eyes glitter with desire, and little breaths escape each time she moves up and down.

"God, Thiago, I needed you inside me," she says breathlessly while she rides me.

Fuck, she looks so damn beautiful, but this pace is killing me tonight. I slip my hand down between us and stroke her. Slowly at first, I gradually speed up and her hips follow. Her body tightens and I grind my jaw, trying to hold on. When I think she's close, I pinch. The second her body clenches mine, I rise and flip us over. Driving hard and fast, I get the friction I need. My cock swells, and I come hard inside her.

Breathing heavily, I give us a minute to recover, then pull out. "Hold on, I'll get us a towel."

After cleaning us up, I climb into bed and pull her in my arms. "You're amazing and I fucking love seeing you in my bed." Her body relaxes beside mine and within minutes, she's asleep.

I needed this—her in my arms tonight. Reminding me of what's at stake tomorrow. Everyone I care about is going to be in that hangar. I send a little prayer to Marcos, asking him to help me keep everyone safe, then I run through every detail over and over in my mind.

CHAPTER 35

HENLEY

The jet carrying Mateo, Raider, and Paulo, along with their security, arrives around five p.m. Paulo Costa Fontes, one of the most powerful drug lords in the world, is a surprisingly handsome man with a strong jaw, dark hair, and the darkest of eyes. His wide shoulders and lean waist are similar to Grayson's. But the similarities end when I look into his eyes. Cold, determined, lethal. Not predatory like Thiago's. Lethal—they remind me of Raider's eyes. Different color, same death stare.

Thiago reluctantly introduces me to Paulo.

"Olá, so you are the one who found the thief in my kingdom," he remarks softly.

"I'm the one who found your money, but the thief was already there," I remark lightly. I open my laptop and show him the three identities and explain the trail I followed. "I'm not able to access the safe deposit box, but maybe you will find a Ron Silva somewhere to help you." It's the closest thing to telling him to send someone in using a fake identity. Or he could bribe someone. There are options. "For the two accounts, there's roughly twenty-one million dollars in

242

SAVAGE RUIN

them. Once I change the password, you'll have everything you need to electronically transfer the money to your accounts."

"Thank you. You're quite talented. Would you be interested in taking on a client?" he inserts the question smoothly.

"Thank you for the offer, but I'm retired. Trying to stay clean, you know?" I quip.

The stern mouth lifts in amusement, but before I can blink, it's gone. "I wish you the best of luck."

Zane and Raider come over to ask Paulo if he'd like to see the surveillance they set up.

"No surveillance. Shut it off," he says adamantly. "I'll listen with my own ears. What is the security team wearing?"

Zane points to himself. "Black fatigues, t-shirt."

Paulo snaps his fingers, and his shadow steps forward. Pointing to Zane's outfit, he orders him to purchase the same.

Raider stops him. "I've got an extra set with me. Or you can order from the supply store about twenty minutes away and your team can pick it up."

The shadow whispers in his ear, but Paulo waves him off. "I'll take the set, thank you. My men have camouflage, but they'll stay with the team outside where they won't be noticed in the dark."

Raider shrugs. "Let me get them."

Without the surveillance, there seems little to do while we wait for the time to pass. Paulo changes into Raider's extra fatigues on our jet. When he emerges, he looks... not relaxed exactly, but maybe more comfortable in his skin?

He comes to stand by me while he slides the dark ball cap onto his head.

"Comfortable clothes make all the difference, don't they? I can't imagine wearing a suit all the time, like Thiago or Grayson. Or yourself. I get it. It's a control and power thing. I'm just glad I don't have to worry about it much. I mean, I do have to wear a dress for events, but... never mind." I stop babbling when he gives me an incredulous look. "Sorry, I'm nervous. I'll go stand over there."

"Stay... please." He softens his demand with some manners. "If

243

not, I'll have to stand here by myself while everyone looks at me like I'm the devil."

"You're not, are you?" I murmur. "If you are, I need a few minutes to ask for forgiveness from the big guy first. You know, to give myself a fighting chance."

"I doubt you've done enough to warrant a meeting with the devil," he says dryly. "I'm well acquainted with him, and he doesn't accept lightweight offenders."

I can't contain the laughter that spills out.

The entire room stops to stare at the two of us.

Thiago, Grayson, and Mateo head toward us.

"I have a few calls to make," he remarks quietly and strides off. When he passes the Santos men, he inclines his head and says something to them.

When they reach me, all three are scowling.

I cock an eyebrow. "What?"

Grayson leans in close. "Stop charming the damn drug lord. We don't have time to add a rescue to our very busy plate." His lips drop a kiss onto mine.

"All I did was speak to him. No charming. None, I swear," I protest.

Mateo parks himself by my side and hands me an earpiece. "It's almost time." He points to the clock on the wall above the hangar door—fifteen minutes until eight.

Grayson and Thiago casually stand talking to each other. Or at least it looks that way, but I hear them giving orders to the others. The jet starts up, hangar doors open, and the security team, including Paulo, take their places around us.

At exactly eight o'clock, a dark sedan pulls up and Ronaldo gets out. He pauses to look at the men around the hangar. Thiago ignores him and raises a finger to the pilot of the plane. SEI's jet slowly turns and rolls out of the hangar.

Grayson hands Thiago the stack of fake newspapers we created, and he walks outside to meet his father. "Tomorrow's paper," he says, shoving the pile into Ronaldo's hands.

The old man takes his time reading the article, then switches his attention to the rest of the paper. Once he's done, he pulls today's paper from the bag at his side and rubs the two between his finger and thumb.

He finally nods in satisfaction. "Very good. The jet will take me wherever I want to go?"

Thiago gives him a short nod. "It will. What made you decide to leave after all this time? I thought you lived and breathed the cartel."

"It was never my intent to stay forever, but after I got caught stealing when you were a boy, I was trapped. Paulo's father, Luiz, watched my every move. Or at least most of them," he informs us with a laugh. "It worked well until Luiz died. Paulo is too interested in changing things. Digitizing the accounting system."

"Which would be bad for your side business, wouldn't it?" Thiago taunts him.

His father stills. "If you have something to say, spit it out. I want to get going."

Thiago shakes his head. "You've been stealing from the cartel for years, haven't you, Ron Silva? To the tune of almost twenty-one million dollars."

"Plus, a safety deposit box filled with diamonds," I speculate.

He narrows his eyes. "What do you want?"

"Initially, we were looking for leverage to keep you permanently out of our lives. When we uncovered your secret, we decided it wasn't up to us to decide your fate," Thiago informs him.

Mateo grabs me a seat. Sitting down, I open my laptop and access the accounts. I change the first password and hit save.

A second later, Ronaldo's phone pings with an incoming text. He pulls it out and, in a rage, tries to smash it on the ground before we can get the code.

Thiago rips it from his hand and tosses it to Mateo, who reads it to me.

I enter the security code and the password saves. I repeat the steps for the smaller account. Writing the password down, I hand it to the security guard standing behind me. Mateo passes the phone to Paulo's right-hand man.

"That's mine!" Ronaldo shouts, his old face reddened with rage. "How dare you! One call to Paulo and you'll all be dead. And I'll start with her first. Then you'll know how devastated your precious Marcos was when I took his wife from him."

I gasp.

Thiago lunges for his father, but Grayson and Zane wrap their arms around him and hold him back.

Mateo grabs my laptop and pulls me up behind him.

The security guard behind me steps forward and removes his hat. "No need to call me, Ronaldo. As you can see, I'm right here." Paulo hands the piece of paper to his right-hand man, who immediately opens his own laptop and enters the passwords. He gives Paulo a thumbs up. The phone dings a couple of times telling me he changed the passwords again. Smart.

"When they told me a member of our organization betrayed us not just once, but repeatedly, I couldn't believe it. We've given you everything—money, prestige, respect. And this is how you repay us? By stealing from us?" Paulo reaches up and lightly taps Ronaldo's ashen face.

He signals to another man, and his jet fires to life.

"Greed makes man blind and foolish and makes him an easy prey for death. Rumi was a great poet, don't you think? They would have been good words for you to know before you stole from me. Put him on the plane," he orders his guards.

Ronaldo is quiet when they take him away.

Raider steps up and clasps Paulo arm to arm. "You owe me one."

Paulo lifts a shoulder. "One."

Each of the Santos men steps forward to shake his hand.

Thiago pauses before he steps back. "If we see him again, we won't hesitate to kill him." It's clear he isn't sure if Paulo will do what needs to be done.

"Ghosts can't be seen," Paulo replies with a cold look in his eyes. "Dealing with traitors is never a pleasant task, is it? Especially when they're an integral part of our organization. Elimination is always the answer." He shoots Thiago a knowing glance.

Thiago's gaze sharpens. "It is."

I step up to Thiago's side. "It was nice meeting you, Paulo. I'll work on staying in my weight class."

His mouth quirks, but the smile never appears. "I wouldn't have believed any of you without the evidence. As a thank you, I made a few calls to one of my darker associates. Dr. Harrison Langford owns David Perry's soul. As an enemy, he's formidable. In Henley's case, he's quite psychotic. The two are known for their black hat expertise."

Dr. Langford? Not Aaron?

Shocked, I stand there and try to wrap my head around the information he casually dropped on me. Dr. Langford was my advisor at MIT, but I never met with him, only his graduate assistant, Aaron.

Thiago whispers, "Filho da puta."

Paulo takes a few steps toward the plane, then turns back. "The devil made me do it? Really?"

I shake off the past for a second and laugh. "I thought it would be an easy password for you to remember."

CHAPTER 36

HENLEY

The minute we get to the house, I'm racing for my laptop. Plunking myself down in the middle of the bedroom floor, my fingers fly across the keys, searching for every scrap of information I can find on Dr. Langford.

Dr. Harrison Langford, born 1978, in Greenwich, Connecticut. Parents: Shirley Langford Ross and Harold Ross. I dive into the community. Shockingly, the local paper returns hundreds of Langford results. One article in 1978 stands out. "A Son and Heir for the Langford Millions."

At long last, it's a boy and an heir for the Langford millions! Shirley Langford Ross and Harold Ross of Greenwich welcome Harrison Langford Ross. Baby weight, blah, blah. Shirley Langford's great-great-grandfather, Henry Langford, the youngest son of Baron Baybrooke, settled in Greenwich in the mid-1800s and used his considerable inheritance to buy into the booming railroad industry. Over the next one hundred and twenty-five years, the Langfords diversified their portfolio and continued to increase their wealth, becoming one of Greenwich's wealthiest families.

Harold Ross runs the Langford family business, Baybrooke Enterprises...

Interesting. He must have dropped the Ross at some point.

There's a picture of a man and woman holding a baby in front of a massive colonial home. Sticking with the *local* paper, I click on every mention of Harrison, but so few of them have any pictures of him. Frustrated, I quickly highlight a bunch of them and open them all into new windows.

After checking dozens of articles, I finally find one with a picture, but he's turned away from the camera. What the hell does he look like? Tap, close. Tap, close. Tap, close. Over and over, I tap to open the article and close it when it doesn't give me what I want.

Finally, I get to a graduation article, and he's there in his cap and gown, standing stiffly between his parents. His parents are barely smiling at the camera, but unlike the students in the background, this family is not standing with their arms around each other. In fact, they look uncomfortable.

Tall, with medium brown hair and eyes, he doesn't look like a monster, but on this happy occasion, there isn't an ounce of emotion on his face. How does one go from this boy to the man who terrorized me for years?

The article mentions Harvard as the first stop for the brilliant genius.

A hand touches my shoulder, and I jump.

"It's just me, Henley," Grayson states softly. "It's eight a.m. and you've been at this all night. Why don't you take a break and come eat something? This will be here when you finish."

"I don't want anything to eat," I tell him, returning to the information in front of me. Another article talks about his graduation from Harvard. In it, he informs the reporter Harvard was his father's choice and with that out of the way, he can go to MIT and get his master's degree. Computers are the future, he states. Unfortunately, he doesn't look much different in this picture than he did in the one from high school, but the article does refer to him as Harrison Langford, not Harrison Langford Ross.

"Do you want a tray?"

I blink. What? "I don't want anything to eat," I state firmly. Where was I? Third one down. I click on it. Master's from MIT, returning for PhD, no picture.

Damn it. I keep clicking on articles, but I can't find one image of him as an adult where he's facing the camera. Even on the website where those students published their papers for his class, he's looking down at the desk and grading papers.

He sighs. "How about some coffee? I'll bring you coffee and toast. If you decide you want more, you can let me know, okay?" He lays a hand on my arm. "Henley?"

"Will you please leave me alone?! I told you I'm not hungry!" I yell.

His head rears back as he looks at me in shock, then walks out.

My hand flies to my mouth. *Fuck, fuck.* I scramble to my feet. With Grayson's past abuse, the last thing I should ever do is yell at him. Running to the kitchen, I stop when I see Thiago and Mateo having a serious conversation.

"Where's Grayson?" I ask frantically.

"He left. Went to the yacht to check on the party," Mateo answers solemnly. "Is everything okay? How are you doing?"

"Terrible. I yelled at Grayson," I return, trying to swallow the huge lump in my throat. Tears fall sporadically down my cheeks, and I wipe them off. "Did he say when he'd be back?"

Mateo flashes me a sympathetic look, then hugs me tightly. "He didn't say, but he looked pretty upset. It could be a while. Do you want to eat? He left coffee and toast on the counter for you."

Hearing he left food for me only makes it worse. I shake my head miserably.

Mateo kisses me on the lips softly. "Go get a shower. It's been a long, emotional night for all of us, and it will help you feel better. I know we planned to go into the office today and get the demonstration set up, but it can wait. Thiago's going into the office, but I'll stay here with you."

"No, it can't wait. We need to make a move," I state emphatically. "But I don't want to leave until I've spoken to Grayson. I've got my gun and phone. Is Mitch here?"

Thiago picks up his phone. "Is Mitch on duty?" A pause. "Thanks." He looks at me. "He's here. Do you want him in the house?"

"Do you mind?" I ask, knowing how he feels about letting anyone inside right now.

"Of course, I don't mind," he replies with an irritated huff. "I'll get him."

A few minutes later, the two big men come striding back into the living room. "Mitch will stay with you while we go to the office and get everything set up for tomorrow. Are you sure you're up for it? We can postpone the demonstration." His obsidian eyes regard me with concern.

"Thank you for staying with me, Mitch," I tell the bodyguard I've gotten accustomed to having as a shadow. Turning to Thiago, I give him a firm nod. "I'm positive. I'll be fine."

I kiss Mateo and give him a couple of last-minute instructions for the set-up. It's my baby and I want everything to go off without a hitch.

He rolls his eyes. "I've done a lot of demonstrations over the years. Be good."

When I get close to Thiago, he pulls me in for a hard kiss. "If you need anything, call me. I don't care what it is."

"I will," I murmur.

When they're gone, I wave a hand to the kitchen. "Food and drinks are in there. Help yourself. I'm going to take a shower."

My stupid conversation with Grayson plays repeatedly in my head until I want to scream—at myself. And for what?

Stanley the... I guess I can't call him Stanley anymore. What a pity. I liked the sing song name. It helped eased the fear. Harrison is stuffy and pretentious. And real. Maybe I should use Langford. It's at least a little impersonal.

The shower doesn't make me feel any better, and neither does the sight of the sad face looking back at me in the mirror. Leaving

STELLA BRIE

my hair wet, I contemplate the computer on the floor, but the sight of it makes me sick. Besides, if I stay in here, I won't hear Grayson return.

Upstairs, the door to his room is closed. I knock, but nobody answers, and I don't want to enter without his permission.

Back downstairs, I grab a pillow off the bed, along with the blanket lying on top, then return to his door.

I drop onto the floor with a groan and cover up. Age must be catching up with me if I'm this tired from staying up all night. Fluffing the pillow, I slide down until I'm snuggled in tight. Warm and comfortable, I'm asleep within minutes.

When I wake, I'm no longer on the floor. Propping myself up on my elbow, I shove the hair out of my eyes and look around the unfamiliar room. Deep navy walls and luxurious velvet curtains give the room an air of sophistication. The bed I'm lying has a cream headboard and footboard with brass details. A brass photo gallery covers the wall in front of me, and it's filled with images of the world.

I scan the room, looking for Grayson, but he's not here. Did he come home and leave without speaking to me? I scoot backward on the bed and prop myself up against the headboard. Bringing my knees up, I hug them close, needing something to hold on to while I wait for him to return. At least, I assume he's going to come back.

Ten minutes later, the bedroom door opens, and he strides into the room. When he sees I'm awake, he stops and stares at me, but says nothing. Instead of the slightly amused look I'm used to seeing, his eyes are guarded and wary, and it hurts me to see it.

I grip the blanket tightly. "I'm so, so sorry, Grayson. I shouldn't have yelled at you, and I hope you can forgive me. I know you were trying to help. I fell into a black hole for a while, but it's not an excuse. I tried to catch you right after it happened, but you were gone so quick."

He doesn't say anything for a minute. "Where's Mateo or Thiago?"

"They went to SEI to get the demonstration set up for tomorrow," I remind him. "Tell me how to make this right. Please."

"You stayed here by yourself?"

"Mitch is here," I murmur. He hasn't answered me. My throat starts aching from the hurt bottled up inside. "I set up camp up here because I didn't want to take the chance I'd miss you."

He shoves his hands into his pockets.

Tears slip down my cheeks and a sob escapes. "I'm very, very sorry, and if you let me make it up to you, I will."

The bed dips when he sits. His hands wrap around my head while his thumbs wipe the tears from my face. "Don't cry, sweet Rose. Everything's going to be okay. It was bound to happen sooner or later. We're two damaged souls finally walking in the light, but the past is a trigger capable of pulling us into the shadows. It means we'll have to be more careful with each other."

He places his lips on mine in a soothing kiss. "I should have known you were fighting your own demons, and figured out a way to help you. I let my own past sweep me away, then I left you to deal with all this. I'm sorry too."

Hearing his words only makes me cry harder.

Strong arms wrap around my back and pull me into his chest. "Shh, it's okay."

"It's not. I'm not okay. I'm not okay with hurting you. I'm not okay with yelling at anyone. I'm not okay with all this," I sob, overwhelmed by the emotions bombarding me. Guilt, fear, sadness—I'm so full I can't breathe. "Everything is too much right now and I'm not okay. But I'm sorry. So sorry."

I can't hold back anymore. The gates burst open, and the sobs take over.

Finding out who my stalker is should be something to celebrate, but instead I'm more confused than ever. He's a stranger. We've never even met. Did he randomly pick me out all the students he was supposed to be advising? Is that why he wouldn't meet with me?

And the one question disturbing me the most—why does he avoid the camera?

David. My first real boyfriend. How does he come into it? What did he do to make him so indebted to Harrison? My memories of him and me were bittersweet, but now they're completely tarnished and worthless.

The pictures of my mom, the hatred from Thiago's dad, and all the tension from the last few days, including the incident with Grayson—I cry it all out.

Through it all, he's here, handing me tissues, holding me, murmuring sweet reassurances.

My tears slow until there's only one or two slipping down my face. I must look terrible. Conscious of his stare, the heat rises from my chest to my face, and I excuse myself to the bathroom to clean up. A red, splotchy face looks back at me. It's my ugly cry face.

I come back out and walk over to him. "Sorry, I think everything's been building up inside me, and I couldn't contain it anymore. Thank you for staying with me."

"Anytime," he whispers, pushing a strand of my hair back behind my ear. He opens his mouth to say something but closes it a second later.

My heart whimpers at the distance between us. "Right." I lean over and kiss him slowly. "I'm so incredibly sorry. I wish I could say it would never happen again, but I haven't had a lot of experience with relationships. And no matter how much I try, I'm not always going to get things right between us. But I hope you'll forgive me."

His lips cling to mine, but he says nothing.

"I'll give you some space," I murmur. Grabbing my pillow and blanket, I head toward the door.

"Stop," he calls out hoarsely.

I halt, but don't turn. I can't stand the look in his eyes right now.

"Don't go," he pleads.

My breath catches. "You need time, and I can give that to you. When you're ready, come find me."

I step forward.

His arms band around me from behind. "I don't need time. I need you. In my life. In my arms." He spins me around. "In my bed." His mouth descends and captures mine. Desperate and needy, his lips press against mine until I can't help but open for him.

His hands come up and cup the back of my head, holding me to him, while he pours everything he's feeling into this kiss. His anger, the hurt, the fear of going forward, but underneath it all, is need. Hard lips relentlessly hold mine hostage while his tongue plunges into me, demanding my response.

Tears leak from the corner of my eyes at the vulnerability he's exposing, and I immediately surrender. Matching his need with my own, I try to silently show him how much I need him, too, knowing he's trying to find his way through the pain to me.

Desire rises swift and fast, and we strip off the barriers between us. Skin meets skin, and I gasp. He pulls me up into his arms, and I wrap my legs around him.

The kiss is never-ending. I move my head to breathe, but he immediately pulls it back to his. He shifts us both until he's lined up and plunges into me.

I moan and squeeze him tightly with my legs. My fingers grip his shoulders, holding on, while I beg him to move.

His mouth and tongue in sync, he takes everything I have to give and uses it to fuel the fire between us. "God, I need you, Henley. Don't give up on me."

I cry out from the fire racing through my veins. "Never." My body explodes into a million pieces.

We sink to the floor, and without missing a beat, he sets a punishing rhythm. Thrusting into me, hard and fast, his navy-blue eyes locked on me, he refuses to let up.

"Again," he demands.

My body clenches in response, but it's not there yet. His fingers reach down between us and when he finds the most sensitive part of me, he's merciless, pinching and stroking, until I'm at the peak.

"Now," he orders, and sends me over the edge.

Moaning, I fall, again and again. Instead of subsiding, it keeps spreading outward with every stroke and all I can do is hold on.

He groans and comes hard inside me.

Breathing heavily, he tenderly places his lips on mine. When he pulls back, the darkness is gone from his eyes. He found his way back to me.

CHAPTER 37

GRAYSON

With a twirl, I add the pasta to the sauce and mix it with my tongs. For me, pasta is the ultimate food. I inhale deeply and savor the smell of Italian seasonings and garlic, then transfer everything to the platter I set aside.

"The table's set," Henley remarks behind me. "I'll grab the wine."

I follow her to the table, grabbing a seat next to her. Even after this afternoon, I'm finding it hard to be away from her even for a moment.

Thiago glances between the two of us and I give him a reassuring nod. He takes a drink of wine and turns to Henley. "Did you find anything in your search?"

"Dr. Harrison Langford, 44, from Greenwich, Connecticut. Born to old money. The details of his life are scarce. Parents deceased. I didn't get a chance to dig into them, but there was an interesting history about how the family got their wealth," she summarizes.

Her gaze is troubled when she looks at us. "The one thing I want more than anything is a semi-recent photo. He could come up to me on the street and I wouldn't know it was him. That terrifies me."

"What about school pictures?" Mateo asks with a frown.

"The local paper included his high school graduation picture, but it's the only one I could find close to adulthood with his face in it," she laments.

"What do you mean—with his face?" I question.

"He always looks away from the camera. Even his professor pictures show him looking down at papers on his desk, or turned toward the whiteboard," she explains. "It's weird. And creepy." She takes a drink of wine.

I glance at Thiago and Mateo. It's creepy as fuck. His psychosis must have started early.

"What are you going to do next?" Mateo asks.

"Try to find out why he left MIT. Look into Baybrooke Enterprises. Check in with my dark web network." She ticks each item off her finger as she says them.

Thiago tenses. "Did you say Baybrooke Enterprises?"

"Yes, it's the name of their family business. Apparently, their great- whatever was the youngest son of the Baron of Baybrooke, and he came to America. With his inheritance, he bought into the railroad and the rest is history. Why?" she asks, eating the last bite of pasta on her plate. "This was delicious, Grayson. Thank you."

Thiago jumps up and leaves the table. Returning minutes later with his laptop, he types in a few things, then sits back in satisfaction. "I knew I recognized the name. Baybrooke Enterprises is one of the companies that made a deal with Marcos' old partner, Burnett, to betray him. They tried to steal the company, along with the VPN Marcos developed, right out from under him."

He jumps to his feet and starts pacing back and forth. "Unfortunately for them, Marcos registered the patent in his name, not Angel Consultancy. When they found out the company didn't own its major source of revenue, they walked away."

"I remember this happening," Mateo exclaims. "Marcos was furious. It's the reason he decided to shut down Angel Consultancy and sell the company to us. After giving us the money to buy it, of course."

Henley taps a finger on the table. "I wondered how college students could buy a large company like Angel Consultancy."

"About five years after we took over, the company reported a hundred million in revenue for the year. Ten years later, we posted our first billion. Somewhere in between those two, maybe year seven or eight, Harold Ross, the father, tried to stake a claim on SEI.

"He produced documentation, allegedly signed by Burnett, selling Baybrooke Enterprises his half of Angel Consultancy. When we originally bought the company from Marcos, we gave him a percentage of SEI shares as part of the purchase. Baybrooke was trying to get the equivalent," Thiago snarls.

"What did you do?" Henley asks hesitantly.

"He'd made a lot of bad deals over the years. Unfortunately, he'd leveraged all his business and personal assets to cover the losses. We bought all his markers and called them in. He went bankrupt. Lost everything," Thiago states softly, satisfaction resonating in his tone. "Except his house. I made him an offer. If he renounced his claim on SEI, he could keep his house. He signed the papers."

"And now his son is out for revenge. With Diego out of the way, we know three of the main players—Philip Carlton, David Perry, and Harrison Langford. The only unknown is the woman. Is there anyone you put out of business who might have a wife or a daughter out for blood?" She pauses to let us reflect on the question.

Thiago lifts a shoulder. "Probably. We offer fair deals unless you come after us. Then all bets are off."

"Who came first is the big question. My bet is the woman," I interject. "You found evidence of bribes going back four years, right?" Henley and Mateo nod. "We didn't even notice, which means she didn't have the right players. Diego's knowledge of SEI's inner workings stopped at the security door."

"Did we ever find out anything about the bank account in Houston?"

Mateo looks at Thiago, who grimaces. "I forgot to tell Zane and his team."

"Can you send Sterling... Wait, he's in Mexico with Cruz. Can you send Zane a note and ask him to check into it?" Mateo asks, looking at me.

I jump up, take my plate to the kitchen, and grab my phone on the way back. Sitting down, I shoot off a text to Zane.

He replies with an interesting message. "Zane says banks are required to keep records of customer accounts for five years. The tricky part will be getting into the archives. It's typically a different system."

Henley bites her lip. "Once the demonstration is over, I could try looking for the other system. If it's accessible from the bank, I should be able to locate it."

"I guess we keep playing the game," I drawl. "Is everything set up for the demonstration tomorrow? Did you let it slip to Philip?"

"It's ready. Even better, I let the low-level IT person on their payroll overhear me in the elevator. It worked. I saw them enter Philip's office as I was leaving this evening," Mateo retorts.

One way or another, we're going to catch somebody this week. "The yacht is ready. Are we good to schedule the food and send out the invitations for two nights from now?"

"Let me confirm the security team is ready," Thiago replies. He sends a quick text to ask.

"I'm glad some of the research I did paid off. If I could only find a picture of him," she says with a sigh.

My mouth twitches. "What about his driver's license or passport?"

Dumbfounded, she stares at me with her mouth open. "Mother trucker! I'm so used to dealing in fake IDs, I didn't even think about it." She jumps up and runs out of the room. A few seconds later, she returns, plants a kiss on me, then scrambles away again.

"I'm guessing you patched things up?" Mateo speculates. "She was devastated this morning."

Thiago looks up from his phone, waiting for my answer.

"We did. Henley and I don't flow smoothly like you do with her," I remark with a frustrated sigh.

Thiago leans forward. "First, take it easy on yourself. The past isn't going to go away overnight. It's going to take time. This is the first woman you've fallen for since Kira. It's easier for Mateo and me because we're our own worst enemy."

He lifts a hand. "Commit to her. One hundred percent. Right now, you're trying to keep one foot in and one foot out. It's like skydiving. You just leap. When jealousy bites me in the ass, I deal with it, because there's no way in hell I'm walking away."

Mateo nods his agreement. "I made up my mind to go all in. Even if I had to change my life to do it. Which is ironic to me now because she doesn't mind if I work late or fall into a rabbit hole. I'm the one who minds."

"I thought I had committed, but if I'm still questioning..." My voice trails off. Man, why can't I throw off the past?

"Got it," Henley shouts, waving a piece of paper. She slams it face up on the table where we can all see the bastard stalking her.

I tap the image. "Look at his stare. It's like he's empty inside. There's not an ounce of emotion in his face. At six foot three, he's tall, but the rest of him is average. Medium brown hair and eyes. You wouldn't notice him in a crowd unless you caught his gaze."

She peers closer at his eyes. "They're like that in person, even with a mask on." A shudder runs up her spine.

We all snap a copy, then Thiago sends it to Zane and SEI's security teams. The odds of finding him just increased exponentially based on the sheer number of people who have this picture.

She sucks her bottom lip in for a second. "Do you mind if I sleep with you tonight, Mateo?"

A broad smile steals across his face. "Minha linda, I'd love to have you sleep with me tonight."

"I need to do a few things, but I'll meet you in there," she says.

STELLA BRIE

Thiago leans down and gives her a kiss. "Sweet dreams. No nightmares."

"I wish you'd stop ordering me around," she grumbles, but her smile says she doesn't mind.

"Good night, Grayson," she states softly, her lips finding mine in a sweet kiss that makes me want more.

————

WHEN I OPEN the door to my bedroom, I find Henley standing in the hallway. "When you're ready for bed, Mateo and I would love for you to sleep with us. Uhm, sleep in his bed. Only if you want to, but I understand if you need some space." Without waiting for an answer, she spins around and heads down the hallway toward Mateo's room.

After a quick shower, I slip on some loose shorts and follow.

Mateo's sitting up against the headboard when I enter. I raise an eyebrow, and he points to the bathroom.

Slipping into bed, I can't help but think of the last time I was here. "You knew I was awake, didn't you?"

"At the time, I was only thinking of her, but when you didn't move an inch, I guessed. I asked Henley the next morning, and she told me she knew. And she liked it," he adds.

My body stirs. "She did? Is this why she asked me to sleep here tonight?"

He shrugs. "She asked. I said yes. I didn't ask her why."

Henley comes out of the bathroom, her pink hair a tousled cloud around her shoulders, and slips out of her robe.

"I think that's your answer," Mateo mutters. He whistles. "Always my beautiful woman, aren't you? Why don't you come here and give me a kiss?"

The navy satin cami is sexy and follows her curves, but the skimpy shorts are the star, showcasing her gorgeous legs until they look miles long.

She darts a glance at me but strolls over and climbs on top of

262

Mateo's lap. Her satin shorts curve perfectly across her delicious backside when she leans forward to capture Mateo's lips in a hungry kiss.

His hands roam across her satin-covered body to the soft skin left naked. His touch languid, and sure, like he's mapped her lines a thousand times.

Her lips release his, moving to his ear to blow lightly on it, then down his neck with her tongue.

He palms her through the satin cami, thumbs lightly caressing her nipples, until they harden into tight little points.

She moans and arches her breasts toward him.

His fingers move to the hem, and he pulls it over her head. The minute it's clear, he latches on to her nipple and sucks hard.

"Yesss, harder," she urges him.

My cock throbs and I pull it out. Wrapping my hand around, I slowly pump up and down.

He switches to the other breast and lavishes it with attention until she cries out for more. Only then does he move his mouth back to hers.

Her hips rock back and forth on his body.

He slides a finger between her legs.

"Is she wet?" I ask huskily.

He groans. "She's soaked. Want to feel?"

She pushes off the bed and stands up to remove her shorts. Desire is stretched across her rosy cheeks. Climbing back onto Mateo's lap, she turns her body toward me.

"Fuck, yes." I scoot closer and slide a finger down her center. "Even the thought of both of us touching you makes you so damn turned on and wet."

She moans and widens her legs. "Touch me, Grayson."

I slip a finger inside and stroke in and out.

Her hips move to the rhythm, making it easier to go deeper.

Adding a second finger, I keep stroking.

She grabs Mateo by the hair and pulls his head back so she can kiss him deeply while she continues to ride my hand.

He reaches down and frees his cock.

Curling my fingers inside, I stroke until little shudders start taking over her body. She moans when I add my thumb to her body, sliding faster and faster across the most sensitive part.

Her orgasm takes over. She cries out and clenches down on my fingers.

When her body relaxes, I pull my fingers out and place them on my cock wanting to feel her wetness on me.

Her eyes darken while she watches me. Kneeling between Mateo's legs, she takes him in hand and slides his cock inside her mouth.

I watch her pretty pink mouth wrap around his cock and slide up and down. "Does he taste good?"

Without taking him out of her mouth, she nods.

My fist is stroking my cock hard, and her eyes are glued to me while she licks and nibbles on his. "Can you take him deeper?"

Her mouth slides almost all the way down.

He moans. "Just a little more, please."

She takes him another inch.

His hand slides around the back of her neck and she starts sucking and stroking him. Her mouth and hand working in tandem to bring him over the edge.

"That's it. He's so close. Keep going," I urge her, stroking myself faster.

"Look how good she looks, Mateo," I order him.

His eyes stare down at her. "So beautiful. Minha linda," he murmurs. "I'm coming."

Seeing her mouth on him when he comes is enough to trigger my own release. With a low groan, I surrender.

We lie together breathing for a few minutes.

Mateo smooths the hair back from her face. "I'm not complaining, but what's all this about?"

She darts a look at me and blushes. "I want to explore the dynamics of this relationship between us. It's not just me and Mateo or me and Grayson. It's all three of us, too. The sharing thing is new, but it feels right." She bites her lip, then continues. "And I think the pressure of a one-on-one relationship is a trigger for Grayson, and this could help him. After all, it's not just him and me in this relationship. It's all of us and our different dynamics. We can have moments alone or together."

"Come here," I demand huskily. She moves into my arms. "The thought of watching you and Mateo makes me insanely hard." I lower my head and kiss her pink lips. "But I also love our relationship and where we're headed, too."

CHAPTER 38

HENLEY

M y body is deliciously sore the next day. I can't help but think yesterday gave us all a glimpse into the life we could have together. Thiago and I have a personal relationship separate from them, but Thiago protects us all, his family. We can be together and alone. The dynamics are intricate and layered, and I'm so happy. It's utterly terrifying to be this happy.

I shake my hands at my side and look around the brightly lit room at the TV monitors. In every one, my pink hair stands out like a neon sign. I try to shake off the nerves by thinking of something else but nothing helps. Not only did we invite doctors—we invited the entire medical community and Epic Entertainment.

Mateo's hands rub up and down my arms. "Everything worked well this morning. We're repeating the test. That's it."

The TV monitors show Philip Carlton texting into his phone, but whenever he tries to catch my eye, I avert my gaze. If I'm as bad a liar as they tell me, we can't afford for me to give the game away.

When Philip asked Mateo what I was doing here, he gave him a surprised look. "She's CJ Tech. It's her product." And walked off. Philip look stunned.

The camera guy clicks something in his hand, signaling it is time to start. I position myself in the camera and for the next hour, I demonstrate the technology using several phones and tablets, then I switch to a headset. We rigged a camera above another headset in order to show the audience a replica of what I was seeing.

Next, we opened it up for real-time demonstrations. Doctors and hospitals sent in CT, MRI, and ultrasound scans. Almost all of them performed. There were a few older scans that didn't convert well, but we did recommend they use this only on the latest renderings.

The Q&A session is winding down.

Beau Whitman chimes in with the question we primed him to ask. "When will this be available to the market, and what is the cost?"

I smile and take a deep breath. "It's available on your app store now. The licensing fee is a hundred dollars a year per license. Our goal is for the technology to be accessible to all doctors, and we think this nominal cost will achieve that goal. If hospitals or facilities would like to purchase multiple licenses, you can contact SEI directly at the number shown on the screen and we can work with you. And for our last bit of news, I'll pass it over to Beau Whitman, and Epic Entertainment, to share their good news."

While Beau shares the information on the AR/VR glasses, I look over at Philip Carlton. Pure panic. He lifts his phone to text someone, but the security guy next to him slips it from his grasp.

A click on my right has me refocusing my attention on the presentation. "Thank you, Beau. We're incredibly excited to have Epic Entertainment partner with us on the donation of the glasses to any surgeon who requests one. Hospitals or doctors who wish to order can do so directly through their website. We will post this video on the SEI website for everyone to view. Multiple copies will also be available on the InterPlanetary File System in case our website is down." *Or hacked.* "Thank you for your time."

The demonstration ends. Security closes in on Philip.

Mateo walks up to him. "We should talk. If you would like to follow me up to Thiago's office, we would appreciate it."

Philip eyes the men around him, then nods.

When we enter his office, Thiago's on the phone. "Fantastic. We look forward to receiving the first shipment. I've got to run to another meeting, but we'll talk soon. Thanks, Beau."

He winks at me, then directs his attention to Philip. "Philip." He hands him a stack of papers. "These are your bank statements for the last year. The highlighted deposits are the bribes you've taken for betraying SEI. You are terminated, effective immediately."

Philip's shoulders are stiff for a second, but they drop a second later. "I suspected you knew. Mateo's been tense around me, but I couldn't tell if I was just overreacting." He nods. "I understand. For what it's worth. I'm sorry."

Thiago's smile is all teeth like a shark. "Oh, we're not done here. Whether we decide to turn the evidence over to the authorities is largely dependent on you. While we would love to see you prosecuted and sent to prison, we're after bigger fish. If you help us, we'll figure out a way for you to pay your debt without spending time behind bars."

Philip stiffens. "I don't know what you mean."

Thiago tilts his head. "We know David Perry, your son, is involved in the theft of SEI software."

He shakes his head rapidly back and forth. "He didn't steal your software. In fact, he didn't know anything about it. It was entirely me. Diego told me if I didn't, he would kill David."

Mateo scoffs and crosses his arms. "You've been taking bribes for a year. The software wasn't stolen until the week before Marcos died. Want to try again?"

"When we pitched the software to you and you decided not to move forward, David was devastated. It was supposed to be his ticket back to working on legitimate solutions instead of the black hat jobs. His boss heard about the pitch from Diego and offered

David a choice—death or he could convince me to spy on SEI for them. It wasn't even a choice. He's my son," Philip states quietly.

Mateo throws up his hands. "Why didn't you come to me? To any of us? You were like family. We would have helped you and David. Instead, you took away the one person who meant everything to us—Marcos. No matter what excuses you tell yourself, you'll always be responsible for his death."

Thiago, Grayson, and I all nod.

"We want Langford," Thiago informs him. "And the woman—what's her name?"

"What about David?" Philip questions.

"He can walk free, same as you," Thiago generously offers. "We will require some assurance, of course, that neither of you will ever have anything to do with SEI or..."

Philip's phone rings. He raises it for Thiago to see David's name.

"On speaker," Thiago orders.

"What the hell happened? Harrison is furious, and so is she. They're threatening to kill you." David whispers loudly. Shouts can be heard in the background.

"You're on speaker. Thiago, SEI, they know everything. They're willing to make a deal for Harrison Langford and the woman," Philip interjects.

Voices move closer to the phone.

"They're coming," he blurts out.

Given his background with Dr. Langford, the computer with the rootkit on it has to be David's not Langford's. "David, it's Henley. We saw each other in Austin, remember? Write a time and place to meet and save it to the Henley code file on your computer," I rush to spit out the instructions before he hangs up. "I'll grab it."

"How..." he gets out, then hangs up.

Philip looks at Thiago. "Now what?"

"You'd better hope David finds a time and place to meet, or you're going to prison for a long time," Thiago informs him. He jerks his chin. "Get him out of here. Put him in the holding cell."

I open my laptop and access David's computer via the rootkit.

269

Finding the hidden files, I open the folder named Henley. No new files have been uploaded yet. Leaving it open, I lean back on the couch.

"What did Beau have to say?" I ask Thiago to pass the time.

"Epic's thrilled to be a part of the launch. The glasses passed their rigorous testing and they're ready to start production. The first batch should be here within thirty days," he replies. He nods in satisfaction.

"What are we going to do about Philip?" Mateo wonders.

"If he does what we tell him, nothing. He's fired due to espionage. No company will ever hire him again. How he moves on or recovers, I don't care. He's lucky I don't kill him for his role in Marcos' death. Would you rather go that route?" Thiago asks Mateo, his dark eyes glittering with anger.

Mateo groans. "No, I don't like hearing he did it to save his son."

Grayson scoffs. "He sold you, didn't he? Philip Carlton lives in a multi-million dollar paid off house. His accounts are extremely healthy. And the software they pitched last year is solid. Worth probably three to five million. They could have sold it to someone. We offered to broker it, but they turned us down."

Mateo freezes. "I'm so gullible."

I lean forward and pat his leg. "If it makes you feel any better, you suspected CJ Tech. You were obviously wrong about me, but you didn't dismiss the idea."

He glares at me.

Thiago and Grayson laugh.

"Well, technically, you all suspected CJ Tech, but at least Grayson gave me the benefit of doubt," I qualify my previous statement.

"Are you ever going to let us forget it?" Grayson muses.

"Maybe, with a lot of groveling," I return cheekily.

A file appears in the folder. I sit up and click on it.

Tomorrow. Eight a.m. Vice City Bean. North Miami. Henley 1

I type a quick message onto the file. *Not possible. Security*

Okay, no cops.

Thiago looks thunderous. "You're not going alone."

"I'm not going alone. I'll have security with me," I retort.

"If you think I'm letting you go without me, you've lost your beautiful mind," Thiago spits out, his hands on his hips.

He's absolutely serious, and I don't want to go without him.

"Do you think Mitch has an extra uniform?" I wonder aloud. "How about you and Mitch at the coffee shop. Two others on the SUV? Will that work?"

He thinks about it for a minute. "Three on the SUV."

"Deal. Should we seal it with a kiss?" I tease him.

CHAPTER 39

V ice City Coffee is a happening local joint. Modern looking
with an industrial vibe thanks to its concrete floors and
exposed ceiling. It's busy this morning with people popping in and
out on their way to work. A few sit down at the tables or grab a
quick bite at the bar seating by the window, but not many.

I order a cortado and an egg sandwich, not that I'm going to eat
it, but I need an excuse to sit here for a while. David isn't coming
until eight, but Thiago thought it best to arrive early so we're not
seen together. I tap the button on the side of my phone. Seven
fifty-six.

My eyes dart to the man sitting on my right wearing camo and a
fierce expression on his face. Mitch really isn't happy Thiago has
joined his security team. From the corner of the shop, Thiago raises
his mug and gives me a smirk. Instead of the typical security
uniform, he's gone undercover in running shorts, hat, and black
tank. He worried two large men in camo might cause someone to
call the police.

The girl cleaning the tables swings by my table. "Do you need anything?" she asks nervously.

I pick up my coffee and take a sip. "No, it's delicious. Just planning my day."

She leans in closer and whispers, "If you want to move to a table closer to the register, I'd be happy to help you." Her eyes dart to Mitch.

"He looks a little dangerous," I murmur and almost laugh when she shakes her head vigorously. I crook my finger to bring her closer. "Do you think he'd ask me out? I could do with a little excitement in my life."

Her eyes widen. She sneaks a glance at him, then me. "Go for it. You never know." Smiling at the two of us, she leaves a little more relaxed than when she came over.

Mitch grunts at my shenanigans and takes a drink of his water. "Two o'clock."

David's standing by the door in casual business attire, looking like every other commuter on their way to work. He grabs a coffee to go and a cream cheese Danish, then sits across from me.

Conscious of the ears around us, I keep the conversation neutral. "Philip is staying with us until everything is settled. We offered to send you both off in exchange for some information."

He swallows. "If I can't help you?"

"It would be a shame to let him go down alone. It would be almost like prison," I say lightly. Or exactly like prison.

He clears his throat. "He's only in this mess because of me. When I was in college, I did something incredibly stupid. I stole someone else's work and published it as my own. A professor caught me. Instead of turning me in, he used me to steal more. I thought it would end after college, but it was only the beginning."

The table starts rattling, and I peer over the side. His leg is bouncing wildly. It suddenly stops.

He smiles sheepishly. "Sorry. When my mother died a couple years back, I found Philip's contact information in her files. I wanted to know what he was like and reached out. I'm sure he's regretted it ever since," he says derisively.

273

I study him, but other than his obvious nervousness, I can't tell if he's sincere or spouting a bunch of half-truths. "Philip's first concern when we spoke to him yesterday was you. He wants a fresh start for you."

A genuine smile breaks out on his face. Maybe he really cares for Philip.

I tap on the table and lower my voice. "The professor. You know he's a stalker, right?"

He shifts forward with a grimace. "That's kind of my fault. He set up surveillance in my dorm room without me knowing, probably to make sure I didn't go to the authorities. When you and I started dating, he became obsessed with you. Or your mind. It's hard to tell with him. I knew it was bad, though, because you were all he talked about. I broke up with you to save you. It had the opposite effect. Without the daily video feed, he started actively stalking you."

A stupid coincidence or a convenient lie? It doesn't matter. I need two things right now. "Address?"

He pulls out a piece of paper from his sports coat. "This is his."

"How did your two bosses meet?" I ask nonchalantly.

"They're both psychotic and obsessed with the Savages. She posted a job on the dark web. We took it. Built a mega virus to attack their corporation. When he found out who it was, he volunteered our services. It's been a vicious merry-go-round ever since."

I tap the piece of paper. "Her name and address?"

He shakes his head. "No, Philip first. I'll give you her info after you give him to me."

Frustrated, I glance at Thiago, who gives me a single nod.

"We'll do an exchange. Let us know when and where," I inform him. "Use the same method to communicate."

"The rootkit was clever. I assume it was on the drive Diego gave me," he says with a snort.

"I laid it on the table, and he snatched it up," I reply.

David grabs his coffee and gets up. "We need to make the exchange today. She's losing it. After the success you had with Epic in Austin and the demonstration yesterday, she's pinpointed you as the reason she's failing to bring down Santos. All I want to do is get my father and get out of here. You can have them."

He heads out the door.

"Well, that was interesting," I say, but before I can continue, a scream pierces the air. It's coming from outside.

Jumping up, I ignore Mitch's order to wait and collide with Thiago on my way out. He pushes me behind Mitch and sprints outside.

Mitch steps in front of me and clears a path through the crowd. Per protocol, he heads to the SUV where we can pick up reinforcements. A crowd is gathered in the street. I turn my head to the left and see a familiar looking brown shoe by the curb.

"David."

I leave Mitch and run toward the crowd in the center of the road. Pushing through, I drop down on my knees beside David. His body is bent at odd angles, and a weird gurgling noise is coming from his chest.

"David, it's Henley. It's okay. Hold on, the ambulance is coming," I urge him. "Can you hear me? You need to be strong for your dad. He's expecting you to save him."

"Save him," he repeats. "You, Henley."

"I'm here. Stay with us. You need to save your dad. Do you hear me?"

He says something, but I can't quite make it out. I lean down and he whispers one word. "Worthington."

Large hands grip my shoulders and pull me out of the way. The ambulance is here, but they're too late. He's gone.

I turn to the man holding me and lay my head on his chest. "Two down, two to go."

Maybe I should feel something for David, but I can't. He knew. From the beginning. All those years of being stalked and terrorized. He could have helped me. Maybe if he had, my mother would still be alive. Sometimes, karma's a bitch, and she runs you over in the middle of the street.

CHAPTER 40

MATEO

Thiago and Grayson head out with the security team to the address David gave them. Henley and I take the elevator to the holding cell in the basement where Philip Carlton waits for us. When Thiago called to let us know what happened, I thought she would be distraught over David's death, but she isn't.

She calmly sits down and tells Philip every word David said to her. When he asks for clarification about the stalking, she explains how her dating David caught the eye of Langford. When Philip asks to see the paper with the address, she hands it to him.

"It's in his handwriting," he reflects softly, running his finger over the paper. "David's life would have been so different if he hadn't met Harrison Langford. As his professor, he could have helped David turn away from a life of crime. Instead, he's the reason David never got out. It's his fault David is dead. So, what happens now?"

Henley looks at me.

"As Thiago stated earlier, you're fired with cause, but given the circumstances, we won't hand you or the evidence over to the authorities. If you decide to pursue us for any reason, the first thing we'll do is send the information to the FBI. Do you understand?" I ask him.

"I understand," he states quietly.

Sadness hits me and I reach over and clasp his arm. "I wish it hadn't ended like this—for both of us. You helped me build a fabulous team at SEI. We'll go on to do great things." Without you. I don't have to say it, though, the regret is apparent in every line of his face.

Henley and I stand and walk to the door. "You're free to leave immediately. Security won't stop you." I pause for a moment. "One last thing—David's body is at the morgue, under the name David Perry Carlton. We put you down as next of kin."

He closes his eyes for a second and a tear rolls down his face. "Thank you. I can't tell you what that means to me."

Henley wraps her arm around my waist and leans into me while we walk down the hall. "What are we doing now?"

"We're going to the yacht to make sure everything is ready for the party tonight. Later, we're meeting Thiago, Grayson, and... what's that cheeky guy's name?"

She punches me lightly on the arm. "Peyton. You'd better be nice to him. He's my very talented friend and the only reason I'm going to look good tonight."

I tilt her chin up and kiss her. "You always look beautiful to me."

Mitch is waiting for us in the hallway, but he barely looks at us. Thiago said he threw a fit when Henley broke protocol to go to David in the middle of the street.

We pass the security office, and she turns to me. "What are we doing about the name and the license plate number?" She asks.

Some quick thinking guy managed to snap a photo of the license plate from the car that hit David.

"The team is searching SEI files for any mention of Worthington, but it doesn't sound familiar. They're also searching local hotels, car rentals and such, to see if anyone registered a room or a car in that name, but it's going to take a while," I reply, running a hand through my hair in frustration. "The license plate came back registered to

Juan Morales, but he reported it stolen early this morning. We've switched our attention to the vehicle. If we can locate it on city cameras, we might be able to see where it went after it hit him."

My phone buzzes and I answer. "Did you find anything?"

"Nothing. It's empty. Looks like he left in a hurry, though," Grayson says hoarsely.

He pauses. "I'm damn glad Henley didn't come with us. There are pictures of her everywhere, from every angle, covering the walls. And those are just the images from Miami. He's got stacks of photo albums filled with images of her when she was younger. Her picture is the screensaver on his fucking computer."

I hear Thiago yelling in the background. "Is everything okay?"

"He fucking lost it when he saw this place," Grayson reveals. "They recorded everything, but I'd advise against watching it. I'm going to have a hard time letting her out of my sight after seeing this psycho bullshit."

With a weary sigh, I remind him where we're going next. "We're going by the yacht and will meet you at home."

"Be careful. Fucker could be anywhere," Grayson warns me.

Henley's waiting for me to give her an update. "He's gone. Looks like he left in a hurry."

"That's not all, is it? Your face is white," she observes. "What happened? Are Grayson and Thiago okay?"

"There were pictures of you all over the place. It's shaken both Grayson and Thiago," I reluctantly reveal.

She swallows. "As long as they're okay... I can't think about the other."

When we get to the yacht, I'm surprised to see all the workers rushing around in a panic. "Where's Claire?"

"She never showed," a young man tells me as he rushes by.

I motion to security. "How did all these people get on board? I thought we were keeping things contained, including the set-up."

He points to his clipboard. "Everyone on this boat is on the list."

"Who's in charge here?" I shout across the deck.

A blonde-haired young woman pops her head up from behind

the bar. "That would be me, I'm Alyssa. Claire called me earlier, told me to get over here and set everything up. Do you know when the caterers are coming?"

"Where is Claire?" I ask her.

"I'm not sure. She said she was on her way here," she replies, quickly grabbing another box to unload.

"There aren't any caterers. The food is coming from local restaurants. It should have been here by now," Henley states quietly, not wanting to cause an even bigger panic.

I knew Grayson should have come to the yacht instead of me. Panic starts clawing at my throat. I hate these events.

Henley clears her throat. "Why don't you round up everyone? We need to know who's on board and who isn't. I'll call Grayson and let him know what's going on and see if I can get the list of restaurants."

Relieved to have her here, I kiss her on the cheek and walk off to pull everyone together.

When I return twenty minutes later, she's just finishing her call with Grayson. "We have an overabundance of servers, two bartenders, and a few cooks."

"Grayson came up with a new plan. He called Juanita's Mexican Kitchen and offered them triple what they usually make on Thursday evening to close their restaurant tonight and provide all the food for the party. They'll be here in three hours to set-up and will serve everyone buffet style," she says, looking down at a paper filled with notes.

"Two bartenders aren't enough. We'll ask three of the servers to stay and bartend for us. They can handle the simple orders—wine, beer, and non-alcoholic drinks," she remarks, crossing another item off the list. "Get rid of everyone else. After they're gone, Thiago wants the entire yacht swept for people and explosives."

I leave her at the table and head over to the group. I randomly choose three servers and tell everyone else to go home. Angry at having their time wasted, I tell them to call Claire and complain.

Something is bugging my brain. Stepping back a few feet, I tap my fingers in a familiar pattern, trying to figure out what it's trying to tell me. Watching the crowd head toward the stairs, it hits me. "Where's Alyssa?"

"She took a case of champagne down to the kitchen," one of the servers tells me.

That doesn't make sense. The bars are on this deck. We even have a small walk-in refrigerator for the sole purpose of storing alcohol.

I motion for Mitch to move in closer to Henley and call Thiago.

"Something isn't adding up," I blurt out when he answers. "And we have someone missing. A woman."

"Get everyone off the yacht," Thiago orders. "I'll call Jameson and Allison and get it swept immediately. Is there anyone else near the yacht that needs to be warned?"

I scan the marina. "No, it's clear."

"We'll be there in ten minutes. Stay safe," Thiago spits out and hangs up.

Motioning to the servers and bartenders, I let them know we've received a threat and need to evacuate the yacht. I text Mitch and order him to remove Henley.

Spotting the guy with the clipboard, I head toward him. "Where did you get the list?"

"Same place I got the first one," he replies. He picks up his phone and shows me the two emails. "Is something wrong?"

"We need to evacuate the yacht. Can you make sure everyone gets off?" I tell him without answering.

I dial Grayson. "You may want to have someone check on Claire. The revised list came from her email. Either someone hacked it, or they accessed her computer directly, but she isn't here today, which suggests some type of foul play."

He curses. "I'll get security on it. Where are you?"

"Heading for the stairs now," I reply. "How close…"

"I don't think so," a feminine voice says behind me.

When I turn around, Alyssa's standing there with a gun. "Alyssa. What are you doing?"

She grimaces. "It's Kathleen, actually. Kathleen Worthington. Or I should say Kathleen Adair Worthington."

"Kathleen Adair Worthington," I repeat to Grayson on the phone.

"Is that Grayson? Please tell me he's on his way. He's the reason I'm here, after all," she comments in a sing-song kind of way.

"Fuck, fuck, fuck. It's Kira's sister. We're two minutes out," Grayson announces. "Where's Henley?" Fear makes his voice tight.

"Not here," I reassure him.

"Tell him to come alone. Leave Thiago on the ground," she instructs me.

I repeat her message to Grayson.

"Thiago said to tell you—you've got a friend up high," Grayson returns.

Keeping the phone to my ear, I slowly scan the building on the wharf behind us. Something glints on the far corner, but I can't tell if it's a person.

"Uh huh," I continue to make sounds like I'm listening to Grayson say something. "Maybe." Turning a quarter to the left, I see something moving on the roof of a nearby dock.

"I'm here," he notes. "Be there in a few seconds."

A second later, Thiago comes on the line. "Keep the line open as long as you can," he commands. "Are you doing okay?"

"Yes."

"Where is he?" she shouts, waving the gun around wildly.

"Right here," Grayson inserts smoothly from behind her.

I take advantage of the moment and slip the phone into my pocket hoping she'll forget about it.

Kathleen immediately backs up and motions for Grayson to move next to me. She studies Grayson for a second, then her mouth twists. "Of course, you're still handsome as ever. Kira sure could pick them."

"What are you doing here, Kathleen? Kira died ten years ago," Grayson remarks, confusion and weariness lining his face.

"Don't tell me when she died!" she screams. "I know when she died. Every minute of every day, she's on my mind. She was beautiful, and you killed her!"

Grayson stiffens. "Kira committed suicide. You know this, Kathleen. The police told you how she died. The coroner confirmed it. I didn't kill Kira."

"You didn't slit her wrists, but you drove her to it. When she came home for college breaks, she'd be so torn up about you and those other girls. She'd cry for hours. I tried to get her to dump your cheating ass, but she refused to leave you. It made me sick—the way you would manipulate her into forgiving you, telling her you only loved her, and nobody else. You knew how much she loved you and you used it against her," she sneers. "As if you ever loved anyone besides yourself."

Grayson clenches his fists. "I loved her, but her jealousy was over the top. There were no other girls. She made it all up in her head, and she manipulated you into thinking she was the victim."

"You're lying!" she screams. Reaching behind her, she pulls a pink book from behind her back and flings it at Grayson. "Pick it up. Look at the last few pages. Read it."

Grayson bends down slowly and grabs the book. He shows me the cover. It says "Diary." He opens it to the inside cover. "Kira Adair" is written under "This diary belongs to…" He flips to the last few pages. They're filled with pages of newspaper and magazine photos with him and his beauties. Xs across most of their faces.

"Read it out loud," Kathleen demands.

"I can't stand it. He tells me he loves me and wants to get married, but how can I believe him when he hangs out with all these whores!!! Last night, he was so sweet and tender with me, but then I heard he'd been with her all day—Bea Matthews. How can he go from her to me? I keep picturing him and her together in bed and it's driving me crazy. Why does he torment me like this?" His voice is hoarse and his face stricken as he reads the desperate words. "This isn't real. Kira and I broke up in college and never got back together. Kira had a psychotic breakdown before she died."

"Liar! She always told me to keep a diary and tell it all the things

I'd never tell anyone else. It's the truth. She wouldn't lie in her diary," she states, as if the idea is preposterous. "My parents might have believed your lies, but I didn't."

"When she died, our whole world fell apart. My mother drank all the time, and my father stopped going to work. He'd sit in the recliner all day looking at the garden. They couldn't live without her. I tried so hard to keep us going. I got good grades, graduated with honors, and became a lawyer. But in the end, we all wanted things to go back to the way they were. Before Kira died!" She screams. Sobs burst out. The gun waves wildly when she uses her arm to wipe her face and we both step back.

"Are you the one who bribed our employees?" I ask, trying to bring her back to the present. The account in Texas must be hers.

She gives me a smug look. "I did. My parents died and left me a fortune. My husband had an affair, and I added to it when I took him to the cleaners." She snorts. "I had all this lovely money and nobody to share it with. Where was my sister? The one I looked up to my whole life? Dead. Where was my family? Dead. There was just... me. All alone."

Her eyes swing to Grayson. "I was alone and heartbroken, barely living. Then, one day, I'm walking by a bookstore, and I see a photo of Grayson on a magazine. He's on a yacht, smiling, with his arms around a bunch of women, and living his best fucking life. And I could hear Kira telling me it wasn't fair, and I knew he had to be stopped."

She's calmed down a little since she started talking about the present. "Was Diego the first?" I ask as if I don't already know the answer.

"The first and easiest," she admits with a laugh. "A little seduction, some ego pandering, and a lot of money went a long way with him. Unfortunately, he didn't have any brains. The people he recruited couldn't help me."

"That's when you hired David Perry and Harrison Langford, right? To build a virus to attack SEI?" I ask her.

She narrows her eyes. "I suppose David told you that this morning. He didn't give you the entire story, did he? David built the virus for Harrison Langford, who was already planning to attack SEI as revenge for bankrupting his idiot father. We met in a chat room and decided to pool our resources. When David's father, Philip, joined the team, things started happening. We were this close." She holds her fingers a few centimeters apart. "Until your stupid girlfriend comes out of nowhere and ruins every single one of my plans. I think it's time to take her off the board, don't you?"

"Unfortunately, she evacuated the yacht," I reveal with a shrug.

She laughs. "Unfortunately, she never made it. Oh, Henley!" she calls out loudly.

Henley shuffles out from behind the bar with her hands and feet tied, and Grayson swears.

Tear tracks line her face, but with the gag, she can't say anything.

"Untie her feet and remove the gag," she orders me.

I rush over and do what she says. "Where's Mitch?" I whisper.

"Downstairs in a closet. She injected him with something," she whispers back.

"Stop talking and get back over here!" she yells.

Gripping Henley's tied hands, I keep her behind me and move back to Grayson's side.

"Henley, step forward," she instructs her.

"Why don't you—"

The gun goes off and a splinter of wood flies in the air near my feet. Henley's hand squeezes mine tightly.

"If she doesn't step forward, I'll kill you, then her. Do it now," she orders.

I lock my knees. Where the hell is our friend in the sky? "I wish I had a friend right now," I yell.

She gives me a suspicious look and turns the gun on Grayson. "Fine, I'll shoot him first."

"Wait!" Henley shouts behind me. "I'm coming." She jerks her hands from mine and steps around me.

Both Grayson and I step forward.

Kathleen levels the gun on Henley. "I'm an excellent shot, you know. A Texas girl through and through. My daddy taught me to defend myself at an early age." A tinkling laugh fills the air. "Unfortunately, Henley, you've got to go. From the moment you showed up in Miami, you've done nothing but ruin every single one of my plans. Well, except the one to kill Grayson." With the gun raised, she walks toward Henley. "I'm going to enjoy seeing you die."

I bend my knees, preparing to jump when she gets closer, but a second later, blood and matter explodes from the front of her head and Kathleen crumples to the ground.

I cautiously walk over and peer down at the hole in the back of her head. We never even heard a sound.

I blow out a huge breath. Our friend finally came to the party. Better late than never, I guess. I step forward to hug Henley, and something stings my bicep.

"Get down!" Grayson yells, diving toward Henley and me. Another bullet hits right where he was standing a second ago.

Staying low, we scoot across the deck into the covered area. Grayson pulls Henley into his arms while I scramble to get to my phone.

Putting it up to my ear, I hear Thiago yelling orders and directing men to a nearby roof. I guess he's already realized what's happening.

"Thiago!" I yell, trying to get his attention.

"Tell me everyone is alive," he snarls into the phone.

"Henley, Grayson, and I are alive, Kathleen is dead, and we're not sure about Mitch," I respond quietly. "I'm guessing the friend on the roof wasn't ours?"

"Shots came from the dock roof, not the building where one of our security team was supposed to be," he replies in a hard voice. "You can come out now. They're gone. I'll be there in a minute." He hangs up.

I relay everything to Grayson and Henley.

She raises a hand to my arm. "You're bleeding. Is there a first aid kit?"

Grayson nods absentmindedly. "I'll get it."

"He's going to have a tough time with this," I say tiredly. "Guilt will eat him alive for bringing this down on our heads."

She throws up her hands. "He can get over it. We both brought psychos to the party."

Grayson barks a laugh behind her. "On the bright side, three down. One to go?"

"Precisely," she retorts. "Can you bandage him up while I go look for Mitch?"

"No!" Grayson and I shout.

"Don't go anywhere without us. Not right now. Okay?" I plead with her. This was way too close.

After she bandages my arm, we head down to find Mitch. When we get to the lower deck, Thiago's standing there with Mitch propped up against him.

Grayson hurries over to Mitch's other side to help hold him up.

Henley turns a worried face toward Thiago. "Is he going to make it?"

"He's a little fuzzy from the drugs, but thankfully, it's beginning to wear off. He'd already kicked the door open when I saw him," Thiago informs her. "Let's get off the yacht and let the team sweep it for tonight's party."

We all look at him like he's crazy, but his face is set. I guess the show must go on.

After the ambulance drives off with Mitch, the team sweeps the yacht, but thankfully, they don't find anything.

Juanita arrives shortly after and begins to set up the food.

Grayson finds out the bartenders and servers left when the men with guns showed up.

"Fuck it. We'll open several bottles of wine and champagne. If they want something else, they can help themselves to the bar," Grayson says with a frustrated sigh. "We need a fucking vacation."

CHAPTER 41

<u>HENLEY</u>

Peyton's frantic when we arrive. "Where the hell have you been? I arrived hours ago, and they told me you were going to be late." He waves his watch at me. "There's late, and there's impossible. I'm never going to get you ready in time."

I grab onto his shoulders and hug him. "There was an incident on the yacht. We had to evacuate, and it took a while to get it swept and cleared. I'm sorry. I should have called you, but honestly, it was pretty chaotic."

His eyes are round. "Seriously? If this is what it means to be wealthy, you can keep it. I'll take rich. Very rich, maybe. But that's where I draw the line. But why are we standing here talking? We need to get you ready. Go! Shower!"

Chuckling, I head into the bathroom and jump in the shower. Alone, finally, I lean against the wall and let the water flow over me. One second to breathe—it's all I need. We're so close to finishing this thing, but it's taking a toll. At this point, I just pray we don't lose anyone else. The hospital said Mitch would be fine with some rest, but Thomas lost the man on the roof. He'd been shot with a long-distance weapon. My bet is it will match the one that killed Kathleen.

If Kira was anything like her sister, I think Grayson understated the level of psycho. There's only one enemy left. The one who's always been there. Will he show tonight?

The banging on the door startles me.

"Hurry up!" Peyton shouts through the door.

Hurrying, I rush through my shower. Two minutes later, I'm standing in front of Peyton.

He's staring at my hair.

I cock my head to the side, but he immediately straightens it.

"The wet hair look actually works," he mutters to himself. "Smoky eye. Gloss. Leather shorts. It works." He claps his hands and points to the chair in the center of the room.

I sit down and he rolls a cart up beside me.

"We'll let your hair dry some while we do your make-up," Peyton tells me while he searches through a pile of make-up. "We've got twenty minutes. Don't talk, move only when I tell you and in the direction I tell you, and we'll make it."

"Tilt up."

"Straight forward but look up."

"Turn a little to the left."

"Now a little to the right."

"Close your lids."

"Suck in your cheeks."

"Ok, pucker those lips."

He steps back for a second. "Gorgeous. Damn, I'm good. Okay. Your hair is halfway dry. Let's smooth this gel-cream mix on it." His hands spread the mixture on my hair, then he uses a wide-tooth comb to part it on the side and comb it back. He tucks and smooths little pieces around my hairline. "Done!"

I grab the mirror to check it out while he gets the clothes from the closet. My bright pink hair is darker looking, and the slicked back style, with the deep side part, gives off a rocker vibe. "It's sexy!"

"Of course. Put this on. I'm going to the bathroom to get dressed. Don't touch anything," he warns me with a threatening look in his eye.

I slip into the black leather shorts. They tie around the waist and have a ruffle on top. I twist and look at the back. Thankfully, they're not too short.

The flower embroidered corset top is edged in gold, making the whole thing shimmer in the light. When I hold it up, I realize the eye hooks are in the front. Wrapping it around, I quickly get it on.

The short, cropped jacket matches the top. I slip it on.

Who knew shorts could look dressy? I turn side to side, admiring the entire look. The best part—it's comfortable! I grin.

"Turn around," Peyton orders from the bathroom door.

I twirl for him. "Can I wear shorts to every event?"

He hands me a pair of heels with wrap around ties. "No."

I put them on and twirl again.

"Perfect," he remarks, kissing his fingertips.

He's dressed in a sharp black suit with his pink hair slicked back like mine.

"Perfect," I mimic, kissing my fingertips. "Seriously, you look hot. Is your guy coming to the party?"

"He's meeting us there," Peyton replies with a final look in the mirror. "Let's go!"

I take his arm, and we head toward the living room.

Grayson, Thiago, and Mateo are waiting for us in the foyer, and when we round the corner, all talking ceases.

And I forget how to breathe.

Thiago's fierce in an all-black suit.

Mateo is sexy in dark jeans, a black t-shirt, and black sport coat.

Grayson's impeccably dressed in a dark navy suit with a crisp white button-down shirt.

Inhaling, I immediately whistle. "I'm one lucky woman."

"Mateo looks sexy," Peyton whispers to me.

"Hmm, they all do," I murmur. "And they're all mine."

289

He's silent, and I turn my head to find him looking at me in shock. "Damn, girl. Good for you."

"On the down low," I mutter, warning him to keep quiet.

"Good luck with keeping that to yourself," he retorts.

"You're right. You know what? Who cares," I respond rebelliously. Am I really worried about a society that hasn't done a thing to help me all these years? Nope.

Grayson comes over and offers his arm.

I air kiss Peyton because I don't dare smudge the make-up he put on me. "See you at the party."

He and Thiago get in one SUV and leave. Mateo, Grayson, and I get in the second one.

"Minha linda," Mateo says possessively, running a finger down my thigh. "Make sure you save me a dance."

Grayson leans in and kisses along my neck. "Mmm, you even smell beautiful, my sweet rose. And you know what it does to me to see your legs on display."

"What does it do to you?" I slide my hand over the front of his pants until I find what I'm looking for and run my hand lightly up and down. "Hold that thought."

Air hisses between his teeth and he clamps a hand down on top of mine. "Minx. Later." Placing a kiss on my palm, he sets it back down on my thigh.

I sigh.

Mateo slips an earpiece into my ear. "Tonight, we're all wearing one. If you need anything, just speak. We'll hear."

"Got it," I confirm.

We pull up to the yacht a few seconds later.

"Let's celebrate this launch," I state quietly, dreading the evening and the potential danger it holds.

Getting out of the SUV, I walk over to stand with Peyton. The press is specifically stationed here to capture guests when they walk in. "Isn't he fabulous? He designed this gorgeous outfit and styled me from head to toe tonight. I mean, look at the detail on this corset and jacket." I point out the intricate stitching where the gold outlines the flowers and the edges. "Meticulous and beautiful."

Peyton's eyes shine, and he squeezes me into his side.

The press takes several pictures of us both, then up-close images of my outfit, and I leave him to finish the interview. "Come find me later and introduce me to your guy."

The Santos men wait for me to join them. Sliding into the middle, between Thiago and Mateo, I stand tall and proud. The press goes wild. Cameras flash like crazy. Reporters shout questions asking who's dating who. Thiago ignores them and signals for security to let Dan on the yacht as payment for helping us create the fake newspaper.

Thiago gives a mini speech about the product launch and the celebration. He declines any interviews, stating an exclusive with Dan, from the Miami Herald.

We board the yacht and take the elevator up to the party.

Security is everywhere. There's not an inch of this yacht that isn't covered with manpower or surveillance.

Later, we're going to officially announce the launch of the software and show the demonstration video. Right now, it's time to mingle while we wait for all the guests to arrive.

The three men are quickly surrounded by people needing their attention, but I don't want to join a bunch of strangers. I point to the bar to let them know where I'll be.

I'm pouring a glass of wine when I hear a distinct British voice behind me. I turn to find Sterling talking quietly to Zane. As usual, he's dressed to impress in an impeccably cut suit.

"British men certainly know how to dress," I drawl.

Sterling spins around and gives me a dashing grin. "Hmm, you're looking quite smashing yourself, darling."

I reach up and give him a hug. "How is Cruz? I miss him."

His face tightens. "The situation is tense right now. Raider and I switched places. He went to help him so I could fly back here tonight. Zane and I return tomorrow."

I squeeze Sterling's arm. "We can handle this," I say, waving my arm around the party. "If you guys need to leave, go. I'm sure Thiago would agree."

An arm slips around my waist. "I do agree. Leave. Let us know if there's anything you need from us."

Zane and Sterling eye each other, then nod in relief. "Thank you. We'll regroup on the foundation after this mission."

"I'll wire the money tomorrow for the time your team spent helping us," Thiago assures Zane.

Zane rubs his hands together. "That's going to be one hell of a payday."

Thiago winces. "Well deserved. Without your team, we wouldn't have gotten to this point. I appreciate it."

Sterling winces. "I completely forgot about the bank information. Did you find the customer info, or do you need me to carve out some time to investigate it?"

I smile and pat his arm. "We figured it out." It's safe to say it belonged to Kathleen, but I don't tell him. No need for him to feel bad.

Zane reaches over and gives me a hug. "Take care of yourself. Don't let them run over you."

I scoff. "If you need anything, above or below the line, reach out to CJ Tech." Essentially, I told him CJ Tech will provide him with any legal or illegal hacking him or his team needs.

Thiago tightens his arm around my waist but says nothing.

"I've missed Cruz, and now I'll miss them," I murmur. "Good friends are hard to find. And keep." I've called one person "friend" since college—Marcos. Until now. My little circle is growing.

"Mr. Santos, there's a package here for a Henley Night?" A lady wearing an SEI security uniform stands behind Thiago with a small box. "It's been scanned and cleared."

I eye it with trepidation. "The good news is it's too small to be a head."

He signals to Allison. "We're going to the top deck for a second."

Allison raises two fingers, and a pair of her men follow us up. She stops us on the way and removes our earpieces.

Thiago sets the box down on the table in front of the sofa. He carefully lifts the lid. Pink tissue paper is wrapped around the "gift." Peeling it slowly back, he stares down into the box.

I lean over and peer down. It's a frame with a picture in it. He must have taken it with a telephoto lens because it's clear as day and remarkably detailed. Kathleen is standing on the deck with the gun pointed at my head. Sweat is beading on my forehead, and I'm staring straight at her. My chin is lifted, and my jaw locked.

"What's the note say?" I ask, my voice hoarse and tight.

Breathtaking. I've never been more proud of you. Facing death with courage. When Kathleen set her sights on you in Austin, I knew I needed to eliminate her. I was willing to follow the plan and wait, but when the bitch took my sweet David this morning, she became my enemy. A life for a life. You're welcome, little brain. I'll come for you soon.

"I guess he's made other plans tonight," I jest, but my laugh is hollow. I scrutinize Thiago, who hasn't said a word since he saw the picture.

I shove the table back and move in front of him. Cupping his head, I pull it up to meet my eyes. "Are you okay?"

His arms wrap around me like bands of steel. "I hate it. This image. Not being there to protect you," he rasps, his obsidian eyes wild with fury and a hint of fear. "It was too fucking close. And the bastard stopped to take a picture? What the fuck?"

I trail my fingers down the side of his face. "Thiago, my fierce protector. It was close, but I'm here with you. Grayson and Mateo are here. That's what matters." I bend down and seal his lips with mine.

He's stiff at first, his anger front and center, but after a second, the floodgates open and passion comes pouring out. He takes over the kiss, devouring me, until I can't feel or taste anything but him. After several minutes, he pulls back with a shudder.

The sound of an alarm going off in his jacket makes me raise an eyebrow.

"It's time for the announcement," he says gruffly, but his mouth twitches.

"Let's go celebrate," I tell him, my voice even huskier than usual.

Several minutes later, we join the party. Grayson and Mateo look relieved.

Mateo leans in close. "We heard there was a package. Everything okay?"

"We'll show you after the party," I murmur.

Thiago makes a huge speech about the software Marcos and I co-invented, then plays the demonstration video. The crowd exclaims excitedly. Last, he announces the donation partnership with Epic Entertainment and introduces Beau Whitman. Beau makes a speech, and suddenly, it's done. I sigh in relief.

The crowd converges on the two of them, but surprisingly, I gain my own little crowd of people. Mainly comprised of doctors and surgeons, they express their excitement and ask me a ton of questions. At first, it's a little unnerving to talk about my work in public, but I'm passionate about this project. It's remarkable, and I want everyone to use it. Of course, I also make sure to mention Marcos' name when I talk about it. It's his legacy, too.

Is this what it would be like to work for SEI? I don't want to make CJ Tech a legal entity because of the rescues. Surely there's a way for me to do both. Maybe I should start a second—legal company? My eyes slide to my men. Should I talk to them about it? Will they be able to look at this objectively and help me decide what's best for me versus what's best because it's legal?

Grayson excuses himself from the people surrounding him. "Everything okay?"

"It's good. I'm trying to decide some things for the future," I quip.

Grayson looks alarmed. "Don't make decisions until things are settled. We'll all sit down together and talk about it, okay?"

Giving him a bewildered look, I nod. "Is it almost time to go home?"

He laughs loudly, causing several heads to turn. "The business part is done, but the party is just getting started."

I give him an incredulous look because we've been for over two hours. "I'm going to get some wine."

"I'll go with you," he returns with a grin.

When we get to the bar, Peyton's standing with the tall, good-looking man I remember from the ball. "Ahem, can I get an introduction, please?"

"Henley!" Peyton exclaims in a slightly tipsy voice. "This is Alejandro, my incredibly sexy man. Alejandro, this is Henley. My muse. And my friend."

Alejandro looks indulgently at Peyton, then turns to me. "It's nice to meet you," he drawls. "We wouldn't have met if you hadn't invited Peyton to the ball. Thank you."

"I don't think I'm the reason. He looked out the shop window and decided to save me. I was desperate and thankful, so I surrendered instantly," I joke. "He's incredibly talented, and I'm thrilled to have him as a friend. Once things settle down, we'll have dinner together, okay?"

Alejandro's eyes go to Grayson, who smiles. "Absolutely. I'll cook."

Peyton leans over. "He cooks, too?"

"An exceptional cook," I confirm. "He looks hot in an apron, too."

Grayson's hand covers my mouth. "I think the wine is flowing a little too freely tonight."

Alejandro chuckles and pointedly looks at Peyton. "I would agree."

"We'll see you later," I tell them as Grayson drags me off. "Where are we going?"

"Dancing," he responds with a wicked smile, pointing to where Thiago and Mateo are standing on the edge of the dance floor.

All three of them. "Hmm, yes please," I reply with a heartfelt sigh.

For the next however many hours, we dance and drink and dance some more. I live only for the moment. This moment with them. No enemies, stalkers, or ghosts from the past. And when we finally leave the yacht, I'm weaving back and forth. Laughing and singing. On the way home, I'm out.

CHAPTER 42

<u>HENLEY</u>

When the alarm goes off next to me, I lift my head and groan. Blindly reaching out to make it stop, I encounter a hard body beside me. Opening one blurry eye, I see Thiago smirking at me.

"Somebody let loose last night," Thiago teases in a low voice which I greatly appreciate. "I'll get you some water and aspirin."

"Please," I grunt, barely able to get the words out.

He helps me sit up and take the tablets before lying back down.

His finger sweeps the hair from my eyes. "I'm going to work out. Sleep some more, querida."

I bury my head in the covers in response.

It's light when I wake again. Stumbling into the shower, I stand there bleary-eyed until my brain starts to function. When I get out, some wonderful man has laid leggings and a Green Day t-shirt on the bed. I chuckle and get dressed.

"There she is," Grayson says cheerily when I sit down at the island. Coffee and a plate of greasy goodness lands in front of me.

With a huge sigh of relief, I dig in and don't stop until it's gone. My hangover starts to subside.

"Better, thank you," I mumble to Grayson.

He kisses me on the forehead and takes my plate.

"Well, we're down to one enemy. What do we do now? How do we draw him out?" I ask, blowing out a breath.

Thiago leans against the cabinet with his arms crossed. "My workout was longer than usual this morning and it gave me time to think." He smirks at me.

Yeah, yeah. Give a girl a break.

"And?" I prompt him.

"We might have a few options. We can take the evidence we have to the police and see if they think it's enough to charge him with the murder of Kathleen," Thiago suggests, then continues. "We could put his name and picture in the paper and offer a reward for information on his whereabouts. Turn the hunter into the prey." He clears his throat. "Or we could hire someone to hunt him down and take him out."

Grayson likes the idea of the reward.

Mateo frowns. "I'm worried he'll go off the deep end, making it worse for Henley. I don't like any of the options."

They turn to me. "I like the third option. I'm tired of looking over my shoulder, knowing he's there. You saw the pictures. This has been going on for ten years. I want a life. A real one."

"Okay, that's what we'll do," Thiago states, his voice hard.

My conviction lasts for a whole minute. It's so tempting, but I can't let them. Thiago would likely be fine, but the other two would dwell on it. "No, we can't. I don't want this between us. We need to think of a way to trap him. Maybe we can dangle a black hat job in front of him, then inform the FBI."

"Henley—"

Thiago's phone buzzes. "What is it?"

He stands up straight and motions for us to stop talking.

"Where are you?" Thiago asks, grabbing a pen and paper. His hand is poised to write, but a second later, he throws down the pen. "Keep on him. We'll get to SEI and join the teams. Talk to you soon." He hangs up.

His face is filled with a grim satisfaction. "The security team caught Langford on camera early this morning. Thomas and a couple of his men tried to set up surveillance, but Langford hasn't returned to wherever he's holed up now. They've been following him for a couple of hours. Thomas even sent one man back to SEI after he ran into Langford outside a shop. He isn't taking any chances."

"Jameson's got three teams ready to go when Thomas gives the word, but until Langford stops moving, we can't send in more men," Thiago explains in a rush. "Whatever it takes, we're going to ride this one out. We have home field advantage and that won't be the case if he decides to leave Miami. I'm going to grab a quick shower." He motions to Mateo and Grayson. "Tactical gear. We'll split up amongst the teams."

I raise my hand to get his attention. "Umm, I don't have tactical gear. Are jeans and a t-shirt okay?"

Thiago stops and pivots to pull me in close. "Henley, I don't want you to go. If Langford is feeling cornered, it could get ugly. Would you please stay here?"

I think about it for a minute, then nod slowly. "I'll agree to stay, on one condition."

All three men tense, waiting for me to tell them.

"If you kill Harrison Langford, I want to see and touch the body. I need to know beyond a shadow of a doubt, he's dead. If not, I won't have any closure," I state firmly.

The three of them relax.

Thiago holds out his hand to shake mine, and I can't help but remember the first time we made a deal. If I could show him I could shoot, he'd be okay with me having a gun. "It's a deal."

"Thank you. Now, go!" I order them.

Within fifteen minutes, they're dressed in outfits similar to the black fatigues and t-shirts Zane's team wears. As if the black isn't menacing enough, the weapons certainly make the threat real.

299

Mitch walks into the room.

"Stay alert. Keep the radio on and your phone close. When we catch the bastard, you'll need to organize the team and bring Henley to our location, okay?" Thiago commands Mitch.

"Yes, sir," he replies firmly.

After a brief kiss from each of them, they're gone, leaving me to worry and pace. Is it greedy to want them safe and Langford eliminated?

For the next hour, Mitch and I listen to Thomas reporting on the movements of Langford. He's been practically everywhere in Miami, and it doesn't look like he has any intention of stopping.

My phone buzzes with sweet emojis and messages from Grayson and Mateo. Thiago's texts are full of questions and thinly veiled orders disguised as suggestions. I respond sweetly to almost everything. When I don't respond to Thiago's suggestions to lie down for a while, I see dots come and go a few times before finally ceasing.

Thomas groans, and we all tense. "He's turned into a car wash, and the line goes out the door. We're going to be here for a while."

Mitch tosses the phone down and heads to the restroom.

I plop down on the couch. He's got to sleep sometime, right? But night is a hell of a long way away.

Something crashes on the patio, and I cautiously slip to the corner to peer out. A planter has been knocked over. Tilting my head from side to side, I hold my breath and wait, but the only sound I hear is the wind off the ocean. Still, I double check the patio door to make sure it's locked and the security bar is in place. Relieved, I exhale loudly.

The radio is silent except for the ambient traffic noise. I head to the kitchen to get a glass of ice water and a couple of pain tablets. Stress is making my throat dry, and my hangover isn't helping.

When I return, I eye the couch with distaste, but there's no way I can wait this out in my room by myself. With a sigh, I drop back down and sip my water.

I pull my phone out and check for updates, but there's nothing.

After an hour of continuous noise, it's too quiet. Is the radio still on? I set the glass of water on the table and look for the radio. It's not here.

Dropping to my knees, I check under the table, but it's empty. I know the radio was here, and Mitch hasn't come back from the restroom yet. My hand slides to the holster at my side, and I unsnap the strap. Staying low beside the couch, I send a text to all three of them and wait. Nothing. Instead of sliding my phone in my pocket, I put it on silent and slip it into my bra, maneuvering it until it's snug under my arm.

Quietly getting to my feet, I listen for several minutes. Something is wrong. The pit in my gut is screaming for me to get out. After years on the run, it's been a lifesaver more times than I can count. I used to question the logic, but I don't anymore. Sometimes the universe gives you what you need, but it's up to you to act on it.

I hear Mitch coming out of the bathroom. Tense, I silently urge him to hurry. He ambles down the hall and enters the living room.

I raise my finger to my lips.

He pulls his gun and silently makes his way over to my side. His eyes dart to the table, then back to me. He raises an eyebrow, silently asking if I have the radio.

I shake my head.

His brows come together as he realizes we're in trouble and we don't have a way to call for back-up quickly. He pulls out his phone and texts but receives nothing in reply.

Either everyone we know is busy or our cells phone signals are being jammed. My bet is the latter. I look at Mitch and point to the patio door.

He points to the front door. I understand his logic. The security team is out front patrolling. But I glance at the distance and shudder. It's a long way to go.

He motions for me to get behind him.

I grip the back of his bulletproof vest with one hand and hold my gun ready with the other. He quietly walks across the living room, gun held in front of him, and I follow.

301

Right before we cross over the hallway to the foyer, he stops and darts his head around the corner. It's clear. We move onto the tile of the entryway. Only five more feet.

A noise comes from behind me, and I tighten my grip and turn.

Something hard strikes my arm. Pain radiates from my forearm to my fingers, but I still manage to pull the trigger. Unfortunately, the angle is wrong, and I completely miss.

Two more shots are fired, almost simultaneously.

Mitch grunts behind me, and I hear him fall to the ground, but I don't dare turn to check on him. Langford's gun is pointed directly at my head.

Langford grimaces, and I see he's hit in his right shoulder. Mitch's shot would have been the perfect hit to make him drop his gun. Unfortunately, he's holding the gun in his left hand. A southpaw.

He gestures for me to drop the gun.

My fingers grip it tighter, and I stare defiantly at him.

"Do you want to be responsible for another death? Look behind you. I'd say he has about twenty minutes?" he drawls, a smug look on his face.

Keeping him in my sights, I step to the side and dart a glance at the floor where Mitch lays. Langford's aim was true. He hit him between the neck and his shoulder, where the vest doesn't provide cover.

Mitch's blue eyes stare steadily at me. He looks at my gun and shakes his head negatively.

I look at the blood pouring out of him and put my gun on the floor.

Langford kicks it away.

"Someone has to tell them," I murmur. Mitch needs to make it so he can tell them what happened. Not wanting Langford to get any ideas, I stride quickly to the front door.

He rushes after me and jerks me to a halt. "I can still shoot him from here." He smirks.

The handle is in my hand, so I fling the door open. "Are we staying or going?" I glare at him.

His eyes glint, and he places the gun on my temple. "No heroics. Head to the garage."

We only encounter two security men on our way to the garage. Nobody expected him to come from within the house, and most of the team is patrolling the outer edges of the property. With the gun to my head, they quickly back off.

My phone silently vibrates when we enter the garage, and I automatically look up at the camera hidden in the corner. Thiago should be hearing "Garage Door Open" right about now. He shoves me forward.

Noise bursts from his pocket. "Window closing. Car wash done."

His face is pale, and he's sweating. Reaching into his front pocket, with his bloody hand, he extracts a radio. Similar to the one the security team is carrying, but a slightly different model. "Leave the car and meet me at my place. One of those imbecile security guards shot me, and I'm going to need your help to bandage it up." He recites an address.

"Meet you there."

"That sounds like Philip," I say, testing out my theory.

"He contacted me. Offered to help me escape, but I told him I couldn't leave without you. Plus, I wasn't sure of his loyalty with David gone. When I noticed SEI's man earlier, I realized Philip could help me be in two places at once," he explains with a shrug, but his gaze isn't on me, it's on the vehicles in the garage.

I wait for him to pick.

"Which one is Thiago's?" he demands, motioning to the cars.

I point out the dark green Aston Martin DBS.

He smiles. "Get the keys. You're driving."

I look at the blood running down his arm and wince. Thiago's going to have to get rid of his car. Two minutes later, we're rolling down the driveway to the gate.

STELLA BRIE

When we get to the bottom, the car is surrounded by security with guns pointing at the car.

He pushes the gun into my temple. "Move or I'll put a bullet in her head."

One of the men puts his hand to his ear, then turns it in a circle. The gate slowly opens.

We roll through and Langford drops his hand to his lap. The gun is pointed at me, but the wound is taking its toll. He's fading, but I can't tell if it's fast enough for me to have a shot at escaping before we get to the apartment or not.

We clear the security gate to our neighborhood.

He waves the gun. "Floor it."

CHAPTER 43

HENLEY

"Why me?" I ask him the question that's been burning in my throat for ten years. "I used to wonder how you even knew me, but David answered that question for me the other day. Now, I just want to know why."

"Most of the students at MIT are smart, and quite a few of them come from wealthy or privileged backgrounds with every advantage given to them. But here you are, a nobody from nowhere, with no connections, no advantages, and instead of trying to beat everyone to the top, you want to use your brain to help others. You were an anomaly," he muses, his eyes on the distant past.

"I used to listen to you talk about all these ideas you had to help others, and I couldn't help but wonder if it was real. I'd never met anyone who truly wanted to help others. My parents always said they did, making a big deal out of their charitable contributions, but behind the scenes, they were horrible people who only cared about themselves. You seemed sincere, but maybe it was a ruse to get David to fall for you," he admits.

"I had to know, so I watched, and the more I watched, the more

305

intrigued I became with the way you think. But David grew a conscience and broke it off with you. Incensed at first, I made him pay dearly for that decision, but the more I thought about it, the more excited I became. You could be my own little experiment. With very few friends or family, I could isolate you, test you, and determine if you were truly a match for me," he reveals with a gleam of madness in his unnerving eyes.

I grip the steering wheel tighter. "Is that why you killed my mother?"

"She was your safety net, but I knew you could make it on your own," he replies derisively with a smirk. "You exceeded almost all my expectations. Almost. Staging your death could be considered cheating, but I guess I don't mind the initiative you took. Finding you again after all these years… is much more exciting." He runs the barrel of the gun softy down my thigh. "I can't wait to test you. See if you're worthy."

I snort. "Thiago, Grayson, and Mateo think I'm worthy, and they're the only ones who count."

Snarling, he brings the gun up and taps the end of it against my temple. "I haven't forgotten you've been consorting with my enemies. You will not mention their names to me. The Savages took everything from my family. Wealth I was supposed to inherit—mine by right of birth."

"It was my understanding your father made a lot of bad business decisions. He squandered away your inheritance. Maybe you should blame him for losing it all instead of taking revenge against men who did nothing but protect their own," I state passionately, unwilling to let him continue with his delusional rhetoric.

He smiles at me and shoots the driver's side window out. The sound is deafening in the small confines of the car.

I scream and clap one hand over the ear closest to him until the ringing stops.

He turns the gun back toward me. "For weeks I've been dreaming of the punishments I'm going to give you. It's time you learned to show me loyalty and respect." He points to the right. "Slow down. Get off this exit."

Using the paddle shifters, I downshift as we come off the interstate.

"Turn right at the light," he instructs.

After turning, I look in the rearview mirror and notice an SUV coming up fast behind me. Thiago's in the front passenger seat. It pulls back to allow a sedan to move in between us. Thomas is driving.

Langford continues to give me directions until I realize we're going in circles. "What's going on?"

"Just making sure nobody is following us," he says with a smirk.

I say nothing. Every time we turn, the vehicles behind us switch out, but I've recognized several of the drivers. Jameson, Allison, Thomas, and a few other security guys, although I don't remember their names. All driving different vehicles.

Langford messed up when he went to the garage. Once the security system alerted Thiago the garage door was open, he could easily see and hear us through the app. Langford essentially gave his address to his enemy.

He slumps against the window and snarls at the pain. "Fortunately for you, I don't see anyone coming to your rescue. Take a left at the light." After we turn, he points to bright white apartment buildings. "There."

I park the car and look at him.

"Slide to my side and get out," he orders. "Don't try anything."

I do as he says, and we slowly make it to his apartment. When we get closer, Philip opens the door.

"David would be so proud," I say sarcastically toward Philip.

"He will be," Philip returns quietly.

Langford turns to me. "Help me get this shirt off."

I stare at him. "Let your buddy help you."

He locks his jaw, but I look away. Movement at the corner of the kitchen window catches my eye, and I see Thiago slide up to the side of it. His gun is out and ready.

Philip cuts the shirt but when he pulls it away, Langford screams. "Be careful, you idiot. The blood has dried in some places. Grab a wet towel from the kitchen."

Philip walks away to do as he asks. "It doesn't look too bad. We can get you patched up quickly."

Philip's words make me look at the edges of Langford's wound. Very little blood is flowing out now. I think he's going to live. A pity.

The water in the kitchen comes on, and I glance over at Philip. He's whistling. Unable to stand his cheeriness, I look away.

"As soon as he patches me up, we're leaving Miami," Langford announces with a sigh.

"What about your revenge? You're not going to let a little bullet hole stop you, are you?" I taunt him.

"They've been a very bad influence on you. I'll have to correct these misconceptions you have that I'm a tolerant man. I'm not. Insubordination will not be tolerated," he says sarcastically, as if quoting someone from his past.

Philip comes over with the wet towel and soaks the shirt until it softens. He leans closer, grasps it with one hand, and rips it off. He brings the other hand from behind his back, revealing a large chef's knife, and plunges it into Langford's neck, then jerks it out.

Blood spurts out spraying my chest, and I scramble to get away from it.

Langford roars and grabs his throat. Body swaying, he manages to stand and face Philip. He raises his gun.

I scream for Philip to run, but he just laughs. A gunshot fills the air.

Expecting Philip to fall, I'm shocked to see Langford crumple to the ground instead with a hole in the side of his head.

I glance at the kitchen window and see Thiago lowering his gun.

Security bursts in a second later.

Philip's eyes never leave Langford's body.

In a daze, I squat and feel for a pulse, but there isn't one. Thiago's aim was true. "He's dead," I tell Philip, standing to stare down at the bloody mess on the ground. I silently repeat it to myself a few times, too, until I can feel it take root.

Relief and a strange sort of happiness takes over. I can't help feeling glad Philip stabbed him. Watching the knife slam into Langford's body and tear through his muscles and arteries was spectacular, but the brutal efficiency in which Philip yanked it out, was the chef's kiss. I bet it hurt like hell. I smile.

"Maybe now David can rest in peace," Philip replies, then spits on Langford's body.

I nod in agreement. "His death will bring peace to my mother, Marcos, and so many others." I take a step back from the puddle of blood expanding on the floor. "Except him. May he rot in the hell he deserves."

"Henley," Thiago states softly, walking up to us.

Philip turns to face Thiago and raises an eyebrow. "Am I free to go?"

"Yes, but I recommend leaving Miami," Thiago suggests in a hard voice.

"I will," Philip assures him. "Oh, here's your radio." He hands Thiago one of SEI's security radios. "Thomas gave it to me. Asked me to notify him if I saw Langford. Just want to be sure I return it."

Thomas reaches past Thiago and takes the radio. "Thanks, Philip. Good job."

Philip walks out the door.

Thiago crosses his arms and looks at Thomas.

"Tactical warfare. Sometimes a frontal assault is not the answer," he discloses before carefully picking up the knife. He wipes the handle, then places a clear plastic over it. When he lifts the plastic, a couple of partial prints show. "Diego conveniently left his prints on SEI's server. I'll call this into the police and let them deal with the cleanup." Whistling, he walks off.

"Glad he's on our side," I tell Thiago, who nods in agreement.

He reaches out to pull me into his arms, but I hold up my hands. "I'm covered in blood. His blood."

Yanking me into his arms, he holds me tightly. "His blood is on my hands too. You just can't see it." He rocks back and forth with me in his arms.

"I was an experiment," I blurt out, telling him what Langford said to me. My voice shakes when I recount how my isolation made me the perfect target for him. "A single variable with built-in control factors."

He smooths the hair back from my head. "Never again." Black eyes drill into mine, and I grab onto the hope I see in them.

"Where are Mateo and Grayson?" I ask, shifting my attention to the people around us.

"Outside. Thomas didn't want a lot of people inside," he says, smiling wryly. "Now I know why. He didn't want to contaminate the crime scene."

My bra vibrates. I pull out my phone to find dozens of messages from all three of them. I slide it back. I'll read them later. "How's Mitch?"

"He made it, but he wouldn't have if you hadn't gone with Langford," Thiago informs me. "We'll go see him in a few days, okay?" He squeezes me tightly, then turns us toward the door. "Let's go find Mateo and Grayson. I know they need to hold you for a while. Honestly, I'm not sure if any of us will be able to let you out of our sight any time soon."

I glance down at Langford's blood-soaked face one last time, then I turn my back and walk away. My days of running scared are over.

CHAPTER 44

HENLEY

I t took a while to get everything settled with the police. After a Chinese takeout dinner, we're on the back patio, reflecting on the last few days.

"Out of all the scenarios I ran through my mind, Kathleen wasn't even a possibility. We'd have missed her until it was too late. Her rage at Henley helped draw her out," Thiago states in a voice filled with frustration. "The whole thing came down to revenge and money."

"It's hard to believe two months ago, I was sitting in my beautiful loft living the quiet life. Funny thing is... the only thing I miss is Marcos. Even with all the crazy car chases, shootings, and psychos, this is better than my old life. It's real." I can't help but think a lot of it has to do with the men beside me. I'm not sure I would have stuck around on my own.

"I'd give anything to have a conversation with Marcos. A real one where he shares his problems, instead of him only listening to mine. I miss him," Mateo states sadly. "Maybe if he'd have shared his problems, I'd have met Henley sooner."

"We wouldn't have been ready for her," Grayson remarks with a rueful grin. "Plus, I don't think Marcos wanted to share her. He could leave SEI behind and spend time in a world he created doing what he loved most."

I shake my head. "I wasn't ready, and I was too scared. Being forced to change was the only way for me to find a new way forward," I admit with a sigh. "Speaking of forced... I was completely dreading last night, but it turned out to be eye-opening and loads of fun."

Thiago props his elbows on his knees and leans forward. "I thought you were dreading it because of Harrison. Was there something else?"

"Yes and no," I reply trying to think of how to explain it. "I've never celebrated the launch of one of my creations in public. It was nerve-wracking, but it turned out to be incredible. The launch is going great. A two percent adoption rate in the first two days means we've already recouped our development costs and we're in the black. The trajectory is trending upward with exponential daily increases in licenses. If we keep up this rate, we'll hit the fifteen percent mark easily."

Thiago and Grayson share a surprised look.

Mateo laughs. "You should see your faces. She's been running a multi-million-dollar business for years. It might not be entirely legitimate, but that only meant she didn't have to worry about taxes." He leans over to give me a kiss. "Congratulations on a successful launch."

"Thank you. It was nice to see something I helped to create receive so much praise by the public. I never thought it would be possible." I pause, then bring up the thoughts I'd had last night. "I'm thinking about creating a legitimate business, where I can promote the work more. But I don't want to get rid of CJ Tech. It's too valuable for helping people who can't get IDs and other documentation through legal channels. It would be entirely separate, though. What do you think?"

The three of them converse silently, and I wait, with arms crossed, for them to answer.

They move in closer. Thiago sits on the coffee table in front of me and picks up my hand.

"We talked about bringing FJ Technologies into SEI, right? Why don't you run the company? Take whatever role you want, pick the projects you want to work on, and work with SEI to promote and launch them. With you owning shares of SEI, it makes perfect sense."

I bite my lip. "It feels weird. That's Marcos' baby."

"We can change the things you don't like," Grayson offers. "Marcos certainly wouldn't mind. I think he'd be honored."

Mateo jumps in with his thoughts. "One company for you both. If you're working on ideas from Marcos' notebook, you can attribute the work to him. Or if they're your ideas, you retain the credit. It merges all the pieces we've been discussing the last few weeks. Plus, I'd love to have you working at SEI."

The other two nod.

"If I did, I'd want to name it something new," I inform them.

Thiago crosses his arms. "What are you thinking?"

It would need to be something that represents both Marcos and me. The one thing that pops into my mind seems kind of silly, but we shared the two spaces. "NT Labs."

Puzzled, they wait for me to explain.

"We created a lab in the metaverse where we worked on our projects together. After a long day of work, we'd go to Nacho Tequila for a drink. Those are our two places. They belong to Marcos and me. It seems fitting to carry on with a name representing both of us. Something belonging only to us," I proclaim with certainty.

"He would love it," Thiago affirms.

Both Grayson and Mateo agree.

"So, are you stating your intent to run the company?" Thiago presses for an answer. "If you're serious, we'll get things moving to start up a new subsidiary."

STELLA BRIE

I bite my lip nervous to bring up my concern. "What about us?" I wave a hand to indicate all four of us. "I'm not asking for a declaration of love or forever, but we haven't talked about anything. I've been living temporarily in your house. Do I move out when this is over? Get a place in Miami? What?"

Mateo interjects before the other two can get their words out. "What do you want? Do you want to live on your own?" Thiago snarls. "Or move out of Miami?" Grayson cusses. "Or live here? What do you want?"

I think about my answer for a second. "I want to love and be loved. I want to continue doing meaningful work—both the product development and rescues. I want to travel—everywhere. I want to have kids someday."

Mateo clears his throat. "Do you see yourself doing any of that with us?"

I hesitate, then throw caution to the wind. "When I chose to stay and fight a few weeks ago, I promised myself I would find a life and grab it with both hands. This is me fulfilling that promise. I'm crazy about you. All three of you. Honestly, I can't imagine my life without you in it, but if you don't feel the same way, I need to leave and find a life without you. It's too important to me. I'm tired of living my life alone. I want more."

"Henley, I love you. I've known it for weeks, but I didn't want to say anything because I knew you weren't ready. If you leave, I'll follow you," Mateo states passionately, his voice full of love.

I pull him toward me and kiss him until we're both breathless. "I love you, too," I tell him shyly.

Thiago brings my hand up and kisses the palm. "Querida, você é minha. Sweetheart, you are mine. And I am yours. It's as simple and complicated as those words. I want you to stay. Forever. And hopefully, one day, have my child."

Thiago doesn't wait for me to lean over. He pulls me into his lap and takes control with a fierce kiss that leaves no doubt as to the way he feels.

"I love you, too, Thiago," I assure him, watching his eyes close as if he's savoring the words.

I hesitantly look at Grayson, but the darkness he's been carrying with him is gone. I move over to him and smile.

"It's taken me so long to get to this point," Grayson begins. "I could jump out of an airplane, but I couldn't take a leap of faith with you. When I read Kira's diary and looked at the madness in Kathleen's eyes, I realized I was letting fear hold me back. My mind is my own worst enemy. Our path might be rockier, but my heart is yours, without condition."

Tears slip down my cheeks knowing how much this took for him to bet on us. He's all in. "I love you, Grayson, and I won't give up," I promise him. My lips find his, letting the heat sweep us away for a minute.

I look around. This is the life I'm grabbing with both hands. The one with these three men. "NT Labs, Miami, here in our home with you. I guess there's only one thing left to settle," I drawl, turning to stare at Thiago. "Who gets the office? And the couch?"

EPILOGUE

*S*ix months later...

MATEO WALKS into my office and gives me a devilish grin. I motion for him to sit while I finalize the details of our new deal. A robotics engineer in Nigeria has developed a smart bra capable of detecting early breast cancer. The bra utilizes ultrasound technology allowing women to safely use the device in the comfort of their own homes without relying on costly medical tests.

It's ready for the market, but unfortunately, the lifesaving wearable has been held up by lack of materials and funding. Not anymore. The Juliana Silva Santos Foundation is going to fund the entire production. Based on our research, the bra is a better, and more accessible, solution than Marcos' vest. Using the foundation to fund it allows us to follow his last wishes and honor his wife's battle with breast cancer.

With a satisfied sigh, I hang up and tilt my head at the handsome man in front of me. "What are you up to?" He's always surprising me with something, but not at work. Unfortunately, we're all so busy during the day we rarely even see each other.

He stands and holds his hand out. "It's a surprise. Come with me."

I don't even hesitate. Placing my hand in his, I follow him out the door and into the elevator. When the doors open, Thiago and Grayson are waiting for us.

"Hmm, all three of you. Should I be worried?" I tease them.

Thiago bends down and captures my lips. "Of course not." He waves us into his office.

Instead of the couch, four chairs surround the coffee table. A bottle of tequila sits in the middle of the table along with five shot glasses.

I raise an eyebrow. "What are we celebrating?"

Mateo brings me over to a chair and motions for me to sit. He takes the seat next to me.

Grayson comes over and slips a pair of glasses on me. Lips land firmly on mine for a second before he walks away. I hear the tinkling of glasses. Then silence.

A few minutes later, we're sitting in Nacho Tequila.

Unable to help the tears filling my eyes, I turn and look around the colorful bar before swiveling to face the three men in front of me. "How did you know?"

I'd been missing Marcos and our old routine fiercely the last month. The first few months had been insanely busy getting NT Labs up and running and deciding which projects to work on, but once everything settled down, I couldn't help but feel lost without him.

"We feel the same way," Grayson admits softly. "We're just better at hiding it." His hand twirls the glass of tequila sitting in front of him.

"We miss him more at home because that's where we saw him most, but you worked with him every day," Mateo chimes in sadly.

"I could see the grief in your eyes every time you reached a mile-stone or finished a project."

"He may not be physically here, but I don't doubt he's keeping tabs on us," Thiago states gruffly followed by a chuckle. "We thought the idea of celebrating your victories at Nacho Tequila is a tradition we should carry on together. A little piece of him, and the tequila he loved so much. It almost feels like he's right here with us." Thiago's dark eyes stare steadily into mine. "What do you think?"

"I love the idea," I tell him huskily, my voice overcome with emotion for these men. It's been tough adjusting to an entirely new life, but they've been with me every step of the way erasing my doubts and easing my fears. And loving me more than I could have imagined. "It couldn't have come at a better time, either." I explain the deal I made to fund the breast cancer detection bra. "With the AR/VR glasses all distributed and this deal, we've officially achieved Marcos' last wishes. It's time to celebrate." I raise the glass of tequila in my hand. "To Marcos—Saúde!"

"To Marcos! Saúde!" they repeat.

We toast the man who meant so much to us and down the shot of tequila. I silently send an additional prayer of thanks his way for the wonderful men he raised, who I now call mine. And for a split second, I see him at the bar, laughing, with his glass of tequila raised toward me.

THANK YOU!

Thank you for reading. I hope you enjoyed the conclusion of this series. It was a passion project for me and while it may not appeal to everyone, I loved it. I appreciate you giving it a chance.

*If you find an error, feel free to email me at Stellabrie@ stellabrie.com.

Is the technology real??? Get the scoop on the next page!

Cruz, Sterling, Zane, and Raider's book is on pre-order!
Lethal Vengeance

To get a free eBook copy of my first book, My Salvation, just subscribe to my newsletter.
Website: https://www.stellabrie.com/my-salvation

THE TECHNOLOGY

After the first book, a lot of you were curious to know which of the tech is real, coming soon, or completely made up, so I'm dropping this info here. Enjoy!

- The Augmented Reality (AR) Vein Mapping Device is… real! Vein visualization is a new technology and incredibly valuable to medical staff. One of my beta team members is in the medical field and has actually used it!

- NFTs, or non-fungible tokens, are "real". And like the NFT in Grayson's office, these digital assets can be displayed with a new type of digital frame in the real world. You can also display them using an app + device combination. It's pretty fascinating and constantly evolving.

- AR glasses exist. VR headsets exist. AR/VR headset concepts exist. Apple says their version is coming 2023, but we'll see. AR/VR glasses are a few years behind, but one day…

- Full body avatars can now be created for Virtual Reality (VR) worlds using specific apps. It's new technology and in its infancy. There are some issues with spatial awareness, movement, and other things which can cause the images to be clunky, though.

- Metaverse does exist. It's sort of like a multiverse right now with a network of 3D virtual worlds. People are meeting in "rooms" using headsets and apps and reviewing things like PowerPoint decks. There are "bars" in the metaverse, but the drinks are pixe-lated. You can always sip through a straw in real life to enjoy your beverage. :-) NachoTequila does not exist. Streets exist and so do stores. Most of what I mentioned exists, but it's still in its infancy. Incredibly exciting, though!

- Smart clothing, otherwise known as wearables, is happening. Prototypes have been created to detect breast and other types of cancer, monitor pregnant women, help smokers quit, monitor mili-tary vitals, and a myriad of other purposes. The breast cancer detection method I mentioned using fibers embedded in the fabric is real, but it's not the only one out there. Several universities have working prototypes that use a variety of methods. Again, infancy but very exciting.

- The banking technology is *mostly* made up, but I combined real technology with made up scenarios. There are anti money laun-dering algorithms and banks do use daily ledger balances but whether they use them in the way I described… I don't know. :-)

- Insurance algorithms to detect fraud are real.

- Rootkits are real and very, very scary.

- InterPlanetary File System does exist. Its purpose today is to share and store information and data in a distributed file system. It's being used for a wide variety of reasons, including the storing of important information in multiple locations vs. one recording or file location. It's helpful because if one file is taken down, another copy is still available and accessible. This is huge for those who live in a country where information is blocked or censored.

- This series was built around AR technology designed to map a patient's organs and internal systems and overlay them on top of the body for surgeons to use in surgery. Almost like a roadmap. While the display devices and sources of data differs between plat-forms, this is cutting-edge technology TODAY. It's real and it's happening now.

Within the last year, neurosurgeons at Johns Hopkins University have successfully used augmented reality in surgery, and more recently, the FDA cleared several new AR and VR technologies to assist in surgical visualization, navigation, training, and treatment.

- IDs. The average cost for a new identity depends on how much background is set up, but it starts around 0.10 BTC (bitcoin) or USD $2,100+ depending on market value.

- The breast cancer detection bra is real and may hit the market this year!

Some of you thought all or most of the technology was made up when in fact most of it is happening today, maybe just not in the exact way I described. Kind of blows your mind, doesn't it?

BRAZILIAN PORTUGUESE

Special thanks to the beautiful and wonderful Vanessa Santos—from Natal, Brazil—who helped me translate phrases…and so much more. Thank you!

Meu anjo – My angel
Meu amigo – My friend
Você é meu - you are mine
Desgraçado - Bastard
Querida – Sweetheart
Foda / Caralho - Fuck
Meus pequenos selvagens – My little savages
Você está linda – You look beautiful
Que porra é essa? - What the fuck?
Olá, Bom Dia - Hello, Good Morning
Meu Deus – My God
Merda - Shit
Obrigado / Obrigada – Thanks
Saúde! – Cheers!
Meu Filho - My Son
Minha Linda - My Beautiful
Filho da Puta - Son of a Bitch
A Morte Não Me Quis - Death didn't want me

AWESOME PEOPLE

Huge thanks to everyone who make my books possible!

To my readers, friends, and fans! Thanks for all the wonderful words of encouragement, friendship, and love for my books! And for participating in my shenanigans and all the other weird things I post. You guys rock! I couldn't do it without you!!!

My beta readers, who catch so many big and little things, help me with names, show me such amazing friendship, encouragement, and excitement, even when you can't share it with anyone! I know my books are a thousand times better because of your feedback. Thank you, Nia, Bianca, Iliana, Melissa, Rachel, Sandi, and Debbie for everything!

My ARC team who gives me so much support and enthusiasm even though I drop things on them at the last minute. Ooh, look, cover reveal! Book's launching in a week! Seriously, I appreciate all of you!!

My biggest supporters—my husband and mom. I'm so lucky to have you both! Love you!

And always... a special thanks to all the wonderful authors in the why choose community who support each other day in and out. Writing would be a lonely and weird world without you. It would be me and my characters sitting around chatting (drinking) while we plot the next book. Your friendship and support mean a lot to me!

ABOUT THE AUTHOR

Stella Brie lives outside of Nashville, TN, with her husband. After mentioning her desire to write a book a million times to her husband, he challenged her to sit down one day and write a paragraph. Instead, she wrote her first book, *My Salvation*.

She traded in her career in digital marketing, working on big brands, for this wildly creative one. Armed with a notebook crammed full of ideas, she's constantly thinking about bold heroines, sexy men, and HEAs. Whether it's a paranormal book full of creatures and magic or a contemporary romance full of heat and drama, she's always thinking about how she can bring her books to life.

Latest News and Updates:

Facebook Group: Stella's Stalkers

Instagram: @stellabrie_author

TikTok: @stellabrie_author

Join my Newsletter: StellaBrie.com - Exclusive sneak peeks, cover reveals, giveaways, and more!

BOOKS BY STELLA BRIE

PARANORMAL WHY CHOOSE

KILLIAN BLADE SERIES

The Rowan (1)

The Rowan's Stone (2)

The Rowan's Destiny (3)

The Light Falls (4) - Meri's story

The Dark Rises (5) - Meri's story

Spin-offs:

Wicked Savior - Lucifer's story (MF Romance) - Book 3.5

CONTEMPORARY WHY CHOOSE

THE SAVAGES SERIES

Savage Traitor (1)

Savage Ruin (2)

Spin-off:

Lethal Vengeance (Standalone)

My Salvation (Standalone)

To get a free eBook copy of my first book, My Salvation, just subscribe to my newsletter.

Website: https://www.stellabrie.com/my-salvation